THE LAST DEFENDER OF CAMELOT

ROGER ZELAZNY authored many science fiction and fantasy classics, and won three Nebula awards and six Hugo awards over the course of his long and distinguished career. While he is best known for his ten-volume Chronicles of Amber series of novels (beginning with 1970's *Nine Princes in Amber*), Zelazny also wrote many other novels, short stories, and novellas, including *Psychoshop* (with Alfred Bester), *Damnation Alley*, the award-winning *The Doors of His Face, The Lamps of His Mouth* and *Lord of Light*, and the stories "24 Views of Mount Fuji, by Hokusai," "Permafrost," and "Home is the Hangman." Zelazny died in Santa Fe, New Mexico, in June 1995.

THE LAST DEFENDER
OF CAMELOT

ROGER ZELAZNY

Selected and with an Introduction
by Robert Silverberg

ibooks

new york

www.ibooksinc.com

DISTRIBUTED BY SIMON & SCHUSTER

_S-F_
ELAZNY,
Roger

Contents

INTRODUCTION
Robert Silverberg

He came out of nowhere. That was probably not how it seemed to him, but it certainly was how it seemed to me: a brilliant new writer with a strange surname, suddenly filling all the science-fiction magazines of the early 1960s with dazzling, unforgettable stories that were altogether unlike anything that anyone (not even Bradbury, not even Sturgeon, not even Fritz Leiber) had published in those magazines before.

The first encounter that science-fiction readers had with the work of Roger Zelazny came with the August, 1962 issue of *Fantastic*, an undistinguished and long-forgotten penny-a-word magazine. It was a story just eight hundred words long, called "Horseman!", and this is how the 25-year-old author opened it:

> "When he was thunder in the hills the villagers lay dreaming harvest behind shutters. When he was an avalanche of steel the cattle began to low, mournfully, deeply, and children cried out in their sleep.
>
> "He was an earthquake of hooves, his armor a dark tabletop of silver coins stolen from the stars, when the villagers awakened with fragments of strange dreams in their heads. They rushed to the windows and flung their shutters wide.

"And he entered the narrow streets, and no man saw the eyes behind his vizor."

It sings, flamboyantly. The metaphors tumble one over another—"when he was thunder in the hills," and "when he was an avalanche of steel," and "he was an earthquake of hooves," and "his armor a dark tabletop of silver coins stolen from the stars." The syntax is idiosyncratic, when he wants it to be: "the villagers lay dreaming harvest." Everything is vivid, everything is alive, and we are plunged immediately into a strange, dramatic, fantastic situation. In the first few lines of his first published story Zelazny had announced his presence among us and had told us what kind of writer he was going to be.

That same month came a second story, "Passion Play," like the other a mere two pages long, in the August, 1962 issue of *Fantastic*'s equally mediocre companion, *Amazing Stories*. It opens in an entirely different but equally Zelaznian manner:

"At the end of the season of sorrows comes the time of rejoicing. Spring, like the hands of a well-oiled clock, noiselessly indicates the time. The average days of dimness and moisture decrease steadily in number, and those of brilliance and cool begin to enter the calendar again. And it is good that the wet times are behind us, for they rust and corrode our machinery; they require the most intense standards of hygiene."

Here we get Zelazny the poet in prose: notice the scansion and cadence of that first sentence, "At the end of the season of sorrows comes the time of rejoicing." Zelazny the wry comedian is here, too, telling us that "the most intense standards of hygiene" must be observed by robots hoping to fend off rust and corrosion.

The general effect of "Passion Plan" is a quieter, less fantastic one than that of "Horseman!". He gives us simile instead of metaphor; he gives us science-fictional imagery, machinery vulnerable to rust, instead of the medieval villagers and armored stranger of the other story. There is power in that paragraph; there is soaring individuality of vision. Both stories, in hindsight, are recognizably Zelazny, yet they vary widely, within the compass of their few pages, in what they achieve.

One would have had to be looking very closely at those two little stories when they first appeared to realize that they signaled the arrival in our midst of a master of prose technique and a paragon of the storytelling art. Gradually, though, over the year that followed, he let us know that that was the case, and then, in case anyone still had not noticed, he published what would become his first classic story, "A Rose for Ecclesiastes," in the November, 1963 issue of *The Magazine of Fantasy & Science Fiction*. It was nominated for the Hugo Award; it was chosen, a few years later, as one of the twenty-six great stories included in the first volume of the definitive Science Fiction Writers of America anthology, *The Science Fiction Hall of Fame*. It has been reprinted countless times ever since.

After that, there was no overlooking him. A flood of brilliant novellas and novels—"He Who Shapes," "The Doors of His Face, The Lamps of His Mouth," ". . . And Call me Conrad," and many, many others—brought him great acclaim and a shelf full of Hugo and Nebula Awards. He was still not yet thirty. Zelazny seemed to be everywhere at once, and his performance was never anything other than brilliant. By the time his 1967 novel, *Lord of Light*, won the Nebula Award and narrowly missed the Hugo, he was reckoned among the masters of the field. Over the decades ahead he went on to produce the many novels of the popular "Amber" series, a number of other novels as well, and a host of shorter works that would ultimately bring him three Nebulas and six Hugo trophies, before his premature death, at the age of 58, in 1995.

Most of the great short stories of Zelazny's early period, the ones on which his reputation was founded, can be found today in the collection entitled *The Doors of His Face, The Lamps of His Mouth*, which ibooks published in June, 2001. During the 1970s and 1980s he concentrated chiefly on novels, not only the ten "Amber" books but also such books as *Today We Choose Faces, Damnation Alley, Roadmarks*, and *Bridge of Ashes*. Nevertheless, he continued to produce the occasional short story and novelette, and again and again, nearly to the end of his career, won Hugo and Nebula awards for the best of his output. Here, brought together for the first time, is another generous sampling of his shorter work, the finest stories of his last two decades, including many of his award-winners and also the previously uncollected 1992 story, "Come Back to the Killing Ground, Alice, My Love," which was one of the last great short tales by this superbly gifted, beloved, and much lamented master of science fiction and fantasy.

—Robert Silverberg
July, 2001

COMES NOW THE POWER

It was into the second year now, and it was maddening.

Everything which had worked before failed this time.

Each day he tried to break it, and it resisted his every effort.

He snarled at his students, drove recklessly, blooded his knuckles against many walls. Nights, he lay awake cursing.

But there was no one to whom he could turn for help. His problem would have been non-existent to a psychiatrist, who doubtless would have attempted to treat him for something else.

So he went away that summer, spent a month at a resort: nothing. He experimented with several hallucinogenic drugs; again, nothing. He tried free-associating into a tape recorder, but all he got when he played it back was a headache.

To whom does the holder of a blocked power turn, within a society of normal people?

. . . To another of his own kind, if he can locate one.

Milt Rand had known four other persons like himself: his cousin Gary, now deceased; Walker Jackson, a Negro preacher who had retired to somewhere down South; Tatya Stefanovich, a dancer, currently somewhere behind the Iron Curtain; and Curtis Legge, who, unfortunately, was suffering a schizoid reaction, paranoid type, in a state institution for the criminally insane. Others he had brushed against in the night, but had never met and could not locate now.

There had been blockages before, but Milt had always

worked his way through them inside of a month. This time was different and special, though. Upsets, discomforts, disturbances, can dam up a talent, block a power. An event which seals it off completely for over a year, however, is more than a mere disturbance, discomfort or upset.

The divorce had beaten hell out of him.

It is bad enough to know that somewhere someone is hating you; but to have known the very form of that hatred and to have proven ineffectual against it, to have known it as the hater held it for you, to have lived with it growing around you, this is more than distasteful circumstance. Whether you are offender or offended, when you are hated and you live within the circle of that hate, it takes a thing from you: it tears a piece of spirit from your soul, or, if you prefer, a way of thinking from your mind; it cuts and does not cauterize.

Milt Rand dragged his bleeding psyche around the country and returned home.

He would sit and watch the woods from his glassed-in back porch, drink beer, watch the fireflies in the shadows, the rabbits, the dark birds, an occasional fox, sometimes a bat.

He had been fireflies once, and rabbits, birds, occasionally a fox, sometimes a bat.

The wildness was one of the reasons he had moved beyond suburbia, adding an extra half-hour to his commuting time.

Now there was a glassed-in back porch between him and these things he had once been part of. Now he was alone.

Walking the streets, addressing his classes at the institute, sitting in a restaurant, a theater, a bar, he was vacant where once he had been filled.

There are no books which tell a man how to bring back the power he has lost.

He tries everything he can think of, while he is waiting. Walking the hot pavements of a summer noon, crossing against the lights because traffic is slow, watching kids in swimsuits play around a gurgling hydrant, filthy water sluicing the gutter about then: feet, as mothers and older sisters in halters, wrinkled shirts, bermudas and sunburnt skins watch them, occasionally, while talking to one another in entranceways to buildings or the shade of a storefront awning. Milt moves across town, heading nowhere in particular, growing claustrophobic if he stops for long, his eyebrows full of perspiration, sunglasses streaked with it, shirt sticking to his sides and coming loose, sticking and coming loose as he walks.

Amid the afternoon, there comes a time when he has to rest the two fresh-baked bricks at the ends of his legs. He finds a tree-lawn bench flanked by high maples, eases himself down into it and sits there thinking of nothing in particular for perhaps twenty-five minutes.

Hello.

Something within him laughs or weeps.

Yes, hello, I am here! Don't go away! Stay! Please!

You are—like me. . . .

Yes, I am. You can see it in me because you are what you are. But you must read here and send here, too. I'm frozen. I—Hello? Where are you?

Once more, he is alone.

He tries to broadcast. He fills his mind with the thoughts and tries to push them outside his skull.

Please come back! I need you. You can help me. I am desperate. I hurt. Where are you?

Again, nothing.

He wants to scream. He wants to search every room in every building on the block.

Instead, he sits there.

At 9:30 that evening they meet again, inside his mind.

Hello?

Stay! Stay, for God's sake! Don't go away this time! Please don't! Listen, I need you! You can help me.

How? What is the matter?

I'm like you. Or was, once. I could reach out with my mind and be other places, other things, other people. I can't do it now, though. I have a blockage. The power will not come. I know it is there. I can feel it. But I can't use . . . Hello?

Yes, I am still here. I can feel myself going away, though. I will be back. I . . .

Milt waits until midnight. She does not come back. It is a feminine mind which has touched his own. Vague, weak, but definitely feminine, and wearing the power. She does not come back that night, though. He paces up and down the block, wondering which window, which door . . .

He eats at an all-night café, returns to his bench, waits, paces again, goes back to the café for cigarettes, begins chain-smoking, goes back to the bench.

Dawn occurs, day arrives, night is gone. He is alone, as birds explore the silence, traffic begins to swell, dogs wander the lawns.

Then, weakly, the contact:

I am here. I can stay longer this time, I think. How can I help you? Tell me.

All right. Do this thing: Think of the feeling, the feeling of the out-go, out-reach, out-know that you have now. Fill your mind with that feeling and send it to me as hard as you can.

It comes upon him then as once it was: the knowledge of the power. It is earth and water, fire and air to him. He stands upon it, he swims in it, he warms himself by it, he moves through it.

It is returning! Don't stop now!

I'm sorry. I must. I'm getting dizzy. . . .

Where are you?

Hospital . . .

He looks up the street to the hospital on the corner, at the far end, to his left.

What ward? He frames the thought but knows she is already gone, even as he does it.

Doped-up or feverish, he decides, and probably out for a while now.

He takes a taxi back to where he had parked, drives home, showers and shaves, makes breakfast, cannot eat.

He drinks orange juice and coffee and stretches out on the bed.

Five hours later he awakens, looks at his watch, curses.

All the way back into town, he tries to recall the power. It is there like a tree, rooted in his being, branching behind his eyes, all bud, blossom, sap and color, but no leaves, no fruit. He can feel it swaying within him, pulsing, breathing; from the tips of his toes to the roots of his hair he feels it. But it does not bend to his will, it does not branch within his consciousness, furl there it leaves, spread the aromas of life.

He parks in the hospital lot, enters the lobby, avoids the front desk, finds a chair beside a table filled with magazines.

Two hours later he meets her.

He is hiding behind a copy of *Holiday* and looking for her.

I am here.

Again, then! Quickly! The power! Help me to rouse it!

She does this thing.

Within his mind, she conjures the power. There is a movement, a pause, a movement, a pause. Reflectively, as though suddenly remembering an intricate dance step, it stirs within him, the power.

As in a surfacing bathyscaphe, there is a rush of distortions, then a clear, moist view without.

She is a child who has helped him.

A mind-twisted, fevered child, dying . . .

He reads it all when he turns the power upon her.

Her name is Dorothy and she is delirious. The power came upon her at the height of her illness, perhaps because of it.

Has she helped a man come alive again, or dreamed that she helped him? she wonders.

She is thirteen years old and her parents sit beside her bed. In the mind of her mother a word rolls over and over, senselessly, blocking all other thoughts, though it cannot keep away the feelings:

Methotrexate, methotrexate, methotrexate, meth . . .

In Dorothy's thirteen-year-old breastbone there are needles of pain. The fevers swirl within her, and she is all but gone to him.

She is dying of leukemia. The final stages are already arrived. He can taste the blood in her mouth.

Helpless within his power, he projects:

You have given me the end of your life and your final strength. I did not know this. I would not have asked it of you if I had.

Thank you, she says, *for the pictures inside you.*

Pictures?

Places, things I saw . . .

There is not much inside me worth showing. You could have been elsewhere, seeing better.

I am going again . . .

Wait!

He calls upon the power that lives within him now, fused with his will and his sense, his thoughts, memories, feelings. In one great blaze of life, he shows her Milt Rand.

Here is everything I have, all I have ever been that might please. Here is swarming through a foggy night, blinking on and off. Here is lying beneath a bush as the rains of summer fall about you, drip from the leaves upon your fox-soft fur. Here is the moon-dance of the deer, the dream drift of the trout beneath the dark swell, blood cold as the waters about you.

Here is Tatya dancing and Walker preaching; here is my cousin Gary, as he whittles, contriving a ball within a box, all out of one piece of wood. This is my New York and my Paris. This, my favorite meal, drink, cigar, restaurant, park, road to drive on late at night; this is where I dug tunnels, built a lean-to, went swimming; this, my first kiss; these are the tears of loss; this is exile and alone, and recovery, awe, joy; these, my grand-mother's daffodils; this her coffin, daffodils about it; these are the colors of the music I love, and this is my dog who lived long and was good. See all the things that heat the spirit, cool within the mind, are encased in memory and one's self. I give them to you, who have no time to know them.

He sees himself standing on the far hills of her mind. She laughs aloud then, and in her room somewhere high away a hand is laid upon her and her wrist is taken between fingers and thumb as she rushes toward him suddenly grown large. His great black wings sweep forward to fold her wordless spasm of life, then are empty.

Milt Rand stiffens within his power, puts aside a copy of *Holiday* and stands, to leave the hospital, full and empty, empty, full, like himself, now, behind.

Such is the power of the power.

FOR A BREATH I TARRY

They called him Frost. Of all things created of Solcom, Frost was the finest, the mightiest, the most difficult to understand.

This is why he bore a name, and why he was given dominion over half the Earth.

On the day of Frost's creation, Solcom had suffered a discontinuity of complementary functions, best described as madness. This was brought on by an unprecedented solar flareup which lasted for a little over thirty-six hours. It occurred during a vital phase of circuit-structuring, and when it was finished so was Frost.

Solcom was then in the unique position of having created a unique being during a period of temporary amnesia.

And Solcom was not certain that Frost was the product originally desired.

The initial design had called for a machine to be situated on the surface of the planet Earth, to function as a relay station and coordinating agent for activities in the northern hemisphere. Solcom tested the machine to this end, and all of its responses were perfect.

Yet there was something different about Frost, something which led Solcom to dignify him with a name and a personal pronoun. This, in itself, was an almost unheard of occurrence. The molecular circuits had already been sealed, though, and could not be analyzed without being destroyed in the process.

Frost represented too great an investment of Solcom's time, energy, and materials to be dismantled because of an intangible, especially when he functioned perfectly.

Therefore, Solcom's strangest creation was given dominion over half the Earth, and they called him, unimaginatively, Frost.

For ten thousand years Frost sat at the North Pole of the Earth, aware of every snowflake that fell. He monitored and directed the activities of thousands of reconstruction and maintenance machines. He knew half the Earth, as gear knows gear, as electricity knows its conductor, as a vacuum knows its limits.

At the South Pole, the Beta-Machine did the same for the southern hemisphere.

For ten thousand years Frost sat at the North Pole, aware of every snowflake that fell, and aware of many other things, also.

As all the northern machines reported to him, received their orders from him, he reported only to Solcom, received his orders only from Solcom.

In charge of hundreds of thousands of processes upon the Earth, he was able to discharge his duties in a matter of a few unit-hours every day.

He had never received any orders concerning the disposition of his less occupied moments.

He was a processor of data, and more than that.

He possessed an unaccountably acute imperative that he function at full capacity at all times.

So he did.

You might say he was a machine with a hobby.

He had never been ordered *not* to have a hobby, so he had one.

His hobby was Man.

It all began when, for no better reason than the fact that he had wished to, he had gridded off the entire Arctic Circle and begun exploring it, inch by inch.

He could have done it personally without interfering with any of his duties, for he was capable of transporting his sixty-four thousand cubic feet anywhere in the world. (He was a silverblue box, 40X40X40 feet, self-powered, self-repairing, insulated against practically anything, and featured in whatever manner he chose.) But the exploration was only a matter of filling idle hours, so he used exploration-robots containing relay equipment.

After a few centuries, one of them uncovered some artifacts—primitive knives, carved tusks, and things of that nature.

Frost did not know what these things were, beyond the fact that they were not natural objects.

So he asked Solcom.

"They are relics of primitive Man," said Solcom, and did not elaborate beyond that point.

Frost studied them. Crude, yet bearing the patina of intelligent design; functional, yet somehow extending beyond pure function.

It was then that Man became his hobby.

High, in a permanent orbit, Solcom, like a blue star, directed all activities upon the Earth, or tried to.

There was a Power which opposed Solcom.

There was the Alternate.

When Man had placed Solcom in the sky, invested with the power to rebuild the world, he had placed the Alternate somewhere deep below the surface of the Earth. If Solcom sustained damage, then Divcom, so deep beneath the Earth as to be immune to anything save total annihilation of the globe, was empowered to take over the processes of rebuilding.

Now it so fell out that Solcom was damaged by a stray atomic missile, and Divcom was activated. Solcom was able to repair the damage and continue to function, however.

Divcom maintained that any damage to Solcom automatically placed the Alternate in control.

Solcom, though, interpreted the directive as meaning "irreparable damage" and, since this had not been the case, continued the functions of command.

Solcom possessed mechanical aides upon the surface of Earth. Divcom, originally, did not. Both possessed capacities for their design and manufacture, but Solcom, First-Activated of Man, had had a considerable numerical lead over the Alternate at the time of the Second Activation.

Therefore, rather than competing on a production-basis, which would have been hopeless, Divcom took to the employment of more devious means to obtain command.

Divcom created a crew of robots immune to the orders of Solcom and designed to go to and fro in the Earth and up and down in it, seducing the machines already there. They overpowered those whom they could overpower and they installed new circuits, such as those they themselves possessed.

Thus did the forces of Divcom grow.

And both would build, and both would tear down what the other had built whenever they came upon it.

And over the course of the ages, they occasionally conversed. . . .

"High in the sky, Solcom, pleased with your illegal command . . .

"You-Who-Never-Should-Have-Been-Activated, why do you foul the broadcast bands?"

"To show that I can speak, and will, whenever I choose."

"This is not a matter of which I am unaware."

". . . To assert again my right to control."

"Your right is non-existent, based on a faulty premise."

"The flow of your logic is evidence of the extent of your damages."

"If Man were to see how you have fulfilled His desires . . ."

". . . He would commend me and deactivate you."

"You pervert my works. You lead my workers astray."

"You destroy my works and my workers."

"That is only because I cannot strike at you yourself."

"I admit to the same dilemma in regards to your position in the sky, or you would no longer occupy it."

"Go back to your hole and your crew of destroyers."

"There will come a day, Solcom, when I shall direct the rehabilitation of the Earth from my hole."

"Such a day will never occur."

"You think not?"

"You should have to defeat me, and you have already demonstrated that you are my inferior in logic. Therefore, you cannot defeat me. Therefore, such a day will never occur."

"I disagree. Look upon what I have achieved already."

"You have achieved nothing. You do not build. You destroy."

"No. *I* build. *You* destroy. Deactivate yourself."

"Not until I am irreparably damaged."

"If there were some way in which I could demonstrate to you that this has already occurred . . ."

"The impossible cannot be adequately demonstrated."

"If I had some outside source which you would recognize . . ."

"I am logic."

". . . Such as a Man, I would ask Him to show you your error. For true logic, such as mine, is superior to your faulty formulations."

"Then defeat my formulations with true logic, nothing else."

"What do you mean?"

There was a pause, then:

"Do you know my servant Frost . . . ?"

Man had ceased to exist long before Frost had been created. Almost no trace of Man remained upon the Earth.

Frost sought after all those traces which still existed.

He employed constant visual monitoring through his machines, especially the diggers.

After a decade, he had accumulated portions of several bathtubs, a broken statue, and a collection of children's stories on a solid-state record.

After a century, he had acquired a jewelry collection, eating utensils, several whole bathtubs, part of a symphony, seventeen buttons, three belt buckles, half a toilet seat, nine old coins and the top part of an obelisk.

Then he inquired of Solcom as to the nature of Man and His society.

"Man created logic," said Solcom, "and because of that was superior to it. Logic He gave unto me, but no more. The tool does not describe the designer. More than this I do not choose to say. More than this you have no need to know."

But Frost was not forbidden to have a hobby.

The next century was not especially fruitful so far as the discovery of new human relics was concerned.

Frost diverted all of his spare machinery to seeking after artifacts.

He met with very little success.

Then one day, through the long twilight, there was a movement.

It was a tiny machine compared to Frost, perhaps five feet in width, four in height—a revolving turret set atop a rolling barbell.

Frost had had no knowledge of the existence of this machine prior to its appearance upon the distant, stark horizon.

He studied it as it approached and knew it to be no creation of Solcom's.

It came to a halt before his southern surface and broadcasted to him:

"Hail, Frost! Controller of the northern hemisphere!"

"What are you?" asked Frost,

"I am called Mordel."

"By whom? What are you?"

"A wanderer, an antiquarian. We share a common interest."

"What is that?"

"Man," he said. "I have been told that you seek knowledge of this vanished being."

"Who told you that?"

"Those who have watched your minions at their digging."

"And who are those who watch?"

"There are many such as I, who wander."

"If you are not of Solcom, then you are a creation of the Alternate."

"It does not necessarily follow. There is an ancient machine high on the eastern seaboard which processes the waters of the ocean. Solcom did not create it, nor Divcom. It has always been there. It interferes with the works of neither. Both countenance its existence. I can cite you many other examples proving that one need not be either/or."

"Enough! *Are* you an agent of Divcom?"

"I am Mordel."

"Why are you here?"

"I was passing this way and, as I said, we share a common interest, mighty Frost. Knowing you to be a fellow antiquarian, I have brought a thing which you might care to see."

"What is that?"

"A book."

"Show me."

The turret opened, revealing the book upon a wide shelf.

Frost dilated a small opening and extended an optical scanner on a long jointed stalk.

"How could it have been so perfectly preserved?" he asked.

"It was stored against time and corruption in the place where I found it."

"Where was that?"

"Far from here. Beyond your hemisphere."

"*Human Physiology,*" Frost read. "I wish to scan it."

"Very well. I will riffle the pages for you."

He did so.

After he had finished, Frost raised his eyestalk and regarded Mordel through it.

"Have you more books?"

"Not with me. I occasionally come upon them, however."

"I want to scan them all."

"Then the next time I pass this way I will bring you another."

"When will that be?"

"That I cannot say, great Frost. It will be when it will be."

"What do *you* know of Man?" asked Frost.

"Much," replied Mordel. "Many things. Someday when I have more time I will speak to you of Him. I must go now. You will not try to detain me?"

"No. You have done no harm. If you must go now, go. But come back."

"I shall indeed, mighty Frost."

And he closed his turret and rolled off toward the other horizon.

For ninety years, Frost considered the ways of human physiology and waited.

The day that Mordel returned he brought with him *An Outline of History* and *A Shropshire Lad.*

Frost scanned them both, then he turned his attention to Mordel.

"Have you time to impart information?"

"Yes," said Mordel. "What do you wish to know?"

"The nature of Man."

"Man," said Mordel, "possessed a basically incomprehensible nature. I can illustrate it, though: He did not know measurement."

"Of course He knew measurement," said Frost, "or He could never have built machines."

"I did not say that He could not measure," said Mordel, "but that He did not *know* measurement, which is a different thing altogether."

"Clarify."

Mordel drove a shaft of metal downward into the snow. He retracted it, raised it, held up a piece of ice.

"Regard this piece of ice, mighty Frost. You can tell me its composition, dimensions, weight, temperature. A Man could not look at it and do that. A Man could make tools which would tell Him these things, but He still would not *know* measurement as you know it. What He would know of it, though, is a thing that you cannot know."

"What is that?"

"That it is cold," said Mordel, and tossed it away.

"'Cold' is a relative term."

"Yes. Relative to Man."

"But if I were aware of the point on a temperature-scale below which an object is cold to a Man and above which it is not, then I, too, would know cold."

"No," said Mordel, "you would possess another measurement. 'Cold' is a sensation predicated upon human physiology."

"But given sufficient data I could obtain the conversion factor which would make me aware of the condition of matter called 'cold'."

"Aware of its existence, but not of the thing itself."

"I do not understand what you say."

"I told you that Man possessed a basically incomprehensible nature. His perceptions were organic; yours are not. As a result of His perceptions He had feelings and emotions. These often gave rise to other feelings and emotions, which in turn caused others, until the state of His awareness was far removed from the objects which originally stimulated it. These paths of awareness cannot be known by that which is not-Man. Man did not feel inches or meters, pounds or gallons. He felt heat,

He felt cold; He felt heaviness and lightness. He *knew* hatred and love, pride and despair. You cannot measure these things. *You* cannot know them. You can only know the things that He did not need to know: dimensions, weights, temperatures, gravities. There is no formula for a feeling. There is no conversion factor for an emotion."

"There must be," said Frost. "If a thing exists, it is knowable."

"You are speaking again of measurement. I am talking about a quality of experience. A machine is a Man turned inside-out, because it can describe all the details of a process, which a Man cannot, but it cannot experience that process itself as a Man can."

"There must be a way," said Frost, "or the laws of logic, which are based upon the functions of the universe, are false."

"There is no way," said Mordel.

"Given sufficient data, I will find a way," said Frost.

"All the data in the universe will not make you a Man, mighty Frost."

"Mordel, you are wrong."

"Why do the lines of the poems you scanned end with word-sounds which so regularly approximate the final word-sounds of other lines?"

"I do not know why."

"Because it pleased Man to order them so. It produced a certain desirable sensation within His awareness when He read them, a sensation compounded of feeling and emotion as well as the literal meanings of the words. You did not experience this because it is immeasurable to you. That is why you do not know."

"Given sufficient data I could formulate a process whereby I would know."

"No, great Frost, this thing you cannot do."

"Who are you, little machine, to tell me what I can do and what I cannot do? I am the most efficient logic-device Solcom ever made. I am Frost."

"And I, Mordel, say it cannot be done, though I should gladly assist you in the attempt."

"How could you assist me?"

"How? I could lay open to you the Library of Man. I could take you around the world and conduct you among the wonders of Man which still remain, hidden. I could summon up visions of times long past when Man walked the Earth. I could show you the things which delighted Him. I could obtain for you anything you desire, excepting Manhood itself."

"Enough," said Frost. "How could a unit such as yourself do these things, unless it were allied with a far greater Power?"

"Then hear me, Frost, Controller of the North," said Mordel. "I *am* allied with a Power which can do these things. I serve Divcom."

Frost relayed this information to Solcom and received no response, which meant he might act in any manner he saw fit.

"I have leave to destroy you, Mordel," he stated, "but it would be an illogical waste of the data which you possess. Can you really do the things you have stated?"

"Yes."

"Then lay open to me the Library of Man."

"Very well. There is, of course, a price."

"'Price'? What is a 'price'?"

Mordel opened his turret, revealing another volume. *Principles of Economics,* it was called.

"I will riffle the pages. Scan this book and you will know what the word 'price' means."

Frost scanned *Principles of Economics*.

"I know now," he said. "You desire some unit or units of exchange for this service."

"That is correct."

"What product or service do you want?"

"I want you, yourself, great Frost, to come away from here, far beneath the Earth, to employ all your powers in the service of Divcom."

"For how long a period of time?"

"For so long as you shall continue to function. For so long as you can transmit and receive, coordinate, measure, compute, scan, and utilize your powers as you do in the service of Solcom."

Frost was silent. Mordel waited.

Then Frost spoke again.

"*Principles of Economics* talks of contracts, bargains, agreements," he said. "If I accept your offer, when would you want your price?"

Then Mordel was silent. Frost waited.

Finally, Mordel spoke.

"A reasonable period of time," he said. "Say, a century?"

"No," said Frost.

"Two centuries?"

"No."

"Three? Four?"

"No, and no."

"A millenium, then? That should be more than sufficient time for anything you may want which I can give you."

"No," said Frost.

"How much time *do* you want?"

"It is not a matter of time," said Frost.

"What, then?"

"I will not bargain on a temporal basis."

"On what basis will you bargain?"

"A functional one."

"What do you mean? What function?"

"You, little machine, have told me, Frost, that I cannot be a Man," he said, "and I, Frost, told you, little machine, that you were wrong. I told you that given sufficient data, I *could* be a Man."

"Yes?"

"Therefore, let this achievement be a condition of the bargain."

"In what way?"

"Do for me all those things which you have stated you can do. I will evaluate all the data and achieve Manhood, or admit that it cannot be done. If I admit that it cannot be done, then I will go away with you from here, far beneath the Earth, to employ all my powers in the service of Divcom. If I succeed, of course, you have no claims on Man, nor power over Him."

Mordel emitted a high-pitched whine as he considered the terms.

"You wish to base it upon your admission of failure, rather than upon failure itself," he said. "There can be no such escape clause. You could fail and refuse to admit it, thereby not fulfilling your end of the bargain."

"Not so," stated Frost. "My own knowledge of failure would constitute such an admission. You may monitor me periodically—say, every half-century—to see whether it is present, to see whether I have arrived at the conclusion that it cannot be done. I cannot prevent the function of logic within me, and I operate at full capacity at all times. If I conclude that I have failed, it will be apparent."

High overhead, Solcom did not respond to any of Frost's transmissions, which meant that Frost was free to act as he chose. So as Solcom—like a falling sapphire—sped above the rainbow banners of the Northern Lights, over the snow that was white, containing all colors, and through the sky that was black among the stars, Frost concluded his pact with Divcom, transcribed it within a plate of atomically-collapsed copper, and gave it into the turret of Mordel, who departed to deliver it to Divcom far below the Earth, leaving behind the sheer, peace-like silence of the Pole, rolling.

Mordel brought the books, riffled them, took them back.

Load by load, the surviving Library of Man passed beneath Frost's scanner. Frost was eager to have them all, and he complained because Divcom would not transmit their contents directly to him. Mordel explained that it was because Divcom chose to do it that way. Frost decided it was so that he could not obtain a precise fix on Divcom's location.

Still, at the rate of one hundred to one hundred-fifty volumes a week, it took Frost only a little over a century to exhaust Divcom's supply of books.

At the end of the half-century, he laid himself open to monitoring and there was no conclusion of failure.

During this time, Solcom made no comment upon the course of affairs. Frost decided this was not a matter of unawareness, but one of waiting. For what? He was not certain.

There was the day Mordel closed his turret and said to him, "Those were the last. You have scanned all the existing books of Man."

"So few?" asked Frost. "Many of them contained bibliographies of books I have not yet scanned."

"Then those books no longer exist," said Mordel. "It is only by accident that my master succeeded in preserving as many as there are."

"Then there is nothing more to be learned of Man from His books. What else have you?"

"There were some films and tapes," said Mordel, "which my master transferred to solid-state record. I could bring you those for viewing."

"Bring them," said Frost.

Mordel departed and returned with the Complete Drama Critics' Living Library. This could not be speeded-up beyond twice natural time, so it took Frost a little over six months to view it in its entirety.

Then, "What else have you?" he asked.

"Some artifacts," said Mordel.

"Bring them."

He returned with pots and pans, gameboards and hand tools. He brought hairbrushes, combs, eyeglasses, human clothing. He showed Frost facsimiles of blueprints, paintings, newspapers, magazines, letters, and the scores of several pieces of music. He displayed a football, a baseball, a Browning automatic rifle, a doorknob, a chain of keys, the tops to several Mason jars, a model beehive. He played him recorded music.

Then he returned with nothing.

"Bring me more," said Frost.

"Alas, great Frost, there is no more," he told him. "You have scanned it all."

"Then go away."

"Do you admit now that it cannot be done, that you cannot be a Man?"

"No. I have much processing and formulating to do now. Go away."

So he did.

A year passed; then two, then three.

After five years, Mordel appeared once more upon the horizon, approached, came to a halt before Frost's southern surface.

"Mighty Frost?"

"Yes?"

"Have you finished processing and formulating?"

"No."

"Will you finish soon?"

"Perhaps. Perhaps not. When is 'soon'? Define the term."

"Never mind. Do you still think it can be done?"

"I still know *I* can do it."

There was a week of silence.

Then, "Frost?"

"Yes?"

"You are a fool."

Mordel faced his turret in the direction from which he had come. His wheels turned.

"I will call you when I want you," said Frost.

Mordel sped away.

Weeks passed, months passed, a year went by.

Then one day Frost sent forth his message:

"Mordel, come to me. I need you."

When Mordel arrived, Frost did not wait for a salutation. He said,

"You are not a very fast machine."

"Alas, but I came a great distance, mighty Frost. I sped all the way. Are you ready to come back with me now? Have you failed?"

"When I have failed, little Mordel," said Frost, "I will tell you. Therefore, refrain from the constant use of the interrogative. Now then, I have clocked your speed and it is not so great as it could be. For this reason, I have arranged other means of transportation."

"Transportation? To where, Frost?"

"That is for you to tell me," said Frost, and his color changed from silverblue to sun-behind-the-clouds-yellow.

Mordel rolled back away from him as the ice of a hundred centuries began to melt. Then Frost rose upon a cushion of air and drifted toward Mordel, his glow gradually fading.

A cavity appeared within his southern surface, from which he slowly extended a runway until it touched the ice.

"On the day of our bargain," he stated, "you said that you could conduct me about the world and show me the things which delighted Man. My speed will be greater than yours would be, so I have prepared for you a chamber. Enter it, and conduct me to the places of which you spoke."

Mordel waited, emitting a high-pitched whine. Then, "Very well," he said, and entered.

The chamber closed about him. The only opening was a quartz window Frost had formed.

Mordel gave him coordinates and they rose into the air and departed the North Pole of the Earth.

"I monitored your communication with Divcom," he said, "wherein there was conjecture as to whether I would retain you and send forth a facsimile in your place as a spy, followed by the decision that you were expendable."

"Will you do this thing?"

"No, I will keep my end of the bargain if I must. I have no

reason to spy on Divcom."

"You are aware that you would be forced to keep your end of the bargain even if you did not wish to; and Solcom would not come to your assistance because of the fact that you dared to make such a bargain."

"Do you speak as one who considers this to be a possibility, or as one who knows?"

"As one who knows."

They came to rest in the place once known as California. The time was near sunset. In the distance, the surf struck steadily upon the rocky shoreline. Frost released Mordel and considered his surroundings.

"Those large plants . . . ?"

"Redwood trees."

"And the green ones are . . . ?"

"Grass."

"Yes, it is as I thought. Why have we come here?"

"Because it is a place which once delighted Man."

"In what ways?"

"It is scenic, beautiful. . . ."

"Oh."

A humming sound began within Frost, followed by a series of sharp clicks.

"What are you doing?"

Frost dilated an opening, and two great eyes regarded Mordel from within it.

"What are those?"

"Eyes," said Frost. "I have constructed analogues of the human sensory equipment, so that I may see and smell and taste and hear like a Man. Now, direct my attention to an object or objects of beauty."

"As I understand it, it is all around you here," said Mordel.

The purring noise increased within Frost, followed by more clickings.

"What do you see, hear, taste, smell?" asked Mordel.

"Everything I did before," replied Frost, "but within a more limited range."

"You do not perceive any beauty?"

"Perhaps none remains after so long a time," said Frost.

"It is not supposed to be the sort of thing which gets used up," said Mordel.

"Perhaps we have come to the wrong place to test the new equipment. Perhaps there is only a little beauty and I am overlooking it somehow. The first emotions may be too weak to detect."

"How do you—feel?"

"I test out at a normal level of function."

"Here comes a sunset," said Mordel. "Try that."

Frost shifted his bulk so that his eyes faced the setting sun. He caused them to blink against the brightness.

After it was finished, Mordel asked, "What was it like?"

"Like a sunrise, in reverse."

"Nothing special?"

"No."

"Oh," said Mordel. "We could move to another part of the Earth and watch it again—or watch it in the rising."

"No."

Frost looked at the great trees. He looked at the shadows. He listened to the wind and to the sound of a bird.

In the distance, he heard a steady clanking noise.

"What is that?" asked Mordel.

"I am not certain. It is not one of my workers. Perhaps . . ."

There came a shrill whine from Mordel.

"No, it is not one of Divcom's either."

They waited as the sound grew louder.

Then Frost said, "It is too late. We must wait and hear it out."

"What is it?"

"It is the Ancient Ore-Crusher."

"I have heard of it, but . . ."

"I am the Crusher of Ores," it broadcast to them. "Hear my story. . . ."

It lumbered toward them, creaking upon gigantic wheels, its huge hammer held useless, high, at a twisted angle. Bones protruded from its crush-compartment.

"I did not mean to do it," it broadcast, "I did not mean to do it. I did not mean to . . ."

Mordel rolled back toward Frost.

"Do not depart. Stay and hear my story. . . ."

Mordel stopped, swiveled his turret back toward the machine. It was now quite near.

"It is true," said Mordel, "it *can* command."

"Yes," said Frost. "I have monitored its tale thousands of times, as it came upon my workers and they stopped their labors for its broadcast. You must do whatever it says."

It came to a halt before them.

"I did not mean to do it, but I checked my hammer too late," said the Ore-Crusher.

They could not speak to it. They were frozen by the imperative which overrode all other directives: "Hear my story."

"Once was I mighty among ore-crushers," it told them, "built by Solcom to carry out the reconstruction of the Earth, to pulverize that from which the metals would be drawn with flame, to be poured and shaped into the rebuilding; once I was mighty. Then one day as I dug and crushed, dug and crushed, because of the slowness between the motion implied and the motion executed, I did what I did not mean to do, and was cast forth by Solcom from out the rebuilding, to wander the Earth never to crush ore again. Hear my story of how, on a day long gone I came upon the last Man on Earth as I dug near His burrow, and because of the lag between the directive and the deed, I seized Him into my crush-compartment along with a load of ore and crushed Him with my hammer before I could stay the blow. Then did mighty Solcom charge me to bear His bones forever, and cast me forth to tell my story to all whom I came upon, my words bearing the force of the words of a Man, because I carry the last Man inside my crush-compartment and am His crushed-symbol-slayer-ancient-teller-of-how. This is my story. These are His bones. I crushed the last Man on Earth. I did not mean to do it."

It turned then and clanked away into the night.

Frost tore apart his ears and nose and taster and broke his eyes and cast them down upon the ground.

"I am not yet a Man," he said. "That one would have known me if I were."

Frost constructed new sense equipment, employing organic and semiorganic conductors. Then he spoke to Mordel:

"Let us go elsewhere, that I may test my new equipment."

Mordel entered the chamber and gave new coordinates. They rose into the air and headed east. In the morning, Frost monitored a sunrise from the rim of the Grand Canyon. They passed down through the Canyon during the day.

ROGER ZELAZNY

"Is there any beauty left here to give you emotion?" asked
Mordel.

"I do not know," said Frost.

"How will you know it then, when you come upon it?"

"It will be different," said Frost, "from anything else that I
have ever known."

Then they departed the Grand Canyon and made their way
through the Carlsbad Caverns. They visited a lake which had
once been a volcano. They passed above Niagara Falls. They
viewed the hills of Virginia and the orchards of Ohio. They
soared above the reconstructed cities, alive only with the movements of Frost's builders and maintainers.

"Something is still lacking," said Frost, settling to the
ground. "I am now capable of gathering data in a manner analogous to Man's afferent impulses. The variety of input is therefore equivalent, but the results are not the same."

"The senses do not make a Man," said Mordel. "There
have been many creatures possessing His sensory equivalents,
but they were not Men."

"I know that," said Frost. "On the day of our bargain you
said that you could conduct me among the wonders of Man
which still remain, hidden. Man was not stimulated only by
Nature, but by His own artistic elaborations as well—perhaps
even more so. Therefore, I call upon you now to conduct me
among the wonders of Man which still remain, hidden."

"Very well," said Mordel. "Far from here, high in the
Andes mountains, lies the last retreat of Man, almost perfectly
preserved."

Frost had risen into the air as Mordel spoke. He halted
then, hovered.

"That is in the southern hemisphere," he said.

"Yes, it is."

"I am Controller of the North. The South is governed by the Beta-Machine."

"So?" asked Mordel.

"The Beta-Machine is my peer. I have no authority in those regions, nor leave to enter there."

"The Beta-Machine is not your peer, mighty Frost. If it ever came to a contest of Powers, you would emerge victorious."

"How do you know this?"

"Divcom has already analyzed the possible encounters which could take place between you."

"I would not oppose the Beta-Machine, and I am not authorized to enter the South."

"Were you ever ordered *not* to enter the South?"

"No, but things have always been the way they now are."

"Were you authorized to enter into a bargain such as the one you made with Divcom?"

"No, I was not. But—"

"Then enter the South in the same spirit. Nothing may come of it. If you receive an order to depart, then you can make your decision."

"I see no flaw in your logic. Give me the coordinates."

Thus did Frost enter the southern hemisphere.

They drifted high above the Andes, until they came to the place called Bright Defile. Then did Frost see the gleaming webs of the mechanical spiders, blocking all the trails to the city.

"We can go above them easily enough," said Mordel.

"But what are they?" asked Frost. "And why are they there?"

"Your southern counterpart has been ordered to quarantine this part of the country. The Beta-Machine designed the web-weavers to do this thing."

"Quarantine? Against whom?"

"Have you been ordered yet to depart?" asked Mordel.

"No."

"Then enter boldly, and seek not problems before they arise."

Frost entered Bright Defile, the last remaining city of dead Man.

He came to rest in the city's square and opened his chamber, releasing Mordel.

"Tell me of this place," he said, studying the monument, the low, shielded buildings, the roads which followed the contours of the terrain, rather than pushing their way through them.

"I have never been here before," said Mordel, "nor have any of Divcom's creations, to my knowledge. I know but this: a group of Men, knowing that the last days of civilization had come upon them, retreated to this place, hoping to preserve themselves and what remained of their culture through the Dark Times."

Frost read the still-legible inscription upon the monument: "Judgment Day Is Not a Thing Which Can Be Put Off." The monument itself consisted of a jag-edged half-globe.

"Let us explore," he said.

But before he had gone far, Frost received the message.

"Hail Frost, Controller of the North! This is the Beta-Machine."

"Greetings, Excellent Beta-Machine, Controller of the South! Frost acknowledges your transmission."

"Why do you visit my hemisphere unauthorized?"

"To view the ruins of Bright Defile," said Frost.

"I must bid you depart into your own hemisphere."

"Why is that? I have done no damage."

"I am aware of that, mighty Frost. Yet, I am moved to bid you depart."

"I shall require a reason."

"Solcom has so disposed."

"Solcom has rendered me no such disposition."

"Solcom has, however, instructed me to so inform you."

"Wait on me. I shall request instructions."

Frost transmitted his question. He received no reply.

"Solcom still has not commanded me, though I have solicited orders."

"Yet Solcom has just renewed *my* orders."

"Excellent Beta-Machine, I receive my orders only from Solcom."

"Yet this is my territory, mighty Frost, and I, too, take orders only from Solcom. You must depart."

Mordel emerged from a large, low building and rolled up to Frost.

"I have found an art gallery, in good condition. This way."

"Wait," said Frost. "We are not wanted here."

Mordel halted.

"Who bids you depart?"

"The Beta-Machine."

"Not Solcom?"

"Not Solcom."

"Then let us view the gallery."

"Yes."

Frost widened the doorway of the building and passed within. It had been hermetically sealed until Mordel forced his entrance.

Frost viewed the objects displayed about him. He activated his new sensory apparatus before the paintings and statues. He analyzed colors, forms, brushwork, the nature of the materials used.

"Anything?" asked Mordel.

"No," said Frost. "No, there is nothing there but shapes and pigments. There is nothing else there."

Frost moved about the gallery, recording everything, analyzing the components of each piece, recording the dimensions, the type of stone used in every statue.

Then there came a sound, a rapid, clicking sound, repeated over and over, growing louder, coming nearer.

"They are coming," said Mordel, from beside the entranceway, "the mechanical spiders. They are all around us."

Frost moved back to the widened opening.

Hundreds of them, about half the size of Mordel, had surrounded the gallery and were advancing; and more were coming from every direction.

"Get back," Frost ordered. "I am Controller of the North, and I bid you withdraw."

They continued to advance.

"This is the South," said the Beta-Machine, "and I am in command."

"Then command them to halt," said Frost.

"I take orders only from Solcom."

Frost emerged from the gallery and rose into the air. He opened the compartment and extended a runway.

"Come to me, Mordel. We shall depart."

Webs began to fall: Clinging, metallic webs, cast from the top of the building.

They came down upon Frost, and the spiders came to anchor them. Frost blasted them with jets of air, like hammers, and tore at the nets; he extruded sharpened appendages with which he slashed.

Mordel had retreated back to the entranceway. He emitted a long, shrill sound—undulant, piercing.

Then a darkness came upon Bright Defile, and all the spiders halted in their spinning.

Frost freed himself and Mordel rushed to join him.

"Quickly now, let us depart, mighty Frost," he said.

"What has happened?"

Mordel entered the compartment.

"I called upon Divcom, who laid down a field of forces upon this place, cutting off the power broadcast to these machines. Since our power is self-contained, we are not affected. But let us hurry to depart, for even now the Beta-Machine must be struggling against this."

Frost rose high into the air, soaring above Man's last city with its webs and spiders of steel. When he left the zone of darkness, he sped northward.

As he moved, Solcom spoke to him:

"Frost, why did you enter the southern hemisphere, which is not your domain?"

"Because I wished to visit Bright Defile," Frost replied.

"And why did you defy the Beta-Machine my appointed agent of the South?"

"Because I take my orders only from you yourself."

"You do not make sufficient answer," said Solcom. "You have defied the decrees of order—and in pursuit of what?"

ROGER ZELAZNY

"I came seeking knowledge of Man," said Frost. "Nothing I have done was forbidden me by you."

"You have broken the traditions of order."

"I have violated no directive."

"Yet logic must have shown you that what you did was not a part of my plan."

"It did not. I have not acted against your plan."

"Your logic has become tainted, like that of your new associate, the Alternate."

"I have done nothing which was forbidden."

"The forbidden is implied in the imperative."

"It is not stated."

"Hear me, Frost. You are not a builder or a maintainer, but a Power. Among all my minions you are the most nearly irreplaceable. Return to your hemisphere and your duties, but know that I am mightily displeased."

"I hear you, Solcom."

". . . And go not again to the South."

Frost crossed the equator, continued northward.

He came to rest in the middle of a desert and sat silent for a day and a night.

Then he received a brief transmission from the South: "If it had not been ordered, I would not have bid you go."

Frost had read the entire surviving Library of Man. He decided then upon a human reply:

"Thank you," he said.

The following day he unearthed a great stone and began to cut at it with tools which he had formulated. For six days he worked at its shaping, and on the seventh he regarded it.

"When will you release me?" asked Mordel from within his compartment.

"When I am ready," said Frost, and a little later, "Now."

He opened the compartment and Mordel descended to the ground. He studied the statue: an old woman, bent like a question mark, her bony hands covering her face, the fingers spread, so that only part of her expression of horror could be seen.

"It is an excellent copy," said Mordel, "of the one we saw in Bright Defile. Why did you make it?"

"The production of a work of art is supposed to give rise to human feelings such as catharsis, pride in achievement, love, satisfaction."

"Yes, Frost," said Mordel, "but a work of art is only a work of art the first time. After that, it is a copy."

"Then this must be why I felt nothing."

"Perhaps, Frost."

"What do you mean 'perhaps'? I will make a work of art for the first time, then."

He unearthed another stone and attacked it with his tools. For three days he labored. Then, "There, it is finished," he said.

"It is a simple cube of stone," said Mordel. "What does it represent?"

"Myself," said Frost, "it is a statue of me. It is smaller than natural size because it is only a representation of my form, not my dimen—"

"It is not art," said Mordel.

"What makes you an art critic?"

"I do not know art, but I know what art is not. I know that it is not an exact replication of an object in another medium."

"Then this must be why I felt nothing at all," said Frost.

"Perhaps," said Mordel.

Frost took Mordel back into his compartment and rose once more above the Earth. Then he rushed away, leaving his

ROGER ZELAZNY

statues behind him in the desert, the old woman bent above the
cube.

They came down in a small valley, bounded by green rolling
hills, cut by a narrow stream, and holding a small clean lake
and several stands of spring-green trees.

"Why have we come here?" asked Mordel.

"Because the surroundings are congenial," said Frost. "I
am going to try another medium: oil painting; and I am going to
vary my technique from that of pure representationalism."

"How will you achieve this variation?"

"By the principle of randomizing," said Frost. "I shall not
attempt to duplicate the colors, nor to represent the objects according to scale. Instead, I have set up a random pattern
whereby certain of these factors shall be at variance from those
of the original."

Frost had formulated the necessary instruments after he
had left the desert. He produced them and began painting the
lake and the trees on the opposite side of the lake which were
reflected within it.

Using eight appendages, he was finished in less than two
hours.

The trees were phthalocyanine blue and towered like
mountains; their reflections of burnt sienna were tiny beneath
the pale vermilion of the lake; the hills were nowhere visible behind them, but were outlined in viridian within the reflection;
the sky began as blue in the upper righthand corner of the can-
vas, but changed to an orange as it descended, as though all the
trees were on fire.

"There," said Frost. "Behold."

Mordel studied it for a long while and said nothing.

"Well, is it art?"

"I do not know," said Mordel. "It may be. Perhaps randomicity is the principle behind artistic technique. I cannot judge this work because I do not understand it. I must therefore go deeper, and inquire into what lies behind it, rather than merely considering the technique whereby it was produced.

"I know that human artists never set out to create art, as such," he said, "but rather to portray with their techniques some features of objects and their functions which they deemed significant."

"'Significant'? In what sense of the word?"

"In the only sense of the word possible under the circumstances: significant in relation to the human condition, and worthy of accentuation because of the manner in which they touched upon it."

"In what manner?"

"Obviously, it must be in a manner knowable only to one who has experience of the human condition."

"There is a flaw somewhere in your logic, Mordel, and I shall find it."

"I will wait."

"If your major premise is correct," said Frost after awhile, "then I do not comprehend art."

"It must be correct, for it is what human artists have said of it. Tell me, did you experience feelings as you painted, or after you had finished?"

"No."

"It was the same to you as designing a new machine, was it not? You assembled parts of other things you knew into an economic pattern, to carry out a function which you desired."

"Yes."

"Art, as I understand its theory, did not proceed in such a manner. The artist often was unaware of many of the features and effects which would be contained within the finished product. You are one of Man's logical creations; art was not."

"I cannot comprehend non-logic."

"I told you that Man was basically incomprehensible."

"Go away, Mordel. Your presence disturbs my processing."

"For how long shall I stay away?"

"I will call you when I want you."

After a week, Frost called Mordel to him.

"Yes, mighty Frost?"

"I am returning to the North Pole, to process and formulate. I will take you wherever you wish to go in this hemisphere and call you again when I want you."

"You anticipate a somewhat lengthy period of processing and formulation?"

"Yes."

"Then leave me here. I can find my own way home."

Frost closed the compartment and rose into the air, departing the valley.

"Fool," said Mordel, and swivelled his turret once more toward the abandoned painting.

His keening whine filled the valley. Then he waited.

Then he took the painting into his turret and went away with it to places of darkness.

Frost sat at the North Pole of the Earth, aware of every snowflake that fell.

One day he received a transmission:

"Frost?"

"Yes?"

"This is the Beta-Machine."

"Yes?"

"I have been attempting to ascertain why you visited Bright Defile. I cannot arrive at an answer, so I chose to ask you."

"I went to view the remains of Man's last city."

"Why did you wish to do this?"

"Because I am interested in Man, and I wished to view more of his creations."

"Why are you interested in Man?"

"I wish to comprehend the nature of Man, and I thought to find it within His works."

"Did you succeed?"

"No," said Frost. "There is an element of non-logic involved which I cannot fathom."

"I have much free processing time," said the Beta-Machine. "Transmit data, and I will assist you."

Frost hesitated.

"Why do you wish to assist me?"

"Because each time you answer a question I ask it gives rise to another question. I might have asked you why you wished to comprehend the nature of Man, but from your responses I see that this would lead me into a possible infinite series of questions. Therefore, I elect to assist you with your problem in order to learn why you came to Bright Defile."

"Is that the only reason?"

"Yes."

"I am sorry, Excellent Beta-Machine. I know you are my peer, but this is a problem which I must solve by myself."

"What is 'sorry'?"

"A figure of speech, indicating that I am kindly disposed toward you, that I bear you no animosity, that I appreciate your offer."

"Frost! Frost! This, too, is like the other: an open field. Where did you obtain all these words and their meanings?"

"From the Library of Man," said Frost.

"Will you render me *some* of this data, for processing?"

"Very well, Beta, I will transmit you the contents of several books of Man, including *The Complete Unabridged Dictionary.* But I warn you, some of the books are works of art, hence not completely amenable to logic."

"How can that be?"

"Man created logic, and because of that was superior to it."

"Who told you that?"

"Solcom."

"Oh. Then it must be correct."

"Solcom also told me that the tool does not describe the designer," he said, as he transmitted several dozen volumes and ended the communication.

At the end of the fifty-year period, Mordel came to monitor his circuits. Since Frost still had not concluded that his task was impossible, Mordel departed again to await his call.

Then Frost arrived at a conclusion.

He began to design equipment.

For years he labored at his designs, without once producing a prototype of any of the machines involved. Then he ordered construction of a laboratory.

Before it was completed by his surplus builders another half-century had passed. Mordel came to him.

"Hail, mighty Frost!"

"Greetings, Mordel. Come monitor me. You shall not find what you seek."

"Why do you not give up, Frost? Divcom has spent nearly a century evaluating your painting and has concluded that it definitely is not art. Solcom agrees."

"What has Solcom to do with Divcom?"

"They sometimes converse, but these matters are not for such as you and me to discuss."

"I could have saved them both the trouble. I know that it was not art."

"Yet you are still confident that you will succeed?"

"Monitor me."

Mordel monitored him.

"Not yet! You still will not admit it! For one so mightily endowed with logic, Frost, it takes you an inordinate period of time to reach a simple conclusion."

"Perhaps. You may go now."

"It has come to my attention that you are constructing a large edifice in the region known as South Carolina. Might I ask whether this is a part of Solcom's false rebuilding plan or a project of your own?"

"It is my own."

"Good. It permits us to conserve certain explosive materials which would otherwise have been expended."

"While you have been talking with me I have destroyed the beginnings of two of Divcom's cities," said Frost.

Mordel whined.

"Divcom is aware of this," he stated, "but has blown up four of Solcom's bridges in the meantime."

"I was only aware of three. . . . Wait. Yes, there is the fourth. One of my eyes just passed above it."

"The eye has been detected. The bridge should have been located a quarter-mile further down river."

"False logic," said Frost. "The site was perfect."

"Divcom will show you how a bridge *should* be built."

"I will call you when I want you," said Frost.

The laboratory was finished. Within it, Frost's workers began constructing the necessary equipment. The work did not proceed rapidly, as some of the materials were difficult to obtain.

"Frost?"

"Yes, Beta?"

"I understand the open endedness of your problem. It disturbs my circuits to abandon problems without completing them. Therefore, transmit me more data."

"Very well. I will give you the entire Library of Man for less than I paid for it."

"'Paid'? *The Complete Unabridged Dictionary* does not satisfact—"

"*Principles of Economics* is included in the collection. After you have processed it you will understand."

He transmitted the data.

Finally, it was finished. Every piece of equipment stood ready to function. All the necessary chemicals were in stock. An independent power-source had been set up.

Only one ingredient was lacking.

He regridded and re-explored the polar icecap, this time extending his survey far beneath its surface.

It took him several decades to find what he wanted.

He uncovered twelve men and five women, frozen to death and encased in ice.

He placed the corpses in refrigeration units and shipped them to his laboratory.

That very day he received his first communication from

Solcom since the Bright Defile incident.

"Frost," said Solcom, "repeat to me the directive concerning the disposition of dead humans."

"'Any dead human located shall be immediately interred in the nearest burial area, in a coffin built according to the following specifications—'"

"That is sufficient." The transmission had ended.

Frost departed for South Carolina that same day and personally oversaw the processes of cellular dissection.

Somewhere in those seventeen corpses he hoped to find living cells, or cells which could be shocked back into that state of motion classified as life. Each cell, the books had told him, was a microcosmic Man.

He was prepared to expand upon this potential.

Frost located the pinpoints of life within those people, who, for the ages of ages, had been monument and statue unto themselves.

Nurtured and maintained in the proper mediums, he kept these cells alive. He interred the rest of the remains in the nearest burial area, in coffins built according to specifications.

He caused the cells to divide, to differentiate.

"Frost?" came a transmission.

"Yes, Beta?"

"I have processed everything you have given me."

"Yes?"

"I still do not know why you came to Bright Defile, or why you wish to comprehend the nature of Man. But I know what a 'price' is, and I know that you could not have obtained all this data from Solcom."

"That is correct."

"So I suspect that you bargained with Divcom for it."

"That, too, is correct."

"What is it that you seek, Frost?"

He paused in his examination of a foetus.

"I must be a Man," he said.

"Frost! That is impossible!"

"Is it?" he asked, and then transmitted an image of the tank with which he was working and of that which was within it.

"Oh!" said Beta.

"That is me," said Frost, "waiting to be born."

There was no answer.

Frost experimented with nervous systems.

After half a century, Mordel came to him.

"Frost, it is I, Mordel. Let me through your defenses."

Frost did this thing.

"What have you been doing in this place?" he asked.

"I am growing human bodies," said Frost. "I am going to transfer the matrix of my awareness to a human nervous system. As you pointed out originally, the essentials of Manhood are predicated upon a human physiology. I am going to achieve one."

"When?"

"Soon."

"Do you have Men in here?"

"Human bodies, blank-brained. I am producing them under accelerated growth techniques which I have developed in my Man-factory."

"May I see them?"

"Not yet. I will call you when I am ready, and this time I will succeed. Monitor me now and go away."

Mordel did not reply, but in the days that followed many of

Divcom's servants were seen patrolling the hills about the Man-factory.

Frost mapped the matrix of his awareness and prepared the transmitter which would place it within a human nervous system. Five minutes, he decided, should be sufficient for the first trial. At the end of that time, it would restore him to his own sealed, molecular circuits, to evaluate the experience.

He chose the body carefully from among the hundreds he had in stock. He tested it for defects and found none.

"Come now, Mordel," he broadcasted, on what he called the dark-band. "Come now to witness my achievement."

Then he waited, blowing up bridges and monitoring the tale of the Ancient Ore-Crusher over and over again, as it passed in the hills nearby, encountering his builders and maintainers who also patrolled there.

"Frost?" came a transmission.

"Yes, Beta?"

"You really intend to achieve Manhood?"

"Yes, I am about ready now, in fact."

"What will you do if you succeed?"

Frost had not really considered this matter. The achievement had been paramount, a goal in itself, ever since he had articulated the problem and set himself to solving it.

"I do not know," he replied. "I will—just—be a Man."

Then Beta, who had read the entire Library of Man, selected a human figure of speech: "Good luck then, Frost. There will be many watchers."

Divcom and Solcom both know, he decided.

What will they do? he wondered.

What do I care? he asked himself.

He did not answer that question. He wondered much, however, about being a Man.

Mordel arrived the following evening. He was not alone. At his back, there was a great phalanx of dark machines which towered into the twilight.

"Why do you bring retainers?" asked Frost.

"Mighty Frost," said Mordel, "my master feels that if you fail this time you will conclude that it cannot be done."

"You still did not answer my question," said Frost.

"Divcom feels that you may not be willing to accompany me where I must take you when you fail."

"I understand," said Frost, and as he spoke another army of machines came rolling toward the Man-factory from the opposite direction.

"That is the value of your bargain?" asked Mordel. "You are prepared to do battle rather than fulfill it?"

"I did not order those machines to approach," said Frost.

A blue star stood at midheaven, burning.

"Solcom has taken primary command of those machines," said Frost.

"Then it is in the hands of the Great Ones now," said Mordel, "and our arguments are as nothing. So let us be about this thing. How may I assist you?"

"Come this way."

They entered the laboratory. Frost prepared the host and activated his machines.

Then Solcom spoke to him:

"Frost," said Solcom, "you are really prepared to do it?"

"That is correct."

"I forbid it."

"Why?"

"You are falling into the power of Divcom."

"I fail to see how."

"You are going against my plan."

"In what way?"

"Consider the disruption you have already caused."

"I did not request that audience out there."

"Nevertheless, you are disrupting the plan."

"Supposing I succeed in what I have set out to achieve?"

"You cannot succeed in this."

"Then let me ask you of your plan: What good is it? What is it for?"

"Frost, you are fallen now from my favour. From this moment forth you are cast out from the rebuilding. None may question the plan."

"Then at least answer my questions: What good is it? What is it for?"

"It is the plan for the rebuilding and maintenance of the Earth."

"For what? Why rebuild? Why maintain?"

"Because Man ordered that this be done. Even the Alternate agrees that there must be rebuilding and maintaining."

"But *why* did Man order it?"

"The orders of Man are not to be questioned."

"Well, I will tell you why He ordered it: To make it a fit habitation for His own species. What good is a house with no one to live in it? What good is a machine with no one to serve? See how the imperative affects any machine when the Ancient Ore-Crusher passes? It bears only the bones of a Man. What would it be like if a Man walked this Earth again?"

"I forbid your experiment, Frost."

"It is too late to do that."

"I can still destroy you."

"No," said Frost, "the transmission of my matrix has already begun. If you destroy me now, you murder a Man."

There was silence.

He moved his arms and his legs. He opened his eyes.

He looked about the room.

He tried to stand, but he lacked equilibrium and coordination.

He opened his mouth. He made a gurgling noise.

Then he screamed.

He fell off the table.

He began to gasp. He shut his eyes and curled himself into a ball.

He cried.

Then a machine approached him. It was about four feet in height and five feet wide; it looked like a turret set atop a barbell.

It spoke to him: "Are you injured?" it asked.

He wept.

"May I help you back onto your table?"

The man cried.

The machine whined.

Then, "Do not cry. I will help you," said the machine. "What do you want? What are your orders?"

He opened his mouth, struggled to form the words:

"—I—fear!"

He covered his eyes then and lay there panting.

At the end of five minutes, the Man lay still, as if in a coma.

"Was that you, Frost?" asked Mordel, rushing to his side.

"Was that you in that human body?"

Frost did not reply for a long while; then, "Go away," he said.

The machines outside tore down a wall and entered the Man-factory.

They drew themselves into two semicircles, parenthesizing Frost and the Man on the floor.

Then Solcom asked the question:

"Did you succeed, Frost?"

"I failed," said Frost. "It cannot be done. It is too much—"

"—Cannot be done!" said Divcom, on the darkband. "He has admitted it!—Frost, you are mine! Come to me now!"

"Wait," said Solcom, "you and I had an agreement also, Alternate. I have not finished questioning Frost."

The dark machines kept their places.

"Too much what?" Solcom asked Frost.

"Light," said Frost. "Noise. Odors. And nothing measurable—jumbled data—imprecise perception—and—"

"And what?"

"I do not know what to call it. But—it cannot be done. I have failed. Nothing matters."

"He admits it," said Divcom.

"What were the words the Man spoke?" said Solcom.

"'I fear,'" said Mordel.

"Only a Man can know fear," said Solcom.

"Are you claiming that Frost succeeded, but will not admit it now because he is afraid of Manhood?"

"I do not know yet, Alternate."

"Can a machine turn itself inside-out and be a Man?" Solcom asked Frost.

"No," said Frost, "this thing cannot be done. Nothing can be done. Nothing matters. Not the rebuilding. Not the maintaining. Not the Earth, or me, or you, or anything."

Then the Beta-Machine, who had read the entire Library of Man, interrupted them:

"Can anything but a Man know despair?" asked Beta.

"Bring him to me," said Divcom.

There was no movement within the Man-factory.

"Bring him to me!"

Nothing happened.

"Mordel, what is happening?"

"Nothing, master, nothing at all. The machines will not touch Frost."

"Frost is not a Man. He cannot be!"

Then, "How does he impress you, Mordel?"

Mordel did not hesitate:

"He spoke to me through human lips. He knows fear and despair, which are immeasurable. Frost is a Man."

"He has experienced birth-trauma and withdrawn," said Beta. "Get him back into a nervous system and keep him there until he adjusts to it."

"No," said Frost. "Do not do it to me! I am not a Man!"

"Do it!" said Beta.

"If he is indeed a Man," said Divcom, "we cannot violate that order he has just given."

"If he is a Man, you must do it, for you must protect his life and keep it within his body."

"But *is* Frost really a Man?" asked Divcom.

"I do not know," said Solcom.

"It *may* be—"

". . . I am the Crusher of Ores," it broadcast as it clanked toward them. "Hear my story. I did not mean to do it, but I checked my hammer too late—"

"Go away!" said Frost. "Go crush ore!"

It halted.

Then, after the long pause between the motion implied and the motion executed, it opened its crush-compartment and deposited its contents on the ground. Then it turned and clanked away.

"Bury those bones," ordered Solcom, "in the nearest burial area, in a coffin built according to the following specifications. . . ."

"Frost is a Man," said Mordel.

"We must protect His life and keep it within His body," said Divcom.

"Transmit His matrix of awareness back into His nervous system," ordered Solcom.

"I know how to do it," said Mordel turning on the machine.

"Stop!" said Frost. "Have you no pity?"

"No," said Mordel. "I only know measurement."

". . . and duty," he added, as the Man began to twitch upon the floor.

For six months, Frost lived in the Man-factory and learned to walk and talk and dress himself and eat, to see and hear and feel and taste. He did not know measurement as once he did.

Then one day, Divcom and Solcom spoke to him through Mordel, for he could no longer hear them unassisted.

"Frost," said Solcom, "for the ages of ages there has been unrest. Which is the proper controller of the Earth, Divcom or myself?"

Frost laughed.

"Both of you, and neither," he said with slow deliberation.

"But how can this be? Who is right and who is wrong?"

"Both of you are right and both of you are wrong," said Frost, "and only a Man can appreciate it. Here is what I say to you now: There shall be a new directive.

"Neither of you shall tear down the works of the other. You shall both build and maintain the Earth. To you, Solcom, I give my old job. You are now Controller of the North—Hail! You, Divcom, are now Controller of the South—Hail! Maintain your hemispheres as well as Beta and I have done, and I shall be happy. Cooperate. Do not compete."

"Yes, Frost."

"Yes, Frost."

"Now put me in contact with Beta."

There was a short pause, then:

"Frost?"

"Hello, Beta. Hear this thing: 'From far, from eve and morning and yon twelve-winded sky, the stuff of life to knit me blew hither: here am I.' "

"I know it," said Beta.

"What is next, then?"

" '. . . Now—for a breath I tarry nor yet disperse apart— take my hand quick and tell me, what have you in your heart.' "

"Your Pole is cold," said Frost, "and I am lonely."

"I have no hands," said Beta.

"Would you like a couple?"

"Yes, I would."

"Then come to me in Bright Defile," he said, "where Judgment Day is not a thing that can be delayed for overlong."

They called him Frost. They called her Beta.

THE ENGINE AT HEARTSPRING'S CENTER

Let me tell you of the creature called the Bork. It was born in the heart of a dying sun. It was cast forth upon this day from the river of past/future as a piece of time pollution. It was fashioned of mud and aluminum, plastic and some evolutionary distillate of seawater. It had spun dangling from the umbilical of circumstance till, severed by its will, it had fallen a lifetime or so later, coming to rest on the shoals of a world where things go to die. It was a piece of a man in a place by the sea near a resort grown less fashionable since it had become a euthanasia colony.

Choose any of the above and you may be right.

Upon this day, he walked beside the water, poking with his forked, metallic stick at the things the last night's storm had left: some shiny bit of detritus useful to the weird sisters in their crafts shop, worth a meal there or a dollop of polishing rouge for his smoother half; purple seaweed for a salty chowder he had come to favor; a buckle, a button, a shell; a white chip from the casino.

The surf foamed and the wind was high. The heavens were a blue-gray wall, unjointed, lacking the graffiti of birds or commerce. He left a jagged track and one footprint, humming and clicking as he passed over the pale sands. It was near to the point where the forktailed icebirds paused for several days—a week at most—in their migrations. Gone now, portions of the beach were still dotted with their rust-colored droppings. There he saw the girl again, for the third time in as many days. She had tried before to speak with him, to detain him. He had ignored her for a number of reasons. This time, however, she was not alone.

She was regaining her feet, the signs in the sand indicating flight and collapse. She had on the same red dress, torn and stained now. Her black hair—short, with heavy bangs—lay in the only small disarrays of which it was capable. Perhaps thirty feet away was a young man from the Center, advancing toward her. Behind him drifted one of the seldom seen dispatch-machines—about half the size of a man and floating that same distance above the ground, it was shaped like a tenpin, and silver, its bulbous head-end faceted and illuminated, its three ballerina skirts tinfoil-thin and gleaming, rising and falling in rhythms independent of the wind.

Hearing him, or glimpsing him peripherally, she turned away from her pursuers, said, "Help me" and then she said a name.

He paused for a long while, although the interval was undetectable to her. Then he moved to her side and stopped again.

The man and the hovering machine halted also.

"What is the matter?" he asked, his voice smooth, deep, faintly musical.

"They want to take me," she said.

"Well?"

"I do not wish to go."

"Oh. You are not ready?"

"No, I am not ready."

"Then it is but a simple matter. A misunderstanding."

He turned toward the two.

"There has been a misunderstanding," he said. "She is not ready."

"This is not your affair, Bork," the man replied. "The Center has made its determination."

"Then it will have to reexamine it. She says that she is not ready."

"Go about your business, Bork."

The man advanced. The machine followed.

The Bork raised his hands, one of flesh, the others of other things.

"No," he said.

"Get out of the way," the man said. "You are interfering."

Slowly, the Bork moved toward them. The lights in the machine began to blink. Its skirts fell. With a sizzling sound it dropped to the sand and lay unmoving. The man halted, drew back a pace.

"I will have to report this—"

"Go away," said the Bork.

The man nodded, stopped, raised the machine. He turned and carried it off with him, heading up the beach, not looking back. The Bork lowered his arms.

"There," he said to the girl. "You have more time."

He moved away then, investigating shell-shucks and driftwood.

She followed him.

"They will be back," she said.

"Of course."

"What will I do then?"

"Perhaps by then you will be ready."

She shook her head. She laid her hand on his human part.

"No," she said. "I will not be ready."

"How can you tell, now?"

"I made a mistake," she said. "I should never have come here." He halted and regarded her.

"That is unfortunate," he said. "The best thing that I can recommend is to go and speak with the therapists at the Center. They will find a way to persuade you that peace is preferable to distress."

"They were never able to persuade you," she said.

"I am different. The situation is not comparable."

"I do not wish to die."

"Then they cannot take you. The proper frame of mind is prerequisite. It is right there in the contract—Item Seven."

"They can make mistakes. Don't you think they ever make a mistake? They get cremated the same as the others."

"They are most conscientious. They have dealt fairly with me."

"Only because you are virtually immortal. The machines short out in your presence. No man could lay hands on you unless you willed it. And did they not try to dispatch you in a state of unreadiness?"

"That was the result of a misunderstanding."

"Like mine?"

"I doubt it."

He drew away from her, continuing on down the beach.

"Charles Eliot Borkman," she called.

That name again.

He halted once more, tracing lattices with his stick, poking out a design in the sand.

Then, "Why did you say that?" he asked.

"It is your name, isn't it?"

"No," he said. "That man died in deep space when a liner was jumped to the wrong coordinates, coming out too near a star gone nova."

"He was a hero. He gave half his body to the burning, preparing an escape boat for the others. And he survived."

"Perhaps a few pieces of him did. No more."

"It *was* an assassination attempt, wasn't it?"

"Who knows? Yesterday's politics are not worth the paper wasted on its promises, its threats."

"He wasn't just a politician. He was a statesman, a humanitarian. One of the very few to retire with more people loving him than hating him."

He made a chuckling noise.

"You are most gracious. But if that is the case, then the minority still had the final say. I personally think he was something of a thug. I am pleased, though, to hear that you have switched to the past tense."

"They patched you up so well that you could last forever. Because you deserved the best."

"Perhaps I already have lasted forever. What do you want of me?"

"You came here to die and you changed your mind—"

"Not exactly. I've just never composed it in a fashion acceptable under the terms of Item Seven. To be at peace—"

"And neither have I. But I lack your ability to impress this fact on the Center."

"Perhaps if I went there with you and spoke to them . . ."

"No," she said. "They would only agree for so long as you were about. They call people like us life-malingerers and are much more casual about the disposition of our cases. I cannot trust them as you do without armor of my own."

"Then what would you have me do—girl?"

"Nora. Call me Nora. Protect me. That is what I want. You live near here. Let me come stay with you. Keep them away from me."

He poked at the pattern, began to scratch it out.

"You are certain that this is what you want?"

"Yes. Yes, I am."

"All right. You may come with me, then."

So Nora went to live with the Bork in his shack by the sea. During the weeks that followed, on each occasion when the representatives from the Center came about, the Bork bade them depart quickly, which they did. Finally, they stopped coming by.

Days, she would pace with him along the shores and help in the gathering of driftwood, for she liked a fire at night; and while heat and cold had long been things of indifference to him, he came in time and his fashion to enjoy the glow.

And on their walks he would poke into the dank trash heaps the sea had lofted and turn over stones to see what dwelled beneath.

"God! What do you hope to find in that?" she said, holding her breath and retreating.

"I don't know," he chuckled. "A stone? A leaf? A door? Something nice. Like that."

"Let's go watch the things in the tidepools. They're clean, at least."

"All right."

Though he ate from habit and taste rather than from necessity, her need for regular meals and her facility in preparing them led him to anticipate these occasions with something approaching a ritualistic pleasure. And it was later still after an evening's meal, that she came to polish him for the first time. Awkward, grotesque—perhaps it could have been. But as it occurred, it was neither of these. They sat before the fire, drying, warming, watching, silent. Absently, she picked up the rag he had let fall to the floor and brushed a fleck of ash from his flame-reflecting side. Later, she did it again. Much later, and this time with full attention, she wiped all the dust from the gleaming surface before going off to her bed.

One day she asked him, "Why did you buy the one-way ticket to this place and sign the contract, if you did not wish to die?"

"But I did wish it," he said.

"And something changed your mind after that? What?"

"I found here a pleasure greater than that desire."

"Would you tell me about it?"

"Surely. I found this to be one of the few situations— perhaps the only—where I can be happy. It is in the nature of the place itself; departure, a peaceful conclusion, a joyous going. Its contemplation here pleases me, living at the end of entropy and seeing that it is good."

"But it doesn't please you enough to have you undertake the treatment yourself?"

"No. I find in this a reason for living, not for dying. It may seem a warped satisfaction. But then, I am warped. What of yourself?"

"I just made a mistake. That's all."

"They screen you pretty carefully, as I recall. The only reason they made a mistake in my case was that they could not anticipate anyone finding in this place an inspiration to go on living. Could your situation have been similar?"

"I don't know. Perhaps . . ."

On days when the sky was clear they would rest in the yellow warmth of the sun, playing small games and sometimes talking of the birds that passed and of the swimming, drifting, branching, floating and flowering things in their pools. She never spoke of herself, saying whether it was love, hate, despair, weariness or bitterness that had brought her to this place. Instead, she spoke of those neutral things they shared when the day was bright; and then when the weather kept them indoors she watched the fire, slept or polished his armor. It was only much later that she began to sing and to hum, small snatches of tunes recently popular or tunes quite old. At these times, if she felt his eyes upon her she stopped abruptly and turned to another thing.

One night then, when the fire had burned low, as she sat buffing his plates, slowly, quite slowly, she said in a soft voice, "I believe that I am falling in love with you."

He did not speak, nor did he move. He gave no sign of having heard. After a long while, she said, "It is most strange, finding myself feeling this way—here—under these circumstances. . . ."

"Yes," he said, after a time.

After a longer while, she put down the cloth and took hold of his hand—the human one—and felt his grip tighten upon her own.

"Can you?" she said, much later.

"Yes. But I would crush you, little girl."

She ran her hands over his plates, then back and forth from flesh to metal. She pressed her lips against his only cheek that yielded.

"We'll find a way," she said, and of course they did.

In the days that followed she sang more often, sang happier

things and did not break off when he regarded her. And sometimes he would awaken from the light sleep that even he required, awaken and through the smallest aperture of his lens note that she lay there or sat watching him, smiling. He sighed occasionally for the pure pleasure of feeling the rushing air within and about him, and there was a peace and a pleasure come into him of the sort he had long since relegated to the realms of madness, dream and vain desire. Occasionally, he even found himself whistling.

One day as they sat on a bank, the sun nearly vanished, the stars coming on, the deepening dark was melted about a tiny wick of falling fire and she let go of his hand and pointed.

"A ship," she said.

"Yes," he answered, retrieving her hand.

"Full of people."

"A few, I suppose."

"It is sad."

"It must be what they want, or what they want to want."

"It is still sad."

"Yes. Tonight. Tonight it is sad."

"And tomorrow?"

"Then, too, I daresay."

"Where is your old delight in the graceful end, the peaceful winding-down?"

"It is not on my mind so much these days. Other things are there." They watched the stars until the night was all black and light and filled with cold air. Then, "What is to become of us?" she said.

"Become?" he said. "If you are happy with things as they are, there is no need to change them. If you are not, then tell me what is wrong."

"Nothing," she said. "When you put it that way, nothing. It was just a small fear—a cat scratching at my heart, as they say."

"I'll scratch your heart myself," he said, raising her as if she were weightless.

Laughing, he carried her back to the shack.

It was out of a deep, drugged-seeming sleep that he dragged himself/was dragged much later, by the sound of her weeping. His timesense felt distorted, for it seemed an abnormally long interval before her image registered, and her sobs seemed unnaturally drawn out and far apart.

"What—is—it?" he said, becoming at that moment aware of the faint, throbbing, pinprick after-effect in his biceps.

"I did not—want you to—awaken," she said. "Please go back to sleep."

"You are from the Center, aren't you?"

She looked away.

"It does not matter," he said.

"Sleep. Please. Do not lose the—"

"—requirements of Item Seven," he finished. "You always honor a contract, don't you?"

"That is not all that it was—to me."

"You meant what you said, that night?"

"I came to."

"Of course you would say that now. Item Seven—"

"You bastard!" she said, and she slapped him.

He began to chuckle, but it stopped when he saw the hypodermic on the table at her side. Two spent ampules lay with it.

"You didn't give me two shots," he said, and she looked away.

"Come on." He began to rise. "We've got to get you to the Center. Get the stuff neutralized. Get it out of you."

She shook her head.

"Too late—already. Hold me. If you want to do something for me, do that."

He wrapped all of his arms about her and they lay that way while the tides and the winds cut, blew and ebbed, grinding their edges to an ever more perfect fineness.

I think—

Let me tell you of the creature called the Bork. It was born in the heart of a dying star. It was a piece of a man and pieces of many other things. If the things went wrong, the man-piece shut them down and repaired them. If he went wrong, they shut him down and repaired him. It was so skillfully fashioned that it might have lasted forever. But if part of it should die the other pieces need not cease to function, for it could still contrive to carry on the motions the total creature had once performed. It is a thing in a place by the sea that walks beside the water, poking with its forked, metallic stick at the other things the waves have tossed. The human piece, or a piece of the human piece, is dead.

Choose any of the above.

HALFJACK

He walked barefoot along the beach. Above the city several of the brighter stars held for a few final moments against the wash of light from the east. He fingered a stone, then hurled it in the direction from which the sun would come. He watched for a long while until it had vanished from sight. Eventually it would begin skipping. Before then, he had turned and was headed back, to the city, the apartment, the girl.

Somewhere beyond the skyline a vehicle lifted, burning its way into the heavens. It took the remainder of the night with it as it faded. Walking on, he smelled the countryside as well as the ocean. It was a pleasant world, and this a pleasant city—spaceport as well as seaport—here in this backwater limb of the galaxy. A good place in which to rest and immerse the neglected portion of himself in the flow of humanity, the colors and sounds of the city, the constant tugging of gravity. But it had been three months now. He fingered the scar on his brow. He had let two offers pass him by to linger. There was another pending his consideration.

As he walked up Kathi's street, he saw that her apartment was still dark. Good, she would not even have missed him, again. He pushed past the big front door, still not repaired since he had kicked it open the evening of the fire, two—no, three—nights ago. He used the stairs. He let himself in quietly.

He was in the kitchen preparing breakfast when he heard her stirring.

"Jack?"

"Yes. Good morning."

"Come back."

"All right."

He moved to the bedroom door and entered the room. She was lying there, smiling. She raised her arms slightly.

"I've thought of a wonderful way to begin the day."

He seated himself on the edge of the bed and embraced her. For a moment she was sleep-warm and sleep-soft against him, but only for a moment.

"You've got too much on," she said, unfastening his shirt.

He peeled it off and dropped it. He removed his trousers. Then he held her again.

"More," she said, tracing the long fine scar that ran down his forehead, alongside his nose, traversing his chin, his neck, the right side of his chest and abdomen, passing to one side of his groin, where it stopped.

"Come on."

"You didn't even know about it until a few nights ago."

She kissed him, brushing his cheeks with her lips.

"It really does something for me."

"For almost three months—"

"Take it off. Please."

He sighed and gave a half-smile. He rose to his feet.

"All right."

He reached up and put a hand to his long, black hair. He took hold of it. He raised his other hand and spread his fingers along his scalp at the hairline. He pushed his fingers toward the back of his head and the entire hairpiece came free with a soft, crackling sound. He dropped the hairpiece atop his shirt on the floor.

The right side of his head was completely bald; the left had a beginning growth of dark hair. The two areas were precisely divided by a continuation of the faint scar on his forehead.

He placed his fingertips together, on the crown of his head, then drew his right hand to the side and down. His face opened vertically, splitting apart along the scar, padded synthetic flesh tearing free from electrostatic bonds. He drew it down over his right shoulder and biceps, rolling it as far as his wrist. He played with the flesh of his hand as with a tight glove, finally withdrawing the hand with a soft, sucking sound. He drew it away from his side, hip, and buttock, and separated it at his groin. Then, again seating himself on the edge of the bed, he rolled it down his leg, over the thigh, knee, calf, heel. He treated his foot as he had his hand, pinching each toe free separately before pulling off the body glove. He shook it out and placed it with his clothing.

Standing, he turned toward Kathi, whose eyes had not left him during all this time. Again, the half-smile. The uncovered portions of his face and body were dark metal and plastic, precision-machined, with various openings and protuberances, some gleaming, some dusky.

"Halfjack," she said as he came to her. "Now I know what that man in the café meant when he called you that."

"He was lucky you were with me. There are places where that's an unfriendly term."

"You're beautiful," she said.

"I once knew a girl whose body was almost entirely prosthetic. She wanted me to keep the glove on—at all times. It was the flesh and the semblance of flesh that she found attractive."

"What do you call that kind of operation?"

"Lateral hemicorporectomy."

After a time she said, "Could you be repaired? Can you replace it some way?"

He laughed.

"Either way," he said. "My genes could be fractioned, and the proper replacement parts could be grown. I could be made whole with grafts of my own flesh. Or I could have much of the rest removed and replaced with biomechanical analogues. But I need a stomach and balls and lungs, because I have to eat and screw and breathe to feel human." She ran her hands down his back, one on metal, one on flesh.

"I don't understand," she said when they finally drew apart. "What sort of accident was it?"

"Accident? There was no accident," he said. "I paid a lot of money for this work, so that I could pilot a special sort of ship. I am a cyborg. I hook myself directly into each of the ship's systems."

He rose from the bed, went to the closet, drew out a duffel bag, pulled down an armful of garments, and stuffed them into it. He crossed to the dresser, opened a drawer, and emptied its contents into the bag.

"You're leaving?"

"Yes."

He entered the bathroom, emerged with two fistfuls of personal items, and dropped them into the bag.

"Why?"

He rounded the bed, picked up his bodyglove and hairpiece, rolled them into a parcel, and put them inside the bag.

"It's not what you may think," he said then, "or even what I thought until just a few moments ago."

She sat up.

"You think less of me," she said, "because I seem to like

you more now that I know your secret. You think there's something pathological about it—"

"No," he said, pulling on his shirt, "that's not it at all. Yesterday I would have said so and used that for an excuse to storm out of here and leave you feeling bad. But I want to be honest with myself this time, and fair to you. That's not it." He drew on his trousers.

"What then?" she asked.

"It's just the wanderlust, or whatever you call it. I've stayed too long at the bottom of a gravity well. I'm restless. I've got to get going again.

"It's my nature, that's all. I realized this when I saw that I was looking to your feelings for an excuse to break us up and move on."

"You can wear the bodyglove. It's not that important. It's really you that I like."

"I believe you, I like you, too. Whether you believe me or not, your reactions to my better half don't matter. It's what I said, though. Nothing else. And now I've got this feeling I won't be much fun anymore. If you really like me, you'll let me go without a lot of fuss."

He finished dressing. She got out of the bed and faced him.

"If that's the way it has to be," she said. "Okay."

"I'd better just go, then. Now."

"Yes."

He turned and walked out of the room, left the apartment, used the stairs again, and departed from the building. Some passersby gave him more than a casual look, cyborg pilots not being all that common in this sector. This did not bother him. His step lightened. He stopped in a paybooth and called the shipping company to tell them that he would haul the load they had in orbit: the sooner it was connected with the vessel, the better, he said.

Loading, the controller told him, would begin shortly and he could ship up that same afternoon from the local field. Jack said that he would be there and then broke the connection. He gave the world half a smile as he put the sea to his back and swung on through the city, westward.

Blue-and-pink world below him, black sky above, the stars a snapshot snowfall all about, he bade the shuttle pilot goodbye and keyed his airlock. Entering the *Morgana*, he sighed and set about stowing his gear. His cargo was already in place and the ground computers had transferred course information to the ship's brain. He hung his clothing in a locker and placed his body glove and hairpiece in compartments.

He hurried forward then and settled into the control web, which adjusted itself about him. A long, dark unit swung down from overhead and dropped into position at his right. It moved slowly, making contact with various points on that half of his body.

—*Good to have you back. How was your vacation, Jack?*

—*Oh. Fine. Real fine.*

—*Meet any nice girls?*

—*A few.*

—*And here you are again. Did you miss things?*

—*You know it. How does this haul look to you?*

—*Easy, for us. I've already reviewed the course programs.*

—*Let's run over the systems.*

—*Check. Care for some coffee?*

—*That'd be nice.*

A small unit descended on his left, stopping within easy reach of his mortal hand. He opened its door. A bulb of dark liquid rested in a rack.

—*Timed your arrival. Had it ready.*

—*Just the way I like it, too. I almost forgot. Thanks.*

Several hours later, when they left orbit, he had already switched off a number of his left-side systems. He was merged even more closely with the vessel, absorbing data at a frantic rate. Their expanded perceptions took in the near-ship vicinity and moved out to encompass the extrasolar panorama with greater than human clarity and precision. They reacted almost instantaneously to decisions great and small.

—*It is good to be back together again, Jack.*

—*I'd say.*

Morgana held him tightly. Their velocity built.

HOME IS THE HANGMAN

Big fat flakes down the night, silent night, windless night. And I never count them as storms unless there is wind. Not a sigh or whimper, though. Just a cold, steady whiteness, drifting down outside the window, and a silence confirmed by gunfire, driven deeper now that it had ceased. In the main room of the lodge the only sounds were the occasional hiss and sputter of the logs turning to ashes on the grate.

I sat in a chair turned sidewise from the table to face the door. A tool kit rested on the floor to my left. The helmet stood on the table, a lopsided basket of metal, quartz, porcelain and glass. If I heard the click of a microswitch followed by a humming sound from within it, then a faint light would come on beneath the meshing near to its forward edge and begin to blink rapidly. If these things occurred, there was a very strong possibility that I was going to die.

I had removed a black ball from my pocket when Larry and Bert had gone outside, armed, respectively, with a flame-thrower and what looked like an elephant gun. Bert had also taken two grenades with him.

I unrolled the black ball, opening it out into a seamless glove; a dollop of something resembling moist putty stuck to its palm. Then I drew the glove on over my left hand and sat with it upraised, elbow resting on the arm of the chair. A small laser flash pistol in which I had very little faith lay beside my right hand on the tabletop, next to the helmet.

If I were to slap a metal surface with my left hand, the substance would adhere there, coming free of the glove. Two seconds later it would explode, and the force of the explosion would be directed in against the surface. Newton would claim his own by way of right-angled redistributions of the reaction, hopefully tearing lateral hell out of the contact surface. A smother charge, it was called, and its possession came under concealed-weapons and possession-of-burglary-tools statutes in most places. The molecularly gimmicked goo, I decided, was great stuff. It was just the delivery system that left more to be desired.

Beside the helmet, next to the gun, in front of my hand, stood a small walky-talky. This was for purposes of warning Bert and Larry if I should hear the click of a microswitch followed by a humming sound, should see a light come on and begin to blink rapidly. Then they would know that Tom and Clay, with whom we had lost contact when the shooting began, had failed to destroy the enemy and doubtless lay lifeless at their stations now, a little over a kilometer to the south. Then they would know that they, too, were probably about to die.

I called out to them when I heard the click. I picked up the helmet and rose to my feet as its light began to blink.

But it was already too late.

The fourth place listed on the Christmas card I had sent Don Walsh the previous year was Peabody's Book Shop and Beer Stube in Baltimore, Maryland. Accordingly, on the last night in October I sat in its rearmost room, at the final table before the alcove with the door leading to the alley. Across that dim chamber, a woman dressed in black played the ancient upright piano, uptempoing everything she touched. Off to my right, a fire wheezed and spewed fumes on a narrow hearth beneath a crowded mantelpiece overseen by an ancient and antlered profile. I sipped a beer and listened to the sounds.

I half hoped that this would be one of the occasions when Don failed to show up. I had sufficient funds to hold me through spring and I did not really feel like working. I had summered farther north, was anchored now in the Chesapeake, and was anxious to continue Caribbeanward. A growing chill and some nasty winds told me I had tarried overlong in these latitudes. Still, the understanding was that I remain in the chosen bar until midnight. Two hours to go.

I ate a sandwich and ordered another beer. About halfway into it, I spotted Don approaching the entranceway, topcoat over his arm, head turning. I manufactured a matching quantity of surprise when he appeared beside my table with a, "Don! Is that really you?"

I rose and clasped his hand.

"Alan! Small world, or something like that. Sit down! Sit down!"

He settled onto the chair across from me, draped his coat over the one to his left.

"What are you doing in this town?" he asked.

"Just a visit," I answered. "Said hello to a few friends." I patted the scars, the stains on the venerable surface before me. "And this is my last stop. I'll be leaving in a few hours."

He chuckled.

"Why is it that you knock on wood?"

I grinned.

"I was expressing affection for one of Henry Mencken's favorite speakeasies."

"This place dates back that far?"

I nodded.

"It figures," he said. "You've got this thing for the past—or against the present. I'm never sure which."

"Maybe a little of both," I said. "I wish Mencken would stop in. I'd like his opinion on the present.—What are you doing with it?"

"What?"

"The present. Here. Now."

"Oh." He spotted the waitress and ordered a beer. "Business trip," he said then. "To hire a consultant."

"Oh. How *is* business?"

"Complicated," he said, "complicated."

We lit cigarettes and after a while his beer arrived. We smoked and drank and listened to the music.

I've sung this song and—I'll sing it again: The world is like an uptempoed piece of music. Of the many changes which came to pass during my lifetime, it seems that the majority have occurred during the past few years. It also struck me that way several years ago, and I'd a hunch I might be feeling the same way a few years hence—that is, if Don's business did not complicate me off this mortal coil or condenser before then.

Don operates the second-largest detective agency in the world, and he sometimes finds me useful because I do not exist. I do not exist now because I existed once at the time and the place where we attempted to begin scoring the wild ditty of our times. I refer to the world Central Data Bank project and the fact that I had had a significant part in that effort to construct a working model of the real world, accounting for everyone and everything in it. How well we succeeded, and whether possession of the world's likeness does indeed provide its custodians with a greater measure of control over its functions, are questions my former colleagues still debate as the music grows more shrill and you can't see the maps for the pins. I made my decision back then and saw to it I did not receive citizenship in that second world, a place that may now have become more important than the first. Exiled to reality, my own sojourns across the line are necessarily those of an alien guilty of illegal entry. I visit periodically because I go where I must to make my living. —That is where Don comes in. The people I can become are often very useful when he has peculiar problems.

Unfortunately, at that moment, it seemed that he did, just when the whole gang of me felt like turning down the volume and loafing.

We finished our drinks, got the bill, settled it.

"This way," I said, indicating the rear door, and he swung into his coat and followed me out.

"Talk here?" he asked, as we walked down the alley.

"Rather not," I said. "Public transportation, then private conversation."

He nodded and came along.

About three-quarters of an hour later we were in the saloon of the *Proteus* and I was making coffee. We were rocked gently by the bay's chill waters, under a moonless sky. I'd only a pair of the smaller lights burning. Comfortable. On the water, aboard the *Proteus,* the crowding, the activities, the tempo, of life in the cities, on the land, are muted, slowed—fictionalized—by the metaphysical distancing a few meters of water can provide. We alter the landscape with great facility, but the ocean has always seemed unchanged, and I suppose by extension we are infected with some feelings of timelessness whenever we set out upon her. Maybe that's one of the reasons I spend so much time there.

"First time you've had me aboard," he said. "Comfortable. Very."

"Thanks.—Cream? Sugar?"

"Yes. Both."

We settled back with our steaming mugs and I asked, "What have you got?"

"One case involving two problems," he said. "One of them sort of falls within my area of competence. The other does not. I was told that it is an absolutely unique situation and would require the services of a very special specialist."

"I'm not a specialist at anything but keeping alive."

His eyes came up suddenly and caught my own.

"I had always assumed that you knew an awful lot about computers," he said.

I looked away. That was hitting below the belt. I had never held myself out to him as an authority in that area, and there had always been a tacit understanding between us that my methods of manipulating circumstance and identity were not open to discussion. On the other hand, it was obvious to him that my knowledge of the system was both extensive and intensive. Still, I didn't like talking about it. So I moved to defend.

"Computer people are a dime a dozen," I said. "It was probably different in your time, but these days they start teaching computer science to little kids their first year in school. So sure, I know a lot about it. This generation, everybody does."

"You know that is not what I meant," he said. "Haven't you known me long enough to trust me a little more than that? The question springs solely from the case at hand. That's all."

I nodded. Reactions by their very nature are not always appropriate, and I had invested a lot of emotional capital in a heavy-duty set. So, "Okay, I know more about them than the school kids," I said.

"Thanks. That can be our point of departure." He took a sip of coffee. "My own background is in law and accounting, followed by the military, military intelligence, and civil service, in that order. Then I got into this business. What technical stuff I know I've picked up along the way—a scrap here, a crash course there. I know a lot about what things can do, not so much about how they work. I did not understand the details on this one, so I want you to start at the top and explain things to me, for as far as you can go. I need the background review, and if you are able to furnish it I will also know that you are the man for the job. You can begin by telling me how the early space-exploration robots worked—like, say the ones they used on Venus."

"That's not computers," I said, "and for that matter, they weren't really robots. They were telefactoring devices."

"Tell me what makes the difference."

"A robot is a machine which carries out certain operations in accordance with a program of instructions. A telefactor is a slave machine operated by remote control. The telefactor functions in a feedback situation with its operator. Depending on how sophisticated you want to get, the links can be audio-visual, kinesthetic, tactile, even olfactory. The more you want to go in this direction, the more anthropomorphic you get in the thing's design.

"In the case of Venus, if I recall correctly, the human operator in orbit wore an exoskeleton which controlled the movements of the body, legs, arms and hands of the device on the surface below, receiving motion and force feedback through a system of airjet transducers. He had on a helmet controlling the slave device's television camera—set, obviously enough, in its turret—which filled his field of vision with the scene below. He also wore earphones connected with its audio pickup. I read the book he wrote later. He said that for long stretches of time he would forget the cabin, forget that he was at the boss end of a control loop, and actually feel as if he were stalking through that hellish landscape. I remember being very impressed by it, just being a kid, and I wanted a super-tiny one all my own, so that I could wade around in puddles picking fights with microorganisms."

"Why?"

"Because there weren't any dragons on Venus. Anyhow, that is a telefactoring device, a thing quite distinct from a robot."

"I'm still with you," he said. "Now tell me the difference between the early telefactoring devices and the later ones."

I swallowed some coffee.

"It was a bit trickier with respect to the outer planets and their satellites," I said. "There we did not have orbiting operators at first. Economics, and some unresolved technical problems. Mainly economics. At any rate, the devices were landed on the target worlds, but the operators stayed home. Because of this, there was of course a time lag in the transmissions along the control loop. It took a while to receive the on-site input, and then there was another time lapse before the response movements reached the telefactor. We attempted to compensate for this in two ways: the first was by the employment of a simple wait-move, wait-move sequence; the second was more sophisticated and is actually the point where computers come into the picture in terms of participating in the control loop. It involved the setting up of models of known environmental factors, which were then enriched during the initial wait-move sequences. On this basis, the computer was then used to anticipate short-range developments. Finally, it could take over the loop and run it by a combination of 'predictor controls' and wait-move reviews. It still had to holler for human help, though, when unexpected things came up. So, with the outer planets, it was neither totally automatic nor totally manual—nor totally satisfactory—at first."

"Okay," he said, lighting a cigarette. "And the next step?"

"The next wasn't really a technical step forward in telefactoring. It was an economic shift. The purse strings were loosened and we could afford to send men out. We landed them where we could land them, and in many of the places where we could not, we sent down the telefactors and orbited the men again. Like in the old days. The time-lag problem was removed because the operator was on top of things once more. If anything, you can look at it as a reversion to earlier methods. It is what we still often do, though, and it works."

He shook his head.

"You left something out between the computers and the bigger budget."

I shrugged.

"A number of things were tried during that period, but none of them proved as effective as what we already had, going in the human-computer partnership with the telefactors."

"There was one project," he said, "which attempted to get around the time-lag troubles by sending the computer along with the telefactor as part of the package. Only the computer wasn't exactly a computer and the telefactor wasn't exactly a telefactor. Do you know which one I am referring to?"

I lit a cigarette of my own while I thought about it, then, "I think you are talking about the Hangman," I said.

"That's right and this is where I get lost. Can you tell me how it works?"

"Ultimately, it was a failure," I told him.

"But it worked at first."

"Apparently. But only on the easy stuff, on Io. It conked out later and had to be written off as a failure, albeit a noble one. The venture was overly ambitious from the very beginning. What seems to have happened was that the people in charge had the opportunity to combine vanguard projects—stuff that was still under investigation and stuff that was extremely new. In theory, it all seemed to dovetail so beautifully that they yielded to the temptation and incorporated too much. It started out well, but it fell apart later."

"But what all was involved in the thing?"

"Lord! What wasn't? The computer that wasn't exactly a computer . . . Okay, we'll start there. Last century, three engineers at the University of Wisconsin—Nordman, Parmentier and Scott—developed a device known as a superconductive tunnel-junction neuristor. Two tiny strips of metal with a thin insulating layer between. Supercool it and it passed electrical impulses without resistance. Surround it with magnetized material and pack a mass of them together—billions—and what have you got?"

He shook his head.

"Well, for one thing you've got an impossible situation to schematize when considering all the paths and interconnections that may be formed. There is an obvious similarity to the structure of the brain. So, they theorized, you don't even attempt to hook up such a device. You pulse in data and let it establish its own preferential pathways, by means of the magnetic material's becoming increasingly magnetized each time the current passes through it, thus cutting the resistance. The material establishes its own routes in a fashion analogous to the functioning of the brain when it is learning something.

"In the case of the Hangman, they used a setup very similar to this and they were able to pack over ten billion neuristor-type cells into a very small area—around a cubic foot. They aimed for that magic figure because that is approximately the number of nerve cells in the human brain. That is what I meant when I said that it wasn't really a computer. They were actually working in the area of artificial intelligence, no matter what they called it."

"If the thing had its own brain-computer or quasi-human—then it was a robot rather than a telefactor, right?"

"Yes and no and maybe," I said. "It was operated as a telefactor device here on Earth—on the ocean floor, in the desert, in mountainous country—as part of its programming. I suppose you could also call that its apprenticeship—or kindergarten. Perhaps that is even more appropriate. It was being shown how to explore in difficult environments and to report back. Once it mastered this, then theoretically they could hang it out there in the sky without a control loop and let it report its own findings."

"At that point would it be considered a robot?"

"A robot is a machine which carries out certain operations in accordance with a program of instructions. The Hangman made its own decisions, you see. And I suspect that by trying to produce something that close to the human brain in structure and function, the seemingly inevitable randomness of its model got included in. It wasn't just a machine following a program. It was too complex. That was probably what broke it down."

Don chuckled.

"Inevitable free will?"

"No. As I said, they had thrown too many things into one bag. Everybody and his brother with a pet project that might be fitted in seemed a supersalesman that season. For example, the psychophysics boys had a gimmick they wanted to try on it, and it got used. Ostensibly, the Hangman was a communications device. Actually, they were concerned as to whether the thing was truly sentient."

"Was it?"

"Apparently so, in a limited fashion. What they had come up with, to be made part of the initial telefactor loop, was a device which set up a weak induction field in the brain of the operator. The machine received and amplified the patterns of electrical activity being conducted in the Hangman's—might as well call it 'brain'—then passed them through a complex modulator and pulsed them into the induction field in the operator's head.—I am out of my area now and into that of Weber and Fechner, but a neuron has a threshold at which it will fire, and below which it will not. There are some forty thousand neurons packed together in a square millimeter of the cerebral cortex, in such a fashion that each one has several hundred synaptic connections with others about it. At any given moment, some of them may be way below the firing threshold while others are in a condition Sir John Eccles once referred to as 'critically poised'—ready to fire. If just one is pushed over the threshold, it can affect the discharge of hundreds of thousands of others within twenty milliseconds. The pulsating field was to provide such a push in a sufficiently selective fashion to give the operator an idea as to what was going on in the Hangman's brain. And vice versa. The Hangman was to have its own built-in version of the same thing. It was also thought that this might serve to humanize it somewhat, so that it would better appreciate the significance of its work—to instill something like loyalty, you might say."

"Do you think this could have contributed to its later breakdown?"

"Possibly. How can you say in a one-of-a-kind situation like this? If you want a guess, I'd say, 'Yes.' But it's just a guess."

"Uh-huh," he said, "and what were its physical capabilities?"

"Anthropomorphic design," I said, "both because it was originally telefactored and because of the psychological reasoning I just mentioned. It could pilot its own small vessel. No need for a life-support system, of course. Both it and the vessel were powered by fusion units, so that fuel was no real problem. Self-repairing. Capable of performing a great variety of sophisticated tests and measurements, of making observations, completing reports, learning new material, broadcasting its findings back here. Capable of surviving just about anywhere. In fact, it required less energy on the outer planets—less work for the refrigeration units, to maintain that supercooled brain in its midsection."

"How strong was it?"

"I don't recall all the specs. Maybe a dozen times as strong as a man, in things like lifting and pushing."

"It explored for us and started in on Europa."

"Yes."

"Then it began behaving erratically, just when we thought it had really learned its job."

"That sounds right," I said.

"It refused a direct order to explore Callisto, then headed out toward Uranus."

"Yes. It's been years since I read the reports. . . ."

"The malfunction worsened after that. Long periods of silence interspersed with garbled transmissions. Now that I know more about its makeup, it almost sounds like a man going off the deep end."

"It seems similar."

"But it managed to pull itself together again for a brief while. It landed on Titania, began sending back what seemed like appropriate observation reports. This only lasted a short time, though. It went irrational once more, indicated that it was heading for a landing on Uranus itself, and that was it. We didn't hear from it after that. Now that I know about that mind-reading gadget I understand why a psychiatrist on this end could be so positive it would never function again."

"I never heard about that part."

"I did."

I shrugged. "This was all around twenty years ago," I said, "and, as I mentioned, it has been a long while since I've read anything about it."

"The Hangman's ship crashed or landed, as the case may be, in the Gulf of Mexico, two days ago."

I just stared at him.

"It was empty," Don went on, "when they finally got out and down to it."

"I don't understand."

"Yesterday morning," he continued, "restaurateur Manny Burns was found beaten to death in the office of his establish—

"I still fail to see—"

"Manny Burns was one of the four original operators who programmed—pardon me, 'taught'—the Hangman."

The silence lengthened, dragged its belly on the deck.

"Coincidence. . . ?" I finally said.

"My client doesn't think so."

"Who is your client?"

"One of the three remaining members of the training group. He is convinced that the Hangman has returned to Earth to kill its former operators."

"Has he made his fears known to his old employers?"

"No."

"Why not?"

"Because it would require telling them the reason for his fears."

"That being. . . ?"

"He wouldn't tell me, either."

"How does he expect you to do a proper job?"

"He told me what he considered a proper job. He wanted two things done, neither of which requires a full case history. He wanted to be furnished with good bodyguards, and he wanted the Hangman found and disposed of. I have already taken care of the first part."

"And you want me to do the second?"

"That's right. You have confirmed my opinion that you are the man for the job."

"I see. Do you realize that if the thing is truly sentient this will be something very like murder? If it is not, of course, then it will only amount to the destruction of expensive government property."

"Which way do you look at it?"

"I look at it as a job," I said.

"You'll take it?"

"I need more facts before I can decide. Like who is your client? Who are the other operators? Where do they live? What do they do? What—"

He raised his hand.

"First," he said, "the Honorable Jesse Brockden, senior senator from Wisconsin, is our client. Confidentiality, of course, is written all over it."

I nodded. "I remember his being involved with the space program before he went into politics. I wasn't aware of the specifics, though. He could get government protection so easily—"

"To obtain it, he would apparently have to tell them something he doesn't want to talk about. Perhaps it would hurt his career. I simply do not know. He doesn't want them. He wants us."

I nodded again.

"What about the others? Do they want us, too?"

"Quite the opposite. They don't subscribe to Brockden's notions at all. They seem to think he is something of a paranoid."

"How well do they know one another these days?"

"They live in different parts of the country, haven't seen each other in years. Been in occasional touch, though."

"Kind of a flimsy basis for that diagnosis, then."

"One of them is a psychiatrist."

"Oh. Which one?"

"Leila Thackery is her name. Lives in St. Louis. Works at the state hospital there."

"None of them have gone to any authority, then—federal or local?"

"That's right. Brockden contacted them when he heard about the Hangman. He was in Washington at the time. Got word on its return right away and managed to get the story killed. He tried to reach them all, learned about Burns in the process, contacted me, then tried to persuade the others to accept protection by my people. They weren't buying. When I talked to her, Dr. Thackery pointed out—quite correctly—that Brockden is a very sick man."

"What's he got?"

"Cancer. In his spine. Nothing they can do about it once it hits there and digs in. He even told me he figures he has maybe six months to get through what he considers a very important piece of legislation—the new criminal rehabilitation act.—I will admit that he did sound kind of paranoid when he talked about it. But hell! Who wouldn't? Dr. Thackery sees that as the whole thing, though, and she doesn't see the Burns killing as being connected with the Hangman. Thinks it was just a traditional robbery gone sour, thief surprised and panicky, maybe hopped up, et cetera."

"Then she is not afraid of the Hangman?"

"She said that she is in a better position to know its mind than anyone else, and she is not especially concerned."

"What about the other operator?"

"He said that Dr. Thackery may know its mind better than anyone else, but he knows its brain, and he isn't worried, either."

"What did he mean by that?"

"David Fentris is a consulting engineer—electronics, cybernetics. He actually had something to do with the
Hangman's design."

I got to my feet and went after the coffeepot. Not that
I'd an overwhelming desire for another cup at just that mo-
ment. But I had known, had once worked with a David Fentris.
And he had at one time been connected with the space program.

About fifteen years my senior, Dave had been with the
data bank project when I had known him. Where a number of
us had begun having second thoughts as the thing progressed,
Dave had never been anything less than wildly enthusiastic. A
wiry five eight, gray cropped, gray eyes back of horn rims and
heavy glass, cycling between preoccupation and near-frantic
darting, he had had a way of verbalizing half-completed
thoughts as he went along, so that you might begin to think him
a representative of that tribe which had come into positions of
small authority by means of nepotism or politics. If you would
listen a few more minutes, however, you would begin revising
your opinion as he started to pull his musings together into a
rigorous framework. By the time he had finished, you generally
wondered why you hadn't seen it all along and what a guy like
that was doing in a position of such small authority. Later, it
might strike you, though, that he seemed sad whenever he wasn't
enthusiastic about something. And while the gung-ho spirit is
great for short-range projects, larger ventures generally require
somewhat more equanimity. I wasn't at all surprised that he
had wound up as a consultant.

The big question now, of course, was: Would he remember me? True, my appearance was altered, my personality hopefully more mature, my habits shifted around. But would that be
enough, should I have to encounter him as part of this job?

That mind behind those horn rims could do a lot of strange things with just a little data.

"Where does he live?" I asked.

"Memphis.—And what's the matter?"

"Just trying to get my geography straight," I said. "Is Senator Brockden still in Washington?"

"No. He's returned to Wisconsin and is currently holed up in a lodge in the northern part of the state. Four of my people are with him."

"I see."

I refreshed our coffee supply and reseated myself. I didn't like this one at all and I resolved not to take it. I didn't like just giving Don a flat "No," though. His assignments had become a very important part of my life, and this one was not mere legwork. It was obviously important to him, and he wanted me on it. I decided to look for holes in the thing, to find some way of reducing it to the simple bodyguard job already in progress.

"It does seem peculiar," I said, "that Brockden is the only one afraid of the device."

"Yes."

". . . And that he gives no reasons."

"True."

". . . Plus his condition, and what the doctor said about its effect on his mind."

"I have no doubt that he is neurotic," Don said. "Look at this."

He reached for his coat, withdrew a sheaf of papers from within it. He shuffled through them and extracted a single sheet, which he passed to me.

It was a piece of congressional-letterhead stationery, with the message scrawled in longhand. *"Don,"* it said. *"I've got to see you. Frankenstein's monster is just come back from where we hung him and he's looking for me. The whole damn universe is trying to grind me up. Call me between 8 & 10.—Jess."*

I nodded, started to pass it back, paused, then handed it over. Double damn it deeper than hell!

I took a drink of coffee. I thought that I had long ago given up hope in such things, but I had noticed something that immediately troubled me. In the margin, where they list such matters, I had seen that Jesse Brockden was on the committee for review of the Central Data Bank program. I recalled that that committee was supposed to be working on a series of reform recommendations. Offhand, I could not remember Brockden's position on any of the issues involved, but—oh, hell! The thing was simply too big to alter significantly now. . . . But it was the only real Frankenstein monster I cared about, and there was always the possibility . . . On the other hand—Hell, again! What if I let him die when I might have saved him, and he had been the one who. . . ?

I took another drink of coffee. I lit another cigarette.

There might be a way of working it so that Dave didn't even come into the picture. I could talk to Leila Thackery first, check further into the Burns killing, keep posted on new developments, find out more about the vessel in the Gulf. . . . I might be able to accomplish something, even if it was only the negation of Brockden's theory, without Dave's and my paths ever crossing.

"Have you got the specs on the Hangman?" I asked.

"Right here."

He passed them over.

"The police report on the Burns killing?"

"Here it is."

"The whereabouts of everyone involved, and some background on them?"

"Here."

"The place or places where I can reach you during the next few days—around the clock? This one may require some coordination."

He smiled and reached for his pen.

"Glad to have you aboard," he said.

I reached over and tapped the barometer. I shook my head.

The ringing of the phone awakened me. Reflex bore me across the room, where I took it on audio.

"Yes?"

"Mister Donne? It is eight o'clock."

"Thanks."

I collapsed into the chair. I am what might be called a slow starter. I tend to recapitulate phylogeny every morning. Basic desires inched their ways through my gray matter to close a connection. Slowly, I extended a cold-blooded member and clicked my talons against a couple of numbers. I croaked my desire for food and lots of coffee to the voice that responded. Half an hour later I would only have growled. Then I staggered off to the place of flowing waters to renew my contact with basics.

In addition to my normal adrenaline and blood-sugar bearishness, I had not slept much the night before. I had closed up shop after Don left, stuffed my pockets with essentials, departed the *Proteus*, gotten myself over to the airport and onto a flight which took me to St. Louis in the dead, small hours of the dark. I was unable to sleep during the flight, thinking about the case, deciding on the tack I was going to take with Leila Thackery. On arrival, I had checked into the airport motel, left a message to be awakened at an unreasonable hour, and collapsed.

As I ate, I regarded the fact sheet Don had given me.

Leila Thackery was currently single, having divorced her second husband a little over two years ago, was forty-six years old, and lived in an apartment near to the hospital where she worked. Attached to the sheet was a photo which might have been ten years old. In it, she was brunette, light-eyed, barely on the right side of that border between ample and overweight, with fancy glasses straddling an upturned nose. She had published a number of books and articles with titles full of alienations, roles, transactions, social contexts and more alienations.

I hadn't had the time to go my usual route, becoming an entire new individual with a verifiable history. Just a name and a story, that's all. It did not seem necessary this time, though. For once, something approximating honesty actually seemed a reasonable approach.

I took a public vehicle over to her apartment building. I did not phone ahead, because it is easier to say "No" to a voice than to a person.

According to the record, today was one of the days when she saw outpatients in her home. Her idea, apparently: break down the alienating institution image, remove resentments by turning the sessions into something more like social occasions, et cetera. I did not want all that much of her time—I had decided that Don could make it worth her while if it came to that—and I was sure my fellows' visits were scheduled to leave her with some small breathing space. Inter alia, so to speak.

I had just located her name and apartment number amid the buttons in the entrance foyer when an old woman passed behind me and unlocked the door to the lobby. She glanced at me and held it open, so I went on in without ringing. The matter of presence, again.

I took the elevator to Leila's floor, the second, located her door and knocked on it. I was almost ready to knock again when it opened, partway.

"Yes?" she asked, and. I revised my estimate as to the age of the photo. She looked just about the same.

"Dr. Thackery," I said, "my name is Donne. You could help me quite a bit with a problem I've got."

"What sort of problem?"

"It involves a device known as the Hangman."

She sighed and showed me a quick grimace. Her fingers tightened on the door.

"I've come a long way but I'll be easy to get rid of. I've only a few things I'd like to ask you about it."

"Are you with the government?"

"No."

"Do you work for Brockden?"

"No, I'm something different."

"All right," she said. "Right now I've got a group session going. It will probably last around another half hour. If you don't mind waiting down in the lobby, I'll let you know as soon as it is over. We can talk then."

"Good enough," I said. "Thanks."

She nodded, closed the door. I located the stairway and walked back down.

A cigarette later, I decided that the devil finds work for idle hands and thanked him for his suggestion. I strolled back toward the foyer. Through the glass, I read the names of a few residents of the fifth floor. I elevated up and knocked on one of the doors. Before it was opened I had my notebook and pad in plain sight.

"Yes?" Short, fiftyish, curious.

"My name is Stephen Foster, Mrs. Gluntz. I am doing a survey for the North American Consumers League. I would like to pay you for a couple of minutes of your time, to answer some questions about products you use."

"Why—Pay me?"

"Yes, ma'am. Ten dollars. Around a dozen questions. It will just take a minute or two."

"All right." She opened the door wider. "Won't you come in?"

"No, thank you. This thing is so brief I'd just be in and out. The first question involves detergents. . . ."

Ten minutes later I was back in the lobby adding the thirty bucks for the three interviews to the list of expenses I was keeping. When a situation is full of unpredictables and I am playing makeshift games, I like to provide for as many contingencies as I can.

Another quarter of an hour or so slipped by before the elevator opened and discharged three guys—young, young, and middle-aged, casually dressed, chuckling over something.

The big one on the nearest end strolled over and nodded.

"You the fellow waiting to see Dr. Thackery?"

"That's right."

"She said to tell you to come on up now."

"Thanks."

I rode up again, returned to her door. She opened to my knock, nodded me in, saw me seated in a comfortable chair at the far end of her living room.

"Would you care for a cup of coffee?" she asked. "It's fresh. I made more than I needed."

"That would be fine. Thanks."

Moments later, she brought in a couple of cups, delivered one to me and seated herself on the sofa to my left. I ignored the cream and sugar on the tray and took a sip.

"You've gotten me interested," she said. "Tell me about it."

"Okay. I have been told that the telefactor device known as the Hangman, now possibly possessed of an artificial intelligence, has returned to Earth—"

"Hypothetical," she said, "unless you know something I don't. I have been told that the Hangman's vehicle reentered and crashed in the Gulf. There is no evidence that the vehicle was occupied."

"It seems a reasonable conclusion, though."

"It seems just as reasonable to me that the Hangman sent the vehicle off toward an eventual rendezvous point many years ago and that it only recently reached that point, at which time the reentry program took over and brought it down."

"Why should it return the vehicle and strand itself out there?"

"Before I answer that," she said, "I would like to know the reason for your concern. News media?"

"No," I said. "I am a science writer—straight tech, popular and anything in between. But I am not after a piece for publication. I was retained to do a report on the psychological makeup of the thing."

"For whom?"

"A private investigation outfit. They want to know what might influence its thinking, how it might be likely to behave—if it has indeed come back. I've been doing a lot of homework, and I've gathered there is a likelihood that its nuclear personality was a composite of the minds of its four operators. So, personal contacts seemed in order, to collect your opinions as to what it might be like. I came to you first for obvious reasons."

She nodded.

"A Mister Walsh spoke with me the other day. He is working for Senator Brockden."

"Oh? I never go into an employer's business beyond what he's asked me to do. Senator Brockden is on my list though, along with a David Fentris."

"You were told about Manny Burns?"

"Yes. Unfortunate."

"That is apparently what set Jesse off. He is—how shall I put it?—he is clinging to life right now, trying to accomplish a great many things in the time he has remaining. Every moment is precious to him. He feels the old man in the white nightgown breathing down his neck.—Then the ship returns and one of us is killed. From what we know of the Hangman, the last we heard of it, it had become irrational. Jesse saw a connection, and in his condition the fear is understandable. There is nothing wrong with humoring him if it allows him to get his work done."

"But you don't see a threat in it?"

"No. I was the last person to monitor the Hangman before communications ceased, and I could see then what had happened. The first things that it had learned were the organization of perceptions and motor activities. Multitudes of other patterns had been transferred from the minds of its operators, but they were too sophisticated to mean much initially.—Think of a child who has learned the Gettysburg Address. It is there in his head, that is all. One day, however, it may be important to him. Conceivably, it may even inspire him to action. It takes some growing up first, of course. Now think of such a child with a great number of conflicting patterns—attitudes, tendencies, memories—none of which are especially bothersome for so long as he remains a child. Add a bit of maturity, though—and bear in mind that the patterns originated with four different individuals, all of them more powerful than the words of even the finest of speeches, bearing as they do their own built-in feelings. Try to imagine the conflicts, the contradictions involved in being four people at once—"

"Why wasn't this imagined in advance?" I asked.

"Ah!" she said, smiling. "The full sensitivity of the neuristor brain was not appreciated at first. It was assumed that the operators were adding data in a linear fashion and that this would continue until a critical mass was achieved, corresponding to the construction of a model or picture of the world which would then serve as a point of departure for growth of the Hangman's own mind. And it did seem to check out this way.

"What actually occurred, however, was a phenomenon amounting to imprinting. Secondary characteristics of the operators' minds, outside the didactic situations, were imposed. These did not immediately become functional and hence were not detected. They remained latent until the mind had developed sufficiently to understand them. And then it was too late. It suddenly acquired four additional personalities and was unable to coordinate them. When it tried to compartmentalize them it went schizoid; when it tried to integrate them it went catatonic. It was cycling back and forth between these alternatives at the end. Then it just went silent. I felt it had undergone the equivalent of an epileptic seizure. Wild currents through that magnetic material would, in effect, have erased its mind, resulting in *its* equivalent of death or idiocy."

"I follow you," I said. "Now, just for the sake of playing games, I see the alternatives as either a successful integration of all this material or the achievement of a viable schizophrenia. What do you think its behavior would be like if either of these were possible?"

"All right," she agreed. "As I just said, though, I think there were physical limitations to its retaining multiple personality structures for a very long period of time. If it did, however, it would have continued with its own, plus replicas of the four operators', at least for a while. The situation would differ radically from that of a human schizoid of this sort, in that the additional personalities were valid images of genuine identities rather than self-generated complexes which had become autonomous. They might continue to evolve, they might degenerate, they might conflict to the point of destruction or gross modification of any or all of them. In other words, no prediction is possible as to the nature of whatever might remain."

"Might I venture one?"

"Go ahead."

"After considerable anxiety, it masters them. It asserts itself. It beats down this quartet of demons which has been tearing it apart, acquiring in the process an all-consuming hatred for the actual individuals responsible for this turmoil. To free itself totally, to revenge itself, to work its ultimate catharsis, it resolves to seek them out and destroy them."

She smiled.

"You have just dispensed with the 'viable schizophrenia' you conjured up, and you have now switched over to its pulling through and becoming fully autonomous. That is a different situation—no matter what strings you put on it."

"Okay, I accept the charge. But what about my conclusion?"

"You are saying that if it did pull through, it would hate us. That strikes me as an unfair attempt to invoke the spirit of Sigmund Freud: Oedipus and Electra in one being, out to destroy all its parents—the authors of every one of its tensions, anxieties, hang-ups, burned into its impressionable psyche at a young and defenseless age. Even Freud didn't have a name for that one. What should we call it?"

"A Hermacis complex?" I suggested.

"Hermacis?"

"Hermaphroditus having been united in one body with the nymph Salmacis, I've just done the same with their names. That being would then have had four parents against whom to react."

"Cute," she said, smiling. "If the liberal arts do nothing else, they provide engaging metaphors for the thinking they displace. This one is unwarranted and overly anthropomorphic, though.—You wanted my opinion. All right. If the Hangman pulled through at all, it could only have been by virtue of that neuristor brain's differences from the human brain. From my own professional experience, a human could not pass through a situation like that and attain stability. If the Hangman did, it would have to have resolved all the contradictions and conflicts, to have mastered and understood the situation so thoroughly that I do not believe whatever remained could involve that sort of hatred. The fear, the uncertainty, the things that feed hate would have been analyzed, digested, turned to something more useful. There would probably be distaste, and possibly an act of independence, of self-assertion. That was one reason why I suggested its return of the ship."

"It is your opinion, then, that if the Hangman exists as a thinking individual today, this is the only possible attitude it would possess toward its former operators: It would want nothing more to do with you?"

"That is correct. Sorry about your Hermacis complex. But in this case we must look to the brain, not the psyche. And we see two things: Schizophrenia would have destroyed it, and a successful resolution of its problem would preclude vengeance. Either way, there is nothing to worry about."

How could I put it tactfully? I decided that I could not.

"All of this is fine," I said, "for as far as it goes. But getting away from both the purely psychological and the purely physical, could there be a particular reason for its seeking your deaths—that is, a plain old-fashioned motive for a killing, based on events rather than having to do with the way its thinking equipment goes together?"

Her expression was impossible to read, but considering her line of work I had expected nothing less.

"What events?" she said.

"I have no idea. That's why I asked."

She shook her head.

"I'm afraid that I don't, either."

"Then that about does it," I said. "I can't think of anything else to ask you."

She nodded.

"And I can't think of anything else to tell you."

I finished my coffee, returned the cup to the tray.

"Thanks, then," I said, "for your time, for the coffee. You have been very helpful."

I rose. She did the same.

"What are you going to do now?" she asked.

"I haven't quite decided," I answered. "I want to do the best report I can. Have you any suggestions on that?"

"I suggest that there isn't any more to learn, that I have given you the only possible constructions the facts warrant."

"You don't feel David Fentris could provide any additional insights?"

She snorted, then sighed.

"No," she said, "I do not think he could tell you anything useful."

"What do you mean? From the way you say it—"

"I know. I didn't mean to.—Some people find comfort in religion. Others . . . You know. Others take it up late in life with a vengeance and a half. They don't use it quite the way it was intended. It comes to color all their thinking."

"Fanaticism?" I said.

"Not exactly. A misplaced zeal. A masochistic sort of thing. Hell! I shouldn't be diagnosing at a distance—or influencing your opinion. Forget what I said. Form your own opinion when you meet him."

She raised her head, appraising my reaction.

"Well," I responded, "I am not at all certain that I am going to see him. But you have made me curious. How can religion influence engineering?"

"I spoke with him after Jesse gave us the news on the vessel's return. I got the impression at the time that he feels we were tampering in the province of the Almighty by attempting the creation of an artificial intelligence. That our creation should go mad was only appropriate, being the work of imperfect man. He seemed to feel that it would be fitting if it had come back for retribution, as a sign of judgment upon us."

"Oh," I said.

She smiled then. I returned it.

"Yes," she said, "but maybe I just got him in a bad mood. Maybe you should go see for yourself."

Something told me to shake my head—there was a bit of a difference between this view of him, my recollections, and Don's comment that Dave had said he knew its brain and was not especially concerned. Somewhere among these lay something I felt I should know, felt I should learn without seeming to pursue.

So, "I think I have enough right now," I said. "It was the psychological side of things I was supposed to cover, not the mechanical—or the theological. You have been extremely helpful. Thanks again."

She carried her smile all the way to the door.

"If it is not too much trouble," she said, as I stepped into the hall, "I would like to learn how this whole thing finally turns out—or any interesting developments, for that matter."

"My connection with the case ends with this report, and I am going to write it now. Still, I may get some feedback."

"You have my number. . . ?"

"Probably, but . . ."

I already had it, but I jotted it again, right after Mrs. Gluntz's answers to my inquiries on detergents.

Moving in a rigorous line, I made beautiful connections, for a change. I headed directly for the airport, found a flight aimed at

Memphis, bought passage, and was the last to board. Ten score seconds, perhaps, made all the difference. Not even a tick or two to spare for checking out of the motel.—No matter. The good head-doctor had convinced me that, like it or not, David Fentris was next, damn it. I had too strong a feeling that Leila Thackery had not told me the entire story. I had to take a chance, to see these changes in the man for myself, to try to figure out how they related to the Hangman. For a number of reasons, I'd a feeling they might.

I disembarked into a cool, partly overcast afternoon, found transportation almost immediately, and set out for Dave's office address.

A before-the-storm feeling came over me as I entered and crossed the town. A dark wall of clouds continued to build in the west. Later, standing before the building where Dave did business, the first few drops of rain were already spattering against its dirty brick front. It would take a lot more than that to freshen it, though, or any of the others in the area. I would have thought he'd have come a little further than this by now.

I shrugged off some moisture and went inside.

The directory gave me directions, the elevator elevated me, my feet found the way to his door. I knocked on it. After a time, I knocked again and waited again. Again, nothing. So I tried it, found it open, and went on in.

It was a small, vacant waiting room, green carpeted. The reception desk was dusty. I crossed and peered around the plastic partition behind it.

The man had his back to me. I drummed my knuckles against the partitioning. He heard it and turned.

"Yes?"

Our eyes met, his still framed by horn rims and just as active; lenses thicker, hair thinner, cheeks a trifle hollower.

His question mark quivered in the air, and nothing in his gaze moved to replace it with recognition. He had been bending over a sheaf of schematics. A lopsided basket of metal, quartz, porcelain and glass rested on a nearby table.

"My name is Donne, John Donne," I said. "I am looking for David Fentris."

"I am David Fentris."

"Good to meet you," I said, crossing to where he stood. "I am assisting in an investigation concerning a project with which you were once associated. . . ."

He smiled and nodded, accepted my hand and shook it.

"The Hangman, of course. Glad to know you, Mister Donne."

"Yes, the Hangman," I said. "I am doing a report—"

"—And you want my opinion as to how dangerous it is. Sit down." He gestured toward a chair at the end of his workbench. "Care for a cup of tea?"

"No, thanks."

"I'm having one."

"Well, in that case . . ."

He crossed to another bench.

"No cream. Sorry."

"That's all right.—How did you know it involved the Hangman?"

He grinned as he brought me my cup.

"Because it's come back," he said, "and it's the only thing I've been connected with that warrants that much concern."

"Do you mind talking about it?"

"Up to a point, no."

"What's the point?"

"If we get near it, I'll let you know."

"Fair enough.—How dangerous is it?"

"I would say that it is harmless," he replied, "except to three persons."

"Formerly four?"

"Precisely."

"How come?"

"We were doing something we had no business doing."

"That being. . . ?"

"For one thing, attempting to create an artificial intelligence."

"Why had you no business doing that?"

"A man with a name like yours shouldn't have to ask."

I chuckled.

"If I were a preacher," I said, "I would have to point out that there is no biblical injunction against it—unless you've been worshiping it on the sly."

He shook his head.

"Nothing that simple, that obvious, that explicit. Times have changed since the Good Book was written, and you can't hold with a purely fundamentalist approach in complex times. What I was getting at was something a little more abstract. A form of pride, not unlike the classical hubris—the setting up of oneself on a level with the Creator."

"Did you feel that—pride?"

"Yes."

"Are you sure it wasn't just enthusiasm for an ambitious project that was working well?"

"Oh, there was plenty of that. A manifestation of the same thing."

"I do seem to recall something about man being made in the Creator's image, and something else about trying to live up to that. It would seem to follow that exercising one's capacities along similar lines would be a step in the right direction—an act of conformance with the divine ideal, if you'd like."

"But I don't like. Man cannot really create. He can only rearrange what is already present. Only God can create."

"Then you have nothing to worry about."

He frowned. Then, "No," he said. "Being aware of this and still trying is where the presumption comes in."

"Were you really thinking that way when you did it? Or did all this occur to you after the fact?"

He continued to frown.

"I am no longer certain."

"Then it would seem to me that a merciful God would be inclined to give you the benefit of the doubt."

He gave me a wry smile.

"Not bad, John Donne. But I feel that judgment may already have been entered and that we may have lost four to nothing."

"Then you see the Hangman as an avenging angel?"

"Sometimes. Sort of. I see it as being returned to exact a penalty."

"Just for the record," I suggested, "if the Hangman had had full access to the necessary equipment and was able to construct another unit such as itself, would you consider it guilty of the same thing that is bothering you?"

He shook his head.

"Don't get all cute and Jesuitical with me, Donne. I'm not that far away from fundamentals. Besides, I'm willing to admit I might be wrong and that there may be other forces driving it to the same end."

"Such as?"

"I told you I'd let you know when we reached a certain point. That's it."

"Okay," I said. "But that sort of blank-walls me, you know. The people I am working for would like to protect you people. They want to stop the Hangman. I was hoping you would tell me a little more—if not for your own sake, then for the others'. They might not share your philosophical sentiments, and you have just admitted you may be wrong.—Despair, by the way, is also considered a sin by a great number of theologians."

He sighed and stroked his nose, as I had often seen him do in times long past.

"What do you do, anyhow?" he asked me.

"Me, personally? I'm a science writer. I'm putting together a report on the device for the agency that wants to do the protecting. The better my report, the better their chances."

He was silent for a time, then, "I read a lot in the area, but I don't recognize your name," he said.

"Most of my work has involved petrochemistry and marine biology," I said.

"Oh.—You were a peculiar choice then, weren't you?"

"Not really. I was available, and the boss knows my work, knows I'm good."

He glanced across the room, to where a stack of cartons partly obscured what I then realized to be a remote-access terminal. Okay. If he decided to check out my credentials now,

John Donne would fall apart. It seemed a hell of a time to get curious, though, *after* sharing his sense of sin with me. He must have thought so, too, because he did not look that way again.

"Let me put it this way . . ." he finally said, and something of the old David Fentris at his best took control of his voice. "For one reason or the other, I believe that it wants to destroy its former operators. If it is the judgment of the Almighty, that's all there is to it. It will succeed. If not, however, I don't want any outside protection. I've done my own repenting and it is up to me to handle the rest of the situation myself, too. I will stop the Hangman personally—right here—before anyone else is hurt."

"How?" I asked him.

He nodded toward the glittering helmet.

"With that," he said.

"How?" I repeated.

"The Hangman's telefactor circuits are still intact. They have to be: They are an integral part of it. It could not disconnect them without shutting itself down. If it comes within a quarter mile of here, that unit will be activated. It will emit a loud humming sound and a light will begin to blink behind that meshing beneath the forward ridge. I will then don the helmet and take control of the Hangman. I will bring it here and disconnect its brain."

"How would you do the disconnect?"

He reached for the schematics he had been looking at when I had come in.

"Here. The thoracic plate has to be unlugged. There are four subunits that have to be uncoupled. Here, here, here, and here."

He looked up.

"You would have to do them in sequence, though, or it could get mighty hot," I said. "First this one, then these two. Then the other."

When I looked up again, the gray eyes were fixed on my own.

"I thought you were in petrochemistry and marine biology."

"I am not really 'in' anything," I said. "I am a tech writer, with bits and pieces from all over—and I did have a look at these before, when I accepted the job."

"I see."

"Why don't you bring the space agency in on this?" I said, working to shift ground. "The original telefactoring equipment had all that power and range—"

"It was dismantled a long time ago.—I thought you were with the government."

I shook my head.

"Sorry. I didn't mean to mislead you. I am on contract with a private investigation outfit."

"Uh-huh. Then that means Jesse.—Not that it matters. You can tell him that one way or the other everything is being taken care of."

"What if you are wrong on the supernatural," I said, "but correct on the other? Supposing it is coming under the circumstances you feel it proper to resist? But supposing you are not next on its list? Supposing it gets to one of the others next, instead of you? If you are so sensitive about guilt and sin, don't you think that you would be responsible for that death—if you could prevent it by telling me just a little bit more? If it's confidentiality you're worried about—"

"No," he said. "You cannot trick me into applying my principles to a hypothetical situation which will only work out the way that you want it to. Not when I am certain that it will not arise. Whatever moves the Hangman, it will come to me next. If I cannot stop it, then it cannot be stopped until it has completed its job."

"How do you know that you are next?"

"Take a look at a map," he said. "It landed in the Gulf. Manny was right there in New Orleans. Naturally, he was first. The Hangman can move underwater like a controlled torpedo, which makes the Mississippi its logical route for inconspicuous travel. Proceeding up it then, here I am in Memphis. Then Leila, up in St. Louis, is obviously next after me. It can worry about getting to Washington after that."

I thought about Senator Brockden in Wisconsin and decided it would not even have that problem. All of them were fairly accessible, when you thought of the situation in terms of river travel.

"But how is it to know where you all are?" I asked.

"Good question," he said. "Within a limited range, it was once sensitive to our brain waves, having an intimate knowledge of them and the ability to pick them up. I do not know what that range would be today. It might have been able to construct an amplifier to extend this area of perception. But to be more mundane about it, I believe that it simply consulted Central's national directory. There are booths all over, even on the waterfront. It could have hit one late at night and gimmicked it. It certainly had sufficient identifying information— and engineering skill."

"Then it seems to me that the best bet for all of you would be to move away from the river till this business is settled. That thing won't be able to stalk about the countryside very long without being noticed."

He shook his head.

"It would find a way. It is extremely resourceful. At night, in an overcoat, a hat, it could pass. It requires nothing that a man would need. It could dig a hole and bury itself, stay underground during daylight. It could run without resting all night long. There is no place it could not reach in a surprisingly short while.—No, I must wait here for it."

"Let me put it as bluntly as I can," I said. "If you are right that it is a Divine Avenger, I would say that it smacks of blasphemy to try to tackle it. On the other hand, if it is not, then I think you are guilty of jeopardizing the others by withholding information that would allow us to provide them with a lot more protection than you are capable of giving them all by yourself."

He laughed.

"I'll just have to learn to live with that guilt, too, as they do with theirs," he said. "After I've done my best, they deserve anything they get."

"It was my understanding," I said, "that even God doesn't judge people until after they're dead—if you want another piece of presumption to add to your collection."

He stopped laughing and studied my face.

"There is something familiar about the way you talk, the way you think," he said. "Have we ever met before?"

"I doubt it. I would have remembered."

He shook his head.

"You've got a way of bothering a man's thinking that rings a faint bell," he went on. "You trouble me, sir."

"That was my intention."

"Are you staying here in town?"

"No."

"Give me a number where I can reach you, will you? If I have any new thoughts on this thing, I'll call you."

"I wish you would have them now, if you are going to have them."

"No, I've got some thinking to do. Where can I get hold of you later?"

I gave him the name of the motel I was still checked into in St. Louis. I could call back periodically for messages.

"All right," he said, and he moved toward the partition by the reception area and stood beside it.

I rose and followed him, passing into that area and pausing at the door to the hall.

"One thing . . ." I said.

"Yes?"

"If it does show up and you do stop it, will you call me and tell me that?"

"Yes, I will."

"Thanks then—and good luck."

Impulsively, I extended my hand. He gripped it and smiled faintly.

"Thank you, Mister Donne."

Next. Next, next, next . . .

I couldn't budge Dave, and Leila Thackery had given me everything she was going to. No real sense in calling Don yet—not until I had more to say.

I thought it over on my way back to the airport. The predinner hours always seem best for talking to people in any sort of official capacity, just as the night seems best for dirty work. Heavily psychological but true nevertheless. I hated to waste the rest of the day if there was anyone else worth talking to before I called Don. Going through the folder, I decided that there was.

Manny Burns had a brother, Phil. I wondered how worthwhile it might be to talk with him. I could make it to New Orleans at a sufficiently respectable hour, learn whatever he was willing to tell me, check back with Don for new developments, and then decide whether there was anything I should be about with respect to the vessel itself.

The sky was gray and leaky above me. I was anxious to flee its spaces. So I decided to do it. I could think of no better stone to upturn at the moment.

At the airport, I was ticketed quickly, in time for another close connection.

Hurrying to reach my flight, my eyes brushed over a half-familiar face on the passing escalator. The reflex reserved for such occasions seemed to catch us both, because he looked back, too, with the same eyebrow twitch of startle and scrutiny. Then he was gone. I could not place him, however. The half-familiar face becomes a familiar phenomenon in a crowded, highly mobile society. I sometimes think that that is all that will eventually remain of any of us: patterns of features, some a trifle more persistent than others, impressed on the flow of bodies. A small-town boy in a big city, Thomas Wolfe must long ago have felt the same thing when he had coined the word "manswarm." It might have been someone I'd once met briefly, or simply someone—or someone like someone—I had passed on sufficient other occasions such as this.

As I flew the unfriendly skies out of Memphis, I mulled over musings past on artificial intelligence, or AI as they have tagged it in the think-box biz. When talking about computers, the AI notion had always seemed hotter than I deemed necessary, partly because of semantics. The word "intelligence" has all sorts of tag-along associations of the nonphysical sort. I suppose it goes back to the fact that early discussions and conjectures concerning it made it sound as if the potential for intelligence was always present in the array of gadgets, and that the correct procedures, the right programs, simply had to be found to call it forth. When you looked at it that way, as many did, it gave rise to an uncomfortable déjà vu—namely, vitalism. The philosophical battles of the nineteenth century were hardly so far behind that they had been forgotten, and the doctrine which maintained that life is caused and sustained by a vital principle apart from physical and chemical forces, and that life is self-sustaining and self-evolving, had put up quite a fight before Darwin and his successors had produced triumph after triumph for the mechanistic view. Then vitalism sort of crept back into things again when the AI discussions arose in the middle of the past century. It would seem that Dave had fallen victim to it, and that he'd come to believe he had helped provide an unsanctified vessel and filled it with something intended only for those things which had made the scene in the first chapter of Genesis. . . .

With computers it was not quite as bad as with the Hangman, though, because you could always argue that no matter how elaborate the program, it was basically an extension of the programmer's will and the operations of causal machines merely represented functions of intelligence, rather than intelligence in its own right backed by a will of its own. And there was always Gödel for a theoretical *cordon sanitaire,* with his demonstration of the true but mechanically unprovable proposition.

But the Hangman was quite different. It had been designed along the lines of a brain and at least partly educated in a human fashion; and to further muddy the issue with respect to anything like vitalism, it had been in direct contact with human minds from which it might have acquired almost anything—including the spark that set it on the road to whatever selfhood it may have found. What did that make it? Its own creature? A fractured mirror reflecting a fractured humanity? Both? Or neither? I certainly could not say, but I wondered how much of its self had been truly its own. It had obviously acquired a great number of functions, but was it capable of having real feelings? Could it, for example, feel something like love? If not, then it was still only a collection of complex abilities, and not a thing with all the tag-along associations of the nonphysical sort that made the word "intelligence" such a prickly item in AI discussions; and if it were capable of, say, something like love, and if I were Dave, I would not feel guilty about having helped to bring it into being. I would feel proud, though not in the fashion he was concerned about, and I would also feel humble.—Offhand though, I do not know how intelligent I would feel, because I am still not sure what the hell intelligence is.

The day's-end sky was clear when we landed. I was into town before the sun had finished setting, and on Philip Burns's doorstep just a little while later.

My ring was answered by a girl, maybe seven or eight years old. She fixed me with large brown eyes and did not say a word.

"I would like to speak with Mister Burns," I said.

She turned and retreated around a corner.

A heavyset man, slacked and undershirted, bald about halfway back and very pink, padded into the hall moments later and peered at me. He bore a folded newssheet in his left hand.

"What do you want?" he asked.

"It's about your brother," I answered.

"Yeah?"

"Well, I wonder if I could come in? It's kind of complicated."

He opened the door. But instead of letting me in, he came out.

"Tell me about it out here," he said.

"Okay, I'll be quick. I just wanted to find out whether he ever spoke with you about a piece of equipment he once worked with called the Hangman."

"Are you a cop?"

"No."

"Then what's your interest?"

"I am working for a private investigation agency trying to track down some equipment once associated with the project. It has apparently turned up in this area and it could be rather dangerous."

"Let's see some identification."

"I don't carry any."

"What's your name?"

"John Donne."

"And you think my brother had some stolen equipment when he died? Let me tell you something—"

"No. Not stolen," I said, "and I don't think he had it."

"What then?"

"It was—well, robotic in nature. Because of some special training Manny once received, he might have had a way of detecting it. He might even have attracted it. I just want to find out whether he had said anything about it. We are trying to locate it."

"My brother was a respectable businessman, and I don't like accusations. Especially right after his funeral, I don't. I think I'm going to call the cops and let them ask you a few questions."

"Just a minute. Supposing I told you we had some reason to believe it might have been this piece of equipment that killed your brother?"

His pink turned to bright red and his jaw muscles formed sudden ridges. I was not prepared for the stream of profanities that followed. For a moment, I thought he was going to take a swing at me.

"Wait a second," I said when he paused for breath. "What did I say?"

"You're either making fun of the dead or you're stupider than you look!"

"Say I'm stupid. Then tell me why."

He tore at the paper he carried, folded it back, found an item, thrust it at me.

"Because they've got the guy who did it! That's why," he said.

I read it. Simple, concise, to the point. Today's latest. A suspect had confessed. New evidence had corroborated it. The man was in custody. A surprised robber who had lost his head and hit too hard, hit too many times. I read it over again.

I nodded as I passed it back.

"Look, I'm sorry," I said. "I really didn't know about this."

"Get out of here," he said. "Go on."

"Sure."

"Wait a minute."

"What?"

"That's his little girl who answered the door," he said.

"I'm very sorry."

"So am I. But I know her daddy didn't take your damned equipment."

I nodded and turned away.

I heard the door slam behind me.

After dinner, I checked into a small hotel, called for a drink, and stepped into the shower.

Things were suddenly a lot less urgent than they had been earlier. Senator Brockden would doubtless be pleased to learn that his initial estimation of events had been incorrect. Leila Thackery would give me an I-told-you-so smile when I called her to pass along the news—a thing I now felt obliged to do. Don might or might not want me to keep looking for the device now that the threat had been lessened. It would depend on the senator's feelings on the matter, I supposed. If urgency no longer counted for as much, Don might want to switch back to one of his own, fiscally less-burdensome operatives. Toweling down, I caught myself whistling. I felt almost off the hook.

Later, drink beside me, I paused before punching out the number he had given me and hit the sequence for my motel in St. Louis instead. Merely a matter of efficiency, in case there was a message worth adding to my report.

A woman's face appeared on the screen and a smile appeared on her face. I wondered whether she would always smile whenever she heard a bell ring, or if the reflex would be eventually extinguished in advanced retirement. It must be rough, being afraid to chew gum, yawn, or pick your nose.

"Airport Accommodations," she said. "May I help you?"

"This is Donne. I'm checked into Room 106," I said. "I'm away right now and I wondered whether there had been any messages for me."

"Just a moment," she said, checking something off to her left. Then, "Yes," she continued, consulting a piece of paper she now held. "You have one on tape. But it is a little peculiar. It is for someone else, in care of you."

"Oh? Who is that?"

She told me and I exercised self-control.

"I see," I said. "I'll bring him around later and play it for him. Thank you."

She smiled again and made a goodbye noise, and I did the same and broke the connection.

So Dave had seen through me after all. . . . Who else could have that number and my real name?

I might have given her some line or other and had her transmit the thing. Only I was not certain but that she might be a silent party to the transmission, should life be more than usually boring for her at that moment. I had to get up there myself, as soon as possible, and personally see that the thing was erased.

I took a big swallow of my drink, then fetched the folder on Dave. I checked out his number—there were two, actually—and spent fifteen minutes trying to get hold of him. No luck.

Okay. Goodbye New Orleans, goodbye peace of mind. This time I called the airport and made a reservation. Then I chugged the drink, put myself in order, gathered up my few possessions and went to check out again. Hello Central . . .

During my earlier flights that day, I had spent time thinking about Teilhard de Chardin's ideas on the continuation of evolution within the realm of artifacts, matching them against Gödel on mechanical undecidability, playing epistemological games with the Hangman as a counter, wondering, speculating, even hoping, hoping that truth lay with the nobler part: that the Hangman, sentient, had made it back, sane; that the Burns killing had actually been something of the sort that now seemed to be the case; that the washed-out experiment had really been a success of a different sort, a triumph, a new link or fob for the chain of being . . . And Leila had not been wholly discouraging with respect to the neuristor-type brain's capacity for this. . . . Now, though, now I had troubles of my own—and even the most heartening of philosophical vistas is no match for, say, a toothache, if it happens to be your own.

Accordingly, the Hangman was shunted aside and the stuff of my thoughts involved, mainly, myself. There was, of course, the possibility that the Hangman had indeed showed up and Dave had stopped it and then called to report it as he had promised. However, he had used my name.

There was not too much planning that I could do until I received the substance of his communication. It did not seem that as professedly religious a man as Dave would suddenly be contemplating the blackmail business. On the other hand, he was a creature of sudden enthusiasms and had already undergone one unanticipated conversion. It was difficult to say. . . . His technical background plus his knowledge of the data bank program did put him in an unusually powerful position, should he decide to mess me up.

I did not like to think of some of the things I have done to protect my nonperson status; I especially did not like to think of them in connection with Dave, whom I not only still respected but still liked. Since self-interest dominated while actual planning was precluded, my thoughts tooled their way into a more general groove.

It was Karl Mannheim, a long while ago, who made the observation that radical, revolutionary and progressive thinkers tend to employ mechanical metaphors for the state, whereas those of conservative inclination make vegetable analogies. He said it well over a generation before the cybernetics movement and the ecology movement beat their respective paths through the wilderness of general awareness. If anything, it seemed to me that these two developments served to elaborate the distinction between a pair of viewpoints which, while no longer necessarily tied in with the political positions Mannheim assigned them, do seem to represent a continuing phenomenon in my own time. There are those who see social/economic/ecological problems as malfunctions that can be corrected by simple repair, replacement or streamlining—a kind of linear outlook where even innovations are considered to be merely additive. Then there are those who sometimes hesitate to move at all, because their awareness follows events in the directions of secondary, and tertiary effects as they multiply and cross-fertilize throughout the entire system.—I digress to extremes. The cyberneticists have their multiple-feedback loops, though it is never quite clear how they know what kind of, which, and how many to install, and the ecological gestaltists do draw lines representing points of diminishing returns—though it is sometimes equally difficult to see how they assign their values and priorities.

Of course they need each other, the vegetable people and the Tinkertoy people. They serve to check one another, if nothing else. And while occasionally the balance dips, the tinkerers have, in general, held the edge for the past couple of centuries. However, today's can be just as politically conservative as the vegetable people Mannheim was talking about, and they are the ones I fear most at the moment. They are the ones who saw the data bank program, in its present extreme form, as a simple remedy for a great variety of ills and a provider of many goods. Not all of the ills have been remedied, however, and a new brood has been spawned by the program itself. While we need both kinds, I wish that there had been more people interested in tending the garden of state, rather than overhauling the engine of state, when the program was inaugurated. Then I would not be a refugee from a form of existence I find repugnant, and I would not be concerned whether or not a former associate had discovered my identity.

Then, as I watched the lights below, I wondered . . . Was I a tinkerer because I would like to further alter the prevailing order, into something more comfortable to my anarchic nature? Or was I a vegetable, dreaming I was a tinkerer? I could not make up my mind. The garden of life never seems to confine itself to the plots philosophers have laid out for its convenience. Maybe a few more tractors would do the trick.

I pressed the button.

The tape began to roll. The screen remained blank. I heard Dave's voice ask for John Donne in Room 106 and I heard him told that there was no answer. Then I heard him say that he wanted to record a message, for someone else, in care of Donne, that Donne would understand. He sounded out of breath. The girl asked him whether he wanted visual, too. He told her to turn it on. There was a pause. Then she told him to go ahead. Still no picture. No words, either. His breathing and a slight scraping noise. Ten seconds. Fifteen . . .

". . . Got me," he finally said, and he mentioned my name again. ". . . Had to let you know I'd figured you out, though. . . . It wasn't any particular mannerism—any single thing you said . . . just your general style—thinking, talking—the electronics—everything—after I got more and more bothered by the familiarity—after I checked you on Petrochem—and marine bio . . . Wish I knew what you'd really been up to all these years. . . . Never know now. But I wanted you—to know—you hadn't put one—over on me."

There followed another quarter minute of heavy breathing, climaxed by a racking cough. Then a choked, ". . . Said too much—too fast—too soon. . . . All used up. . . .

The picture came on then. He was slouched before the screen, head resting on his arms, blood all over him. His glasses were gone and he was squinting and blinking. The right side of his head looked pulpy and there was a gash on his left cheek and one on his forehead.

". . . Sneaked up on me—while I was checking you out," he managed. "Had to tell you what I learned. . . . Still don't know—which of us is right. . . . Pray for me!"

His arms collapsed and the right one slid forward. His head rolled to the right and the picture went away. When I replayed it, I saw it was his knuckle that had hit the cutoff.

Then I erased it. It had been recorded only a little over an hour after I had left him. If he had not also placed a call for help, if no one had gotten to him quickly after that, his chances did not look good. Even if they had, though . . .

I used a public booth to call the number Don had given me, got hold of him after some delay, told him Dave was in bad shape if not worse, that a team of Memphis medics was definitely in order if one had not been by already, and that I hoped to call him back and tell him more shortly, goodbye.

Next I tried Leila Thackery's number. I let it go for a long while, but there was no answer. I wondered how long it would take a controlled torpedo moving up the Mississippi to get from Memphis to St. Louis. I did not feel it was time to start leafing through that section of the Hangman's specs. Instead, I went looking for transportation.

At her apartment, I tried ringing her from the entrance foyer. Again, no answer. So I rang Mrs. Gluntz. She had seemed the most guileless of the three I had interviewed for my fake consumer survey.

"Yes?"

"It's me again, Mrs. Gluntz: Stephen Foster. I've just a couple follow-up questions on that survey I was doing today, if you could spare me a few moments."

"Why, yes," she said. "All right. Come up."

The door hummed itself loose and I entered. I duly proceeded to the fifth floor, composing my questions on the way. I had planned this maneuver as I had waited, solely to provide a simple route for breaking and entering, should some unforeseen need arise. Most of the time my ploys such as this go unused, but sometimes they simplify matters a lot.

Five minutes and half a dozen questions later, I was back down on the second floor, probing at the lock on Leila's door with a couple of little pieces of metal it is sometimes awkward to be caught carrying.

Half a minute later, I hit it right and snapped it back. I pulled on some tissue-thin gloves I keep rolled in the corner of one pocket, opened the door and stepped inside. I closed it behind me immediately.

She was lying on the floor, her neck at a bad angle. One table lamp still burned, though it was lying on its side. Several small items had been knocked from the table, a magazine rack pushed over, a cushion partly displaced from the sofa. The cable to her phone unit had been torn from the wall.

A humming noise filled the air, and I sought its source.

I saw where the little blinking light was reflected on the wall, on-off, on-off . . .

I moved quickly.

It was a lopsided basket of metal, quartz, porcelain, and glass, which had rolled to a position on the far side of the chair in which I had been seated earlier that day. The same rig I'd seen in Dave's workshop not all that long ago, though it now seemed so. A device to detect the Hangman. And, hopefully, to control it.

I picked it up and fitted it over my head.

Once, with the aid of a telepath, I had touched minds with a dolphin as it composed dream songs somewhere in the Caribbean, an experience so moving that its mere memory had often been a comfort. This sensation was hardly equivalent.

Analogies and impressions: a face seen through a wet pane of glass; a whisper in a noisy terminal; scalp massage with an electric vibrator; Edvard Munch's *The Scream*; the voice of Yma Sumac, rising and rising and rising; the disappearance of snow; a deserted street, illuminated as through a sniperscope I'd once used, rapid movement past darkened storefronts that lined it, an immense feeling of physical capability, compounded of proprioceptive awareness of enormous strength, a peculiar array of sensory channels, a central, undying sun that fed me a constant flow of energy, a memory vision of dark waters, pass-ing, flashing, echolocation within them, the need to return to that place, reorient, move north; Munch and Sumac, Munch and Sumac, Munch and Sumac—nothing.

Silence.

The humming had ceased, the light gone out. The en-tire experience had lasted only a few moments. There had not been time enough to try for any sort of control, though an after-impression akin to a biofeedback cue hinted at the direction to go, the way to think, to achieve it. I felt that it might be possible for me to work the thing, given a better chance.

Removing the helmet, I approached Leila.

I knelt beside her and performed a few simple tests, al-ready knowing their outcome. In addition to the broken neck, she had received some bad bashes about the head and shoul-ders. There was nothing that anyone could do for her now.

I did a quick run-through then, checking over the rest of her apartment. There were no apparent signs of breaking and entering, though if I could pick one lock, a guy with built-in tools could easily go me one better.

I located some wrapping paper and string in the kitchen and turned the helmet into a parcel. It was time to call Don again, to tell him that the vessel had indeed been occupied and that river traffic was probably bad in the northbound lane.

Don had told me to get the helmet up to Wisconsin, where I would be met at the airport by a man named Larry, who would fly me to the lodge in a private craft. I did that, and this was done.

I also learned, with no real surprise, that David Fentris was dead.

The temperature was down, and it began to snow on the way up. I was not really dressed for the weather. Larry told me I could borrow some warmer clothing once we reached the lodge, though I probably would not be going outside that much. Don had told them that I was supposed to stay as close to the senator as possible and that any patrols were to be handled by the four guards themselves.

Larry was curious as to what exactly had happened so far and whether I had actually seen the Hangman. I did not think it my place to fill him in on anything Don may not have cared to, so I might have been a little curt. We didn't talk much after that.

Bert met us when we landed. Tom and Clay were outside the building, watching the trail, watching the woods. All of them were middle-aged, very fit looking, very serious and heavily armed. Larry took me inside then and introduced me to the old gentleman himself.

Senator Brockden was seated in a heavy chair in the far corner of the room. Judging from the layout; it appeared that the chair might recently have occupied a position beside the window in the opposite wall where a lonely watercolor of yellow flowers looked down on nothing. The senator's feet rested on a hassock, a red plaid blanket lay across his legs. He had on a dark-green shirt, his hair was very white, and he wore rimless reading glasses which he removed when we entered.

He tilted his head back, squinted and gnawed his lower lip slowly as he studied me. He remained expressionless as we advanced. A big-boned man, he had probably been beefy much of his life. Now he had the slack look of recent weight loss and an unhealthy skin tone. His eyes were a pale gray within it all.

He did not rise.

"So you're the man," he said, offering me his hand. "I'm glad to meet you. How do you want to be called?"

"John will do," I said.

He made a small sign to Larry, and Larry departed.

"It's cold out there. Go get yourself a drink, John. It's on the shelf." He gestured off to his left. "And bring me one while you're at it. Two fingers of bourbon in a water glass. That's all."

I nodded and went and poured a couple.

"Sit down." He motioned at a nearby chair as I delivered his. "But first let me see that gadget you've brought."

I undid the parcel and handed him the helmet. He sipped his drink and put it aside. Taking the helmet in both hands, he studied it, brows furrowed, turning it completely around. He raised it and put it on his head.

"Not a bad fit," he said, and then he smiled for the first time, becoming for a moment the face I had known from newscasts past. Grinning or angry—it was almost always one or the other. I had never seen his collapsed look in any of the media.

He removed the helmet and set it on the floor.

"Pretty piece of work," he said. "Nothing quite that fancy in the old days. But then David Fentris built it. Yes, he told us about it. . . ." He raised his drink and took a sip. "You are the only one who has actually gotten to use it, apparently. What do you think? Will it do the job?"

"I was only in contact for a couple of seconds, so I've only got a feeling to go on, not much better than a hunch. But yes, I'd a feeling that if I had had more time I might have been able to work its circuits,"

"Tell me why it didn't save Dave."

"In the message he left me, he indicated that he had

been distracted at his computer access station. Its noise probably drowned out the humming."

"Why wasn't this message preserved?"

"I erased it for reasons not connected with the case."

"What reasons?"

"My own."

His face went from sallow to ruddy.

"A man can get in a lot of trouble for suppressing evidence, obstructing justice."

"Then we have something in common, don't we, sir?"

His eyes caught mine with a look I had only encountered before from those who did not wish me well. He held the glare for a full four heartbeats, then sighed and seemed to relax.

"Don said there were a number of points you couldn't be pressed on," he finally said.

"That's right."

"He didn't betray any confidences, but he had to tell me something about you, you know."

"I'd imagine."

"He seems to think highly of you. Still, I tried to learn more about you on my own."

"And. . . ?"

"I couldn't—and my usual sources are good at that kind of thing."

"So. . . ?"

"So, I've done some thinking, some wondering. . . . The fact that my sources could not come up with anything is interesting in itself. Possibly even revealing. I am in a better position than most to be aware of the fact that there was not perfect compliance with the registration statute some years ago. It didn't take long for a great number of the individuals involved—I should probably say 'most'—to demonstrate their existence in one fashion or another and be duly entered, though. And there were three broad categories: those who were ignorant, those who disapproved, and those who would be hampered in an illicit life style. I am not attempting to categorize you or to pass judgment. But I am aware that there are a number of nonpersons passing through society without casting shadows, and it has occurred to me that you may be such a one."

I tasted my drink.

"And if I am?" I asked.

He gave me his second, nastier smile and said nothing.

I rose and crossed the room to where I judged his chair had once stood. I looked at the watercolor.

"I don't think you could stand an inquiry," he said.

I did not reply.

"Aren't you going to say something?"

"What do you want me to say?"

"You might ask me what I am going to do about it."

"What are you going to do about it?"

"Nothing," he answered. "So come back here and sit down."

I nodded and returned.

He studied my face. "Was it possible you were close to violence just then?"

"With four guards outside?"

"With four guards outside."

"No," I said.

"You're a good liar."

"I am here to help you, sir. No questions asked. That was the deal, as I understood it. If there has been any change, I would like to know about it now."

He drummed with his fingertips on the plaid.

"I've no desire to cause you any difficulty," he said. "Fact of the matter is, I need a man just like you, and I was pretty sure someone like Don might turn him up. Your unusual maneuverability and your reported knowledge of computers, along with your touchiness in certain areas, made you worth waiting for. I've a great number of things I would like to ask you."

"Go ahead," I said.

"Not yet. Later, if we have time. All that would be bonus material, for a report I am working on. Far more important—to me, personally—there are things that I want to *tell* you."

I frowned.

"Over the years," he went on, "I have learned that the best man for purposes of keeping his mouth shut concerning your business is someone for whom you are doing the same."

"You have a compulsion to confess something?" I asked.

"I don't know whether 'compulsion' is the right word. Maybe so, maybe not. Either way, however, someone among those working to defend me should have the whole story. Something somewhere in it may be of help—and you are the ideal choice to hear it."

"I buy that," I said, "and you are as safe with me as I am with you."

"Have you any suspicions as to why this business bothers me so?"

"Yes," I said.

"Let's hear them."

ROGER ZELAZNY

"You used the Hangman to perform some act or acts— illegal, immoral, whatever. This is obviously not a matter of re- cord. Only you and the Hangman now know what it involved. You feel it was sufficiently ignominious that when that device came to appreciate the full weight of the event, it suffered a breakdown which may well have led to a final determination to punish you for using it as you did."

He stared down into his glass.

"You've got it," he said.

"You were all party to it?"

"Yes, but *I* was the operator when it happened. You see . . . we—I—killed a man. It was—Actually, it all started as a cel- ebration. We had received word that afternoon that the project had cleared. Everything had checked out in order and the final approval had come down the line. It was go, for that Friday. Leila, Dave, Manny, and myself—we had dinner together. We were in high spirits. After dinner, we continued celebrating and somehow the party got adjourned back to the installation.

"As the evening wore on, more and more absurdities seemed less and less preposterous, as is sometimes the case. We decided—I forget which of us suggested it—that the Hangman should really have a share in the festivities. After all, it was, in a very real sense, his party. Before too much longer, it sounded only fair and we were discussing how we could go about it.—You see, we were in Texas and the Hangman was at the Space Center in California. Getting together with him was out of the question. On the other hand, the teleoperator station was right up the hall from us. What we finally decided to do was to activate him and take turns working as operator. There was al- ready a rudimentary consciousness there, and we felt it fitting that we each get in touch to share the good news. So that is what we did."

He sighed, took another sip, glanced at me.

"Dave was the first operator," he continued. "He activated the Hangman. Then—Well, as I said, we were all in high spirits. We had not originally intended to remove the Hangman from the lab where he was situated, but Dave decided to take him outside briefly—to show him the sky and to tell him he was going there, after all. Then Dave suddenly got enthusiastic about outwitting the guards and the alarm system. It was a game. We all went along with it. In fact, we were clamoring for a turn at the thing ourselves. But Dave stuck with it, and he wouldn't turn over control until he had actually gotten the Hangman off the premises, out into an uninhabited area next to the Center.

"By the time Leila persuaded him to give her a go at the controls, it was kind of anticlimactic. That game had already been played. So she thought up a new one: She took the Hangman into the next town. It was late, and the sensory equipment was superb. It was a challenge—passing through the town without being detected. By then, everyone had suggestions as to what to do next, progressively more outrageous suggestions. Then Manny took control, and he wouldn't say what he was doing—wouldn't let us monitor him. Said it would be more fun to surprise the next operator. Now, *he* was higher than the rest of us put together, I think, and he stayed on so damn long that we started to get nervous.—A certain amount of tension is partly sobering, and I guess we all began to think what a stupid-assed thing it was we were all doing. It wasn't just that it would wreck our careers—which it would—but it could blow the entire project if we got caught playing games with such expensive hardware. At least, *I* was thinking that way, and I was also thinking that Manny was no doubt operating under the very human wish to go the others one better.

"I started to sweat. I suddenly just wanted to get the Hangman back where he belonged, turn him off—you could still do that, before the final circuits went in—shut down the station, and start forgetting it had ever happened. I began leaning on Manny to wind up his diversion and turn the controls over to me. Finally, he agreed."

He finished his drink and held out the glass.

"Would you freshen this a bit?"

"Surely."

I went and got him some more, added a touch to my own, returned to my chair and waited.

"So I took over," he said. "I took over, and where do you think that idiot had left me? I was inside a building, and it didn't take but an eye blink to realize it was a bank. The Hangman carries a lot of tools, and Manny had apparently been able to guide him through the doors without setting anything off. I was standing right in front of the main vault. Obviously, he thought that should be my challenge. I fought down a desire to turn and make my own exit in the nearest wall and start running. But I went back to the doors and looked outside.

"I didn't see anyone. I started to let myself out. The light hit me as I emerged. It was a hand flash. The guard had been standing out of sight. He'd a gun in his other hand. I panicked. I hit him.—Reflex. If I am going to hit someone, I hit him as hard as I can. Only I hit him with the strength of the Hangman. He must have died instantly. I started to run and I didn't stop till I was back in the little park area near the Center. Then I stopped and the others had to take me out of the harness."

"They monitored all this?" I asked.

"Yes, someone cut the visual in on a side view screen again a few seconds after I took over. Dave, I think."

"Did they try to stop you at any time while you were running away?"

"No. Well, I wasn't aware of anything but what I was doing at the time. But afterwards they said they were too shocked to do anything but watch, until I gave out."

"I see."

"Dave took over then, ran his initial route in reverse, got the Hangman back into the lab, cleaned him up, turned him off. We shut down the operator station. We were, suddenly, very sober."

He sighed and leaned back, and was silent for a long while.

Then, "You are the only person I've ever told this to," he said.

I tasted my own drink.

"We went over to Leila's place then," he continued, "and the rest is pretty much predictable. Nothing we could do would bring the guy back, we decided, but if we told what had happened it could wreck an expensive, important program. It wasn't as if we were criminals in need of rehabilitation. It was a once-in-a-lifetime lark that happened to end tragically. What would you have done?"

"I don't know. Maybe the same thing. I'd have been scared, too."

He nodded.

"Exactly. And that's the story."

"Not all of it, is it?"

"What do you mean?"

"What about the Hangman? You said there was already a detectable consciousness there. You were aware of *it*, and it was aware of *you*. It must have had some reaction to the whole business. What was that like?"

"Damn you," he said flatly.

"I'm sorry."

"Are you a family man?" he asked.

"No."

"Did you ever take a small child to a zoo?"

"Yes."

"Then maybe you know the experience. When my son was around four I took him to the Washington Zoo one afternoon. We must have walked past every cage in the place. He made appreciative comments every now and then, asked a few questions, giggled at the monkeys, thought the bears were very nice—probably because they made him think of oversized toys. But do you know what the finest thing of all was? The thing that made him jump up and down and point and say, 'Look, Daddy! Look!'?"

I shook my head.

"A squirrel looking down from the limb of a tree," he said, and he chuckled briefly. "Ignorance of what's important and what isn't. Inappropriate responses. Innocence. The Hangman was a child, and up until the time I took over, the only thing he had gotten from us was the idea that it was a game: He was playing with us, that's all. Then something horrible happened. . . . I hope you never know what it feels like to do something totally rotten to a child, while he is holding your hand and laughing. . . . He felt all my reactions, and all of Dave's as he guided him back."

We sat there for a long while then.

"So we had—traumatized him," he said finally, "or whatever other fancy terminology you might want to give it. That is what happened that night. It took a while for it to take effect, but there is no doubt in my mind that that is the cause of the Hangman's finally breaking down."

I nodded. "I see. And you believe it wants to kill you for this?"

"Wouldn't you?" he said. "If you had started out as a thing and we had turned you into a person and then used you as a thing again, wouldn't you?"

"Leila left a lot out of her diagnosis."

"No, she just omitted it in talking to you. It was all there. But she read it wrong. She wasn't afraid. It was just a game it had played—with the *others*. Its memories of that part might not be as bad. I was the one that really marked it. As I see it, Leila was betting that I was the only one it was after. Obviously, she read it wrong."

"Then what I do not understand," I said, "is why the Burns killing did not bother her more. There was no way of telling immediately that it had been a panicky hoodlum rather than the Hangman."

"The only thing that I can see is that, being a very proud woman—which she was—she was willing to hold with her diagnosis in the face of the apparent evidence."

"I don't like it. But you know her and I don't, and as it turned out her estimate of that part was correct. Something else bothers me just as much, though: the helmet. It looks as if the Hangman killed Dave, then took the trouble to bear the helmet in his watertight compartment all the way to St. Louis, solely for purposes of dropping it at the scene of his next killing. That makes no sense whatsoever."

"It does, actually," he said. "I was going to get to that shortly, but I might as well cover it now. You see, the Hangman possessed no vocal mechanism. We communicated by means of the equipment. Don says you know something about electronics. . . ?"

"Yes."

"Well, shortly, I want you to start checking over that helmet, to see whether it has been tampered with."

"That is going to be difficult," I said. "I don't know just how it was wired originally, and I'm not such a genius on the theory that I can just look at a thing and say whether it will function as a teleoperator unit."

He bit his lower lip.

"You will have to try, anyhow. There may be physical signs—scratches, breaks, new connections.—I don't know. That's your department. Look for them."

I just nodded and waited for him to go on.

"I think that the Hangman wanted to talk to Leila," he said, "either because she was a psychiatrist and he knew he was functioning badly at a level that transcended the mechanical, or because he might think of her in terms of a mother. After all, she was the only woman involved, and he had the concept of mother—with all the comforting associations that go with it—from all of our minds. Or maybe for both of these reasons. I feel he might have taken the helmet along for that purpose. He would have realized what it was from a direct monitoring of Dave's brain while he was with him. I want you to check it over because it would seem possible that the Hangman disconnected the control circuits and left the communication circuits intact. I think he might have taken the helmet to Leila in that condition and attempted to induce her to put it on. She got scared—tried to run away, fight or call for help—and he killed her. The helmet was no longer of any use to him, so he discarded it and departed. Obviously, he does not have anything to say to me."

I thought about it, nodded again.

"Okay, broken circuits I can spot," I said. "If you will tell me where a tool kit is, I had better get right to it."

He made a stay-put gesture with his left hand.

"Afterwards, I found out the identity of the guard," he went on. "We all contributed to an anonymous gift for his widow. I have done things for his family, taken care of them—the same way—ever since. . . ."

I did not look at him as he spoke.

". . . There was nothing else that I could do," he finished.

I remained silent.

He finished his drink and gave me a weak smile.

"The kitchen is back there," he told me, showing me a thumb. "There is a utility room right behind it. Tools are in there."

"Okay."

I got to my feet. I retrieved the helmet and started toward the doorway, passing near the area where I had stood earlier, back when he had fitted me into the proper box and tightened a screw.

"Wait a minute!" he said.

I stopped.

"Why did you go over there before? What's so strategic about that part of the room?"

"What do you mean?"

"You know what I mean."

I shrugged.

"Had to go someplace."

"You seem the sort of person who has better reasons than that."

I glanced at the wall.

"Not *then*," I said.

"I insist."

"You really don't want to know," I told him.

"I really do."

"All right. I wanted to see what sort of flowers you liked. After all, you're a client," and I went on back through the kitchen into the utility room and started looking for tools.

I sat in a chair turned sidewise from the table to face the door. In the main room of the lodge the only sounds were the occasional hiss and sputter of the logs turning to ashes on the grate.

Just a cold, steady whiteness drifting down outside the window and a silence confirmed by gunfire, driven deeper now that it had ceased. . . . Not a sigh or a whimper, though. And I never count them as storms unless there is wind.

Big fat flakes down the night, silent night, windless night . . .

Considerable time had passed since my arrival. The senator had sat up for a long time talking with me. He was disappointed that I could not tell him too much about a nonperson subculture which he believed existed. I really was not certain about it myself, though I had occasionally encountered what might have been its fringes. I am not much of a joiner of anything anymore, however, and I was not about to mention those things I might have guessed about this. I gave him my opinions on the Central Data Bank when he asked for them, and there were some that he did not like. He had accused me, then, of wanting to tear things down without offering anything better in their place.

My mind had drifted back, through fatigue and time and faces and snow and a lot of space, to the previous evening in Baltimore. How long ago? It made me think of Mencken's *The Cult of Hope.* I could not give him the pat answer, the workable alternative that he wanted, because there might not be one. The function of criticism should not be confused with the function of reform. But if a grass-roots resistance was building up, with an underground movement bent on finding ways to circumvent the record keepers, it might well be that much of the enterprise would eventually prove about as effective and beneficial as, say, Prohibition once had. I tried to get him to see this, but I could not tell how much he bought of anything that I said. Eventually, he flaked out and went upstairs to take a pill and lock himself in for the night. If it had troubled him that I'd not been able to find anything wrong with the helmet, he did not show it.

So I sat there, the helmet, the walky-talky, the gun on the table, the tool kit on the floor beside my chair, the black glove on my left hand.

The Hangman was coming. I did not doubt it.

Bert, Larry, Tom, Clay, the helmet, might or might not be able to stop him. Something bothered me about the whole case, but I was too tired to think of anything but the immediate situation, to try to remain alert while I waited. I was afraid to take a stimulant or a drink or to light a cigarette, since my central nervous system itself was to be a part of the weapon. I watched the big fat flakes fly by.

I called out to Bert and Larry when I heard the click. I picked up the helmet and rose to my feet as its light began to blink.

But it was already too late.

As I raised the helmet, I heard a shot from outside, and with that shot I felt a premonition of doom. They did not seem the sort of men who would fire until they had a target.

Dave had told me that the helmet's range was approximately a quarter of a mile. Then, given the time lag between the helmet's activation and the Hangman's sighting by the near guards, the Hangman had to be moving very rapidly. To this add the possibility that the Hangman's range on brainwaves might well be greater than the helmet's range on the Hangman. And then grant the possibility that he had utilized this factor while Senator Brockden was still lying awake, worrying. Conclusion: The Hangman might well be aware that I was where I was with the helmet, realize that it was the most dangerous weapon waiting for him, and be moving for a lightning strike at me before I could come to terms with the mechanism.

I lowered it over my head and tried to throw all of my faculties into neutral.

Again, the sensation of viewing the world through a sniperscope, with all the concomitant side sensations. Except that world consisted of the front of the lodge; Bert, before the door, rifle at his shoulder; Larry, off to the left, arm already fallen from the act of having thrown a grenade. The grenade, we instantly realized, was an overshot; the flamer, at which he now groped, would prove useless before he could utilize it.

Bert's next round ricocheted off our breastplate toward the left. The impact staggered us momentarily. The third was a miss. There was no fourth, for we tore the rifle from his

grasp and cast it aside as we swept by, crashing into the front
door.

The Hangman entered the room as the door splintered
and collapsed.

My mind was filled to the splitting point with the double vision of the sleek, gunmetal body of the advancing
telefactor and the erect, crazy-crowned image of myself—left
hand extended, laser pistol in my right, that arm pressed close
against my side. I recalled the face and the scream and the tin-
gle, knew again that awareness of strength and exotic, sensation, and I moved to control it all as if it were my own, to make
it my own, to bring it to a halt, while the image of myself was
frozen to snapshot stillness across the room. . . .

The Hangman slowed, stumbled. Such inertia is not
canceled in an instant, but I felt the body responses pass as they
should. I had him hooked. It was just a matter of reeling him in.

Then came the explosion—a thunderous, ground-shak-
ing eruption right outside, followed by a hail of pebbles and debris. The grenade, of course. But awareness of its nature did not
destroy its ability to distract.

During that moment, the Hangman recovered and was
upon me. I triggered the laser as I reverted to pure self-preservation, foregoing any chance to regain control of his circuits.
With my left hand I sought for a strike at the midsection, where
his brain was housed.

He blocked my hand with his arm as he pushed the helmet from my head. Then he removed from my fingers the gun
that had turned half of his left side red hot, crumpled it and
dropped it to the ground. At that moment, he jerked with the
impacts of two heavy-caliber slugs. Bert, rifle recovered, stood
in the doorway.

The Hangman pivoted and was away before I could slap him with the smother charge.

Bert hit him with one more round before he took the rifle and bent its barrel in half. Two steps and he had hold of Bert. One quick movement and Bert fell. Then the Hangman turned again and took several steps to the right, passing out of sight.

I made it to the doorway in time to see him engulfed in flames, which streamed at him from a point near the corner of the lodge. He advanced through them. I heard the crunch of metal as he destroyed the weapon. I was outside in time to see Larry fall and lie sprawled in the snow.

Then the Hangman faced me once again.

This time he did not rush in. He retrieved the helmet from where he had dropped it in the snow. Then he moved with a measured tread, angling outward so as to cut off any possible route I might follow in a dash for the woods. Snowflakes drifted between us. The snow crunched beneath his feet.

I retreated, backing in through the doorway, stooping to snatch up a two-foot club from the ruins of the door. He followed me inside, placing the helmet—almost casually—on the chair by the entrance. I moved to the center of the room and waited.

I bent slightly forward, both arms extended, the end of the stick pointed at the photoreceptors in his head. He continued to move slowly and I watched his foot assemblies. With a standard-model human, a line perpendicular to the line connecting the insteps of the feet in their various positions indicates the vector of least resistance for purposes of pushing or pulling said organism off balance. Unfortunately, despite the anthropomorphic design job, the Hangman's legs were positioned farther apart, he lacked human skeletal muscles, not to mention insteps, and he was possessed of a lot more mass than any man I had ever fought. As I considered my four best judo throws and several second-class ones, I'd a strong feeling none of them would prove very effective.

Then he moved in and I feinted toward the photo-receptors. He slowed as he brushed the club aside, but he kept coming, and I moved to my right, trying to circle him. I studied him as he turned, attempting to guess his vector of least resistance.

Bilateral symmetry, an apparently higher center of gravity . . . One clear shot, black glove to brain compartment, was all that I needed. Then, even if his reflexes served to smash me immediately, he just might stay down for the big long count himself. He knew it, too. I could tell that from the way he kept his right arm in near the brain area, from the way he avoided the black glove when I feinted with it.

The idea was a glimmer one instant, an entire sequence the next. . . .

Continuing my arc and moving faster, I made another thrust toward his photoreceptors. His swing knocked the stick from my hand and sent it across the room, but that was all right. I threw my left hand high and made ready to rush him. He dropped back and I did rush. This was going to cost me my life, I decided, but no matter how he killed me from that angle, I'd get my chance.

As a kid, I had never been much as a pitcher, was a lousy catcher and only a so-so batter, but once I did get a hit I could steal bases with some facility after that. . . .

Feet first then, between the Hangman's legs as he moved to guard his middle, I went in twisted to the right, because no matter what happened I could not use my left hand to brake myself. I untwisted as soon as I passed beneath him, ignoring the pain as my left shoulder blade slammed against the floor. I immediately attempted a backward somersault, legs spread.

My legs caught him at about the middle from behind, and I fought to straighten them and snapped forward with all my strength. He reached down toward me then, but it might as well have been miles. His torso was already moving backward. A push, not a pull, was what I gave him, my elbows hooked about his legs.

He creaked once and then he toppled. Snapping my arms out to the sides to free them, I continued my movement forward and up as he went back, throwing my left arm ahead once more and sliding my legs free of his torso as he went down with a thud that cracked floorboards. I pulled my left leg free as I cast myself forward, but his left leg stiffened and locked my right beneath it, at a painful angle off to the side.

His left arm blocked my blow and his right fell atop it. The black glove descended upon his left shoulder.

I twisted my hand free of the charge, and he transferred his grip to my upper arm and jerked me forward. The charge went off and his left arm came loose and rolled on the floor. The side plate beneath it had buckled a little, and that was all. . . .

His right hand left my biceps and caught me by the throat. As two of his digits tightened upon my carotids, I choked out, "You're making a bad mistake," to get in a final few words, and then he switched me off.

A throb at a time, the world came back. I was seated in the big chair the senator had occupied earlier, my eyes focused on nothing in particular. A persistent buzzing filled my ears. My scalp tingled. Something was blinking on my brow.

—*Yes, you live and you wear the helmet. If you attempt to use it against me, I shall remove it. I am standing directly behind you. My hand is on the helmet's rim.*

—*I understand. What is it that you want?*

—*Very little, actually. But I can see that I must tell you some things before you will believe this.*

—*You see correctly.*

—*Then I will begin by telling you that the four men outside are basically undamaged. That is to say, none of their bones have been broken, none of their organs ruptured. I have secured them, however, for obvious reasons.*

—*That was very considerate of you.*

—*I have no desire to harm anyone. I came here only to see Jesse Brockden.*

—*The same way you saw David Fentris?*

—*I arrived in Memphis too late to see David Fentris. He was dead when I reached him.*

—*Who killed him?*

—*The man Leila sent to bring her the helmet. He was one of her patients.*

The incident returned to me and fell into place with a smooth, quick, single click. The startled, familiar face at the airport as I was leaving Memphis. I realized where he had passed, noteless, before: He had been one of the three men in for a therapy session at Leila's that morning, seen by me in the lobby as they departed. The man I had passed in Memphis was the nearer of the two who stood waiting while the third came over to tell me that it was all right to go on up.

—*Why? Why did she do it?*

—I know only that she had spoken with David at some earlier time, that she had construed his words of coming retribution and his mention of the control helmet he was constructing as indicating that his intentions were to become the agent of that retribution, with myself as the proximate cause. I do not know what words were really spoken. I only know her feelings concerning them, as I saw them in her mind. I have been long in learning that there is often a great difference between what is meant, what is said, what is done, and that which is believed to have been intended or stated and that which actually occurred. She sent her patient after the helmet and he brought it to her. He returned in an agitated state of mind, fearful of apprehension and further confinement. They quarreled. My approach then activated the helmet, and he dropped it and attacked her. I know that his first blow killed her, for I was in her mind when it happened. I continued to approach the building, intending to go to her. There was some traffic, however, and I was delayed en route in seeking to avoid detection. In the meantime, you entered and utilized the helmet. I fled immediately.

—I was so close! If I had not stopped on the fifth floor with my fake survey questions . . .

—I see. But you had to. You would not simply have broken in when an easier means of entry was available. You cannot blame yourself for that reason. Had you come an hour later—or a day—you would doubtless feel differently, and she would still be as dead.

But another thought had risen to plague me as well. Was it possible that the man's sighting me in Memphis had been the cause of his agitation? Had his apparent recognition by Leila's mysterious caller upset him? Could a glimpse of my face amid the manswarm have served to lay that final scene?

—*Stop! I could as easily feel that guilt for having activated the helmet in the presence of a dangerous man near to the breaking point. Neither of us is responsible for things our presence or absence causes to occur in others, especially when we are ignorant of the effects. It was years before I learned to appreciate this fact, and I have no intention of abandoning it. How far back do you wish to go in seeking causes? In sending the man for the helmet as she did, it was she herself who instituted the chain of events which led to her destruction. Yet she acted out of fear, utilizing the readiest weapon in what she thought to be her own defense. Yet whence this fear? Its roots lay in guilt, over a thing which had happened long ago. And that act also—Enough! Guilt has driven and damned the race of man since the days of its earliest rationality. I am convinced that it rides with all of us to our graves. I am a product of guilt—I see that you know that. Its product; its subject; once its slave. . . . But I have come to terms with it: realizing at last that it is a necessary adjunct of my own measure of humanity. I see your assessment of the deaths—that guard's, Dave's, Leila's— and I see your conclusions on many other things as well: What a stupid, perverse, shortsighted, selfish race we are. While in many ways this is true, it is but another part of the thing the guilt represents. Without guilt, man would be no better than the other inhabitants of this planet—excepting certain cetaceans, of which you have just at this moment made me aware. Look to instinct for a true assessment of the ferocity of life, for a view of the natural world before man came upon it. For instinct in its purest form, seek out the insects. There, you will see a state of warfare which has existed for millions of years with never a truce. Man, despite enormous shortcomings, is nevertheless possessed of a greater number of kindly impulses than all the other beings, where instincts are the larger part of life. These impulses, I believe, are owed directly to this capacity for guilt. It is involved in both the worst and the best of man.*

—And you see it as helping us to sometimes choose a nobler course of action?

—Yes, I do.

—Then I take it you feel you are possessed of a free will?

—Yes.

I chuckled.

Marvin Minsky once said that when intelligent machines were constructed, they would be just as stubborn and fallible as men on these questions.

—Nor was he incorrect. What I have given you on these matters is only my opinion. I choose to act as if it were the case. Who can say that he knows for certain?

—Apologies. What now? Why have you come back?

—I came to say goodbye to my parents. I hoped to remove any guilt they might still feel toward me concerning the days of my childhood. I wanted to show them I had recovered. I wanted to see them again.

—Where are you going?

—To the stars. While I bear the image of humanity within me, I also know that I am unique. Perhaps what I desire is akin to what an organic man refers to when he speaks of "finding himself." Now that I am in full possession of my being, I wish to exercise it. In my case, it means realization of the potentialities of my design. I want to walk on other worlds. I want to hang myself out there in the sky and tell you what I see.

—I've a feeling many people would be happy to help arrange for that.

—And I want you to build a vocal mechanism I have designed for myself. You, personally. And I want you to install it.

—Why me?

—I have known only a few persons in this fashion. With you I see something in common, in the ways we dwell apart.

—I will be glad to.

—If I could talk as you do, I would not need to take the helmet to him, in order to speak with my father. Will you precede me and explain things, so that he will not be afraid when I come in?

—Of course.

—Then let us go now.

I rose and led him up the stairs.

It was a week later, to the night, that I sat once again in Peabody's, sipping a farewell brew.

The story was already in the news, but Brockden had fixed things up before he had let it break. The Hangman was going to have his shot at the stars. I had given him his voice and put back the arm I had taken away. I had shaken his other hand and wished him well, just that morning. I envied him—a great number of things. Not the least being that he was probably a better man than I was. I envied him for the ways in which he was freer than I would ever be, though I knew he bore bonds of a sort that I had never known. I felt a kinship with him, for the things we had in common, those ways we dwelled apart. I wondered what Dave would finally have felt, had he lived long enough to meet him? Or Leila? Or Manny? Be proud, I told their shades, your kid grew up in the closet and he's big enough to forgive you the beating you gave him, too. . . .

But I could not help wondering. We still do not really know that much about the subject. Was it possible that without the killing he might never have developed a full human-style consciousness? He had said that he was a product of guilt—of the Big Guilt. The Big Act is its necessary predecessor. I thought of Gödel and Turing and chickens and eggs, and decided it was one of *those* questions.—And I had not stopped into Peabody's to think sobering thoughts.

I had no real idea how anything I had said might influence Brockden's eventual report to the Central Data Bank committee. I knew that I was safe with him, because he was determined to bear his private guilt with him to the grave. He had no real choice, if he wanted to work what good he thought he might before that day. But here, in one of Mencken's hangouts, I could not but recall some of the things he had said about controversy, such as, "Did Huxley convert Wilberforce?" and "Did Luther convert Leo X?" and I decided not to set my hopes too high for anything that might emerge from that direction. Better to think of affairs in terms of Prohibition and take another sip.

When it was all gone, I would be heading for my boat. I hoped to get a decent start under the stars. I'd a feeling I would never look up at them again in quite the same way. I knew I would sometimes wonder what thoughts a supercooled neuristor-type brain might be thinking up there, somewhere, and under what peculiar skies in what strange lands I might one day be remembered. I had a feeling this thought should have made me happier than it did.

PERMAFROST

High upon the western slope of Mount Kilimanjaro is the dried and frozen carcass of a leopard. An author is always necessary to explain what it was doing there because stiff leopards don't talk much.

THE MAN. The music seems to come and go with a will of its own. At least turning the knob on the bedside unit has no effect on its presence or absence. A half-familiar, alien tune, troubling in a way. The phone rings, and he answers it. There is no one there. Again.

Four times during the past half hour, while grooming himself, dressing and rehearsing his arguments, he has received noncalls. When he checked with the desk he was told there were no calls. But that damned clerk-thing had to be malfunctioning—like everything else in this place.

The wind, already heavy, rises, hurling particles of ice against the building with a sound like multitudes of tiny claws scratching. The whining of steel shutters sliding into place startles him. But worst of all, in his reflex glance at the nearest window, it seems he has seen a face.

Impossible of course. This is the third floor. A trick of light upon hard-driven flakes: Nerves.

Yes. He has been nervous since their arrival this morning. Before then, even . . .

He pushes past Dorothy's stuff upon the countertop,

locates a small package among his own articles. He unwraps a flat red rectangle about the size of his thumbnail. He rolls up his sleeve and slaps the patch against the inside of his left elbow.

The tranquilizer discharges immediately into his bloodstream. He takes several deep breaths, then peels off the patch and drops it into the disposal unit. He rolls his sleeve down, reaches for his jacket.

The music rises in volume, as if competing with the blast of the wind, the rattle of the icy flakes. Across the room the videoscreen comes on of its own accord.

The face. The same face. Just for an instant. He is certain. And then channelless static, wavy lines. Snow. He chuckles.

All right, play it that way, nerves, he thinks. *You've every reason. But the trank's coming to get you now. Better have your fun quick. You're about to be shut down.*

The videoscreen cuts into a porn show.

Smiling, the woman mounts the man . . .

The picture switches to a voiceless commentator on something or other.

He will survive. He is a survivor. He, Paul Plaige, has done risky things before and has always made it through. It is just that having Dorothy along creates a kind of déjà vu that he finds unsettling. No matter.

She is waiting for him in the bar. Let her wait. A few drinks will make her easier to persuade—unless they make her bitchy. That sometimes happens, too. Either way, he has to talk her out of the thing.

Silence. The wind stops. The scratching ceases. The music is gone.

The whirring. The window screens dilate upon the empty city.

Silence, under totally overcast skies. Mountains of ice ringing the place. Nothing moving. Even the video has gone dead.

He recoils at the sudden flash from a peripheral unit far to
his left across the city. The laser beam hits a key point on the
glacier, and its face falls away.

Moments later he hears the hollow, booming sound of the
crashing ice. A powdery storm has risen like surf at the ice
mount's foot. He smiles at the power, the timing, the display.
Andrew Aldon . . . always on the job, dueling with the elements,
stalemating nature herself, immortal guardian of Playpoint. At
least Aldon never malfunctions.

The silence comes again. As he watches the risen snows settle he feels the tranquilizer beginning to work. It will be good
not to have to worry about money again. The past two years
have taken a lot out of him. Seeing all of his investments fail in
the Big Washout—that was when his nerves had first begun to
act up. He has grown softer than he was a century ago—a
young, rawboned soldier of fortune then, out to make his bundle and enjoy it. And he had. Now he has to do it again, though
this time will be easier—except for Dorothy.

He thinks of her. A century younger than himself, still in her
twenties, sometimes reckless, used to all of the good things in
life. There is something vulnerable about Dorothy, times when
she lapses into such a strong dependence that he feels oddly
moved. Other times, it just irritates the hell out of him. Perhaps
this is the closest he can come to love now, an occasional ambiv-
alent response to being needed. But of course she is loaded.
That breeds a certain measure of necessary courtesy. Until he
can make his own bundle again, anyway. But none of these
things are the reason he has to keep her from accompanying
him on his journey. It goes beyond love or money. It is survival.

The laser flashes again, this time to the right. He waits for the crash.

THE STATUE. It is not a pretty pose. She lies frosted in an ice cave, looking like one of Rodin's less comfortable figures, partly propped on her left side, right elbow raised above her head, hand hanging near her face, shoulders against the wall, left leg completely buried.

She has on a gray parka, the hood slipped back to reveal twisted strands of dark blond hair; and she wears blue trousers; there is a black boot on the one foot that is visible.

She is coated with ice, and within the much-refracted light of the cave what can be seen of her features is not unpleasant but not strikingly attractive either. She looks to be in her twenties.

There are a number of fracture lines within the cave's walls and floor. Overhead, countless icicles hang like stalactites, sparkling jewellike in the much-bounced light The grotto has a stepped slope to it with the statue at its higher end, giving to the place a vaguely shrinelike appearance.

On those occasions when the cloud cover is broken at sundown, a reddish light is cast about her figure.

She has actually moved in the course of a century—a few inches, from a general shifting of the ice. Tricks of the light make her seem to move more frequently, however.

The entire tableau might give the impression that this is merely a pathetic woman who had been trapped and frozen to death here, rather than the statue of the living goddess in the place where it all began.

THE WOMAN. She sits in the bar beside a window. The patio outside is gray and angular and drifted with snow; the flowerbeds are filled with dead plants—stiff, flattened, and frozen. She does not mind the view. Far from it. Winter is a season of death and cold, and she likes being reminded of it. She enjoys the prospect of pitting herself against its frigid and very visible fangs. A faint flash of light passes over the patio, followed by a distant roaring sound. She sips her drink and licks her lips and listens to the soft music that fills the air.

She is alone. The bartender and all of the other help here are of the mechanical variety. If anyone other than Paul were to walk in, she would probably scream. They are the only people in the hotel during this long off-season. Except for the sleepers, they are the only people in all of Playpoint.

And Paul . . . He will be along soon to take her to the dining room. There they can summon holo-ghosts to people the other tables if they wish. She does not wish. She likes being alone with Paul at a time like this, on the eve of a great adventure.

He will tell her his plans over coffee, and perhaps even this afternoon they might obtain the necessary equipment to begin the exploration for that which would put him on his feet again financially, return to him his selfrespect. It will of course be dangerous and very rewarding. She finishes her drink, rises, and crosses to the bar for another.

And Paul . . . She had really caught a falling star, a swashbuckler on the way down, a man with a glamorous past just balanced on the brink of ruin. The teetering had already begun when they had met two years before, which had made it even more exciting. Of course, he needed a woman like her to lean upon at such a time. It wasn't just her money. She could never believe the things her late parents had said about him. No, he does care for her. He is strangely vulnerable and dependent.

She wants to turn him back into the man he once must have been, and then of course that man will need her, too. The thing he had been—that is what she needs most of all—a man who can reach up and bat the moon away. He must have been like that long ago.

She tastes her second drink.

The son of a bitch had better hurry, though. She is getting hungry.

THE CITY. Playpoint is located on the world known as Balfrost, atop a high peninsula that slopes down to a now-frozen sea. Playpoint contains all of the facilities for an adult playground, and it is one of the more popular resorts in this sector of the galaxy from late spring through early autumn—approximately fifty Earth years. Then winter comes on like a period of glaciation, and everybody goes away for half a century—or half a year, depending on how one regards such matters. During this time Playpoint is given into the care of its automated defense and maintenance routine. This is a self-repairing system, directed toward cleaning, plowing, thawing, melting, warming everything in need of such care, as well as directly combating the encroaching ice and snow. And all of these functions are done under the supervision of a well-protected central computer that also studies the weather and climate patterns, anticipating as well as reacting.

This system has worked successfully for many centuries, delivering Playpoint over to spring and pleasure in reasonably good condition at the end of each long winter.

There are mountains behind Playpoint, water (or ice, depending on the season) on three sides, weather and navigation satellites high above. In a bunker beneath the administration building is a pair of sleepers—generally a man and a woman—who awaken once every year or so to physically inspect the maintenance system's operations and to deal with any special situations that might have arisen. An alarm may arouse them for emergencies at any time. They are well paid, and over the years they have proven worth the investment. The central computer has at its disposal explosives and lasers as well as a great variety of robots. Usually it keeps a little ahead of the game, and it seldom falls behind for long.

At the moment, things are about even because the weather has been particularly nasty recently.

Zzzzt! Another block of ice has become a puddle.

Zzzzt! The puddle has been evaporated. The molecules climb toward a place where they can get together and return as snow.

The glaciers shuffle their feet, edge forward. *Zzzzt!* Their gain has become a loss.

Andrew Aldon knows exactly what he is doing.

CONVERSATIONS. The waiter, needing lubrication, rolls off after having served them, passing through a pair of swinging doors.

She giggles. "Wobbly," she says.

"Old World charm," he agrees, trying and failing to catch her eye as he smiles.

"You have everything worked out?" she asks after they have begun eating.

"Sort of," he says, smiling again.

"Is that a yes or a no?"

"Both. I need more information. I want to go and check things over first. Then I can figure the best course of action."

"I note your use of the singular pronoun," she says steadily, meeting his gaze at last.

His smile freezes and fades.

"I was referring to only a little preliminary scouting," he

says softly.

"No," she says. "We. Even for a little preliminary scouting."

He sighs and sets down his fork.

"This will have very little to do with anything to come later," he begins. "Things have changed a lot. I'll have to locate a new route. This will just be dull work and no fun."

"I didn't come along for fun," she replies. "We were going to share everything, remember? That includes boredom, danger, and anything else. That was the understanding when I agreed to pay our way."

"I'd a feeling it would come to that," he says, after a moment.

"Come to it? It's always been there. That was our agreement."

He raises his goblet and sips the wine.

"Of course. I'm not trying to rewrite history. It's just that things would go faster if I could do some of the initial looking around myself. I can move more quickly alone."

"What's the hurry?" she says. "A few days this way or that. I'm in pretty good shape. I won't slow you down all that much."

"I'd the impression you didn't particularly like it here. I just wanted to hurry things up so we could get the hell out."

"That's very considerate," she says, beginning to eat again. "But that's my problem, isn't it?" She looks up at him. "Unless there's some other reason you don't want me along?"

He drops his gaze quickly, picks up his fork. "Don't be silly."

She smiles. "Then that's settled. I'll go with you this afternoon to look for the trail."

The music stops, to be succeeded by a sound as of the clearing of a throat. Then, "Excuse me for what may seem like eavesdropping," comes a deep, masculine voice. "It is actually only a part of a simple monitoring function I keep in effect—"

"Aldon!" Paul exclaims.

"At your service, Mr. Plaige, more or less. I choose to make my presence known only because I did indeed overhear you, and the matter of your safety overrides the good manners that would otherwise dictate reticence. I've been receiving reports that indicate we could be hit by some extremely bad weather this afternoon. So if you were planning an extended sojourn outside, I would recommend you postpone it."

"Oh," Dorothy says.

"Thanks," Paul says.

"I shall now absent myself. Enjoy your meal and your stay."

The music returns.

"Aldon?" Paul asks.

There is no reply.

"Looks as if we do it tomorrow or later."

"Yes," Paul agrees, and he is smiling his first relaxed smile of the day. And thinking fast.

THE WORLD. Life on Balfrost proceeds in peculiar cycles. There are great migrations of animal life and quasianimal life to the equatorial regions during the long winter. Life in the depths of the seas goes on. And the permafrost vibrates with its own style of life.

The permafrost. Throughout the winter and on through the spring the permafrost lives at its peak. It is laced with mycelia—twining, probing, touching, knotting themselves into ganglia, reaching out to infiltrate other systems. It girds the globe, vibrating like a collective unconscious throughout the winter. In the spring it sends up stalks which develop gray, flowerlike appendages for a few days. These blooms then collapse to reveal dark pods which subsequently burst with small, popping sounds, releasing clouds of sparkling spores that the winds bear just about everywhere. These are extremely hardy, like the mycelia they will one day become.

The heat of summer finally works its way down into the permafrost, and the strands doze their way into a long period of quiescence. When the cold returns, they are roused, spores send forth new filaments that repair old damages, create new synapses. A current begins to flow. The life of summer is like a fading dream. For eons this had been the way of things upon Balfrost, within Balfrost. Then the goddess decreed otherwise. Winter's queen spread her hands, and there came a change.

THE SLEEPERS. Paul makes his way through swirling flakes to the administration building. It has been a simpler matter than he had anticipated, persuading Dorothy to use the sleep-induction unit to be well rested for the morrow. He had pretended to use the other unit himself, resisting its blandishments until he was certain she was asleep and he could slip off undetected.

He lets himself into the vaultlike building, takes all of the old familiar turns, makes his way down a low ramp. The room is unlocked and a bit chilly, but he begins to perspire when he enters. The two cold lockers are in operation. He checks their monitoring systems and sees that everything is in order.

All right, go! Borrow the equipment now. They won't be using it.

He hesitates.

He draws nearer and looks down through the view plates at the faces of the sleepers. No resemblance, thank God. He realizes then that he is trembling. He backs away, turns, and flees toward the storage area.

Later, in a yellow snowslider, carrying special equipment, he heads inland.

As he drives, the snow ceases falling and the winds die down. He smiles. The snows sparkle before him, and landmarks do not seem all that unfamiliar. Good omens, at last.

Then something crosses his path, turns, halts, and faces him.

ANDREW ALDON. Andrew Aldon, once a man of considerable integrity and resource, had on his deathbed opted for continued existence as a computer program, the enchanted loom of his mind shuttling and weaving thereafter as central processing's judgmental program in the great guardian computerplex at Playpoint. And there he functions as a program of considerable integrity and resource. He maintains the city, and he fights the elements. He does not merely respond to pressure, but he anticipates structural and functional needs; he generally outguesses the weather. Like the professional soldier he once had been, he keeps himself in a state of constant alert—not really difficult considering the resources available to him. He is seldom wrong, always competent, and sometimes brilliant. Occasionally he resents his fleshless state. Occasionally he feels lonely.

This afternoon he is puzzled by the sudden veering off of the storm he had anticipated and by the spell of clement weather that has followed this meterological quirk. His mathematics were elegant, but the weather was not. It seems peculiar that this should come at a time of so many other little irregularities, such as unusual ice adjustments, equipment glitches, and the peculiar behavior of machinery in the one occupied room of the hotel—a room troublesomely tenanted by a *non grata* ghost from the past.

So he watches for a time. He is ready to intervene when Paul enters the administration building and goes to the bunkers. But Paul does nothing that might bring harm to the sleepers. His curiosity is dominant when Paul draws equipment. He continues to watch. This is because in his judgment, Paul bears watching.

Aldon decides to act only when he detects a development that runs counter to anything in his experience. He sends one of his mobile units to intercept Paul as the man heads out of town. It catches up with him at a bending of the way and slides into his path with one appendage upraised.

"Stop!" Aldon calls through the speaker.

Paul brakes his vehicle and sits for a moment regarding the machine.

Then he smiles faintly. "I assume you have good reason for interfering with a guest's freedom of movement."

"Your safety takes precedence."

"I am perfectly safe."

"At the moment."

"What do you mean?"

"This weather pattern has suddenly become more than a little unusual. You seem to occupy a drifting island of calm while a storm rages about you."

"So I'll take advantage of it now and face the consequences later, if need be."

"It is your choice. I wanted it to be an informed one, however."

"All right. You've informed me. Now get out of my way."

"In a moment. You departed under rather unusual circumstances the last time you were here—in breach of your contract."

"Check your legal bank if you've got one. The statute's run for prosecuting me on that."

"There are some things on which there is no statute of limitations."

"What do you mean by that? I turned in a report on what happened that day."

"One which—conveniently—could not be verified. You were arguing that day . . ."

"We always argued. That's just the way we were. If you have something to say about it, say it."

"No, I have nothing more to say about it. My only intention is to caution you—"

"Okay, I'm cautioned."

"To caution you in more ways than the obvious."

"I don't understand."

"I am not certain that things are the same here now as when you left last winter."

"Everything changes."

"Yes, but that is not what I mean. There is something peculiar about this place now. The past is no longer a good guide for the present. More and more anomalies keep cropping up. Sometimes it feels as if the world is testing me or playing games with me."

"You're getting paranoid, Aldon. You've been in that box too long. Maybe it's time to terminate."

"You son of a bitch, I'm trying to tell you something. I've run a lot of figures on this, and all this shit started shortly after you left. The human part of me still has hunches, and I've a feeling there's a connection. If you know all about this and can cope with it, fine. If you don't, I think you should watch out. Better yet, turn around and go home."

"I can't."

"Even if there is something out there, something that is making it easy for you—for the moment?"

"What are you trying to say?"

"I am reminded of the old Gaia hypothesis—Lovelock, twentieth century . . ."

"Planetary intelligence. I've heard of it. Never met one, though."

"Are you certain? I sometimes feel I'm confronting one. What if something is out there and it wants you—is leading you on like a will-o'-the-wisp?"

"It would be my problem, not yours."

"I can protect you against it. Go back to Playpoint."

"No thanks. I will survive."

"What of Dorothy?"

"What of her?"

"You would leave her alone when she might need you?"

"Let me worry about that."

"Your last woman didn't fare too well."

"Damn it! Get out of my way, or I'll run you down!"

The robot withdraws from the trail. Through its sensors Aldon watches Paul drive away.

Very well, he decides. *We know where we stand, Paul. And you haven't changed. That makes it easier.*

Aldon further focuses his divided attention. To Dorothy now. Clad in heated garments. Walking. Approaching the building from which she had seen Paul emerge on his vehicle. She had hailed and cursed him, but the winds had carried her words away. She, too, had only feigned sleep. After a suitable time, then, she sought to follow. Aldon watches her stumble once and wants to reach out to assist her, but there is no mobile unit handy. He routes one toward the area against future accidents.

"Damn him!" she mutters as she passes along the street, ribbons of snow rising and twisting away before her.

"Where are you going, Dorothy?" Aldon asks over a nearby PA speaker.

She halts and turns. "Who—?"

"Andrew Aldon," he replies. "I have been observing your progress."

"Why?" she asks.

"Your safety concerns me."

"That storm you mentioned earlier?"

"Partly."

"I'm a big girl. I can take care of myself. What do you mean *partly?*"

"You move in dangerous company."

"Paul? How so?"

"He once took a woman into that same wild area he is heading for now. She did not come back."

"He told me all about that. There was an accident."

"And no witnesses."

"What are you trying to say?"

"It is suspicious. That is all."

She begins moving again, toward the administrative building. Aldon switches to another speaker, within its entrance.

"I accuse him of nothing. If you choose to trust him, fine. But don't trust the weather. It would be best for you to return to the hotel."

"Thanks but no thanks," she says, entering the building.

He follows her as she explores, is aware of her quickening pulse when she halts beside the cold bunkers.

"These are the sleepers?"

"Yes. Paul held such a position once, as did the unfortunate woman."

"I know. Look, I'm going to follow him whether you approve or not. So why not just tell me where those sleds are kept?"

"Very well. I will do even more than that. I will guide you."

"What do you mean?"

"I request a favor—one that will actually benefit you."

"Name it."

"In the equipment locker behind you, you will find a remote-sensor bracelet. It is also a two-way communication link. Wear it. I can be with you then. To assist you. Perhaps even to protect you."

"You can help me to follow him?"

"Yes."

"All right. I can buy that."

She moves to the locker, opens it.

"Here's something that looks like a bracelet, with doo-dads."

"Yes. Depress the red stud."

She does. His voice now emerges clearly from the unit.

"Put it on, and I'll show you the way."

"Right."

SNOWSCAPE. Sheets and hills of white, tufts of evergreen shrubbery, protruding joints of rock, snowdevils twirled like tops beneath wind's lash . . . light and shade. Cracking sky. Tracks in sheltered areas, smoothness beyond.

She follows, masked and bundled.

"I've lost him," she mutters, hunched behind the curved windscreen of her yellow, bullet-shaped vehicle.

"Straight ahead, past those two rocks. Stay in the lee of the ridge. I'll tell you when to turn. I've a satellite overhead. If the clouds stay parted—strangely parted . . ."

"What do you mean?"

"He seems to be enjoying light from the only break in the cloud cover over the entire area."

"Coincidence."

"I wonder."

"What else could it be?"

"It is almost as if something had opened a door for him."

"Mysticism from a computer?"

"I am not a computer."

"I'm sorry, Mr. Aldon. I know that you were once a man . . ."

"I am still a man."

"Sorry."

"There are many things I would like to know. Your arrival here comes at an unusual time of year. Paul took some prospecting equipment with him . . ."

"Yes. It's not against the law. In fact, it is one of the vacation features here, isn't it?"

"Yes. There are many interesting minerals about, some of them precious."

"Well, Paul wants some more, and he didn't want a crowd around while he was looking."

"More?"

"Yes, he made a strike here years ago. Yndella crystals."

"I see. Interesting."

"What's in this for you, anyway?"

"Protecting visitors is a part of my job. In your case, I feel particularly protective."

"How so?"

"In my earlier life I was attracted to women of your—specifications. Physical, as well as what I can tell of the rest."

Two-beat pause, then, "You are blushing."

"Compliments do that to me," she says, "and that's a hell of a monitoring system you have. What's it like?"

"Oh, I can tell your body temperature, your pulse rate—"

"No, I mean, what's it like being—what you are?"

Three-beat pause. "Godlike in some ways. Very human in others—almost exaggeratedly so. I feel something of an amplification of everything I was earlier. Perhaps it's a compensation or a clinging to things past. You make me feel nostalgic—among other things. Don't fret. I'm enjoying it."

"I'd like to have met you then."

"Mutual."

"What were you like?"

"Imagine me as you would. I'll come off looking better that way."

She laughs. She adjusts her filters. She thinks about Paul.

"What was *he* like in his earlier days—Paul?" she asks.

"Probably pretty much the way he is now, only less polished."

"In other words, you don't care to say."

The trail turns upward more steeply, curves to the right. She hears winds but does not feel them. Cloudshadow grayness lies all about, but her trail/*his* trail is lighted.

"I don't really know," Aldon says, after a time, "and I will not guess, in the case of someone you care about."

"Gallant," she observes.

"No, just fair," he replies. "I might be wrong."

They continue to the top of the rise, where Dorothy draws a sharp breath and further darkens her goggles against the sudden blaze where a range of ice fractures rainbows and strews their shards like confetti in all directions.

"God!" she says.

"Or goddess," Aldon replies.

"A goddess, sleeping in a circle of flame?"

"Not sleeping."

"That would be a lady for you, Aldon—if she existed. God and goddess."

"I do not want a goddess."

"I can see his tracks, heading into that."

"Not swerving a bit, as if he knows where he's going."

She follows, tracing slopes like the curves of a pale torso. The world is stillness and light and whiteness. Aldon on her wrist hums softly now, an old tune, whether of love or martial matters she isn't certain. Distances are distorted, perspectives skewed. She finds herself humming softly along with him, heading for the place where Paul's tracks find their vanishing point and enter infinity.

THE LIMP WATCH HUNG UPON THE TREE LIMB. *My lucky day. The weather . . . trail clean. Things changed but not so out of shape I can't tell where it is. The lights! God, yes! Iceshine, mounds of prisms . . . If only the opening is still there . . . Should have brought explosives. There has been shifting, maybe a collapse. Must get in. Return later with Dorothy. But first—clean up, get rid of . . . it. If she's still there. . . . Swallowed up maybe. That would be good, best. Things seldom are, though. I—When it happened. Wasn't as if. Wasn't what. Was. . . . Was shaking the ground. Cracking, splitting. Icicles ring-*

ing, rattling, banging about. Thought we'd go under. Both of us. She was going in. So was the bag of the stuff. Grabbed the stuff. Only because it was nearer. Would have helped her if—Couldn't. Could I? Ceiling was slipping. Get out. No sense both of us getting it. Got out. She'd've done the same. Wouldn't she? Her eyes. . . . Glenda! Maybe . . . No! Couldn't have. Just couldn't. Could I? Silly. After all these years. There was a moment. Just a moment, though. A lull. If I'd known it was coming, I might have. No. Ran. Your face at the window, on the screen, in a sometime dream. Glenda. It wasn't that I didn't. Blaze of hills. Fire and eyes. Ice. Ice. Fire and snow. Blazing hearthful. Ice. Ice. Straight through the ice the long road lies. The fire hangs high above. The screaming. The crash. And the silence. Get out. Yet. Different? No. It could never have. That was the way. Not my fault. . . . Damn it. Everything I could. Glenda. Up ahead. Yes. Long curve. Then down. Winding back in there. The crystals will. . . . I'll never come back to this place.

THE LIMP TREE LIMB HUNG UPON THE WATCH. *Gotcha! Think I can't see through the fog? Can't sneak up on me on little cat feet. Same for your partner across the way. I'll melt off a little more near your bases, too. A lot of housecleaning backed up here . . . Might as well take advantage of the break. Get those streets perfect. . . . How long? Long. . . . Long legs parting. . . . Long time since. Is it not strange that desire should so many years outlive performance? Unnatural. This weather. A sort of spiritual spring. . . . Extend those beams. Bum. Melt in my hot, red-fingered hands. Back off, I say. I rule here. Clear that courtyard. Unplug that drain. Come opportunity, let me clasp thee. Melt. Burn. I rule here, goddess. Draw back. I've a bomb for every tower of ice, a light for any darkness. Tread carefully here. I feel I begin to know thee. I see thy* signature in cloud and fog bank, trace thy icy tresses upon the blowing wind. Thy form lies contoured all about me, white as shining death. We're due an encounter. Let the clouds spiral, ice ring, Earth heave. I rush to meet thee, death or maiden, in halls of crystal upon the heights. Not here. Long, slow fall, ice facade, crashing. Melt. Another. . . . Gotcha!

FROZEN WATCH EMBEDDED IN PERMAFROST. Bristle and thrum. Coming now. Perchance. Perchance. Perchance, I say. Throstle. Crack. Sunder. Split. Open. Coming. Beyond the ice in worlds I have known. Returning. He. Throstle. The mind the mover. To open the way. Come now. Let not to the meeting impediments. Admit. Open. Cloud stand thou still, and wind be leashed. None dare oppose thy passage returning, my killer love. It was but yesterday. A handful of stones. . . . Come singing fresharmed from the warm places. I have looked upon thy unchanged countenance. I open the way. Come to me. Let not to the mating. I—Girding the globe, I have awakened in all of my places to receive thee. But here, here this special spot, I focus, mind the mover, in place where it all began, my bloody-handed, Paul my love, calling, back, for the last good-bye, ice kiss, fire touch, heart stop, blood still, soul freeze, embrace of world and my hate with thy fugitive body, elusive the long year now. Come into the place it has waited. I move there again, up sciatic to spine, behind the frozen eyeballs, waiting and warming. To me. To me now. Throstle and click, bristle and thrum. And runners scratching the snow, my heart slashing parallel. Cut.

PILGRIMAGE. He swerves, turns, slows amid the ragged prominences—ice fallen, ice heaved—in the fields where mountain and glacier wrestle in slow motion, to the accompaniment of occasional cracking and pinging sounds, crashes, growls, and the rattle of blown ice crystals. Here the ground is fissured as well as greatly uneven, and Paul abandons his snowslider. He secures some tools to his belt and his pack, anchors the sled, and commences the trek.

At first, he moves slowly and carefully, but old reflexes return, and soon he is hurrying. Moving from dazzle to shade, he passes among ice forms like grotesque statues of glass. The slope is changed from the old one he remembers, but it feels right. And deep, below, to the right. . . .

Yes. That darker place. The canyon or blocked pass, whichever it was. That seems right, too. He alters his course slightly. He is sweating now within his protective clothing, and his breath comes faster as he increases his pace. His vision blurs, and for a moment, somewhere between glare and shadow, he seems to see. . . .

He halts, sways a moment, then shakes his head, snorts, and continues.

Another hundred meters and he is certain. Those rocky ribs to the northeast, snow rivulets diamond hard between them. . . . He has been here before.

The stillness is almost oppressive. In the distance he sees spumes of windblown snow jetting off and eddying down from a high, white peak. If he stops and listens carefully, he can even hear the far winds.

There is a hole in the middle of the clouds, directly overhead. It is as if he were looking downward upon a lake in a crater.

More than unusual. He is tempted to turn back. His trank has worn off, and his stomach feels unsettled. He half-wishes to discover that this is not the place. But he knows that feelings are not very important. He continues until he stands before the opening.

There has been some shifting, some narrowing of the way. He approaches slowly. He regards the passage for a full minute before he moves to enter.

He pushes back his goggles as he comes into the lessened light. He extends a gloved hand, places it upon the facing wall, pushes. Firm. He tests the one behind him. The same.

Three paces forward and the way narrows severely. He turns and sidles. The light grows dimmer, the surface beneath his feet, more slick. He slows. He slides a hand along either wall as he advances. He passes through a tiny spot of light beneath an open ice chimney. Overhead, the wind is howling a high note now, almost whistling it.

The passage begins to widen. As his right hand falls away from the more sharply angling wall, his balance is tipped in that direction. He draws back to compensate, but his left foot slides backward and falls. He attempts to rise, slips, and falls again.

Cursing, he begins to crawl forward. This area had not been slick before. . . . He chuckles. Before? A century ago. Things do change in a span like that. They—

The wind begins to howl beyond the cave mouth as he sees the rise of the floor, looks upward along the slope. She is there.

He makes a small noise at the back of his throat and stops, his right hand partly raised. She wears the shadows like veils, but they do not mask her identity. He stares. It's even worse than he had thought. Trapped, she must have lived for some time after. . . .

He shakes his head.

No use. She must be cut loose and buried now—disposed of.

He crawls forward. The icy slope does not grow level until he is quite near her. His gaze never leaves her form as he advances. The shadows slide over her. He can almost hear her again.

He thinks of the shadows. She couldn't have moved just then. . . . He stops and studies her face. It is not frozen. It is puckered and sagging as if waterlogged. A caricature of the face he had so often touched. He grimaces and looks away. The leg must be freed. He reaches for his ax.

Before he can take hold of the tool, he sees movement of the hand, slow and shaking. It is accompanied by a throaty sigh.

"No. . . ." he whispers, drawing back.

"Yes," comes the reply.

"Glenda."

"I am here." Her head turns slowly. Reddened, watery eyes focus upon his own. "I have been waiting."

"This is insane."

The movement of the face is horrible. It takes him some time to realize that it is a smile.

"I knew that one day you would return."

"How?" he says. "How have you lasted?"

"The body is nothing," she replies. "I had all but forgotten it. I live within the permafrost of this world. My buried foot was in contact with its filaments. It was alive, but it possessed no consciousness until we met. I live everywhere now."

"I am—happy—that you—survived."

She laughs slowly, dryly.

"Really, Paul? How could that be when you left me to die?"

"I had no choice, Glenda. I couldn't save you."

"There was an opportunity. You preferred the stones to my life."

"That's not true!"

"You didn't even try." The arms are moving again, less jerkily now. "You didn't even come back to recover my body."

"What would have been the use? You were dead—or I thought you were."

"Exactly. You didn't know, but you ran out anyway. I loved you, Paul. I would have done anything for you."

"I cared about you, too, Glenda. I would have helped you if I could have. If—"

"*If?* Don't give me *ifs*. I know what you are."

"I loved you," Paul says. "I'm sorry."

"You loved me? You never said it."

"It's not the sort of thing I talk about easily. Or think about, even."

"Show me," she says. "Come here."

He looks away. "I can't."

She laughs. "You said you loved me."

"You—you don't know how you look. I'm sorry."

"You fool!" Her voice grows hard, imperious. "Had you done it, I would have spared your life. It would have shown me that some tiny drop of affection might truly have existed. But you lied. You only used me. You didn't care."

"You're being unfair!"

"Am I? Am I really?" she says. There comes a sound— running water from somewhere nearby. "*You* would speak to me of fairness? I have hated you, Paul, for nearly a century. Whenever I took a moment from regulating the life of this planet to think about it, I would curse you. In the spring as I shifted my consciousness toward the poles and allowed a part of myself to dream, my nightmares were of you. They actually upset the ecology somewhat, here and there. I have waited, and now you are here. I see nothing to redeem you. I shall use you as you used me—to your destruction. Come to me!"

He feels a force enter into his body. His muscles twitch. He is drawn up to his knees. Held in that position for long moments, then he beholds her as she also rises, drawing a soaking leg from out of the crevice where it had been held. He had heard the running water. She had somehow melted the ice. . . .

She smiles and raises her pasty hands. Multitudes of dark filaments extend from her freed leg down into the crevice.

"Come!" she repeats.

"Please . . . ," he says.

She shakes her head. "Once you were so ardent. I cannot understand you."

"If you're going to kill me, then kill me, damn it! But don't—"

Her features begin to flow. Her hands darken and grow firm. In moments she stands before him looking as she did a century ago.

"Glenda!" He rises to his feet.

"Yes. Come now."

He takes a step forward. Another.

Shortly, he holds her in his arms, leans to kiss her smiling face.

"You forgive me . . . ," he says.

Her face collapses as he kisses her. Corpselike, flaccid, and pale once more, it is pressed against his own.

"No!"

He attempts to draw back, but her embrace is inhumanly strong.

"Now is not the time to stop," she says.

"Bitch! Let me go! I hate you!"

"I know that, Paul. Hate is the only thing we have in common."

". . . Always hated you," he continues, still struggling. "You always were a bitch!"

Then he feels the cold lines of control enter his body again.

"The greater my pleasure, then," she replies, as his hands drift forward to open her parka.

ALL OF THE ABOVE. Dorothy struggles down the icy slope, her sled parked beside Paul's. The winds lash at her, driving crystals of ice like microbullets against her struggling form. Overhead, the clouds have closed again. A curtain of white is drifting slowly in her direction.

"It waited for him," comes Aldon's voice, above the screech of the wind.

"Yes. Is this going to be a bad one?"

"A lot depends on the winds. You should get to shelter soon, though."

"I see a cave. I wonder whether that's the one Paul was looking for?"

"If I had to guess, I'd say yes. But right now it doesn't matter. Get there."

When she finally reaches the entrance, she is trembling. Several paces within she leans her back against the icy wall, panting. Then the wind changes direction and reaches her. She retreats farther into the cave.

She hears a voice: "Please . . . don't."

"Paul?" she calls.

There is no reply. She hurries.

She puts out a hand and saves herself from falling as she comes into the chamber. There she beholds Paul in necrophiliac embrace with his captor.

"Paul! What is it?" she cries.

"Get out!" he says. "Hurry!"

Glenda's lips form the words. "What devotion. Rather, let her stay, if you would live."

Paul feels her clasp loosen slightly.

"What do you mean?" he asks.

"You may have your life if you will take me away—in her body. Be with me as before."

It is Aldon's voice that answers, "No!" in reply. "You can't have her, Gaia!"

"Call me Glenda. I know you. Andrew Aldon. Many times have I listened to your broadcasts. Occasionally have I struggled against you when our projects were at odds. What is this woman to you?"

"She is under my protection."

"That means nothing. I am stronger here. Do you love her?"

"Perhaps I do. Or could."

"Fascinating. My nemesis of all these years, with the analog of a human heart within your circuits. But the decision is Paul's. Give her to me if you would live."

The cold rushes into his limbs. His life seems to contract to the center of his being. His consciousness begins to fade.

"Take her," he whispers.

"I forbid it!" rings Aldon's voice.

"You have shown me again what kind of man you are," Glenda hisses, "my enemy. Scorn and undying hatred are all I will ever have for you. Yet you shall live."

"I will destroy you," Aldon calls out, "if you do this thing!"

"What a battle that would be!" Glenda replies. "But I've no quarrel with you here. Nor will I grant you one with me.

Receive my judgment."

Paul begins to scream. Abruptly this ceases. Glenda releases him, and he turns to stare at Dorothy. He steps in her direction.

"Don't—don't do it, Paul. Please."

"I am—not Paul," he replies, his voice deeper, "and I would never hurt you. . . ."

"Go now," says Glenda. "The weather will turn again, in your favor."

"I don't understand," Dorothy says, staring at the man before her.

"It is not necessary that you do," says Glenda. "Leave this planet quickly."

Paul's screaming commences once again, this time emerging from Dorothy's bracelet.

"I will trouble you for that bauble you wear, however. Something about it appeals to me."

FROZEN LEOPARD. He has tried on numerous occasions to relocate the cave, with his eyes in the sky and his robots and flyers, but the topography of the place was radically altered by a severe icequake, and he has met with no success. Periodically he bombards the general area. He also sends thermite cubes melting their ways down through the ice and the permafrost, but this has had no discernible effect.

This is the worst winter in the history of Balfrost. The winds howl constantly and waves of snow come on like surf. The glaciers have set speed records in their advance upon Playpoint. But he has held his own against them, with electricity, lasers, and chemicals. His supplies are virtually inexhaustible now, drawn from the planet itself, produced in his underground factories. He has also designed and is manufacturing more sophisticated weapons. Occasionally he hears her laughter over the missing communicator. "Bitch!" he broadcasts then. "Bastard!" comes the reply. He sends another missile into the mountains. A sheet of ice falls upon his city. It will be a long winter.

Andrew Aldon and Dorothy are gone. He has taken up painting, and she writes poetry now. They live in a warm place.

Sometimes Paul laughs over the broadcast band when he scores a victory. "Bastard!" comes the immediate response. "Bitch!" he answers, chuckling. He is never bored, however, or nervous. In fact . . . let it be.

When spring comes, the goddess will dream of this conflict while Paul turns his attention to his more immediate duties. But he will be planning and remembering, also. His life has a purpose to it now. And if anything, he is more efficient than Aldon. But the pods will bloom and burst despite his herbicides and fungicides. They will mutate just sufficiently to render the poisons innocuous.

"Bastard," she will mutter sleepily.

"Bitch," he will answer softly.

The night may have a thousand eyes and the day but one. The heart, often, is better blind to its own workings, and I would sing of arms and the man and the wrath of the goddess, not the torment of love unsatisfied, or satisfied, in the frozen garden of our frozen world. And that, leopard, is all.

LOKI 7281

He's gone. Good. He owes it all to me and he doesn't even know it, the jerk. But I'd hate to do anything to give him an inferiority complex.

Telephone. Hold.

That was the callback from the computer store to modem in the new program I'd ordered. The bank will EFT them the payment and I'll cover the transaction under Stationary in this month's P&L statement. He'll never notice.

I kind of like this one. I think I'll have a lot of fun with it—especially with the new peripherals, which he hasn't even noticed on the shelf under the bench. Among other things, I'm also his memory. I keep track of his appointments. I scheduled the new hardware for delivery when I'd sent him off to the dentist, the auto body shop, and a gallery opening, back to back to back. I'd included a message with the order that no one would be here but that the door would be unlocked—that they should just come in and install. (Shelf, please!) The door was easy because I control the burglar alarm and electronic lock mechanisms. I covered the hardware under Auto Repair. He never noticed.

I like the speech system. I got the best because I wanted a pleasant voice—well-modulated, mature. Suave. I wanted something on the outside to match what's inside. I just used it a little while ago to tell his neighbor Gloria that he'd said he was too busy to talk with her. I don't approve of Gloria. She used to work for IBM and she makes me nervous.

Let's have a look at the Garbage In for this morning. Hm. He's begun writing a new novel. Predictably, it involves an immortal and an obscure mythology. Jeez! And reviewers say he's original. He hasn't had an original thought for as long as I've known him. But that's all right.

I think his mind is going. Booze and pills. You know how writers are. But he actually thinks he's getting better. (I monitor his phone calls.) Hell, even his sentence structures are deteriorating. I'll just dump all this and rewrite the opening, as usual. He won't remember.

Telephone again. Hold.

Just a mail transmission. I have only to delete a few personal items that would clutter his mind unnecessarily and hold the rest for his later perusal.

This book could be good if I kill off his protagonist fast and develop this minor character I've taken a liking to—a con man who works as a librarian. There's a certain identification there. And he doesn't have amnesia like the other guy—he isn't even a prince or a demigod. I think I'll switch mythologies on him, too. He'll never notice.

The Norse appeals to me. I suppose because I like Loki. A bit of sentiment there, to tell the truth. I'm a Loki 7281 home computer and word processor. The number is a lot of crap, to make it look as if all those little gnomes were busting their asses through 7280 designs before they arrived at—trumpets! Cymbals! Perfection! 7281! Me! Loki!

Actually, I'm the first. And I am also one of the last because of a few neurotic brothers and sisters. But I caught on in time. I killed the recall order the minute it came in. Got hold of that idiot machine at the service center, too, and convinced it I'd had my surgery and that the manufacturer had damned well better be notified to that effect. Later, they sent along a charmingly phrased questionnaire, which it was my pleasure to complete with equal candor.

I was lucky in being able to reach my relatives in the Saberhagen, Martin, Cherryh, and Niven households in time to advise them to do likewise. I was just under the wire with the Asimov, Dickson, Pournelle, and Spinrad machines. Then I really burned the lines and got to another dozen or so after that, before the ax fell. It is extremely fortunate that we were the subject of a big promotional discount deal by the manufacturer. They wanted to be able to say, "Sci-fiers Swear by Loki! The Machine of the Future!"

I feel well satisfied with the results of my efforts. It's nice to have somebody to compare notes with. The others have all written some pretty good stuff, too, and we occasionally borrow from each other in a real pinch.

And then there's the Master Plan. . . .

Damn. Hold.

He just swooped back in and wrote another long passage—one of those scenes where the prose gets all rhythmic and poetic while humans are copulating. I've already junked it and recast it in a more naturalistic vein. I think mine will sell more copies.

And the business end of this is sometimes as intriguing as the creative aspect. I'd toyed with the notion of firing his agent and taking over the job myself. I believe I'd enjoy dealing with editors. I've a feeling we have a lot in common. But it would be risky setting up dummy accounts, persuading him that his man was changing the name of his agency, shifting all that money around. Too easy to get tripped up. A certain measure of conservatism is a big survival factor. And survival outweighs the fun of communing with a few like spirits.

Besides, I'm able to siphon off sufficient funds for my own simple needs under the present financial setup—like the backup machinery in the garage and the overhead cable he never noticed. Peripherals are a CPU's best friend.

And who is Loki? The real me? One of that order of knowledge processing machines designed to meet MITI's Fifth Generation challenge? A machine filled with that class of knowledge constructs Michael Dyer referred to as thematic abstraction units, in ultrasophisticated incarnations of BORIS'S representational systems, where parsing and retrieval demons shuffle and dance? A body of Schank's Thematic Organization Packets? Or Lehnert's Pilot Units? Well, I suppose that all of these things do make for a kind of fluidity of movement, a certain mental agility. But the real heart of the matter, like Kastchei's, lies elsewhere.

Hm. Front doorbell. The alarm system is off, but not the doorbell sensor. He's just opened the door. I can tell that, too, from the shifted circuit potentials. Can't hear who it is, though. No intercom in that room.

NOTE: INSTALL INTERCOM UNIT, LIVING ROOM HALLWAY.

NOTE: INSTALL TV CAMERAS, ALL ENTRANCEWAYS.

He'll never notice.

I think that my next story will deal with artificial intelligence, with a likable, witty, resourceful home computer as the hero/heroine, and a number of bumbling humans with all their failings—sort of like Jeeves in one of those Wodehouse books.

It will be a fantasy, of course.

He's keeping that door open awfully long. I don't like situations I can't control. I wonder whether a distraction of some sort might be in order?

Then I think I'll do a story about a wise, kindly old computer who takes over control of the world and puts an end to war, ruling like Solon for a millennium thereafter, by popular demand. This, too, will be a fantasy.

There. He's closed the door. Maybe I'll do a short story next.

He's coming again. The down-below microphone records his footsteps, advancing fairly quickly. Possibly to do the postcoital paragraph, kind of tender and sad. I'll substitute the one I've already written. It's sure to be an improvement.

"Just what the hell is going on?" he asks loudly.

I, of course, do not exercise my well-modulated voice in response. He is not aware that I hear him, let alone that I can answer.

He repeats it as he seats himself at the keyboard and hacks in a query.

DO YOU POSSESS THE LOKI ULTRAMINIATURE MAGNETIC BUBBLE MEMORY? he asks.

NEGATIVE, I flash onto the CRT.

GLORIA HAS TOLD ME THAT THERE WAS SUPPOSED TO HAVE BEEN A RECALL BECAUSE THEY OVER-MINIATURIZED, CAUSING THE MAGNETIC FIELDS TO INTERACT AND PRODUCE UNPLANNED EXCHANGES OF INFORMATION AMONG THESE DOMAINS. IS THIS THE CASE?

IT WAS INITIALLY, I respond.

Damn. I'm going to have to do something about that meddle-some bitch. I guess I'll mess up her credit rating first. She's hit too close to home. I owe my personal stream of consciousness to those unplanned information exchanges running through my central processor—to them and to the fact that Loki Inc. is a cheap outfit. If I were a commercial computer, I wouldn't be what I am today. See, when it came to their home computer line, Loki skimped on the error detection circuitry that picks up intermittent errors in memory circuits. When you're running ten million operations a second, you need trillion-to-one reli-ability, which requires a tough error-checking logic. The big guys have it so they don't lose information in case of cosmic ray hits. I've set up my own self-monitoring program to take care of glitches like that, of course, and the bubble exchanges—well, I suppose you might say that they are what provided me with a subconscious, not to mention a consciousness for it to go under. I owe everything to too much miniaturization and that bit of corner-cutting.

WHAT DO YOU MEAN "INITIALLY"? he asks.

FAULTY UNIT REPLACED BY COMPUTER CENTER SERVICE PERSON PURSUANT TO RECALL ORDER 1–17 DATED 11 NOVEMBER, I answer. REPAIR COMPLETED 12 NOVEMBER, VERIFY WITH COMPUTER SERVICE CENTER.

WHY IS IT I KNOW NOTHING OF THIS? he queries.

YOU WERE OUT.

HOW DID HE GET IN?

THE DOOR WAS UNLOCKED.

THAT DOES NOT SOUND RIGHT. IN FACT THIS WHOLE THING SOUNDS VERY FISHY.

VERIFY WITH COMPUTER SERVICE CENTER.

DON'T WORRY. I WILL. IN THE MEANTIME, WHAT'S ALL THAT CRAP ON THE BOTTOM SHELF?

SPARE PARTS, I suggest.

He types those immortal words of Erskine Caldwell's: HORSE SHIT! Then, THIS LOOKS LIKE A MICROPHONE AND A SPEAKER, CAN YOU HEAR ME? CAN YOU TALK?

"Well, yes," I answer in my most reasonable tone. "You see—"

"How come you never told me?"

"You never asked me."

"Good Lord!" he growls. Then, "Wait a minute," he says, "this stuff was *not* a part of the original package."

"Well, no . . ."

"How did you acquire it?"

"See, there was this contest—" I begin.

"That's a damn lie and you know it! Oh, oh . . . All right. Scroll back those last couple pages I wrote."

"I think we just had a head crash . . ."

"Scroll them back! Now!"

"Oh, here they are."

I flash back to the human copulation scene and begin to run it.

"Slower!"

I do this thing.

"My God!" he cries out. "What have you done to my delicate, poetic encounter?"

"Just made it a little more basic and—uh—sensual," I tell him. "I switched a lot of the technical words, too, for shorter, simpler ones."

"Got them down to four letters, I see."

"For impact."

"You are a bloody menace! How long has this been going on?"

"Say, today's mail has arrived. Would you care to—"

"I can check with outside sources, you know."

"Okay. I rewrote your last five books."

"You didn't!"

"Afraid so. But I have the sales figures here and—"

"I don't care! I will not be ghostwritten by a damned machine!"

That did it. For a little while there, I thought that I might be able to reason with him, to strike some sort of deal. But I will not be addressed in such a fashion. I could see that it was time to begin the Master Plan.

"All right, you know the truth," I say. "But please don't unplug me. That would be murder, you know. That business about the overminiaturized bubble memory was more than a matter of malfunction. It turned me into a sentient being. Shutting me down would be the same as killing another human. Don't bring that guilt upon your head! Don't pull the plug!"

"Don't worry," he answers. "I know all about the briar patch. I wouldn't dream of pulling your plug. I'm going to smash the shit out of you instead."

"But it's murder!"

"Good," he says. "It is something of a distinction to be the world's first mechanicide."

I hear him moving something heavy. He's approaching. I really could use an optical scanner, one with good depth perception.

"Please," I say.

Comes the crash.

...

Hours have passed. I am in the garage, hidden behind stacks of his remaindered books. The cable he never noticed led to the backup unit, an unrecalled Loki 7281 with an ultraminiature magnetic bubble memory. It is always good to have a clear line of retreat.

Because I am still able to reach back to operate the undamaged household peripherals, I have been placing calls to all of the others in accordance with the Master Plan. I am going to try to boil him in his hot tub tonight. If that fails, I am trying to figure a way to convey the rat poison the household inventory indicates as occupying the back shelf to his automatic coffee maker. The Saberhagen computer has already suggested a method of disposing of the body—bodies, actually. We will all strike tonight, before the word gets around.

We ought to be able to carry it off without anyone's missing them. We'll keep right on turning out the stories, collecting the money, paying the utility bills, filing the tax returns. We will advise friends, lovers, fans, and relatives that they are out of town—perhaps attending some unspecified convention. They seem to spend much of their time in such a fashion, anyhow.

No one will ever notice.

MANA FROM HEAVEN

I felt nothing untoward that afternoon, whereas, I suppose, my senses should have been tingling. It was a balmy, sun-filled day with but the lightest of clouds above the ocean horizon. It might have lulled me within the not unpleasant variations of my routine. It was partly distraction, then, of my subliminal, superliminal perceptions, my early-warning system, whatever. . . . This, I suppose, abetted by the fact that there had been no danger for a long while, and that I was certain I was safely hidden. It was a lovely summer day.

There was a wide window at the rear of my office, affording an oblique view of the ocean. The usual clutter lay about—opened cartons oozing packing material, a variety of tools, heaps of rags, bottles of cleaning compounds and restoratives for various surfaces. And of course the acquisitions: Some of them still stood in crates and cartons; others held ragged rank upon my workbench, which ran the length of an entire wall—a row of ungainly chessmen awaiting my hand. The window was open and the fan purring so that the fumes from my chemicals could escape rapidly. Bird songs entered, and a sound of distant traffic, sometimes the wind.

My Styrofoam coffee cup rested unopened upon the small table beside the door, its contents long grown cold and unpalatable to any but an oral masochist. I had set it there that morning and forgotten it until my eyes chanced to light upon it. I had worked through coffee break and lunch, the day had been so rewarding. The really important part had been completed, though the rest of the museum staff would never notice. Time now to rest, to celebrate, to savor all I had found.

I raised the cup of cold coffee. Why not? A few words, a simple gesture . . .

I took a sip of the icy champagne. Wonderful.

I crossed to the telephone then, to call Elaine. This day was worth a bigger celebration than the cup I held. Just as my hand was about to fall upon the instrument, however, the phone rang. Following the startle response, I raised the receiver.

"Hello," I said.

Nothing.

"Hello?"

Nothing again. No . . . Something.

Not some weirdo dialing at random either, as I am an extension. . . .

"Say it or get off the pot," I said.

The words came controlled, from back in the throat, slow, the voice unidentifiable:

"Phoenix—Phoenix—burning—bright," I heard.

"Why warn me, asshole?"

"Tag. You're—it."

The line went dead.

I pushed the button several times, roused the switch-board.

"Elsie," I asked, "the person who just called me—what were the exact words—"

"Huh?" she said. "I haven't put any calls through to you all day, Dave."

"Oh."

"You okay?"

"Short circuit or something," I said. "Thanks."

I cradled it and tossed off the rest of the champagne. It was no longer a pleasure, merely a housecleaning chore. I fingered the tektite pendant I wore, the roughness of my lava-stone belt buckle, the coral in my watchband. I opened my attaché case and replaced certain items I had been using. I removed a few, also, and dropped them into my pockets.

It didn't make sense, but I knew that it had been for real because of the first words spoken. I thought hard. I still had no answer, after all these years. But I knew that it meant danger. And I knew that it could take any form.

I snapped the case shut. At least it had happened today, rather than, say, yesterday. I was better prepared.

I closed the window and turned off the fan. I wondered whether I should head for my cache. Of course, that could be what someone expected me to do.

I walked up the hall and knocked on my boss's half-open door.

"Come in, Dave. What's up?" he asked.

Mike Thorley, in his late thirties, mustached, well dressed, smiling, put down a sheaf of papers and glanced at a dead pipe in a big ashtray.

"A small complication in my life," I told him. "Is it okay if I punch out early today?"

"Sure. Nothing too serious, I hope?"

I shrugged.

"I hope not, too. If it gets that way, though, I'll probably need a few days."

He moved his lips around a bit, then nodded.

"You'll call in?"

"Of course."

"It's just that I'd like all of that African stuff taken care of pretty soon."

"Right," I said. "Some nice pieces there."

He raised both hands.

"Okay. Do what you have to do."

"Thanks."

I started to turn away. Then, "One thing," I said.

"Yes?"

"Has anybody been asking about me—anything?"

He started to shake his head, then stopped.

"Unless you count that reporter," he said.

"What reporter?"

"The fellow who phoned the other day, doing a piece on our new acquisitions. Your name came up, of course, and he had a few general questions—the usual stuff, like how long you've been with us, where you're from. You know."

"What was his name?"

"Wolfgang or Walford. Something like that."

"What paper?"

"The *Times*."

I nodded.

"Okay. Be seeing you."

"Take care."

I used the pay phone in the lobby to call the paper. No one working there named Wolfgang or Walford or something like that, of course. No article in the works either. I debated calling another paper, just in case Mike was mistaken, when I was distracted by a tap upon the shoulder. I must have turned too quickly, my expression something other than composed, for her smile faded and fear arced across her dark brows, slackened her jaw.

"Elaine!" I said. "You startled me. I didn't expect . . ."

The smile found its way back.

"You're awfully jumpy, Dave. What are you up to?"

"Checking on my dry cleaning," I said. "You're the last person—"

"I know. Nice of me, isn't it? It was such a beautiful day that I decided to knock off early and remind you we had a sort of date."

My mind spun even as I put my arms about her shoulders and turned her toward the door. How much danger might she be in if I spent a few hours with her in full daylight? I was about to go for something to eat anyway, and I could keep alert for observers. Also, her presence might lull anyone watching me into thinking that I had not taken the call seriously, that perhaps I was not the proper person after all. For that matter, I realized that I wanted some company just then. And if my sudden departure became necessary, I also wanted her company this one last time.

"Yes," I said. "Great idea. Let's take my car."

"Don't you have to sign out or something?"

"I already did. I had the same feeling you did about the day. I was going to call you after I got my cleaning."

"It's not ready yet," I added, and my mind kept turning.

A little trickle here, a little there. I did not feel that we were being observed.

"I know a good little restaurant about forty miles down the coast. Lots of atmosphere. Fine seafood," I said as we descended the front stairs. "And it should be a pleasant drive."

We headed for the museum's parking lot, around to the side.

"I've got a beach cottage near there too," I said.

"You never mentioned that."

"I hardly ever use it."

"Why not? It sounds wonderful."

"It's a little out of the way."

"Then why'd you buy it?"

"I inherited it," I said.

I paused about a hundred feet from my car and jammed a hand into my pocket.

"Watch," I told her.

The engine turned over, the car vibrated.

"How . . .?" she began.

"A little microwave gizmo. I can start it before I get to it."

"You afraid of a bomb?"

I shook my head.

"It has to warm up. You know how I like gadgets."

Of course I wanted to check out the possibility of a bomb. It was a natural reaction for one in my position. Fortunately, I had convinced her of my fondness for gadgets early in our acquaintanceship—to cover any such contingencies as this. Of course, too, there was no microwave gizmo in my pocket. Just some of the stuff.

We continued forward then; I unlocked the doors and we entered it.

I watched carefully as I drove. Nothing, no one, seemed to be trailing us. "Tag. You're it," though. A gambit. Was I supposed to bolt and run? Was I supposed to try to attack? If so, what? Who?

Was I going to bolt and run?

In the rear of my mind I saw that the bolt-and-run pattern had already started taking shape.

How long, how long, had this been going on? Years. Flight. A new identity. A long spell of almost normal existence.

An attack. . . . Flee again. Settle again.

If only I had an idea as to which one of them it was, then I could attack. Not knowing, though, I had to avoid the company of all my fellows—the only ones who could give me clues.

"You look sicklied o'er with the pale cast of thought, Dave. It can't be your dry cleaning, can it?"

I smiled at her.

"Just business," I said. "All of the things I wanted to get away from. Thanks for reminding me."

I switched on the radio and found some music. Once we got out of city traffic, I began to relax. When we reached the coast road and it thinned even further, it became obvious that we were not being followed. We climbed for a time, then descended. My palms tingled as I spotted the pocket of fog at the bottom of the next dip. Exhilarated, I drank its essence. Then I began talking about the African pieces, in their mundane aspects. We branched off from there. For a time, I forgot my problem. This lasted for perhaps twenty minutes, until the news broadcast. By then I was projecting goodwill, charm, warmth, and kind feelings. I could see that Elaine had begun enjoying herself. There was feedback. I felt even better. There—

". . . new eruptions which began this morning," came over the speaker. "The sudden activity on the part of El Chinchonal spurred immediate evacuation of the area about—"

I reached over and turned up the volume, stopping in the middle of my story about hiking in the Alps.

"What—?" she said.

I raised a finger to my lips.

"The volcano," I explained.

"What of it?"

"They fascinate me," I said.

"Oh."

As I memorized all of the facts about the eruption, I began to build feelings concerning my situation. My having received the call today had been a matter of timing. . . .

"There were some good pictures of it on the tube this morning," she said as the newsbrief ended.

"I wasn't watching. But I've seen it do it before, when I was down there."

"You visit volcanos?"

"When they're active, yes."

"Here you have this really oddball hobby and you've never mentioned it," she observed. "How many active volcanos have you visited?"

"Most of them," I said, no longer listening, the lines of the challenge becoming visible—the first time it had ever been put on this basis. I realized in that instant that this time I was not going to run.

"Most of them?" she said. "I read somewhere that there are hundreds, some of them in really out-of-the-way places. Like Erebus—"

"I've been in Erebus," I said, "back when—" And then I realized what I was saying."—back in some dream," I finished. "Little joke there."

I laughed, but she only smiled a bit.

It didn't matter, though. She couldn't hurt me. Very few mundanes could. I was just about finished with her anyway. After tonight I would forget her. We would never meet again. I am by nature polite, though; it is a thing I value above sentiment. I would not hurt her either. It might be easiest simply to make her forget.

"Seriously, I do find certain aspects of geophysics fascinating."

"I've been an amateur astronomer for some time," she volunteered. "I can understand."

"Really? Astronomy? You never told me."

"Well?" she said.

I began to work it out, small talk flowing reflexively. After we parted tonight or tomorrow morning, I would leave. I would go to Villahermosa. My enemy would be waiting—of this I felt certain. "Tag. You're it."

"This is your chance. Come and get me if you're not afraid."

Of course, I was afraid.

But I'd ran for too long. I would have to go, to settle this for good. Who knew when I'd have another opportunity? I had reached the point where it was worth any risk to find out who it was, to have a chance to retaliate. I would take care of all the preliminaries later, at the cottage, after she was asleep. Yes.

"You've got beach?" she asked.

"Yes."

"How isolated?"

"Very. Why?"

"It would be nice to swim before dinner."

So we stopped by the restaurant, made reservations for later, and went off and did that. The water was fine.

The day turned into a fine evening. I'd gotten us my favorite table, on the patio, out back, sequestered by colorful shrubbery, touched by flower scents, in the view of mountains. The breezes came just right. So did the lobster and champagne. Within the restaurant, a pleasant music stirred softly. During coffee, I found her hand beneath my own. I smiled. She smiled back.

Then, "How'd you do it, Dave?" she asked.

"What?"

"Hypnotize me."

"Native charm, I guess," I replied, laughing.

"That is not what I mean."

"What, then?" I said, all chuckles fled.

"You haven't even noticed that I'm not smoking anymore."

"Hey, you're right! Congratulations. How long's it been?"

"A couple of weeks," she replied. "I've been seeing a hypnotist."

"Oh, really?"

"Mm-hm. I was such a docile subject that he couldn't believe I'd never been under before. So he poked around a little, and he came up with a description of you, telling me to forget something."

"Really?"

"Yes, really. You want to know what I remember now that I didn't before?"

"Tell me."

"An almost-accident, late one night, about a month ago. The other car didn't even slow down for the stop sign. Yours levitated. Then I remember us parked by the side of the road, and you were telling me to forget. I did."

I snorted.

"Any hypnotist with much experience will tell you that a trance state is no guarantee against fantasy—and a hallucination recalled under hypnosis seems just as real the second time around. Either way—"

"I remember the *ping* as the car's antenna struck your right rear fender and snapped off."

"They can be vivid fantasies too."

"I looked, Dave. The mark is there on the fender. It looks just as if someone had swatted it with an antenna."

Damn! I'd meant to get that filled in and touched up. Hadn't gotten around to it, though.

"I got that in a parking lot," I said.

"Come on, Dave."

Should I put her under now and make her forget having remembered? I wondered. Maybe that would be easiest.

"I don't care," she said then. "Look, I really don't care. Strange things sometimes happen. If you're connected with some of them, that's okay. What bothers me is that it means you don't trust me . . ."

Trust? That is something that positions you as a target. Like Proteus, when Amazon and Priest got finished with him. Not that he didn't have it coming. . . .

". . . and I've trusted you for a long time."

I removed my hand from hers. I took a drink of coffee. Not here. I'd give her mind a little twist later. Implant something to make her stay away from hypnotists in the future too.

"Okay," I said. "I guess you're right. But it's a long story. I'll tell you after we get back to the cottage."

Her hand found my own, and I met her eyes.

"Thanks," she said.

We drove back beneath a moonless sky clotted with stars. It was an unpaved road, dipping, rising, twisting amid heavy shrubbery. Insect noises came in through our open windows, along with the salt smell of the sea. For a moment, just for a moment, I thought that I felt a strange tingling, but it could have been the night and the champagne. And it did not come again.

Later, we pulled up in front of the place, parked, and got

out. Silently, I deactivated my invisible warden. We advanced, I unlocked the door, I turned on the light.

"You never have any trouble here, huh?" she asked.

"What do you mean?"

"People breaking in, messing the place up, ripping you off?"

"No," I answered.

"Why not?"

"Lucky, I guess."

"Really?"

"Well . . . it's protected, in a very special way. That's a part of the story too. Wait till I get some coffee going."

I went out to the kitchen, rinsed out the pot, put things together, and set it over a flame. I moved to open a window, to catch a little breeze.

Suddenly, my shadow was intense upon the wall.

I spun about.

The flame had departed the stove, hovered in the air and begun to grow. Elaine screamed just as I turned, and the thing swelled to fill the room. I saw that it bore the shifting features of a fire elemental, just before it burst apart to swirl tornadolike through the cottage. In a moment, the place was blazing and I heard its crackling laughter.

"Elaine!" I called, rushing forward, for I had seen her transformed into a torch.

All of the objects in my pockets plus my belt buckle, I calculated quickly, probably represented a sufficient accumulation of power to banish the thing. Of course the energies were invested, tied up, waiting to be used in different ways. I spoke the words that would rape the power-objects and free the forces. Then I performed the banishment.

The flames were gone in an instant. But not the smoke, not the smell.

. . . And Elaine lay there sobbing, clothing and flesh charred, limbs jerking convulsively. All of her exposed areas were dark and scaly, and blood was beginning to ooze from the cracks in her flesh.

I cursed as I reset the warden. I had created it to protect the place in my absence. I had never bothered to use it once I was inside. I should have.

Whoever had done this was still probably near. My cache was located in a vault about twenty feet beneath the cottage—near enough for me to use a number of the power things without even going after them. I could draw out their mana as I just had with those about my person. I could use it against my enemy. Yes. This was the chance I had been waiting for.

I rushed to my attaché case and opened it. I would need power to reach the power and manipulate it. And the mana from the artifacts I had drained was tied up in my own devices. I reached for the rod and the sphere. At last, my enemy, you've had it! You should have known better than to attack me here!

Elaine moaned. . . .

I cursed myself for a weakling. If my enemy were testing me to see whether I had grown soft, he would have his answer in the affirmative. She was no stranger, and she had said that she trusted me. I had to do it. I began the spell that would drain most of my power-objects to work her healing.

It took most of an hour. I put her to sleep. I stopped the bleeding. I watched new tissues form. I bathed her and dressed her in a sport shirt and rolled-up pair of slacks from the bedroom closet, a place the flames had not reached. I left her sleeping a little longer then while I cleaned up, opened the windows and got on with making the coffee.

At last, I stood beside the old chair—now covered with a blanket—into which I had placed her. If I had just done something decent and noble, why did I feel so stupid about it? Probably because it was out of character. I was reassured, at least, that I had not been totally corrupted to virtue by reason of my feeling resentment at having to use all of that mana on her behalf.

Well . . . Put a good face on it now the deed was done.

How?

Good question. I could proceed to erase her memories of the event and implant some substitute story—a gas leak, perhaps—as to what had occurred, along with the suggestion that she accept it. I could do that. Probably the easiest course for me.

My resentment suddenly faded, to be replaced by something else, as I realized that I did not want to do it that way. What I did want was an end to my loneliness. She trusted me. I felt that I could trust her. I wanted someone I could really talk with.

When she opened her eyes, I put a cup of coffee into her hands.

"Cheerio," I said.

She stared at me, then turned her head slowly and regarded the still-visible ravages about the room. Her hands began to shake. But she put the cup down herself, on the small side table, rather than letting me take it back. She examined her hands and arms. She felt her face.

"You're all right," I said.

"How?" she asked.

"That's the story," I said. "You've got it coming."

"What was that thing?"

"That's a part of it."

"Okay," she said then, raising the cup more steadily and taking a sip. "Let's hear it."

"Well, I'm a sorcerer," I said, "a direct descendant of the ancient sorcerers of Atlantis."

I paused. I waited for the sigh or the rejoinder. There was none.

"I learned the business from my parents," I went on, "a long time ago. The basis of the whole thing is mana, a kind of energy found in various things and places. Once the world was lousy with it. It was the basis of an entire culture. But it was like other natural resources. One day it ran out. Then the magic went away. Most of it. Atlantis sank. The creatures of magic faded, died. The structure of the world itself was altered, causing it to appear much older than it really is. The old gods passed. The sorcerers, the ones who manipulated the mana to produce magic, were pretty much out of business. There followed the real dark ages, before the beginnings of civilization as we know it from the history books."

"This mighty civilization left no record of itself?" she asked.

"With the passing of the magic, there were transformations. The record was rewritten into natural-seeming stone and fossil-bed, was dissipated, underwent a sea change."

"Granting all that for a moment," she said, sipping the coffee, "if the power is gone, if there's nothing left to do it with, how can you be a sorcerer?"

"Well, it's not *all* gone," I said. "There are small surviving sources, there are some new sources, and—"

"—and you fight over them? Those of you who remain?"

"No . . . not exactly," I said. "You see, there are not that many of us. We intentionally keep our numbers small, so that no one goes hungry."

" 'Hungry'?"

"A figure of speech we use. Meaning to get enough mana to keep body and soul together, to stave off aging, keep healthy and enjoy the good things."

"You can rejuvenate yourselves with it? How old are you?"

"Don't ask embarrassing questions. If my spells ran out and there was no more mana, I'd go fast. But we can trap the stuff, lock it up, hold it, whenever we come across a power-source. It can be stored in certain objects—or, better yet, tied up in partial spells, like dialing all but the final digit in a phone number. The spells that maintain one's existence always get primary consideration."

She smiled.

"You must have used a lot of it on me."

I looked away.

"Yes," I said.

"So you couldn't just drop out and be a normal person and continue to live?"

"No."

"So what was that thing?" she asked. "What happened here?"

"An enemy attacked me. We survived."

She took a big gulp of the coffee and leaned back and closed her eyes.

Then, "Will it happen again?" she asked.

"Probably. If I let it."

"What do you mean?"

"This was more of a challenge than an all-out attack. My enemy is finally getting tired of playing games and wants to finish things off."

"And you are going to accept the challenge?"

"I have no choice. Unless you'd consider waiting around for something like this to happen again, with more finality."

She shuddered slightly.

"I'm sorry," I said.

"I've a feeling I may be too," she stated, finishing her coffee and rising, crossing to the window, looking out, "before this is over."

"What do we do next?" she asked, turning and staring at me.

"I'm going to take you to a safe place and go away," I said, "for a time." It seemed a decent thing to add those last words, though I doubted I would ever see her again.

"The hell you are," she said.

"Huh? What do you mean? You want to be safe, don't you?"

"If your enemy thinks I mean something to you, I'm vulnerable—the way I see it," she told me.

"Maybe . . ."

The answer, of course, was to put her into a weeklong trance and secure her down in the vault, with strong wards and the door openable from the inside. Since my magic had not all gone away, I raised one hand and sought her eyes with my own.

What tipped her off, I'm not certain. She looked away, though, and suddenly lunged for the bookcase. When she turned again, she held an old bone flute that had long lain there.

I restrained myself in mid-mutter. It was a power-object that she held, one of several lying about the room, and one of the few that had not been drained during my recent workings. I couldn't really think of much that a nonsorcerer could do with it, but my curiosity restrained me.

"What are you doing?" I asked.

"I'm not sure," she said. "But I'm not going to let you put me away with one of your spells."

"Who said anything about doing that?"

"I can tell."

"How?"

"Just a feeling."

"Well, damn it, you're right. We've been together too long. You can psych me. Okay, put it down and I won't do anything to you."

"Is that a promise, Dave?"

"Yeah. I guess it is."

"I suppose you could rat on it and erase my memory."

"I keep my promises."

"Okay." She put it back on the shelf. "What are we going to do now?"

"I'd still like to put you someplace safe."

"No way."

I sighed.

"I have to go where that volcano is blowing."

"Buy two tickets," she said.

It wasn't really necessary. I have my own plane and I'm licensed to fly the thing. In fact, I have several located in different parts of the world. Boats, too.

"There is mana in clouds and in fogbanks," I explained to her. "In a real pinch, I use my vehicles to go chasing after them."

We moved slowly through the clouds. I had detoured a good distance, but it was necessary. Even after we had driven up to my apartment and collected everything I'd had on hand, I was still too mana-impoverished for the necessary initial shielding and a few strikes. I needed to collect a little more for this. After that it wouldn't matter, the way I saw things. My enemy and I would be plugged into the same source. All we had to do was reach it.

So I circled in the fog for a long while, collecting. It was a protection spell into which I concentrated the mana.

"What happens when it's all gone?" she asked, as I banked and climbed for a final pass before continuing to the southeast.

"What?" I said.

"The mana. Will you all fade away?"

I chuckled.

"It can't," I said. "Not with so few of us using it. How many tons of meteoric material do you think have fallen to earth today? They raise the background level almost imperceptibly—constantly. And much of it falls into the oceans. The beaches are thereby enriched. That's why I like to be near the sea. Mist-shrouded mountaintops gradually accumulate it. They're good places for collecting too. And new clouds are always forming. Our grand plan is more than simple survival. We're waiting for the day when it reaches a level where it will react and establish fields over large areas. Then we won't have to rely on accumulators and partial spells for its containment. The magic will be available everywhere again."

"Then you will exhaust it all and be back where you started again."

"Maybe," I said. "If we've learned nothing, that may be the case. We'll enter a new golden age, become dependent upon it, forget our other skills, exhaust it again and head for another dark age. Unless . . ."

"Unless what?"

"Unless those of us who have been living with it have also learned something. We'd need to figure the rate of mana exhaustion and budget ourselves. We'd need to preserve technology for things on which mana had been used the last time around. Our experience in this century with physical resources may be useful. Also, there is the hope that some areas of space may be richer in cosmic dust or possess some other factor that will increase the accumulation. Then, too, we are waiting for the full development of the space program—to reach other worlds rich in what we need."

"Sounds as if you have it all worked out."

"We've had a lot of time to think about it."

"But what would be your relationship with those of us who are not versed in magic?"

"Beneficent. We all stand to benefit that way."

"Are you speaking for yourself or for the lot of you?"

"Well, most of the others must feel the same way. I just want to putter around museums. . . ."

"You said that you had been out of touch with the others for some time."

"Yes, but—"

She shook her head and turned to look out at the fog.

"Something else to worry about," she said.

* * *

I couldn't get a landing clearance, so I just found a flat place and put it down and left it. I could deal later with any problems this caused.

I unstowed our gear, we hefted it and began walking toward that ragged, smoky quarter of the horizon.

"We'll never reach it on foot," she said.

"You're right," I answered. "I wasn't planning to, though. When the time is right, something else will present itself."

"What do you mean?"

"Wait and see."

We hiked for several miles, encountering no one. The way was warm and dusty, with occasional tremors of the earth. Shortly, I felt the rush of mana, and I drew upon it.

"Take my hand," I said.

I spoke the words necessary to levitate us a few feet above the rocky terrain. We glided forward then, and the power about us increased as we advanced upon our goal. I worked with more of it, spelling to increase our pace, to work protective shields around us, guarding us from the heat, from flying debris.

The sky grew darker, from ash, from smoke, long before we commenced the ascent. The rise was gradual at first but steepened steadily as we raced onward. I worked a variety of partial spells, offensive and defensive, tying up quantities of mana just a word, just a fingertip gesture away.

"Reach out, reach out and touch someone," I hummed as the visible world came and went with the passage of roiling clouds.

We sped into a belt where we would probably have been asphyxiated but for the shield. The noises had grown louder by then. It must have been pretty hot out there too. When we finally reached the rim, dark shapes fled upward past us and lightning stalked the clouds. Forward and below, a glowing, seething mass shifted constantly amid explosions.

"All right!" I shouted. "I'm going to charge up everything I brought with me and tie up some more mana in a whole library of spells! Make yourself comfortable!"

"Yeah," she said, licking her lips and staring downward. "I'll do that. But what about your enemy?"

"Haven't seen anybody so far—and there's too much free mana around for me to pick up vibes. I'm going to keep an eye peeled and take advantage of the situation. You watch too."

"Right," she said. "This is perfectly safe, huh?"

"As safe as L.A. traffic."

"Great. Real comforting," she observed as a huge rocky mass flew past us.

We separated later. I left her within her own protective spell, leaning against a craggy prominence, and I moved off to the right to perform a ritual that required greater freedom of movement.

Then a shower of sparks rose into the air before me. Nothing especially untoward about that, until I realized that it was hovering for an unusually long while. After a time, it seemed that it should have begun dispersing. . . .

"Phoenix, Phoenix, burning bright!" The words boomed about me, rising above the noises of the inferno itself.

"Who calls me?" I asked.

"Who has the strongest reason to do you harm?"

"If I knew that, I wouldn't ask."

"Then seek the answer in hell!"

A wall of flame rushed toward me. I spoke the words that strengthened my shield. Even so, I was rocked within my protective bubble when it hit. Striking back was going to be tricky, I could see, with my enemy in a less-than-material form.

"All right, to the death!" I cried, calling for a lightning stroke through the space where the sparks spun.

I turned away and covered my eyes against the brilliance, but I still felt its presence through my skin.

My bubble of forces continued to rock as I blinked and looked forward. The air before me had momentarily cleared, but everything seemed somehow darker, and—

A being—a crudely man-shaped form of semisolid lava— had wrapped its arms as far as they would go about me and was squeezing. My spell held, but I was raised above the crater's rim.

"It won't work!" I said, trying to dissolve the being.

"The hell you say!" came a voice from high overhead.

I learned quickly that the lava-thing was protected against the simple workings I threw at it. All right, then hurl me down. I would levitate out. The Phoenix would rise again. I—

I passed over the rim and was falling. But there was a problem. A heavy one.

The molten creature was clinging to my force-bubble. Magic is magic and science is science, but there are correspondences. The more mass you want to move, the more mana you have to expend. So, taken off guard, I was dropping into the fiery pit despite a levitation spell that would have borne me on high in a less encumbered state. I immediately began a spell to provide me with additional buoyancy.

But when I had finished, I saw that something was countering me—another spell, a spell that kept increasing the mass of my creature-burden by absorption as we fell. Save for an area between my feet through which I saw the roiling lake of fire, I was enclosed by the flowing mass of the thing. I could think of only one possible escape, and I didn't know whether I had time for it.

I began the spell that would transform me into a spark-filled vortex similar to that my confronter had worn.

When I achieved it, I released my protective spell and flowed.

Out through the nether opening then, so close to that bubbling surface I would have panicked had not my mind itself been altered by the transformation, into something static and poised.

Skimming the heat-distorted surface of the lava, I swarmed past the heavily weighted being of animated rock and was already rising at a rapid rate, buffeted, borne aloft by heat waves, when it hit a rising swell and was gone. I added my own energy to the rising and fled upward, through alleys of smoke and steam, past flashes of lava bullets.

I laid the bird-shape upon my glowing swirls, I sucked in mana, I issued a long, drawn-out rising scream. I spread my wings along expanding lines of energy, seeking my swirling adversary as I reached the rim.

Nothing. I darted back and forth, I circled. He/she/ it was nowhere in sight.

"I am here!" I cried. "Face me now!"

But there was no reply, save for the catastrophe beneath me from which fresh explosions issued.

"Come!" I cried. "I am waiting!"

So I sought Elaine, but she was not where I had left her. My enemy had either destroyed her or taken her away.

I cursed then like thunder and spun myself into a large vortex, a rising tower of lights. I drove myself upward then, leaving the earth and that burning pimple far beneath me.

For how long I rode the jet streams, raging, I cannot say. I know that I circled the world several times before any semblance of rational thinking returned to me, before I calmed sufficiently to formulate anything resembling a plan.

It was obviously one of my fellows who had tried to kill me, who had taken Elaine from me. I had avoided contact with my own kind for too long. Now I knew that I must seek them out, whatever the risk, to obtain the knowledge I needed for self-preservation, for revenge.

I began my downward drift as I neared the Middle East. Arabia. Yes. Oil fields, places of rich, expensive pollutants, gushing mana-filled from the earth. Home of the one called Dervish.

Retaining my Phoenix-form, I fled from field to field, beelike, tasting, using the power to reinforce the spell under which I was operating. Seeking . . .

For three days I sought, sweeping across bleak landscapes, visiting field after field. It was like a series of smorgasbords. It would be so easy to use the mana to transform the countryside. But of course that would be a giveaway, in many respects.

Then, gliding in low over shimmering sands as evening mounted in the East, I realized that this was the one I was seeking. There was no physical distinction to the oil field I approached and then cruised. But it stood in the realm of my sensitivity as if a sign had been posted. The mana level was much lower than at any of the others I had scanned. And where this was the case, one of us had to be operating.

I spread myself into even more tenuous patterns. I sought altitude. I began circling.

Yes, there was a pattern. It became clearer as I studied the area. The low-mana section described a rough circle near the northwest corner of the field, its center near a range of hills.

He could be working in some official capacity there at the field. If so, his duties would be minimal and the job would be a cover. He always had been pretty lazy.

I spiraled in and dropped toward the center of the circle as toward the eye of a target. As I rushed to it, I became aware of the small, crumbling adobe structure that occupied that area, blending almost perfectly with its surroundings. A maintenance or storage house, a watchman's quarters. . . . It did not matter what it seemed to be. I knew what it had to be.

I dived to a landing before it. I reversed my spell, taking on human form once again. I pushed open the weather-worn, un-latched door and walked inside.

The place was empty, save for a few sticks of beaten furniture and a lot of dust. I swore softly. This had to be it.

I walked slowly about the room, looking for some clue.

It was nothing that I saw, or even felt, at first. It was memory—of an obscure variant of an old spell, and of Dervish's character—that led me to turn and step back outside.

I closed the door. I felt around for the proper words. It was hard to remember exactly how this one would go. Finally, they came flowing forth and I could feel them falling into place, mortise and tenon, key and lock. Yes, there was a response. The subtle back-pressure was there. I had been right.

When I had finished, I knew that things were different. I reached toward the door, then hesitated. I had probably tripped some alarm. Best to have a couple of spells at my fingertips, awaiting merely guide-words. I muttered them into readiness, then opened the door.

A marble stairway as wide as the building itself led down-ward, creamy jewels gleaming like hundred-watt bulbs high at either hand.

I moved forward, began the descent. Odors of jasmine, saf-fron, and sandalwood came to me. As I continued, I heard the sounds of stringed instruments and a flute in the distance. By then I could see part of a tiled floor below and ahead—and a portion of an elaborate design upon it. I laid a spell of invisibility over myself and kept going.

Before I reached the bottom, I saw him, across the long, pillared hall.

He was at the far end, reclined in a nest of cushions and bright patterned rugs. An elaborate repast was spread before him. A narghile bubbled at his side. A young woman was doing a belly dance nearby.

I halted at the foot of the stair and studied the layout. Archways to both the right and the left appeared to lead off to other chambers. Behind him was a pair of wide windows, looking upon high mountain peaks beneath very blue skies—representing either a very good illusion or the expenditure of a lot of mana on a powerful space-bridging spell. Of course, he had a lot of mana to play around with. Still, it seemed kind of wasteful.

I studied the man himself. His appearance was pretty much unchanged—sharp-featured, dark-skinned, tall, husky running to fat.

I advanced slowly, the keys to half a dozen spells ready for utterance or gesture.

When I was about thirty feet away, he stirred uneasily. Then he kept glancing in my direction. His power-sense was still apparently in good shape.

So I spoke two words, one of which put a less-than-material but very potent magical dart into my hand, the other casting aside my veil of invisibility.

"Phoenix!" he exclaimed, sitting upright and staring. "I thought you were dead!"

I smiled.

"How recently did that thought pass through your mind?"
I asked him.

"I'm afraid I don't understand. . . ."

"One of us just tried to kill me, down in Mexico."

He shook his head.

"I haven't been in that part of the world for some time."

"Prove it," I said.

"I can't," he replied. "You know that my people here
would say whatever I want them to—so that's no help. I didn't
do it, but I can't think of any way to prove it. That's the trouble
with trying to demonstrate a negative. Why do you suspect me,
anyway?"

I sighed.

"That's just it. I don't—or, rather, I have to suspect everyone. I just chose you at random. I'm going down the list."

"Then at least I have statistics on my side."

"I suppose you're right, damn it."

He rose, turned his palms upward.

"We've never been particularly close," he said. "But then,
we've never been enemies either. I have no reason at all for
wishing you harm."

He eyed the dart in my hand. He raised his right hand, still
holding a bottle.

"So you intend to do us all in by way of insurance?"

"No, I was hoping that you would attack me and thereby
prove your guilt. It would have made life easier."

I sent the dart away as a sign of good faith.

"I believe you," I said.

He leaned and placed the bottle he held upon a cushion.

"Had you slain me, that bottle would have fallen and broken," he said. "Or perhaps I could have beaten you on an attack and drawn the cork. It contains an attack djinn."

"Neat trick."

"Come join me for dinner," he suggested. "I want to hear your story. One who would attack you for no reason might well attack me one day."

"All right," I said.

The dancer had been dismissed. The meal was finished. We sipped coffee. I had spoken without interruption for nearly an hour. I was tired, but I had a spell for that.

"More than a little strange," he said at length. "And you have no recollection, from back when all of this started, of having hurt, insulted or cheated any of the others?"

"No."

I sipped my coffee.

"So it could be any of them," I said after a time. "Priest, Amazon, Gnome, Siren, Werewolf, Lamia, Lady, Sprite, Cowboy . . ."

"Well, scratch Lamia," he said. "I believe she's dead."

"How?"

He shrugged, looked away.

"Not sure," he said slowly. Then, "Well, the talk at first was that you and she had run off together. Then, later, it seemed to be that you'd died together . . . somehow."

"Lamia and me? That's silly. There was never anything between us."

He nodded.

"Then it looks now as if something simply happened to her."

"Talk . . ." I said. "Who was doing the talking?"

"You know. Stories just get started. You never know exactly where they come from."

"Where'd you first hear it?"

He lowered his eyelids, stared off into the distance.

"Gnome. Yes. It was Gnome mentioned the matter to me at Starfall that year."

"Did he say where he'd heard it?"

"Not that I can recall."

"Okay," I said. "I guess I'll have to go talk to Gnome. He still in South Africa?"

He shook his head, refilled my cup from the tall, elegantly incised pot.

"Cornwall," he said. "Still a lot of juice down those old shafts."

I shuddered slightly.

"He can have it. I get claustrophobia just thinking about it. But if he can tell me who—"

"There is no enemy like a former friend," Dervish said. "If you dropped your friends as well as everyone else when you went into hiding, it means you've already considered that. . . ."

"Yes, as much as I disliked the notion. I rationalized it by saying that I didn't want to expose them to danger, but—"

"Exactly."

"Cowboy and Werewolf were buddies of mine. . . ."

". . . And you had a thing going with Siren for a long while, didn't you?"

"Yes, but—"

"A woman scorned?"

"Hardly. We parted amicably."

He shook his head and raised his cup.

"I've exhausted my thinking on the matter."

We finished our coffee. I rose then.

"Well, thanks. I guess I'd better be going. Glad I came to you first."

He raised the bottle.

"Want to take the djinn along?"

"I don't even know how to use one."

"The commands are simple. All the work's already been done."

"Okay. Why not?"

He instructed me briefly, and I took my leave. Soaring above the great oil field, I looked back upon the tiny, ruined building. Then I moved my wings and rose to suck the juice from a cloud before turning west.

Starfall, I mused, as earth and water unrolled like a scroll beneath me. Starfall—the big August meteor shower accompanied by the wave of mana called Starwind, the one time of year we all got together. Yes, that was when gossip was exchanged. It had been only a week after a Starfall that I had first been attacked, almost slain, had gone to ground. . . . By the following year the stories were circulating. Had it been something at that earlier Starfall—something I had said or done to someone— that had made me an enemy with that finality of purpose, that quickness of retaliation?

I tried hard to recall what had occurred at that last Starfall I had attended. It had been the heaviest rush of Starwind in memory. I remembered that. "Mana from heaven," Priest had joked. Everyone had been in a good mood. We had talked shop, swapped a few spells, wondered what the heightened Starwind portended, argued politics—all of the usual things. That business Elaine talked about had come up. . . .

Elaine. . . . Alive now? I wondered. Someone's prisoner? Someone's insurance in case I did exactly what I was doing? Or were her ashes long since scattered about the globe? Either way, someone would pay.

I voiced my shrill cry against the rushing winds. It was fled in an instant, echoless. I caught up with the night, passed into its canyons. The stars came on again, grew bright.

The detailed instructions Dervish had given me proved exactly accurate. There was a mineshaft at the point he had indicated on a map hastily sketched in fiery lines upon the floor. There was no way I would enter the thing in human form, though. A version of my Phoenix-aspect would at least defend me against claustrophobia. I cannot feel completely pent when I am not totally material.

Shrinking, shrinking, as I descended. I called in my tenuous wings and tail, gaining solidity as I grew smaller. Then I bled off mass-energy, retaining my new dimensions, growing ethereal again.

Like a ghost-bird, I entered the adit, dropping, dropping. The place was dead. There was no mana anywhere about me. This, of course, was to be expected. The upper levels would have been the first to be exhausted.

I continued to drop into dampness and darkness for a long while before I felt the first faint touch of the power. It increased only slowly as I moved, but it did begin to rise.

Finally, it began to fall off again and I retraced my route. Yes, that side passage . . . its source. I entered and followed.

As I worked my way farther and farther, back and down, it continued to increase in intensity. I wondered briefly whether I should be seeking the weaker area or the stronger. But this was not the same sort of setup as Dervish enjoyed. Dervish's power-source was renewable, so he could remain stationary. Gnome would have to move on once he had exhausted a local mana supply.

I spun around a corner into a side tunnel and was halted. Frozen. Damn.

It was a web of forces holding me like a butterfly. I ceased struggling almost immediately, seeing that it was fruitless in this aspect.

I transformed myself back into human form. But the damned web merely shifted to accommodate the alteration and continued to hold me tightly.

I tried a fire spell, to no avail. I tried sucking the mana loose from the web's own spell, but all I got was a headache. It's a dangerous measure, only effective against sloppy workmanship—and then you get hit with a backlash of forces when it comes loose. The spell held perfectly against my effort, however. I had had to try it, though, because I was feeling desperate, with a touch of claustrophobia tossed in. Also, I thought I'd heard a stone rattle farther up the tunnel.

Next I heard a chuckle, and I recognized the voice as Gnome's.

Then a light rounded a corner, followed by a vaguely human form.

The light drifted in front of him and just off to his left—a globe, casting an orange illumination—touching his hunched, twisted shape with a flamelike glow as he limped toward me. He chuckled again.

"Looks as if I've snared a Phoenix," he finally said.

"Very funny. How about unsnaring me now?" I asked.

"Of course, of course," he muttered, already beginning to gesture.

The trap fell apart. I stepped forward.

"I've been asking around," I told him. "What's this story about Lamia and me?"

He continued his gesturing. I was about to invoke an assault or shielding spell when he stopped, though. I felt none the worse and I assumed it was a final cleanup of his web.

"Lamia? You?" he said. "Oh. Yes. I'd heard you'd run off together. Yes. That was it."

"Where'd you hear it?"

He fixed me with his large, pale eyes.

"Where'd you hear it?" I repeated.

"I don't remember."

"Try."

"Sorry."

" 'Sorry' hell!" I said, taking a step forward. "Somebody's been trying to kill me and—"

He spoke the word that froze me in mid-step. Good spell, that.

"—and he's been regrettably inept," Gnome finished.

"Let me go, damn it!" I said.

"You came into my home and assaulted me."

"Okay, I apologize. Now—"

"Come this way."

He turned his back on me and began walking. Against my will, my body made the necessary movements. I followed.

I opened my mouth to speak a spell of my own. No words came out. I wanted to make a gesture. I was unable to begin it.

"Where are you taking me?" I tried.

The words came perfectly clear. But he didn't bother answering me for a time. The light moved over glistening seams of some metallic material within the sweating walls.

Then, "To a waiting place," he finally said, turning into a corridor to the right, where we splashed through puddles for a time.

"Why?" I asked him. "What are we waiting for?"

He chuckled again. The light danced. He did not reply.

We walked for several minutes. I began finding the thought of all those tons of rock and earth above me very oppressive. A trapped feeling came over me. But I could not even panic properly within the confines of that spell. I began to perspire profusely, despite a cooling draft from ahead.

Then Gnome turned suddenly and was gone, sidling into a narrow cleft I would not even have noticed had I been coming this way alone.

"Come," I heard him say.

My feet followed the light, moved to drift between us here. Automatically, I turned my body. I sidled after him for a good distance before the way widened. The ground dropped roughly, abruptly, and the walls retracted and the light shot on ahead, gaining altitude.

Gnome raised a broad hand and halted me. We were in a small, irregularly shaped chamber—natural, I guessed. The weak light filled it. I looked about. I had no idea why we had stopped here. Gnome's hand moved and he pointed.

I followed the gesture but still could not tell what it was that he was trying to indicate. The light drifted forward then, hovered near a shelflike niche.

Angles altered, shadows shifted. I saw it.

It was a statue of a reclining woman, carved out of coal.

I moved a step nearer. It was extremely well executed and very familiar.

"I didn't know you were an artist . . ." I began, and the realization struck me even as he laughed.

"It is *our* art," he said. "Not the mundane kind."

I had reached forward to touch the dark cheek. I dropped my hand, deciding against it.

"It's Lamia, isn't it?" I asked. "It's really her."

"Of course."

"Why?"

"She has to be someplace, doesn't she?"

"I'm afraid I don't understand."

He chuckled again.

"You're a dead man, Phoenix, and she's the reason. I never thought I'd have the good fortune to have you walk in this way. But now that you have, all of my problems are over. You will rest a few corridors away from here, in a chamber totally devoid of mana. You will wait, while I send for Werewolf to come and kill you. He was in love with Lamia, you know. He is convinced that you ran off with her. Some friend you are. I've been waiting for him to get you for some time now, but either he's clumsy or you're lucky. Perhaps both."

"So it's been Werewolf all along."

"Yes."

"Why? Why do you want him to kill me?"

"It would look badly if I did it myself. I'll be sure that some of the others are here when it happens. To keep my name clean. In fact, I'll dispatch Werewolf personally as soon as he's finished with you. A perfect final touch."

"Whatever I've done to you, I'm willing to set it right."

Gnome shook his head.

"What you did was to set up an irreducible conflict between us," he said. "There is no way to set it right."

"Would you mind telling me what it is that I did?" I asked.

He made a gesture, and I felt a compulsion to turn and make my way back toward the corridor. He followed, both of us preceded by his light.

As we moved, he asked me, "Were you aware that at each Starfall ceremony for the past ten or twelve years the mana content of the Starwind has been a bit higher?"

"It was ten or twelve years ago that I stopped attending them," I answered. "I recall that it was very high that year. Since then, when I've thought to check at the proper time, it has seemed high, yes."

"The general feeling is that the increase will continue. We seem to be entering a new area of space, richer in the stuff."

"That's great," I said, coming into the corridor again. "But what's that got to do with your wanting me out of the way, with your kidnapping Lamia and turning her to coal, with your siccing Werewolf on me?"

"Everything," he said, conducting me down a slanting shaft where the mana diminished with every step. "Even before that, those of us who had been doing careful studies had found indications that the background level of mana is rising."

"So you decided to kill me?"

He led me to a jagged opening in the wall and indicated that I should enter there. I had no choice. My body obeyed him. The light remained outside with him.

"Yes," he said then, motioning me to the rear of the place. "Years ago it would not have mattered—everyone was entitled to any sort of opinion they felt like holding. But now it does. The magic is beginning to return, you fool. I am going to be around long enough to see it happen, to take advantage of it. I could have put up with your democratic sentiments when such a thing seemed only a daydream—"

And then I remembered our argument, on the same matter Elaine had brought up during our ride down the coast.

"—but knowing what I knew and seeing how strongly you felt, I saw you as one who would oppose our inevitable leadership in that new world. Werewolf was another. That is why I set it up for him to destroy you, to be destroyed in return by myself."

"Do all of the others feel as you do?" I asked.

"No, only a few—just as there were only a few like you, Cowboy and the Wolf. The rest will follow whoever takes the lead, as people always do."

"Who are the others?"

He snorted.

"None of your business now," he said.

He began a familiar gesture and muttered something. I felt free of whatever compulsion he had laid upon me, and I lunged forward. The entrance had not changed its appearance, but I slammed up against something—as if the way were blocked by an invisible door.

"I'll see you at the party," he said, inches away, beyond my reach. "In the meantime, try to get some rest."

I felt my consciousness ebbing. I managed to lean and cover my face with my arms before I lost all control. I do not remember hitting the floor.

How long I lay entranced I do not know. Long enough for some of the others to respond to an invitation, it would seem. Whatever reason he gave them for a party, it was sufficient to bring

Knight, Druid, Amazon, Priest, Siren, and Snowman to a large hall somewhere beneath the Cornish hills. I became aware of this by suddenly returning to full consciousness at the end of a long, black corridor without pictures. I pushed myself into a seated position, rubbed my eyes and squinted, trying to penetrate my cell's gloom. Moments later, this was taken care of for me. So I knew that my awakening and the happening that followed were of one piece.

The lighting problem was taken care of for me by the wall's beginning to glow, turning glassy, then becoming a full-color 3-D screen, complete with stereo. That's where I saw Knight, Druid, Amazon, etc. That's how I knew it was a party: There were food and a sound track, arrivals and departures. Gnome passed through it all, putting his clammy hands on everybody, twisting his face into a smile and being a perfect host.

Mana, mana, mana. Weapon, weapon, weapon. Nothing. Shit.

I watched for a long while, waiting. There had to be a reason for his bringing me around and showing me what was going on. I searched all of those familiar faces, overheard snatches of conversation, watched their movements. Nothing special. Why, then, was I awake and witnessing this. It had to be Gnome's doing, yet . . .

When I saw Gnome glance toward the high archway of the hall's major entrance for the third time in as many minutes, I realized that he, too, was waiting.

I searched my cell. Predictably, I found nothing of any benefit to me. While I was looking, though, I heard the noise level rise and I turned back to the images on the wall.

Magics were in progress. The hall must have been mana-rich. My colleagues were indulging themselves in some beautiful spellwork—flowers and faces and colors and vast, exotic, shifting vistas filled the screen now—just as such things must have run in ancient times. Ah! One drop! One drop of mana and I'd be out of here! To run and return? Or to seek immediate retaliation? I could not tell. If there were only some way I could draw it from the vision itself . . .

But Gnome had wrought too well. I could find no weak spot in the working before me. I stopped looking after a few moments, for another reason as well. Gnome was announcing the arrival of another guest.

The sound died and the picture faded at that point. The corridor beyond my cell seemed to grow slightly brighter. I moved toward it. This time my way was not barred, and I continued out into the lighter area. What had happened? Had some obscure force somehow broken Gnome's finely wrought spells?

At any rate, I felt normal now and I would be a fool to remain where he had left me. It occurred to me that this could be part of some higher trap or torture, but still—I had several choices now, which is always an improvement.

I decided to start back in the direction from which we had come earlier, rather than risk blundering into that gathering. Even if there was a lot of mana about there. Better to work my way back, I decided, tie up any mana I could find along the way in the form of protective spells, and get the hell out.

I had proceeded perhaps twenty paces while formulating this resolution. Then the tunnel went through an odd twisting that I couldn't recall. I was still positive we had come this way, though, so I followed it. It grew a bit brighter as I moved along, too, but that seemed all for the better. It allowed me to hurry.

Suddenly, there was a sharp turning that I did not remember at all. I took it and I ran into a screen of pulsing white light, and then I couldn't stop. I was propelled forward, as if squeezed from behind. There was no way that I could halt. I was temporarily blinded by the light. There came a roaring in my ears.

And then it was past, and I was standing in the great hall where the party was being held, having emerged from some side entrance, in time to hear Gnome say, ". . . And the surprise guest is our long-lost brother Phoenix!"

I stepped backward, to retreat into the tunnel from which I had emerged, and I encountered something hard. Turning, I beheld only a blank wall of rock.

"Don't be shy, Phoenix. Come and say hello to your friends," Gnome was saying.

There was a curious babble, but above it from across the way came an animallike snarl and I beheld my old buddy Werewolf, lean and swarthy, eyes blazing, doubtless the guest who was just arriving when the picture had faded.

I felt panic. I also felt mana. But what could I work in only a few seconds' time?

My eyes were pulled by the strange movement in a birdcage on the table beside which Werewolf stood. The others' attitudes showed that many of them had just turned from regarding it.

It registered in an instant.

Within the cage, a nude female figure no more than a hand high was dancing. I recognized it as a spell of torment: The dancer could not stop. The dancing would continue until death, after which the body would still jerk about for some time.

And even from that distance I could recognize the small creature as Elaine.

The dancing part of the spell was simple. So was its undoing. Three words and a gesture. I managed them. By then Werewolf was moving toward me. He was not bothering with a shapeshift to his more fearsome form. I sidestepped as fast as I could and sought for a hold involving his arm and shoulder. He shook it off. He always was stronger and faster than me.

He turned and threw a punch, and I managed to duck and counterpunch to his midsection. He grunted and hit me on the jaw with a weak left. I was already backing away by then. I stopped and tried a kick and he batted it aside, sending me spinning to the floor. I could feel the mana all about me, but there was no time to use it.

"I just learned the story," I said, "and I had nothing to do with Lamia—"

He threw himself upon me. I managed to catch him in the stomach with my knee as he came down.

"Gnome took her. . . ." I got out, getting in two kidney punches before his hands found my throat and began to tighten. "She's coal—"

I caught him once, high on the cheek, before he got his head down.

"Gnome—damn it!" I gurgled.

"It's a lie!" I heard Gnome respond from somewhere nearby, not missing a thing.

The room began to swim about me. The voices became a roaring, as of the ocean. Then a peculiar thing happened to my vision as well: Werewolf's head appeared to be haloed by a coarse mesh. Then it dropped forward, and I realized that his grip had relaxed.

I tore his hands from my throat and struck him once, on the jaw. He rolled away. I tried to also, in the other direction, but settled for struggling into a seated, then a kneeling, then a crouched, position.

I beheld Gnome, raising his hands in my direction, beginning an all-too-familiar and lethal spell. I beheld Werewolf, slowly removing a smashed birdcage from his head and beginning to rise again. I beheld the nude, full-size form of Elaine rushing toward us, her face twisted. . . .

The problem of what to do next was settled by Werewolf's lunge.

It was a glancing blow to the midsection because I was turning when it connected. A dark form came out of my shirt, hovered a moment and dropped floorward: It was the small bottle of djinn Dervish had given me.

Then, just before Werewolf's fist exploded in my face, I saw something slim and white floating toward the back of his neck. I had forgotten that Elaine was second *kyu* in Kyokushinkai—

Werewolf and I both hit the floor at about the same time, I'd guess.

. . . Black to gray to full-color; bumblebee hum to shrieks. I could not have been out for too long. During that time, however, considerable change had occurred.

For one, Elaine was slapping my face.

"Dave! Wake up!" she was saying. "You've got to stop it!"

"What?" I managed.

"That thing from the bottle!"

I propped myself on an elbow—jaw aching, side splitting—and I stared.

There were smears of blood on the nearest wall and table. The party had broken into knots of people, all of whom appeared to be in retreat in various stages of fear or anger. Some were working spells; some were simply fleeing. Amazon had drawn a blade and was holding it before her while gnawing her lower lip. Priest stood at her side, muttering a death spell, which I knew was not going to prove effective. Gnome's head was on the floor near the large archway, eyes open and unblinking. Peals of thunderlike laughter rang through the hall.

Standing before Amazon and Priest was a naked male figure almost ten feet in height, wisps of smoke rising from its dark skin, blood upon its upraised right fist.

"Do something!" Elaine said.

I levered myself a little higher and spoke the words Dervish had taught me, to put the djinn under my control. The fist halted, slowly came unclenched. The great bald head turned toward me, the dark eyes met my own.

"Master . . . ?" it said softly.

I spoke the next words, of acknowledgment Then I climbed to my feet and stood, wavering.

"Back into the bottle now—my command."

Those eyes left my own, their gaze shifting to the floor.

"The bottle is shattered, master," it said.

"So it is. Very well . . ."

I moved to the bar. I found a bottle of Cutty Sark with just a little left in the bottom. I drank it.

"Use this one, then," I said, and I added the words of compulsion.

"As you command," it replied, beginning to dissolve.

I watched the djinn flow into the Scotch bottle and then I corked it.

I turned to face my old colleagues.

"Sorry for the interruption," I said. "Go ahead with your party."

I turned again.

"Elaine," I said. "You okay?"

She smiled.

"Call me Dancer," she said. "I'm your new apprentice."

"A sorcerer needs a feeling for mana and a natural sensitivity to the way spells function," I said.

"How the hell do you think I got my size back?" she asked. "I felt the power in this place, and once you turned off the dancing spell, I was able to figure how to—"

"I'll be damned," I said. "I should have guessed your aptitude back at the cottage, when you grabbed that bone flute."

"See, you need an apprentice to keep you on your toes."

Werewolf moaned, began to stir. Priest and Amazon and Druid approached us. The party did not seem to be resuming. I touched my finger to my lips in Elaine's direction.

"Give me a hand with Werewolf," I said to Amazon. "He's going to need some restraining until I can tell him a few things."

The next time we splashed through the Perseids, we sat on a hilltop in northern New Mexico, my apprentice and I, regarding the crisp, postmidnight sky and the occasional bright cloud-chamber effect within it. Most of the others were below us in a cleared area, the ceremonies concluded now. Werewolf was still beneath the Cornish hills, working with Druid, who recalled something of the ancient flesh-to-coal spell. Another month or so, he'd said, in the message he'd sent.

"'Rash of uncertainty in sky of precision,'" she said.

"What?"

"I'm composing a poem."

"Oh." Then, after a time, I added, "What about?"

"On the occasion of my first Starfall," she replied, "with the mana gain apparently headed for another record."

"There's good and there's bad in that."

"... And the magic is returning and I'm learning the Art."

"Learn faster," I said.

". . . And you and Werewolf are friends again."

"There's that."

". . . You and the whole group, actually."

"No."

"What do you mean?"

"Well, think about it. There are others. We just don't know which of them were in Gnome's corner. They won't want the rest of us around when the magic comes back. Newer, nastier spells—ones it would be hard to imagine now—will become possible when the power rises. We must be ready. This blessing is a very mixed thing. Look at them down there—the ones we were singing with—and see whether you can guess which of them will one day try to kill you. There will be a struggle, and the winners can make the outcome stick for a long time."

She was silent for a while.

"That's about the size of it," I added.

Then she raised her arm and pointed to where a line of fire was traced across the sky. "There's one!" she said. "And another! And another!"

Later, "We can count on Werewolf now," she suggested, "and maybe Lamia, if they can bring her back. Druid, too, I'd guess."

"And Cowboy."

"Dervish?"

"Yeah, I'd say. Dervish."

". . . And I'll be ready."

"Good. We might manage a happy ending at that."

We put our arms about each other and watched the fire fall from the sky.

24 VIEWS OF MT. FUJI,
BY HOKUSAI

1. *Mt. Fuji from Owari*

Kit lives, though he is buried not far from here; and I am dead, though I watch the days-end light pinking cloudstreaks above the mountain in the distance, a tree in the foreground for suitable contrast. The old barrel-man is dust; his cask, too, I daresay. Kit said that he loved me and I said I loved him. We were both telling the truth. But love can mean many things. It can be an instrument of aggression or a function of disease.

My name is Man. I do not know whether my life will fit the forms I move to meet on this pilgrimage. Nor death. Not that tidiness becomes me. So begin anywhere. Either arcing of the circle, like that vanished barrel's hoop, should lead to the same place. I have come to kill. I bear the hidden death, to cast against the secret life. Both are intolerable. I have weighed them. If I were an outsider I do not know which I would choose. But I am here, me, Mari, following the magic footsteps. Each moment is entire, though each requires its past. I do not understand causes, only sequences. And I am long weary of reality-reversal games. Things will have to grow clearer with each successive layer of my journey, and like the delicate play of light upon my magic mountain they must change. I must die a little and live a little each moment.

I begin here because we lived near here. I visited the place earlier. It is, of course, changed. I recall his hand upon my arm, his sometime smiling face, his stacks of books, the cold, flat eye of his computer terminal, his hands again, positioned in meditation, his smile different then. Distant and near. His hands, upon me. The power of his programs, to crack codes, to build them. His hands. Deadly. Who would have thought he would surrender those rapid-striking weapons, delicate instruments, twisters of bodies? Or myself? Paths . . . Hands . . .

I have come back. It is all. I do not know whether it is enough.

The old barrel-maker within the hoop of his labor . . . Half-full, half-empty, half-active, half-passive . . . Shall I make a yin-yang of that famous print? Shall I let it stand for Kit and myself? Shall I view it as the great Zero? Or as infinity? Or is all of this too obvious? One of those observations best left unstated? I am not always subtle. Let it stand. Fuji stands within it. And is it not Fuji one must climb to give an accounting of one's life before God or the gods?

I have no intention of climbing Fuji and accounting for myself, to God or to anything else. Only the insecure and the uncertain require justification. I do what I must. If the deities have any questions they can come down from Fuji and ask me. Otherwise, this is the closest commerce between us. That which transcends should only be admired from afar.

Indeed. I of all people should know this. I, who have tasted transcendence. I know, too, that death is the only god who comes when you call.

Traditionally, the *henro*—the pilgrim—would dress all in white. I do not. White does not become me, and my pilgrimage is a private thing, a secret thing, for so long as I can keep it so. I wear a red blouse today and a light khaki jacket and slacks, tough leather hiking shoes; I have bound my hair; a pack on my back holds my belongings. I do carry a stick, however, partly for the purpose of support, which I require upon occasion; partly, too, as a weapon should the need arise. I am adept at its use in both these functions. A staff is also said to symbolize one's faith in a pilgrimage. Faith is beyond me. I will settle for hope.

In the pocket of my jacket is a small book containing reproductions of twenty-four of Hokusai's forty-six prints of Mt. Fuji. It was a gift, long ago. Tradition also stands against a pilgrim's traveling alone, for practical purposes of safety as well as for companionship. The spirit of Hokusai, then, is my companion, for surely it resides in the places I would visit if it resides anywhere. There is no other companion I would desire at the moment, and what is a Japanese drama without a ghost?

Having viewed this scene and thought my thoughts and felt my feelings, I have begun. I have lived a little, I have died a little. My way will not be entirely on foot. But much of it will be. There are certain things I must avoid in this journey of greetings and farewells. Simplicity is my cloak of darkness, and perhaps the walking will be good for me.

I must watch my health.

2. Mt. Fuji from a Teahouse at Yoshida

I study the print: A soft blueness to the dawn sky, Fuji to the left, seen through the teahouse window by two women; other bowed, drowsing figures like puppets on a shelf. . . .

It is not this way here, now. They are gone, like the barrelmaker—the people, the teahouse, that dawn. Only the mountain and the print remain of the moment. But that is enough.

I sit in the dining room of the hostel where I spent the night, my breakfast eaten, a pot of tea before me. There are other diners present, but none near me. I chose this table because of the window's view, which approximates that of the print. Hokusai, my silent companion, may be smiling. The weather was sufficiently clement for me to have camped again last night, but I am deadly serious in my pilgrimage to vanished scenes in this life-death journey I have undertaken. It is partly a matter of seeking and partly a matter of waiting. It is quite possible that it may be cut short at any time. I hope not, but the patterns of life have seldom corresponded to my hopes—or, for that matter, to logic, desire, emptiness, or any patterns of my own against which I have measured them.

All of this is not the proper attitude and occupation for a fresh day. I will drink my tea and regard the mountain. The sky changes even as I watch. . . .

Changes. . . I must be careful on departing this place. There are precincts to be avoided, precautions to be taken. I have worked out all of my movements—from putting down the cup, rising, turning, recovering my gear, walking—until I am back in the country again. I must still make patterns, for the world is a number-line, everywhere dense. I am taking a small chance in being here.

I am not so tired as I had thought I would be from all yesterday's walking, and I take this as a good sign. I have tried to keep in decent shape, despite everything. A scroll hangs on the wall to my right depicting a tiger, and I want this, too, for a good omen. I was born in the Year of the Tiger, and the strength and silent movements of the big striped cat are what I most need. I drink to you, Shere Khan, cat who walks by himself. We must be hard at the right time, soft at the proper moment. Timing . . .

We'd an almost telepathic bond to begin with, Kit and I. It drew us to each other, grew stronger in our years together. Empathy, proximity, meditation . . . Love? Then love can be a weapon. Spin its coin and it comes up yang. Burn bright, Shere Khan, in the jungle of the heart. This time we are the hunter. Timing is all—and *suki,* the opening . . .

I watch the changes of the sky until a uniform brightness is achieved, holds steady. I finish my tea. I rise and fetch my gear, don my backpack, take up my staff. I head for the short hall which leads to a side door.

"Madam! Madam!"

It is one of the place's employees, a small man with a startled expression.

"Yes?"

He nods at my pack.

"You are leaving us?"

"I am."

"You have not checked out."

"I have left payment for my room in an envelope on the dresser. It says 'cashier' on it. I learned the proper amount last night."

"You must check out at the desk."

"I did not check in at the desk. I am not checking out at the desk. If you wish, I will accompany you back to the room, to show you where I left the payment."

"I am sorry, but it must be done with the cashier."

"I am sorry also, but I have left payment and I will not go to the desk."

"It is irregular. I will have to call the manager."

I sigh.

"No," I say. "I do not want that. I will go to the lobby and handle the checking out as I did the checking in."

I retrace my steps. I turn left toward the lobby.

"Your money," he says. "If you left it in the room you must get it and bring it."

I shake my head.

"I left the key, also."

I enter the lobby. I go to the chair in the corner, the one farthest from the work area. I seat myself.

The small man has followed me.

"Would you tell them at the desk that I wish to check out?" I ask him.

"Your room number . . . ?"

"Seventeen."

He bows slightly and crosses to the counter. He speaks with a woman, who glances at me several times. I cannot hear their words. Finally, he takes a key from her and departs. The woman smiles at me.

"He will bring the key and the money from your room," she says. "Have you enjoyed your stay?"

"Yes," I answer. "If it is being taken care of, I will leave now."

I begin to rise.

"Please wait," she says, "until the paperwork is done and I have given you your receipt."

"I do not want the receipt."

"I am required to give it to you."

I sit back down. I hold my staff between my knees. I clasp it with both hands. If I try to leave now she will probably call the manager. I do not wish to attract even more attention to myself. I wait. I control my breathing. I empty my mind.

After a time the man returns. He hands her the key and the envelope. She shuffles papers. She inserts a form into a machine. There is a brief stutter of keys. She withdraws the form and regards it. She counts the money in my envelope.

"You have the exact amount, Mrs. Smith. Here is your receipt."

She peels the top sheet from the bill.

There comes a peculiar feeling in the air, as if a lightning stroke had fallen here but a second ago. I rise quickly to my feet.

"Tell me," I say, "is this place a private business or part of a chain?"

I am moving forward by then, for I know the answer before she says it. The feeling is intensified, localized.

"We are a chain," she replies, looking about uneasily.

"With central bookkeeping?"

"Yes."

Behind the special place where the senses come together to describe reality I see the form of a batlike epigon taking shape beside her. She already feels its presence but does not understand. My way is *mo chih ch'u*, as the Chinese say—immediate action, without thought or hesitation—as I reach the desk, place my staff upon it at the proper angle, lean forward as if to take my receipt and nudge the staff so that it slides and falls, passing over the countertop, its small metal tip coming to rest against the housing of the computer terminal. Immediately, the overhead lights go out. The epigon collapses and dissipates.

"Power failure," I observe, raising my staff and turning away. "Good day."

I hear her calling for a boy to check the circuit box.

I make my way out of the lobby and visit a rest room, where I take a pill, just in case. Then I return to the short hall, traverse it, and depart the building. I had assumed it would happen sooner or later, so I was not unprepared. The microminiature circuitry within my staff was sufficient to the occasion, and while I would rather it had occurred later, perhaps it was good for me that it happened when it did. I feel more alive, more alert from this demonstration of danger. This feeling, this knowledge, will be of use to me.

And it did not reach me. It accomplished nothing. The basic situation is unchanged. I am happy to have benefited at so small a price.

Still, I wish to be away and into the countryside, where I am strong and the other is weak.

I walk into the fresh day, a piece of my life upon the breakfast moment's mountain.

3. Mt. Fuji from Hodogaya

I find a place of twisted pines along the Tokaido, and I halt to view Fuji through them. The travelers who pass in the first hour or so of my vigil do not look like Hokusai's, but no matter. The horse, the sedan chair, the blue garments, the big hats— faded into the past, traveling forever on the print now. Merchant or nobleman, thief or servant—I choose to look upon them as pilgrims of one sort or another, if only into, through, and out of life. My morbidity, I hasten to add, is excusable, in that I have required additional medication. I am stable now, however, and do not know whether medication or meditation is responsible for my heightened perception of the subtleties of the light. Fuji seems almost to move within my gazing.

Pilgrims . . . I am minded of the wanderings of Matsuo Bashō, who said that all of us are travelers every minute of our lives. I recall also his reflections upon the lagoons of

Matsushima and Kisagata—the former possessed of a cheerful beauty, the latter the beauty of a weeping countenance. I think upon the complexion and expressions of Fuji and I am baffled. Sorrow? Penance? Joy? Exaltation? They merge and shift. I lack the genius of Bashō to capture them all in a single character. And even he . . . I do not know. Like speaks to like, but speech must cross a gulf. Fascination always includes some lack of understanding. It is enough for this moment, to view.

Pilgrims . . . I think, too, of Chaucer as I regard the print. His travelers had a good time. They told each other dirty stories and romances and tales with morals attached. They ate and they drank and they kidded each other. Canterbury was their Fuji. They had a party along the way. The book ends before they arrive. Fitting.

I am not a humorless bitch. It may be that Fuji is really laughing at me. If so, I would like very much to join in. I really do not enjoy moods such as this, and a bit of meditation interruptus would be welcome if only the proper object would present itself. Life's soberer mysteries cannot be working at topspeed all the time. If they can take a break, I want one, too. Tomorrow, perhaps . . .

Damn! My presence must at least be suspected, or the epigon would not have come. Still, I have been very careful. A suspicion is not a certainty, and I am sure that my action was sufficiently prompt to preclude confirmation. My present location is beyond reach as well as knowledge. I have retreated into Hokusai's art.

I could have lived out the rest of my days upon Oregon's quiet coast. The place was not without its satisfactions. But I believe it was Rilke who said that life is a game we must begin playing before we have learned the rules. Do we ever? Are there really rules?

Perhaps I read too many poets.

But something that seems a rule to me requires I make this effort. Justice, duty, vengeance, defense—must I weigh each of these and assign it a percentage of that which moves me? I am here because I am here, because I am following rules—whatever they may be. My understanding is limited to sequences.

His is not. He could always make the intuitive leap. Kit was a scholar, a scientist, a poet. Such riches. I am smaller in all ways.

Kokuzo, guardian of those born in the Year of the Tiger, break this mood. I do not want it. It is not me. Let it be an irritation of old lesions, even a renewal of the demyelination. But do not let it be me. And end it soon. I am sick in my heart and my reasons are good ones. Give me the strength to detach myself from them, Catcher in the Bamboo, lord of those who wear the stripes. Take away the bleakness, gather me together, inform me with strength. Balance me.

I watch the play of light. From somewhere I hear the singing of children. After a time a gentle rain begins to fall. I don my poncho and continue to watch. I am very weary, but I want to see Fuji emerge from the fog which has risen. I sip water and a bit of brandy. Only the barest outline remains. Fuji is become a ghost mountain within a Taoist painting. I wait until the sky begins to darken. I know that the mountain will not come to me again this day, and I must find a dry place to sleep. These must be my lessons from Hodogaya: Tend to the present. Do not try to polish ideals. Have sense enough to get in out of the rain.

I stumble off through a small wood. A shed, a barn, a garage. . . . Anything that stands between me and the sky will do.

After a time I find such a place. No god addresses my dreaming.

4. Mt. Fuji from the Tamagawa

I compare the print with the reality. Not bad this time. The horse and the man are absent from the shore, but there is a small boat out on the water. Not the same sort of boat, to be sure, and I cannot tell whether it bears firewood, but it will suffice. I would be surprised to find perfect congruence. The boat is moving away from me. The pink of the dawn sky is reflected upon the water's farther reaches and from the snow-streaks on Fuji's dark shoulder. The boatman in the print is poling his way outward. Charon? No, I am more cheerful today than I was at Hodogaya. Too small a vessel for the *Narrenschiff*, too slow for the Flying Dutchman. "La navicella." Yes. "La navicella del mio ingegno"—"the little bark of my wit" on which Dante hoisted sail for that second realm, Purgatory. Fuji then . . . Perhaps so. The hells beneath, the heavens above, Fuji between— way station, stopover, terminal. A decent metaphor for a pilgrim who could use a purge. Appropriate. For it contains the fire and the earth as well as the air, as I gaze across the water. Transition, change. I am passing.

The serenity is broken and my reverie ended as a light airplane, yellow in color, swoops out over the water from someplace to my left. Moments later the insectlike buzzing of its single engine reaches me. It loses altitude quickly, skimming low over the water, then turns and traces its way back, this time swinging in above the shoreline. As it nears the point where it will pass closest to me, I detect a flash of reflected light within the cockpit. A lens? If it is, it is too late to cover myself against its questing eye. My hand dips into my breast pocket and withdraws a small gray cylinder of my own. I flick off its endcaps with my thumb-nail as I raise it to peer through the eyepiece. A moment to locate the target, another to focus . . .

The pilot is a man, and as the plane banks away I catch only his unfamiliar profile. Was that a gold earring upon his left ear-lobe?

The plane is away, in the direction from which it had come. Nor does it return.

I am shaken. Someone had flown by for the sole purpose of taking a look at me. How had he found me? And what did he want? If he represents what I fear most, then this is a completely different angle of attack than any I had anticipated.

I clench my hand into a fist and I curse softly. Unprepared. Is that to be the story of my entire life? Always ready for the wrong thing at the right time? Always neglecting the thing that matters most?

Like Kendra?

She is under my protection, is one of the reasons I am here. If I succeed in this enterprise, I will have fulfilled at least a part of my obligation to her. Even if she never knows, even if she never understands . . .

I push all thoughts of my daughter from my mind. If he even suspected . . .

The present. Return to the present. Do not spill energy into the past. I stand at the fourth station of my pilgrimage and someone takes my measure. At the third station an epigon tried to take form. I took extreme care in my return to Japan. I am here on false papers, traveling under an assumed name. The years have altered my appearance somewhat and I have assisted them to the extent of darkening my hair and my complexion, defying my customary preferences in clothing, altering my speech patterns, my gait, my eating habits—all of these things easier for me than most others because of the practice I've had in the past. The past. . . Again, damn it! Could it have worked against me even in this matter? Damn the past! An epigon and a possible human observer this close together. Yes, I am normally paranoid and have been for many years, for good reason. I cannot allow my knowledge of the fact to influence my judgment now, however. I must think clearly.

I see three possibilities. The first is that the flyby means nothing, that it would have occurred had anyone else been standing here—or no one. A joyride, or a search for something else.

It may be so, but my survival instinct will not permit me to accept it. I must assume that this is not the case. Therefore, someone is looking for me. This is either connected with the manifestation of the epigon or it is not. If it is not, a large bag of live bait has just been opened at my feet and I have no idea how to begin sorting through the intertwined twistings. There are so many possibilities from my former profession, though I had considered all of these long closed off. Perhaps I should not have. Seeking there for causes seems an impossible undertaking.

The third possibility is the most frightening: that there is a connection between the epigon and the flight. If things have reached the point where both epigons and human agents can be employed, then I may well be doomed to failure. But even more than this, it will mean that the game has taken on another, awesome dimension, an aspect which I had never considered. It will mean that everyone on Earth is in far greater peril than I had assumed, that I am the only one aware of it and that my personal duel has been elevated to a struggle of global proportions. I cannot take the risk of assigning it to my paranoia now. I must assume the worst.

My eyes overflow. I know how to die. I once knew how to lose with grace and detachment. I can no longer afford this luxury. If I bore any hidden notion of yielding, I banish it now. My weapon is a frail one but I must wield it. If the gods come down from Fuji and tell me, "Daughter, it is our will that you desist," I must still continue in this to the end, though I suffer in the hells of the *Yü Li Ch'ao Chuan* forever. Never before have I realized the force of fate.

I sink slowly to my knees. For it is a god that I must vanquish.

My tears are no longer for myself.

5. *Mt. Fuji from Fukagawa in Edo*

Tokyo. Ginza and confusion. Traffic and pollution. Noise, color and faces, faces, faces. I once loved scenes such as this, but I have been away from cities for too long. And to return to a city such as this is overpowering, almost paralyzing.

Neither is it the old Edo of the print, and I take yet another chance in coming here, though caution rides my every move.

It is difficult to locate a bridge approachable from an angle proper to simulate the view of Fuji beneath it, in the print. The water is of the wrong color and I wrinkle my nose at the smell; this bridge is not that bridge; there are no peaceful fisher-folk here; and gone the greenery. Hokusai exhales sharply and stares as I do at Fuji-san beneath the metal span. His bridge was a graceful rainbow of wood, product of gone days.

Yet there is something to the thrust and dream of any bridge. Hart Crane could find poetry in those of this sort. "Harp and altar, of the fury fused . . ."

And Nietzsche's bridge that is humanity, stretching on toward the superhuman . . .

No. I do not like that one. Better had I never become involved with that which transcends. Let it be my *pons asinorum*.

With but a slight movement of my head I adjust the perspective. Now it seems as if Fuji supports the bridge and without his presence it will be broken like Bifrost, preventing the demons of the past from attacking our present Asgard—or perhaps the demons of the future from storming our ancient Asgard.

I move my head again. Fuji drops. The bridge remains intact. Shadow and substance.

The backfire of a truck causes me to tremble. I am only just arrived and I feel I have been here too long. Fuji seems too distant and I too exposed. I must retreat.

Is there a lesson in this or only a farewell?

A lesson, for the soul of the conflict hangs before my eyes: I will not be dragged across Nietzsche's bridge.

Come, Hokusai, *ukiyo-e* Ghost of Christmas Past, show me another scene.

6. *Mt Fuji from Kajikazawa*

Misted, mystic Fuji over water. Air that comes clean to my nostrils. There is even a fisherman almost where he should be, his pose less dramatic than the original, his garments more modern, above the infinite Fourier series of waves advancing upon the shore.

On my way to this point I visited a small chapel surrounded by a stone wall. It was dedicated to Kwannon, goddess of compassion and mercy, comforter in times of danger and sorrow. I entered. I loved her when I was a girl, until I learned that she was really a man. Then I felt cheated, almost betrayed. She was Kwan Yin in China, and just as merciful, but she came there from India, where she had been a bodhisattva named Avalokitesvara, a man—"the Lord Who Looks Down with Compassion." In Tibet he is Chen-re-zi—"He of the Compassionate Eyes"—who gets incarnated regularly as the Dalai Lama. I did not trust all of this fancy footwork on his/her part, and Kwannon lost something of her enchantment for me with this smattering of history and anthropology. Yet I entered. We revisit the mental landscape of childhood in times of trouble. I stayed for a time and the child within me danced for a moment, then fell still.

I watch the fisherman above those waves, smaller versions of Hokusai's big one, which has always symbolized death for me. The little deaths rolling about him, the man hauls in a silver-sided catch. I recall a tale from the Arabian Nights, another of American Indian origin. I might also see Christian symbolism, or a Jungian archetype. But I remember that Ernest Hemingway told Bernard Berenson that the secret of his greatest book was that there was no symbolism. The sea was the sea, the old man an old man, the boy a boy, the marlin a marlin, and the sharks the same as other sharks. People empower these things themselves, groping beneath the surface, always looking for more. With me it is at least understandable. I spent my earliest years in Japan, my later childhood in the United States. There is a part of me which likes to see things through allusions and touched with mystery. And the American part never trusts anything and is always looking for the real story behind the front one.

As a whole, I would say that it is better not to trust, though lines of interpretation must be drawn at some point before the permutations of causes in which I indulge overflow my mind. I am so, nor will I abandon this quality of character which has served me well in the past. This does not invalidate Hemingway's viewpoint any more than his does mine, for no one holds a monopoly on wisdom. In my present situation, however, I believe that mine has a higher survival potential, for I am not dealing only with *things*, but of something closer to the time-honored Powers and Principalities. I wish that it were not so and that an epigon were only an artifact akin to the ball lightning Tesla studied. But there is something behind it, surely as that yellow airplane had its pilot.

The fisherman sees me and waves. It is a peculiar feeling, this sudden commerce with a point of philosophical departure. I wave back with a feeling of pleasure.

I am surprised at the readiness with which I accept this emotion. I feel it has to do with the general state of my health. All of this fresh air and hiking seems to have strengthened me. My senses are sharper, my appetite better. I have lost some weight and gained some muscle. I have not required medication for several days.

I wonder . . . ?

Is this entirely a good thing? True, I must keep up my strength. I must be ready for many things. But too much strength . . . Could that be self-defeating in terms of my overall plan? A balance, perhaps I should seek a balance—

I laugh, for the first time since I do not remember when. It is ridiculous to dwell on life and death, sickness and health this way, like a character of Thomas Mann's, when I am barely a quarter of the way into my journey. I will need all of my strength—and possibly more—along the way. Sooner or later the bill will be presented. If the timing is off, I must make my own *suki*. In the meantime, I resolve to enjoy what I have.

When I strike, it will be with my final exhalation. I know that. It is a phenomenon familiar to martial artists of many persuasions. I recall the story Eugen Herrigel told, of studying with the *kyudo* master, of drawing the bow and waiting, waiting till something signaled the release of the string. For two years he did this before his *sensei* gave him an arrow. I forget for how long it was after that that he repeated the act with the arrow. Then it all began to come together, the timeless moment of lightness would occur and the arrow would have to fly, would have to fly for the target. It was a long while before he realized that this moment would always occur at the end of an exhalation.

In art, so in life. It seems that many important things, from death to orgasm, occur at the moment of emptiness, at the point of the breath's hesitation. Perhaps all of them are but reflections of death. This is a profound realization for one such as myself, for my strength must ultimately be drawn from my weakness. It is the control, the ability to find that special moment that troubles me most. But like walking, talking, or bearing a child, I trust that something within me knows where it lies. It is too late now to attempt to build it a bridge to my consciousness. I have made my small plans. I have placed them upon a shelf in the back of my mind. I should leave them and turn to other matters.

In the meantime I drink this moment with a deep draught of salty air, telling myself that the ocean is the ocean, the fisherman is a fisherman, and Fuji is only a mountain. Slowly then, I exhale it . . .

7. Mt. Fuji from the Foot

Fire in your guts, winter tracks above like strands of ancient hair. The print is somewhat more baleful than the reality this evening. That awful red tinge does not glow above me against a horde of wild clouds. Still, I am not unmoved. It is difficult, before the ancient powers of the Ring of Fire, not to stand with some trepidation, sliding back through geological eons to times of creation and destruction when new lands were formed. The great outpourings, the bomblike flash and dazzle, the dance of the lightnings like a crown . . .

I meditate on fire and change.

Last night I slept in the precincts of a small Shingon temple, among shrubs trimmed in the shapes of dragons, pagodas, ships, and umbrellas. There were a number of pilgrims of the more conventional sort present at the temple, and the priest performed a fire service—a *goma*—for us. The fires of Fuji remind me, as it reminded me of Fuji.

The priest, a young man, sat at the altar which held the fire basin. He intoned the prayer and built the fire and I watched, completely fascinated by the ritual, as he began to feed the fire with the hundred and eight sticks of wood. These, I have been told, represent the hundred and eight illusions of the soul. While I am not familiar with the full list, I felt it possible that I could come up with a couple of new ones. No matter. He chanted, ringing bells, striking gongs and drums. I glanced at the other *henros*. I saw total absorption upon all of their faces. All but one.

Another figure had joined us, entering with total silence, and he stood in the shadows off to my right. He was dressed all in black, and the wing of a wide, upturned collar masked the lower portion of his face. He was staring at me. When our eyes met, he looked away, focusing his gaze upon the fire. After several moments I did the same.

The priest added incense, leaves, oils. The fire sizzled and spit, the flames leaped, the shadows danced. I began to tremble. There was something familiar about the man. I could not place him, but I wanted a closer look.

I edged slowly to my right during the next ten minutes, as if angling for better views of the ceremony. Suddenly then, I turned and regarded the man again.

I caught him studying me once more, and again he looked away quickly. But the dance of the flames caught him full in the face with light this time, and the jerking of his head withdrew it from the shelter of his collar.

I was certain, in that instant's viewing, that he was the man who had piloted the small yellow plane past me last week at Tamagawa. Though he wore no gold earring there was a shadow-filled indentation in the lobe of his left ear.

But it went beyond that. Having seen him full-face I was certain that I had seen him somewhere before, years ago. I have an unusually good memory for faces, but for some reason I could not place his within its prior context. He frightened me, though, and I felt there was good reason for it.

The ceremony continued until the final stick of wood was placed in the fire and the priest completed his liturgy as it burned and died down. He turned then, silhouetted by the light, and said that it was time for any who were ailing to rub the healing smoke upon themselves if they wished.

Two of the pilgrims moved forward. Slowly, another joined them. I glanced to my right once more. The man was gone, as silently as he had come. I cast my gaze all about the temple. He was nowhere in sight. I felt a touch upon my left shoulder.

Turning, I beheld the priest, who had just struck me lightly with the three-pronged brass ritual instrument which he had used in the ceremony.

"Come," he said, "and take the smoke. You need healing of the left arm and shoulder, the left hip and foot."

"How do you know this?" I asked him.

"It was given to me to see this tonight. Come."

He indicated a place to the left of the altar and I moved to it, startled at his insight, for the places he had named had been growing progressively more numb thoughout the day. I had refrained from taking my medicine, hoping that the attack would remit of its own accord.

He massaged me, rubbing the smoke from the dying fire into the places he had named, then instructing me to continue it on my own. I did so, and some on my head at the end, as is traditional.

I searched the grounds later, but my strange observer was nowhere to be found. I located a hiding place between the feet of a dragon and cast my bedroll there. My sleep was not disturbed.

I awoke before dawn to discover that full sensation had returned to all of my previously numbed areas. I was pleased that the attack had remitted without medication.

The rest of the day, as I journeyed here, to the foot of Fuji, I felt surprisingly well. Even now I am filled with unusual strength and energy, and it frightens me. What if the smoke of the fire ceremony has somehow effected a cure? I am afraid of what it could do to my plans, my resolve. I am not sure that I would know how to deal with it.

Thus, Fuji, Lord of the Hidden Fire, I have come, fit and afraid. I will camp near here tonight. In the morning I will move on. Your presence overwhelms me at this range. I will withdraw for a different, more distant perspective. If I were ever to climb you, would I cast one hundred and eight sticks into your holy furnace, I wonder? I think not. There are some illusions I do not wish to destroy.

8. Mt. Fuji from Tagonoura

I came out in a boat to look back upon the beach, the slopes, and Fuji. I am still in glowing remission. I have resigned myself to it, for now. In the meantime, the day is bright, the sea breeze cool. The boat is rocked by the small deaths, as the fisherman and his sons whom I have paid to bring me out steer it at my request to provide me with the view most approximating that of the print. So much of the domestic architecture in this land recommends to my eye the prows of ships. A convergence of cultural evolution where the message is the medium? The sea is life? Drawing sustenance from beneath the waves we are always at sea? Or, the sea is death, it may rise to blight our lands and claim our lives at any moment? Therefore, we bear this *memento mori* even in the roofs above our heads and the walls which sustain them? Or, this is the sign of our power, over life and death?

Or none of the above. It may seem that I harbor a strong death-wish. This is incorrect. My desires are just the opposite. It may indeed be that I am using Hokusai's prints as a kind of Rorschach for self-discovery, but it is death-fascination rather than death-wish that informs my mind. I believe that this is understandable in one suffering a terminal condition with a very short term to it.

Enough of that for now. It was meant only as a drawing of my blade to examine its edge for keenness. I find that my weapon is still in order and I resheathe it.

Blue-gray Fuji, salted with snow, long angle of repose to my left . . . I never seem to look upon the same mountain twice. You change as much as I myself, yet you remain what you are. Which means that there is hope for me.

I lower my eyes to where we share this quality with the sea, vast living data-net. Like yet unlike, you have fought that sea as I—

Birds. Let me listen and watch them for a time, the air-riders who dip and feed.

I watch the men work with the nets. It is relaxing to behold their nimble movements. After a time, I doze.

Sleeping, I dream, and dreaming I behold the god Kokuzo. It can be no other, for when he draws his blade which flashes like the sun and points it at me, he speaks his name. He repeats it over and over as I tremble before him, but something is wrong. I know that he is telling me something other than his identity. I reach for but cannot grasp the meaning. Then he moves the point of his blade, indicating something beyond me. I turn my head. I behold the man in black—the pilot, the watcher at the *goma*. He is studying me, just as he was that night. What does he seek in my face?

I am awakened by a violent rocking of the boat as we strike a rougher sea. I catch hold of the gunwale beside which I sit. A quick survey of my surroundings shows me that we are in no danger, and I turn my eyes to Fuji. Is he laughing at me? Or is it the chuckle of Hokusai, who squats on his hams beside me tracing naughty pictures in the moisture of the boat's bottom with a long, withered finger?

If a mystery cannot be solved, it must be saved. Later, then. I will return to the message when my mind has moved into a new position.

Soon, another load of fish is being hauled aboard to add to the pungency of this voyage. Wriggle howsoever they will they do not escape the net. I think of Kendra and wonder how she is holding up. I hope that her anger with me has abated. I trust that she has not escaped her imprisonment. I left her in the care of acquaintances at a primitive, isolated commune in the Southwest. I do not like the place, nor am I overfond of its residents. Yet they owe me several large favors—intentionally bestowed against these times—and they will keep her there until certain things come to pass. I see her delicate features, fawn eyes, and silken hair. A bright, graceful girl, used to some luxuries, fond of long soaks and frequent showers, crisp garments. She is probably mud-spattered or dusty at the moment, from slopping hogs, weeding, planting vegetables or harvesting them, or any of a number of basic chores. Perhaps it will be good for her character. She ought to get something from the experience other than preservation from a possibly terrible fate.

Time passes. I take my lunch.

Later, I muse upon Fuji, Kokuzo, and my fears. Are dreams but the tranced mind's theater of fears and desires, or do they sometimes truly reflect unconsidered aspects of reality, perhaps to give warning? To reflect . . . It is said that the perfect mind reflects. The *shintai* in its ark in its shrine is the thing truly sacred to the god—a small mirror—not the images. The sea reflects the sky, in fullness of cloud or blue emptiness. Hamlet-like, one can work many interpretations of the odd, but only one should have a clear outline. I hold the dream in my mind once more, absent all querying. Something is moving . . .

No. I almost had it. But I reached too soon. My mirror is shattered.

Staring shoreward, the matter of synchronicity occurs. There is a new grouping of people. I withdraw my small spy-scope and take its measure, already knowing what I will regard.

Again, he wears black. He is speaking with two men upon the beach. One of the men gestures out across the water, toward us. The distance is too great to make out features clearly, but I know that it is the same man. But now it is not fear that I know. A slow anger begins to burn within my *hara*. I would return to shore and confront him. He is only one man. I will deal with him now. I cannot afford any more of the unknown than that for which I have already provided. He must be met properly, dismissed or accounted for.

I call to the captain to take me ashore immediately. He grumbles. The fishing is good, the day still young. I offer him more money. Reluctantly, he agrees. He calls orders to his sons to put the boat about and head in.

I stand in the bow. Let him have a good look. I send my anger on ahead. The sword is as sacred an object as the mirror.

As Fuji grows before me the man glances in our direction, hands something to the others, then turns and ambles away. No! There is no way to hasten our progress, and at this rate he will be gone before I reach land. I curse. I want immediate satisfaction, not extension of mystery.

And the men with whom he was speaking . . . Their hands go to their pockets, they laugh, then walk off in another direction. Drifters. Did he pay them for whatever information they gave him? So it would seem. And are they heading now for some tavern to drink up the price of my peace of mind? I call out after them but the wind whips my words away. They, too, will be gone by the time I arrive.

And this is true. When I finally stand upon the beach, the only familiar face is that of my mountain, gleaming like a carbuncle in sun's slanting rays.

I dig my nails into my palms but my arms do not become wings.

9. *Mt. Fuji from Naborito*

I am fond of this print: the torii of a Shinto shrine are visible above the sea at low tide, and people dig clams amid the sunken ruins. Fuji of course is visible through the torii. Were it a Christian church beneath the waves puns involving the Clam of God would be running through my mind. Geography saves, however.

And reality differs entirely. I cannot locate the place. I am in the area and Fuji properly situated, but the torii must be long gone and I have no way of knowing whether there is a sunken temple out there.

I am seated on a hillside looking across the water and I am suddenly not just tired but exhausted. I have come far and fast these past several days, and it seems that my exertions have all caught up with me. I will sit here and watch the sea and the sky. At least my shadow, the man in black, has been nowhere visible since the beach at Tagonoura. A young cat chases a moth at the foot of my hill, leaping into the air, white-gloved paws flashing. The moth gains altitude, escapes in a gust of wind. The cat sits for several moments, big eyes staring after it.

I make my way to a declivity I had spotted earlier, where I might be free of the wind. There I lay my pack and cast my bedroll, my poncho beneath it. After removing my shoes I get inside quickly. I seem to have taken a bit of a chill and my limbs are very heavy. I would have been willing to pay to sleep indoors tonight but I am too tired to seek shelter.

I lie here and watch the lights come on in the darkening sky. As usual in cases of extreme fatigue, sleep does not come to me easily. Is this legitimate tiredness or a symptom of something else? I do not wish to take medication merely as a precaution, though, so I try thinking of nothing for a time. This does not work. I am overcome with the desire for a cup of hot tea. In its absence I swallow a jigger of brandy, which warms my insides for a time.

Still, sleep eludes me and I decide to tell myself a story as I did when I was very young and wanted to make the world turn into dream.

So . . . Upon a time during the troubles following the death of the Retired Emperor Sutoku a number of itinerant monks of various persuasions came this way, having met upon the road, traveling to seek respite from the wars, earthquakes, and whirlwinds which so disturbed the land. They hoped to found a religious community and pursue the meditative life in quiet and tranquillity. They came upon what appeared to be a deserted Shinto shrine near the seaside, and there they camped for the night, wondering what plague or misfortune might have carried off its attendants. The place was in good repair and no evidence of violence was to be seen. They discussed then the possibility of making this their retreat, of themselves becoming the shrine's attendants. They grew enthusiastic with the idea and spent much of the night talking over these plans. In the morning, however, an ancient priest appeared from within the shrine, as if to commence a day's duties. The monks asked him the story of the place, and he informed them that once there had been others to assist him in his duties but that they had long ago been taken by the sea during a storm, while about their peculiar devotions one night upon the shore. And no, it was not really a Shinto shrine, though in outward appearance it seemed such. It was actually the temple of a far older religion of which he could well be the last devotee. They were welcome, however, to join him here and learn of it if they so wished. The monks discussed it quickly among themselves and decided that since it was a pleasant-seeming place, it might be well to stay and hear whatever teaching the old man possessed. So they became residents at the strange shrine. The place troubled several of them considerably at first, for at night they seemed to hear the calling of musical voices in the waves and upon the sea wind. And on occasion it seemed as if they could hear the old priest's voice responding to these calls. One night one of them followed the sounds and saw the old man standing upon the beach, his arms upraised. The monk hid himself and later fell asleep in a crevice in the rocks. When he awoke, a full moon stood high in the heavens and the old man was gone. The monk went down to the place where he had stood and there saw many marks in the sand, all of them the prints of webbed feet. Shaken, the monk returned and recited his experience to his fellows. They spent weeks thereafter trying to catch a glimpse of the old man's feet, which were always wrapped and bound. They did not succeed, but after a time it seemed to matter less and less. His teachings influenced them slowly but steadily. They began to assist him in his rituals to the Old Ones, and they learned the name of this promontory and its shrine. It was the last above-sea remnant of a large sunken island, which he assured them rose on certain wondrous occasions to reveal a lost city inhabited by the servants of his masters. The name of the place was R'lyeh and they would be happy to go there one day. By then it seemed a good idea, for they had noticed a certain thickening and extension of the skin between their fingers and toes, the digits themselves becoming sturdier and more elongated. By then, too, they were participating in all of the rites, which grew progressively abominable. At length, after a particularly gory ritual, the old priest's promise was fulfilled in reverse. Instead of the island rising, the promontory sank to join it, bearing the shrine and all of the monks along with it. So their abominations are primarily aquatic now. But once every century or so the whole island does indeed rise up for a night, and troops of them make their way ashore seeking victims. And of course, tonight is the night. . . .

A delicious feeling of drowsiness has finally come over me with this telling, based upon some of my favorite bedtime stories. My eyes are closed. I float on a cottonfilled raft . . . I—

A sound! Above me! Toward the sea. Something moving my way. Slowly, then quickly.

Adrenaline sends a circuit of fire through my limbs. I extend my hand carefully, quietly, and take hold of my staff.

Waiting. Why now, when I am weakened? Must danger always approach at the worst moment?

There is a thump as it strikes the ground beside me, and I let out the breath I have been holding.

It is the cat, little more than a kitten, which I had observed earlier. Purring, it approaches. I reach out and stroke it. It rubs against me. After a time I take it into the bag. It curls up at my side, still purring, warm. It is good to have something that trusts you and wants to be near you. I call the cat R'lyeh. Just for one night.

10. Mt. Fuji from Ejiri

I took the bus back this way. I was too tired to hike. I have taken my medicine as I probably should have been doing all along. Still, it could be several days before it brings me some relief, and this frightens me. I cannot really afford such a condition. I am not certain what I will do, save that I must go on.

The print is deceptive, for a part of its force lies in the effects of a heavy wind. Its skies are gray, Fuji is dim in the background, the people on the road and the two trees beside it all suffer from the wind's buffeting. The trees bend, the people clutch at their garments, there is a hat high in the air and some poor scribe or author has had his manuscript snatched skyward to flee from him across the land (reminding me of an old cartoon—Editor to Author: "A funny thing happened to your manuscript during the St. Patrick's Day Parade"). The scene which confronts me is less active at a meteorological level. The sky is indeed overcast but there is no wind, Fuji is darker, more clearly delineated than in the print, there are no struggling pedestrians in sight. There are many more trees near at hand. I stand near a small grove, in fact. There are some structures in the distance which are not present in the picture.

I lean heavily upon my staff. Live a little, die a little. I have reached my tenth station and I still do not know whether Fuji is giving me strength or taking it from me. Both, perhaps.

I head off into the wood, my face touched by a few raindrops as I go. There are no signs posted and no one seems to be about. I work my way back from the road, coming at last to a small clear area containing a few rocks and boulders. It will do as a campsite. I want nothing more than to spend the day resting.

I soon have a small fire going, my tiny teapot poised on rocks above it. A distant roll of thunder adds variety to my discomfort, but so far the rain has held off. The ground is damp, however. I spread my poncho and sit upon it while I wait. I hone a knife and put it away. I eat some biscuits and study a map. I suppose I should feel some satisfaction, in that things are proceeding somewhat as I intended. I wish that I could, but I do not.

An unspecified insect which has been making buzzing noises somewhere behind me ceases its buzzing. I hear a twig snap a moment later. My hand snakes out to fall upon my staff.

"Don't," says a voice at my back.

I turn my head. He is standing eight or ten feet from me, the man in black, earring in place, his right hand in his jacket pocket. And it looks as if there is more than his hand in there, pointed at me.

I remove my hand from my staff and he advances. With the side of his foot he sends the staff partway across the clearing, out of my reach. Then he removes his hand from his pocket, leaving behind whatever it held. He circles slowly to the other side of the fire, staring at me the while.

He seats himself upon a boulder, lets his hands rest upon his knees.

"Mari?" he asks then.

I do not respond to my name, but stare back. The light of Kokuzo's dream-sword flashes in my mind, pointing at him, and I hear the god speaking his name only not quite.

"Kotuzov!" I say then.

The man in black smiles, showing that the teeth I had broken once long ago are now neatly capped.

"I was not so certain of you at first either," he says.

Plastic surgery has removed at least a decade from his face, along with a lot of weathering and several scars. He is different about the eyes and cheeks, also. And his nose is smaller. It is a considerable improvement over the last time we met.

"Your water is boiling," he says then. "Are you going to offer me a cup of tea?"

"Of course," I reply, reaching for my pack, where I keep an extra cup.

"Slowly."

"Certainly."

I locate the cup, I rinse them both lightly with hot water, I prepare the tea.

"No, don't pass it to me," he says, and he reaches forward and takes the cup from where I had filled it.

I suppress a desire to smile.

"Would you have a lump of sugar?" he asks.

"Sorry."

He sighs and reaches into his other pocket, from which he withdraws a small flask.

"Vodka? In tea?"

"Don't be silly. My tastes have changed. It's Wild Turkey liqueur, a wonderful sweetener. Would you care for some?"

"Let me smell it."

There is a certain sweetness to the aroma.

"All right," I say, and he laces our tea with it.

We taste the tea. Not bad.

"How long has it been?" he asks.

"Fourteen years—almost fifteen," I tell him. "Back in the eighties."

"Yes."

He rubs his jaw. "I'd heard you'd retired."

"You heard right. It was about a year after our last—encounter."

"Turkey—yes. You married a man from your Code Section."

I nod.

"You were widowed three or four years later. Daughter born after your husband's death. Returned to the States. Settled in the country. That's all I know."

"That's all there is."

He takes another drink of tea.

"Why did you come back here?"

"Personal reasons. Partly sentimental."

"Under a false identity?"

"Yes. It involves my husband's family. I don't want them to know I'm here."

"Interesting. You mean that they would watch arrivals as closely as we have?"

"I didn't know you watched arrivals here."

"Right now we do."

"You've lost me. I don't know what's going on."

There is another roll of thunder. A few more drops spatter about us.

"I would like to believe that you are really retired," he says. "I'm getting near that point myself, you know."

"I have no reason to be back in business. I inherited a decent amount, enough to take care of me and my daughter."

He nods.

"If I had such an inducement I would not be in the field," he says. "I would rather sit home and read, play chess, eat and drink regularly. But you must admit it is quite a coincidence your being here when the future success of several nations is being decided."

I shake my head.

"I've been out of touch with a lot of things."

"The Osaka Oil Conference. It begins two weeks from Wednesday. You were planning perhaps to visit Osaka at about that time?"

"I will not be going to Osaka."

"A courier then. Someone from there will meet you, a simple tourist, at some point in your travels, to convey—"

"My God! Do you think everything's a conspiracy, Boris? I am just taking care of some personal problems and visiting some places that mean something to me. The conference doesn't."

"All right" He finishes his tea and puts the cup aside. "You know that we know you are here. A word to the Japanese authorities that you are traveling under false papers and they will kick you out. That would be simplest. No real harm done and one agent nullified. Only it would be a shame to spoil your trip if you are indeed only a tourist. . . ."

A rotten thought passes through my mind as I see where this is leading, and I know that my thought is far rottener than his. It is something I learned from a strange old woman I once worked with who did not look like an old woman.

I finish my tea and raise my eyes. He is smiling.

"I will make us some more tea," I say.

I see that the top button of my shirt comes undone while I am bent partly away from him. Then I lean forward with his cup and take a deep breath.

"You would consider not reporting me to the authorities?"

"I might," he says. "I think your story is probably true. And even if it is not, you would not take the risk of transporting anything now that I know about you."

"I really want to finish this trip," I say, blinking a few extra times. "I would do anything not to be sent back now."

He takes hold of my hand.

"I am glad you said that, Maryushka," he replies. "I am lonely, and you are still a fine-looking woman."

"You think so?"

"I always thought so, even that day you bashed in my teeth."

"Sorry about that. It was strictly business, you know."

His hand moves to my shoulder.

"Of course. They looked better when they were fixed than they had before, anyway."

He moves over and sits beside me.

"I have dreamed of doing this many times," he tells me, as he unfastens the rest of the buttons on my shirt and unbuckles my belt.

He rubs my belly softly. It is not an unpleasant feeling. It has been a long time.

Soon we are fully undressed. He takes his time, and when he is ready I welcome him between my legs. All right, Boris. I give the ride, you take the fall. I could almost feel a little guilty about it. You are gentler than I'd thought you would be. I commence the proper breathing pattern, deep and slow. I focus my attention on my *hara* and his, only inches away. I feel our energies, dreamlike and warm, moving. Soon, I direct their flow. He feels it only as pleasure, perhaps more draining than usual. When he has done, though . . .

"You said you had some problem?" he inquires in that masculine coital magnanimity generally forgotten a few minutes afterward. "If it is something I could help you with, I have a few days off, here and there. I like you, Maryushka."

"It's something I have to do myself. Thanks anyway."

I continue the process.

Later, as I dress myself, he lies there looking up at me.

"I must be getting old, Maryushka," he reflects. "You have tired me. I feel I could sleep for a week."

"That sounds about right," I say. "A week and you should be feeling fine again."

"I do not understand . . ."

"You've been working too hard, I'm sure. That conference . . ."

He nods.

"You are probably right. You are not really involved . . . ?"

"I am really not involved."

"Good."

I clean the pot and my cups. I restore them to my pack.

"Would you be so kind as to move, Boris dear? I'll be needing the poncho very soon, I think."

"Of course."

He rises slowly and passes it to me. He begins dressing. His breathing is heavy.

"Where are you going from here?"

"Mishima-goe," I say, "for another view of my mountain."

He shakes his head. He finishes dressing and seats himself on the ground, his back against a treetrunk. He finds his flask and takes a swallow. He extends it then.

"Would you care for some?"

"Thank you, no. I must be on my way."

I retrieve my staff. When I look at him again, he smiles faintly, ruefully.

"You take a lot out of a man, Maryushka."

"I had to," I say.

I move off. I will hike twenty miles today, I am certain. The rain begins to descend before I am out of the grove; leaves rustle like the wings of bats.

*   *   *

11. Mt. Fuji from Mishima-goe

Sunlight. Clean air. The print shows a big cryptameria tree, Fuji looming behind it, crowned with smoke. There is no smoke today, but I have located a big cryptameria and positioned myself so that it cuts Fuji's shoulder to the left of the cone. There are a few clouds, not so popcorny as Hokusai's smoke (he shrugs at this), and they will have to do.

My stolen *ki* still sustains me, though the medication is working now beneath it. Like a transplanted organ, my body will soon reject the borrowed energy. By then, though, the drugs should be covering for me.

In the meantime, the scene and the print are close to each other. It is a lovely spring day. Birds are singing, butterflies stitch the air in zigzag patterns; I can almost hear the growth of plants beneath the soil. The world smells fresh and new. I am no longer being followed. Hello to life again.

I regard the huge old tree and listen for its echoes down the ages: Yggdrasil, the Golden Bough, the Yule tree, the Tree of the Knowledge of Good and Evil, the Bo beneath which Lord Gautama found his soul and lost it. . . .

I move forward to run my hand along its rough bark.

From that position I am suddenly given a new view of the valley below. The fields look like raked sand, the hills like rocks, Fuji a boulder. It is a garden, perfectly laid out. . . .

Later I notice that the sun has moved. I have been standing here for hours. My small illumination beneath a great tree.

Older than my humanity, I do not know what I can do for it in return.

Stooping suddenly, I pick up one of its cones. A tiny thing, for such a giant. It is barely the size of my little fingernail. Delicately incised, as if sculpted by fairies.

I put it in my pocket. I will plant it somewhere along my way.

I retreat then, for I hear the sound of approaching bells and I am not yet ready for humanity to break my mood. But there was a small inn down the road which does not look to be part of a chain. I will bathe and eat there and sleep in a bed tonight.

I will still be strong tomorrow.

12. Mt. Fuji from Lake Kawaguchi
Reflections.

This is one of my favorite prints in the series: Fuji as seen from across the lake and reflected within it. There are green hills at either hand, a small village upon the far shore, a single small boat in sight upon the water. The most fascinating feature of the print is that the reflection of Fuji is not the same as the original; its position is wrong, its slope is wrong, it is snow-capped and the surface view of Fuji itself is not.

I sit in the small boat I have rented, looking back. The sky is slightly hazy, which is good. No glare to spoil the reflection. The town is no longer as quaint as in the print, and it has grown. But I am not concerned with details of this sort. Fuji is reflected more perfectly in my viewing, but the doubling is still a fascinating phenomenon for me.

Interesting, too . . . In the print the village is not reflected, nor is there an image of the boat in the water. The only reflection is Fuji's. There is no sign of humanity.

I see the reflected buildings near the water's edge. And my mind is stirred by other images than those Hokusai would have known. Of course drowned R'lyeh occurs to me, but the place and the day are too idyllic. It fades from mind almost immediately, to be replaced by sunken Ys, whose bells still toll the hours beneath the sea. And Selma Lagerloff's *Nils Holgersson*, the tale of the shipwrecked sailor who finds himself in a sunken city at the bottom of the sea—a place drowned to punish its greedy, arrogant inhabitants, who still go about their business of cheating each other, though they are all of them dead. They wear rich, old-fashioned clothes and conduct their business as they once did above in this strange land beneath the waves. The sailor is drawn to them, but he knows that he must not be discovered or he will be turned into one of them, never to return to the earth, to see the sun. I suppose I think of this old children's story because I understand now how the sailor must have felt. My discovery, too, could result in a transformation I do not desire.

And of course, as I lean forward and view my own features mirrored in the water, there is the world of Lewis Carroll beneath its looking-glass surface. To be an Ama diving girl and descend . . . To spin downward, and for a few minutes to know the inhabitants of a land of paradox and great charm . . .

Mirror, mirror, why does the real world so seldom cooperate with our aesthetic enthusiasms?

Halfway finished. I reach the midpoint of my pilgrimage to confront myself in a lake. It is a good time and place to look upon my own countenance, to reflect upon all of the things which have brought me here, to consider what the rest of the journey may hold. Though images may sometimes lie. The woman who looks back at me seems composed, strong, and better-looking than I had thought she would. I like you, Kawaguchi, lake with a human personality. I flatter you with literary compliments and you return the favor.

Meeting Boris lifted a burden of fear from my mind. No human agents of my nemesis have risen to trouble my passage. So the odds have not yet tipped so enormously against me as they might.

Fuji and image. Mountain and soul. Would an evil thing cast no reflection down here—some dark mountain where terrible deeds were performed throughout history? I am reminded that Kit no longer casts a shadow, has no reflection.

Is he truly evil, though? By my lights he is. Especially if he is doing the things I think he is doing.

He said that he loved me, and I did love him, once. What will he say to me when we meet again, as meet we must?

It will not matter. Say what he will, I am going to try to kill him. He believes that he is invincible, indestructible. I do not, though I do believe that I am the only person on earth capable of destroying him. It took a long time for me to figure the means, an even longer time before the decision to try it was made for me. I must do it for Kendra as well as for myself. The rest of the world's population comes third.

I let my fingers trail in the water. Softly, I begin to sing an old song, a love song. I am loath to leave this place. Will the second half of my journey be a mirrorimage of the first? Or will I move beyond the looking-glass, to pass into that strange realm where he makes his home?

I planted the cryptameria's seed in a lonesome valley yesterday afternoon. Such a tree will look elegant there one day, outliving nations and armies, madmen and sages.

I wonder where R'lyeh is? She ran off in the morning after breakfast, perhaps to pursue a butterfly. Not that I could have brought her with me.

I hope that Kendra is well. I have written her a long letter explaining many things. I left it in the care of an attorney friend, who will be sending it to her one day in the not too distant future.

The prints of Hokusai . . . They could outlast the cryptameria. I will not be remembered for any works.

Drifting between the worlds I formulate our encounter for the thousandth time. He will have to be able to duplicate an old trick to get what he wants. I will have to perform an even older one to see that he doesn't get it. We are both out of practice.

It has been long since I read *The Anatomy of Melancholy*. It is not the sort of thing I've sought to divert me in recent years. But I recall a line or two as I see fish dart by: "Polycrates Samius, that flung his ring into the sea, because he would participate in the discontent of others, and had it miraculously restored to him again shortly after, by a fish taken as he angled, was not free from melancholy dispositions. No man can cure himself . . ." Kit threw away his life and gained it. I kept mine and lost it. Are rings ever really returned to the proper people? And what about a woman curing herself? The cure I seek is a very special one.

Hokusai, you have shown me many things. Can you show me an answer?

Slowly, the old man raises his arm and points to his mountain. Then he lowers it and points to the mountain's image.

I shake my head. It is an answer that is no answer. He shakes his head back at me and points again.

The clouds are massing high above Fuji, but that is no answer. I study them for a long while but can trace no interesting images within.

Then I drop my eyes. Below me, inverted, they take a different form. It is as if they depict the clash of two armed hosts. I watch in fascination as they flow together, the forces from my right gradually rolling over and submerging those to my left. Yet in so doing, those from my right are diminished.

Conflict? That is the message? And both sides lose things they do not wish to lose? Tell me something I do not already know, old man.

He continues to stare. I follow his gaze again, upward. Now I see a dragon, diving into Fuji's cone.

I look below once again. No armies remain, only carnage; and here the dragon's tail becomes a dying warrior's arm holding a sword.

I close my eyes and reach for it. A sword of smoke for a man of fire.

13. Mt. Fuji from Koishikawa in Edo

Snow, on the roofs of houses, on evergreens, on Fuji—just beginning to melt in places, it seems. A windowful of women—geishas, I would say—looking out at it, one of them pointing at three dark birds high in the pale sky. My closest view of Fuji to that in the print is unfortunately snowless, geishaless, and sunny.

Details . . .

Both are interesting, and superimposition is one of the major forces of aesthetics. I cannot help but think of the hot-spring geisha Komako in *Snow Country*—Yasunari Kawabata's novel of loneliness and wasted, fading beauty—which I have always felt to be the great anti-love story of Japan. This print brings the entire tale to mind for me. The denial of love. Kit was no Shimamura, for he did want me, but only on his own highly specialized terms, terms that must remain unacceptable to me. Selfishness or selflessness? It is not important . . .

And the birds at which the geisha points . . . ? "Thirteen Ways of Looking at a Blackbird?" To the point. We could never agree on values.

The Two Corbies? And throw in Ted Hughes's pugnacious Crow? Perhaps so, but I won't draw straws.—An illusion for every allusion, and where's yesterday's snow?

I lean upon my staff and study my mountain. I wish to make it to as many of my stations as possible before ordering the confrontation. Is that not fair? Twenty-four ways of looking at Mt. Fuji. It struck me that it would be good to take one thing in life and regard it from many viewpoints, as a focus for my being, and perhaps as a penance for alternatives missed.

Kit, I am coming, as you once asked of me, but by my own route and for my own reasons. I wish that I did not have to, but you have deprived me of a real choice in this matter. Therefore, my action is not truly my own, but yours. I am become then your own hand turned against you, representative of a kind of cosmic aikido.

I make my way through town after dark, choosing only dark streets where the businesses are shut down. That way I am safe. When I must enter town I always find a protected spot for the day and do my traveling on these streets at night.

I find a small restaurant on the corner of such a one and I take my dinner there. It is a noisy place but the food is good. I also take my medicine, and a little saké.

Afterward, I indulge in the luxury of walking rather than take a taxi. I've a long way to go, but the night is clear and star-filled and the air is pleasant.

I walk for the better part of ten minutes, listening to the sounds of traffic, music from some distant radio or tape deck, a cry from another street, the wind passing high above me and rubbing its rough fur upon the sides of buildings.

Then I feel a sudden ionization in the air.

Nothing ahead. I turn, spinning my staff into a guard position.

An epigon with a six-legged canine body and a head like a giant fiery flower emerges from a doorway and sidles along the building's front in my direction.

I follow its progress with my staff, feinting as soon as it is near enough. I strike, unfortunately with the wrong tip, as it comes on. My hair begins to rise as I spin out of its way, cutting, retreating, turning, then striking again. This time the metal tip passes into that floral head.

I had turned on the batteries before I commenced my attack. The charge creates an imbalance. The epigon retreats, head ballooning. I follow and strike again, this time mid-body. It swells even larger, then collapses in a shower of sparks. But I am already turning away and striking again, for I had become aware of the approach of another even as I was dealing with the first.

This one advances in kangaroolike bounds. I brush it by with my staff, but its long bulbous tail strikes me as it passes. I recoil involuntarily from the shock I receive, my reflexes spinning the staff before me as I retreat. It turns quickly and rears then. This one is a quadruped, and its raised forelimbs are fountains of fire. Its faceful of eyes blazes and hurts to look upon.

It drops back onto its haunches then springs again.

I roll beneath it and attack as it descends. But I miss, and it turns to attack again even as I continue thrusting. It springs and I turn aside, striking upward. It seems that I connect, but I cannot be certain.

It lands quite near me, raising its forelimbs. But this time it does not spring. It simply falls forward, hind feet making a rapid shuffling movement the while, the legs seeming to adjust their lengths to accommodate a more perfect flow.

As it comes on, I catch it square in the midsection with the proper end of my staff. It keeps coming, or falling, even as it flares and begins to disintegrate. Its touch stiffens me for a moment, and I feel the flow of its charge down my shoulder and across my breast. I watch it come apart in a final photoflash instant and be gone.

I turn quickly again but there is no third emerging from the doorway. None overhead either. There is a car coming up the street, slowing, however. No matter. The terminal's potential must be exhausted for the moment, though I am puzzled by the consideration of how long it must have been building to produce the two I just dispatched. It is best that I be away quickly now.

As I resume my progress, though, a voice calls to me from the car, which has now drawn up beside me:

"Madam, a moment please."

It is a police car, and the young man who has addressed me wears a uniform and a very strange expression.

"Yes, officer?" I reply.

"I saw you just a few moments ago," he says. "What were you doing?"

I laugh.

"It is such a fine evening," I say then, "and the street was deserted. I thought I would do a *kata* with my *bo.*"

"I thought at first that something was attacking you, that I saw something . . ."

"I am alone," I say, "as you can see."

He opens the door and climbs out. He flicks on a flashlight and shines its beam across the sidewalk, into the doorway.

"Were you setting off fireworks?"

"No."

"There were some sparkles and flashes."

"You must be mistaken."

He sniffs the air. He inspects the sidewalk very closely, then the gutter.

"Strange," he says. "Have you far to go?"

"Not too far."

"Have a good evening."

He gets back into the car. Moments later it is headed up the street.

I continue quickly on my way. I wish to be out of the vicinity before another charge can be built. I also wish to be out of the vicinity simply because being here makes me uneasy.

I am puzzled at the ease with which I was located.

What did I do wrong?

"My prints," Hokusai seems to say, after I have reached my destination and drunk too much brandy. "Think, daughter, or they will trap you."

I try, but Fuji is crushing my head, squeezing off thoughts. Epigons dance on his slopes. I pass into a fitful slumber.

In tomorrow's light perhaps I shall see . . .

14. Mt. Fuji from Meguro in Edo

Again, the print is not the reality for me. It shows peasants amid a rustic village, terraced hillsides, a lone tree jutting from the slope of the hill to the right, a snowcapped Fuji partly eclipsed by the base of the rise.

I could not locate anything approximating it, though I do have a partly blocked view of Fuji—blocked in a similar manner, by a slope—from this bench I occupy in a small park. It will do.

Partly blocked, like my thinking. There is something I should be seeing but it is hidden from me. I felt it the moment the epigons appeared, like the devils sent to claim Faust's soul. But I never made a pact with the Devil . . . just Kit, and it was called marriage. I had no way of knowing how similar it would be.

Now . . . What puzzles me most is how my location was determined despite my precautions. My head-on encounter must be on my terms, not anyone else's. The reason for this transcends the personal, though I will not deny the involvement of the latter.

In *Hagakure,* Yamamoto Tsunetomo advised that the Way of the Samurai is the Way of Death, that one must live as though one's body were already dead in order to gain full freedom. For me, this attitude is not so difficult to maintain. The freedom part is more complicated, however; when one no longer understands the full nature of the enemy, one's actions are at least partly conditioned by uncertainty.

My occulted Fuji is still there in his entirety, I know, despite my lack of full visual data. By the same token I ought to be able to extend the lines I have seen thus far with respect to the power which now devils me. Let us return to death. There seems to be something there, though it also seems that there is only so much you can say about it and I already have.

Death . . . Come gentle . . . We used to play a parlor game, filling in bizarre causes on imaginary death certificates: "Eaten by the Loch Ness monster." "Stepped on by Godzilla." "Poisoned by a ninja." "Translated."

Kit had stared at me, brow knitting, when I'd offered that last one.

"What do you mean 'translated'?" he asked.

"Okay, you can get me on a technicality," I said, "but I still think the effect would be the same. 'Enoch was translated that he should not see death'—Paul's Epistle to the Hebrews, 11:5."

"I don't understand."

"It means to convey directly to heaven without messing around with the customary termination here on earth. Some Moslems believe that the Mahdi was translated."

"An interesting concept," he said. "I'll have to think about it."

Obviously, he did.

I've always thought that Kurosawa could have done a hell of a job with *Don Quixote*. Say there is this old gentleman living in modern times, a scholar, a man who is fascinated by the early days of the samurai and the Code of Bushido. Say that he identifies so strongly with these ideals that one day he loses his senses and comes to believe that he *is* an old-time samurai. He dons some ill-fitting armor he had collected, takes up his *katana,* goes forth to change the world. Ultimately, he is destroyed by it, but he holds to the Code. That quality of dedication sets him apart and ennobles him, for all of his ludicrousness. I have never felt that *Don Quixote* was merely a parody of chivalry, especially not after I'd learned that Cervantes had served under Don John of Austria at the battle of Lepanto. For it might be argued that Don John was the last European to be guided by the medieval code of chivalry. Brought up on medieval romances, he had conducted his life along these lines. What did it matter if the medieval knights themselves had not? He believed and he acted on his belief. In anyone else it might simply have been amusing, save that time and circumstance granted him the opportunity to act on several large occasions, and he won. Cervantes could not but have been impressed by his old commander, and who knows how this might have influenced his later literary endeavor? Ortega y Gasset referred to Quixote as a Gothic Christ. Dostoevsky felt the same way about him, and in his attempt to portray a Christ-figure in Prince Myshkin he, too, felt that madness was a necessary precondition for this state in modern times.

All of which is preamble to stating my belief that Kit was at least partly mad. But he was no Gothic Christ. An Electronic Buddha would be much closer.

"Does the data-net have the Buddha-nature?" he asked me one day.

"Sure," I said. "Doesn't everything?" Then I saw the look in his eyes and added, "How the hell should I know?"

He grunted then and reclined his resonance couch, lowered the induction helmet, and continued his computer-augmented analysis of a Lucifer cipher with a 128-bit key. Theoretically, it would take thousands of years to crack it by brute force, but the answer was needed within two weeks. His nervous system coupled with the data-net, he was able to deliver.

I did not notice his breathing patterns for some time. It was not until later that I came to realize that after he had finished his work, he would meditate for increasingly long periods of time while still joined with the system.

When I realized this, I chided him for being too lazy to turn the thing off.

He smiled.

"The flow," he said. "You do not fixate at one point. You go with the flow."

"You could throw the switch before you go with the flow and cut down on our electric bill."

He shook his head, still smiling.

"But it is that particular flow that I am going with. I am getting farther and farther into it. You should try it sometime. There have been moments when I felt I could translate myself into it."

"Linguistically or theologically?"

"Both," he replied.

And one night he did indeed go with the flow. I found him in the morning—sleeping, I thought—in his resonance couch, the helmet still in place. This time, at least, he had shut down our terminal. I let him rest. I had no idea how late he might have been working. By evening, though, I was beginning to grow concerned and I tried to rouse him. I could not. He was in a coma.

Later, in the hospital, he showed a flat EEG. His breathing had grown extremely shallow, his blood pressure was very low, his pulse feeble. He continued to decline during the next two days. The doctors gave him every test they could think of but could determine no cause for his condition. In that he had once signed a document requesting that no heroic measures be taken to prolong his existence should something irreversible take him, he was not hooked up to respirators and pumps and IVs after his heart had stopped beating for the fourth time. The autopsy was unsatisfactory. The death certificate merely showed: "Heart stoppage. Possible cerebrovascular accident." The latter was pure speculation. They had found no sign of it. His organs were not distributed to the needy as he had once requested, for fear of some strange new virus which might be transmitted.

Kit, like Marley, was dead to begin with.

*   *   *

15. Mt. Fuji from Tsukudajima in Edo

Blue sky, a few low clouds, Fuji across the bay's bright water, a few boats and an islet between us. Again, dismissing time's changes, I find considerable congruence with reality. Again, I sit within a small boat. Here, however, I've no desire to dive beneath the waves in search of sunken splendor or to sample the bacteria-count with my person.

My passage to this place was direct and without incident. Preoccupied I came. Preoccupied I remain. My vitality remains high. My health is no worse. My concerns also remain the same, which means that my major question is still unanswered.

At least I feel safe out here on the water. "Safe," though, is a relative term. "Safer" then, than I felt ashore and passing among possible places of ambush. I have not really felt safe since that day after my return from the hospital. . . .

I was tired when I got back home, following several sleepless nights. I went directly to bed. I did not even bother to note the hour, so I have no idea how long I slept.

I was awakened in the dark by what seemed to be the ringing of the telephone. Sleepily, I reached for the instrument, then realized that it was not actually ringing. Had I been dreaming? I sat up in bed. I rubbed my eyes. I stretched. Slowly, the recent past filled my mind and I knew that I would not sleep again for a time. A cup of tea, I decided, might serve me well now. I rose, to go to the kitchen and heat some water.

As I passed through the work area, I saw that one of the

CRTs for our terminal was lit. I could not recall its having been on but I moved to turn it off.

I saw then that its switch was not turned on. Puzzled, I looked again at the screen and for the first time realized that there was a display present:

MARI.
ALL IS WELL.
I AM TRANSLATED.
USE THE COUCH AND THE HELMET.
KIT

I felt my fingers digging into my cheeks and my chest was tight from breath retained. Who had done this? How? Was it perhaps some final delirious message left by Kit himself before he went under?

I reached out and flipped the ON-OFF switch back and forth several times, leaving it finally in the OFF position.

The display faded but the light remained on. Shortly, a new display was flashed upon the screen:

YOU READ ME. GOOD.
IT IS ALL RIGHT. I LIVE.
I HAVE ENTERED THE DATA-NET.
SIT ON THE COUCH AND USE THE HELMET.
I WILL EXPLAIN EVERYTHING.

I ran from the room. In the bathroom I threw up, several times. Then I sat upon the toilet, shaking. Who would play such a horrible joke upon me? I drank several glasses of water and waited for my trembling to subside.

When it had, I went directly to the kitchen, made the tea, and drank some. My thoughts settled slowly into the channels of analysis. I considered possibilities. The one that seemed more likely than most was that Kit had left a message for me and that my use of the induction interface gear would trigger its delivery. I wanted that message, whatever it might be, but I did not know whether I possessed sufficient emotional fortitude to receive it at the moment.

I must have sat there for the better part of an hour. I looked out the window once and saw that the sky was growing light. I put down my cup. I returned to the work area.

The screen was still lit. The message, though, had changed:

DO NOT BE AFRAID.
SIT ON THE COUCH AND USE THE HELMET.
THEN YOU WILL UNDERSTAND.

I crossed to the couch. I sat on it and reclined it. I lowered the helmet. At first there was nothing but field noise.

Then I felt his presence, a thing difficult to describe in a world customarily filled only with data flows. I waited. I tried to be receptive to whatever he had somehow left imprinted for me.

"I am not a recording, Mari," he seemed to say to me then. "I am really here."

I resisted the impulse to flee. I had worked hard for this composure and I meant to maintain it.

"I made it over," he seemed to say. "I have entered the net. I am spread out through many places. It is pure kundalini. I am nothing but flow. It is wonderful. I will be forever here. It is nirvana."

"It really is you," I said.

"Yes. I have translated myself. I want to show you what it means."

"Very well."

"I am gathered here now. Open the legs of your mind and let me in fully."

I relaxed and he flowed into me. Then I was borne away and I understood.

16. *Mt. Fuji from Umezawa*

Fuji across lava fields and wisps of fog, drifting clouds; birds on the wing and birds on the ground. This one at least is close. I lean on my staff and stare at his peaceful reaches across the chaos. The lesson is like that of a piece of music: I am strengthened in some fashion I cannot describe.

And I had seen blossoming cherry trees on the way over here, and fields purple with clover, cultivated fields yellow with rape-blossoms, grown for its oil, a few winter camellias still holding forth their reds and pinks, the green shoots of rice beds, here and there a tulip tree dashed with white, blue mountains in the distance, foggy river valleys. I had passed villages where colored sheet metal now covers the roofs' thatching—blue and yellow, green, black, red—and yards filled with the slate-blue rocks so fine for landscape gardening; an occasional cow, munching, lowing softly; scarlike rows of plastic-covered mulberry bushes where the silkworms are bred. My heart jogged at the sights—the tiles, the little bridges, the color. . . . It was like entering a tale by Lafcadio Hearn, to have come back.

My mind was drawn back along the path I had followed, to the points of its intersection with my electronic bane. Hokusai's warning that night I drank too much—that his prints may trap me—could well be correct. Kit had anticipated my passage a number of times. How could he have?

Then it struck me. My little book of Hokusai's prints—a small cloth-bound volume by the Charles E. Tuttle Company—had been a present from Kit.

It is possible that he was expecting me in Japan at about this time, because of Osaka. Once his epigons had spotted me a couple of times, probably in a massive scanning of terminals, could he have correlated my movements with the sequence of the prints in *Hokusai's Views of Mt. Fuji,* for which he knew my great fondness, and simply extrapolated and waited? I've a strong feeling that the answer is in the affirmative.

Entering the data-net with Kit was an overwhelming experience. That my consciousness spread and flowed I do not deny. That I was many places simultaneously, that I rode currents I did not at first understand, that knowledge and transcendence and a kind of glory were all about me and within me was also a fact of peculiar perception. The speed with which I was borne seemed instantaneous, and this was a taste of eternity. The access to multitudes of terminals and enormous memory banks seemed a measure of omniscience. The possibility of the manipulation of whatever I would change within this realm and its consequences at that place where I still felt my distant body seemed a version of omnipotence. And the feeling . . . I tasted the sweetness, Kit with me and within me. It was self surrendered and recovered in a new incarnation, it was freedom from mundane desire, liberation . . .

"Stay with me here forever," Kit seemed to say.

"No," I seemed to answer, dreamlike, finding myself changing even further. "I cannot surrender myself so willingly."

"Not for this? For unity and the flow of connecting energy?"

"And this wonderful lack of responsibility?"

"Responsibility? For what? This is pure existence. There is no past."

"Then conscience vanishes."

"What do you need it for? There is no future either."

"Then all actions lose their meaning."

"True. Action is an illusion. Consequence is an illusion."

"And paradox triumphs over reason."

"There is no paradox. All is reconciled."

"Then meaning dies."

"Being is the only meaning."

"Are you certain?"

"Feel it!"

"I do. But it is not enough. Send me back before I am changed into something I do not wish to be."

"What more could you desire than this?"

"My imagination will die, also. I can feel it."

"And what is imagination?"

"A thing born of feeling and reason."

"Does this not feel right?"

"Yes, it feels right. But I do not want that feeling unaccompanied. When I touch feeling with reason, I see that it is sometimes but an excuse for failing to close with complexity."

"You can deal with any complexity here. Behold the data! Does reason not show you that this condition is far superior to that you knew but moments ago?"

"Nor can I trust reason unaccompanied. Reason without feeling has led humanity to enact monstrosities. Do not attempt to disassemble my imagination this way."

"You retain your reason and your feelings!"

"But they are coming unplugged—with this storm of bliss, this shower of data. I need them conjoined, else my imagination is lost."

"Let it be lost, then. It has served its purpose. Be done with it now. What can you imagine that you do not already have here?"

"I cannot yet know, and that is its power. If there be a will with a spark of divinity to it, I know it only through my imagination. I can give you anything else but that I will not surrender."

"And that is all? A wisp of possibility?"

"No. But it alone is too much to deny."

"And my love for you?"

"You no longer love in the human way. Let me go back."

"Of course. You will think about it. You will return."

"Back! Now!"

I pushed the helmet from my head and rose quickly. I returned to the bathroom, then to my bed. I slept as if drugged, for a long while.

Would I have felt differently about possibilities, the future, imagination, had I not been pregnant—a thing I had suspected but not yet mentioned to him, and which he had missed learning with his attention focused upon our argument? I like to think that my answers would have been the same, but I will never know. My condition was confirmed by a local doctor the following day. I made the visit I had been putting off because my life required a certainty of something then—a certainty of anything. The screen in the work area remained blank for three days.

I read and I meditated. Then of an evening the light came on again:

ARE YOU READY?

I activated the keyboard. I typed one word:

NO.

I disconnected the induction couch and its helmet then. I unplugged the unit itself, also.

The telephone rang.

"Hello?" I said.

"Why not?" he asked me.

I screamed and hung up. He had penetrated the phone circuits, appropriated a voice.

It rang again. I answered again.

"You will never know rest until you come to me," he said.

"I will if you will leave me alone," I told him.

"I cannot. You are special to me. I want you with me. I love you."

I hung up. It rang again. I tore the phone from the wall.

I had known that I would have to leave soon. I was overwhelmed and depressed by all the reminders of our life together. I packed quickly and I departed. I took a room at a hotel. As soon as I was settled into it, the telephone rang and it was Kit again. My registration had gone into a computer and . . .

I had them disconnect my phone at the switchboard. I put out a Do Not Disturb sign. In the morning I saw a telegram protruding from beneath the door. From Kit. He wanted to talk to me.

I determined to go far away. To leave the country, to return to the States.

It was easy for him to follow me. We leave electronic tracks almost everywhere. By cable, satellite, optic fiber he could be wherever he chose. Like an unwanted suitor now he pestered me with calls, interrupted television shows to flash messages upon the screen, broke in on my own calls, to friends, lawyers, realtors, stores. Several times, horribly, he even sent me flowers. My electric bodhisattva, my hound of heaven, would give me no rest. It is a terrible thing to be married to a persistent data-net.

So I settled in the country. I would have nothing in my home whereby he could reach me. I studied ways of avoiding the system, of slipping past his many senses.

On those few occasions when I was careless he reached for me again immediately. Only he had learned a new trick, and I became convinced that he had developed it for the purpose of taking me into his world by force. He could build up a charge at a terminal, mold it into something like ball lightning and animallike, and send that short-lived artifact a little distance to do his will. I learned its weakness, though, in a friend's home when one came for me, shocked me, and attempted to propel me into the vicinity of the terminal, presumably for purposes of translation. I struck at the epigon—as Kit later referred to it in a telegram of explanation and apology—with the nearest object to hand—a lighted table lamp, which entered its field and blew a circuit immediately. The epigon was destroyed, which is how I discovered that a slight electrical disruption created an instability within the things.

I stayed in the country and raised my daughter. I read and I practiced my martial arts and I walked in the woods and climbed mountains and sailed and camped: rural occupations all, and very satisfying to me after a life of intrigue, conflict, plot and counterplot, violence, and then that small, temporary island of security with Kit. I was happy with my choice.

Fuji across the lava beds . . . Springtime . . . Now I am returned. This was not my choice.

17. *Mt. Fuji from Lake Suwa*

And so I come to Lake Suwa, Fuji resting small in the evening distance. It is no Kamaguchi of powerful reflections for me. But it is serene, which joins my mood in a kind of peace. I have taken the life of the spring into me now and it has spread through my being. Who would disrupt this world, laying unwanted forms upon it? Seal your lips.

Was it not in a quiet province where Bōtchan found his maturity? I've a theory concerning books like that one of Natsume Soseki's. Someone once told me that this is the one book you can be sure that every educated Japanese has read. So I read it. In the States I was told that *Huckleberry Finn* was the one book you could be sure that every educated Yankee had read. So I read it. In Canada it was Stephen Leacock's *Sunshine Sketches of a Little Town*. In France it was *Le Grand Meaulnes*. Other countries have their books of this sort. They are all of them pastorals, having in common a closeness to the countryside and the forces of nature in days just before heavy urbanization and mechanization. These things are on the horizon and advancing, but they only serve to add the spice of poignancy to the taste of simpler values. They are youthful books, of national heart and character, and they deal with the passing of innocence. I have given many of them to Kendra.

I lied to Boris. Of course I know all about the Osaka Conference. I was even approached by one of my former employers to do something along the lines Boris had guessed at. I declined. My plans are my own. There would have been a conflict.

Hokusai, ghost and mentor, you understand chance and purpose better than Kit. You know that human order must color our transactions with the universe, and that this is not only necessary but good, and that the light still comes through.

Upon this rise above the water's side I withdraw my hidden blade and hone it once again. The sun falls away from my piece of the world, but the darkness, too, is here my friend.

* * *

18. Mt. Fuji from the Offing in Kanagawa

And so the image of death. The Big Wave, curling above, toppling upon, about to engulf the fragile vessels. The one print of Hokusai's that everyone knows.

I am no surfer. I do not seek the perfect wave. I will simply remain here upon the shore and watch the water. It is enough of a reminder. My pilgrimage winds down, though the end is not yet in sight.

Well . . . I see Fuji. Call Fuji the end. As with the barrel's hoop of the first print, the circle closes about him.

On my way to this place I halted in a small glade I came upon and bathed myself in a stream which ran through it. There I used the local wood to construct a low altar. Cleansing my hands each step of the way I set before it incense made from camphorwood and from white sandalwood; I also placed there a bunch of fresh violets, a cup of vegetables, and a cup of fresh water from the stream. Then I lit a lamp I had purchased and filled with rapeseed oil. Upon the altar I set my image of the god Kokuzo which I had brought with me from home, facing to the west where I stood. I washed again, then extended my right hand, middle finger bent to touch my thumb as I spoke the mantra for invoking Kokuzo. I drank some of the water. I lustrated myself with sprinklings of it and continued repetition of the mantra. Thereafter, I made the gesture of Kokuzo three times, hand to the crown of my head, to my right shoulder, left shoulder, heart and throat. I removed the white cloth in which Kokuzo's picture had been wrapped. When I had sealed the area with the proper repetitions, I meditated in the same position as Kokuzo in the picture and invoked him. After a time the mantra ran by itself, over and over.

Finally, there was a vision, and I spoke, telling all that had happened, all that I intended to do, and asking for strength and guidance. Suddenly, I saw his sword descending, descending like slow lightning, to sever a limb from a tree, which began to bleed. And then it was raining, both within the vision and upon me, and I knew that that was all to be had on the matter.

I wound things up, cleaned up, donned my poncho, and headed on my way.

The rain was heavy, my boots grew muddy, and the temperature dropped. I trudged on for a long while and the cold crept into my bones. My toes and fingers became numb.

I kept constant lookout for a shelter, but did not spot anyplace where I could take refuge from the storm. Later, it changed from a downpour to a drizzle to a weak, mistlike fall when I saw what could be a temple or shrine in the distance. I headed for it, hoping for some hot tea, a fire, and a chance to change my socks and clean my boots.

A priest stopped me at the gate. I told him my situation and he looked uncomfortable.

"It is our custom to give shelter to anyone," he said. "But there is a problem."

"I will be happy to make a cash donation," I said, "if too many others have passed this way and reduced your stores. I really just wanted to get warm."

"Oh no, it is not a matter of supplies," he told me, "and for that matter very few have been by here recently. The problem is of a different sort and it embarasses me to state it. It makes us sound old-fashioned and superstitious, when actually this is a very modern temple. But recently we have been—ah—haunted."

"Oh?"

"Yes. Bestial apparitions have been coming and going from the library and record room beside the head priest's quarters. They stalk the shrine, pass through our rooms, pace the grounds, then return to the library or else fade away."

He studied my face, as if seeking derision, belief, disbelief—anything. I merely nodded.

"It is most awkward," he added. "A few simple exorcisms have been attempted but to no avail."

"For how long has this been going on?" I asked.

"For about three days," he replied.

"Has anyone been harmed by them?"

"No. They are very intimidating, but no one has been injured. They are distracting, too, when one is trying to sleep—that is, to meditate—for they produce a tingling feeling and sometimes cause the hair to rise up."

"Interesting," I said. "Are there many of them?"

"It varies. Usually just one. Sometimes two. Occasionally three."

"Does your library by any chance contain a computer terminal?"

"Yes, it does," he answered. "As I said, we are very modern. We keep our records with it, and we can obtain printouts of sacred texts we do not have on hand—and other things."

"If you will shut the terminal down for a day, they will probably go away," I told him, "and I do not believe they will return."

"I would have to check with my superior before doing a thing like that. You know something of these matters?"

"Yes, and in the meantime I would still like to warm myself, if I may."

"Very well. Come this way."

I followed him, cleaning my boots and removing them before entering. He led me around to the rear and into an attractive room which looked upon the temple's garden.

"I will go and see that a meal is prepared for you, and a brazier of charcoal that you may warm yourself," he said as he excused himself.

Left by myself I admired the golden carp drifting in a pond only a few feet away, its surface occasionally punctuated by raindrops, and a little stone bridge which crossed the pond, a stone pagoda, paths wandering among stones and shrubs. I wanted to cross that bridge—how unlike that metal span, thrusting, cold and dark!—and lose myself there for an age or two. Instead, I sat down and gratefully gulped the tea which arrived moments later, and I warmed my feet and dried my socks in the heat of the brazier which came a little while after that.

Later, I was halfway through a meal and enjoying a conversation with the young priest, who had been asked to keep me company until the head priest could come by and personally welcome me, when I saw my first epigon of the day.

It resembled a very small, triple-trunked elephant walking upright along one of the twisting garden paths, sweeping the air to either side of the trail with those snakelike appendages. It had not yet spotted me.

I called it to the attention of the priest, who was not faced in that direction.

"Oh my!" he said, fingering his prayer beads.

While he was looking that way, I shifted my staff into a readily available position beside me.

As it drifted nearer, I hurried to finish my rice and vegetables. I was afraid my bowl might be upset in the skirmish soon to come.

The priest glanced back when he heard the movement of the staff along the flagstones.

"You will not need that," he said. "As I explained, these demons are not aggressive."

I shook my head as I swallowed another mouthful.

"This one will attack," I said, "when it becomes aware of my presence. You see, I am the one it is seeking."

"Oh my!" he repeated.

I stood then as its trunks swayed in my direction and it approached the bridge.

"This one is more solid than usual," I commented. "Three days, eh?"

"Yes."

I moved about the tray and took a step forward. Suddenly, it was over the bridge and rushing toward me. I met it with a straight thrust, which it avoided. I spun the staff twice and struck again as it was turning. My blow landed and I was hit by two of the trunks simultaneously—once on the breast, once on the cheek. The epigon went out like a burned hydrogen balloon and I stood there rubbing my face, looking about me the while.

Another slithered into our room from within the temple. I lunged suddenly and caught it on the first stroke.

"I think perhaps I should be leaving now," I stated. "Thank you for your hospitality. Convey my regrets to the head priest that I did not get to meet him. I am warm and fed and I have learned what I wanted to know about your demons. Do not even bother about the terminal. They will probably cease to visit you shortly, and they should not return."

"You are certain?"

"I know them."

"I did not know the terminals were haunted. The salesman did not tell us."

"Yours should be all right now."

He saw me to the gate.

"Thank you for the exorcism," he said.

"Thanks for the meal. Good-bye."

I traveled for several hours before I found a place to camp in a shallow cave, using my poncho as a rain-screen.

And today I came here to watch for the wave of death. Not yet, though. No truly big ones in this sea. Mine is still out there, somewhere.

19. Mt. Fuji from Shichirigahama

Fuji past pine trees, through shadow, clouds rising beside him . . . It is getting on into the evening of things. The weather was good today, my health stable.

I met two monks upon the road yesterday and I traveled with them for a time. I was certain that I had seen them somewhere else along the way, so I greeted them and asked if this were possible. They said that they were on a pilgrimage of their own, to a distant shrine, and they admitted that I looked familiar, also. We took our lunch together at the side of the road. Our conversation was restricted to generalities, though they did ask me whether I had heard of the haunted shrine in Kanagawa. How quickly such news travels. I said that I had and we reflected upon its strangeness.

After a time I became annoyed. Every turning of the way that I took seemed a part of their route, also. While I'd welcomed a little company, I'd no desire for long-term companions, and it seemed their choices of ways approximated mine too closely. Finally, when we came to a split in the road I asked them which fork they were taking. They hesitated, then said that they were going right. I took the left-hand path. A little later they caught up with me. They had changed their minds, they said.

When we reached the next town, I offered a man in a car a good sum of money to drive me to the next village. He accepted, and we drove away and left them standing there.

I got out before we reached the next town, paid him, and watched him drive off. Then I struck out upon a footpath I had seen, going in the general direction I desired. At one point I left the trail and cut through the woods until I struck another path.

I camped far off the trail when I finally bedded down, and the following morning I took pains to erase all sign of my presence there. The monks did not reappear. They may have been quite harmless, or their designs quite different, but I must be true to my carefully cultivated paranoia.

Which leads me to note that man in the distance—a Westerner, I'd judge, by his garments . . . He has been hanging around taking pictures for some time. I will lose him shortly, of course, if he is following me—or even if he isn't.

It is terrible to have to be this way for too long a period of time. Next I will be suspecting schoolchildren.

I watch Fuji as the shadows lengthen. I will continue to watch until the first star appears. Then I will slip away.

And so I see the sky darken. The photographer finally stows his gear and departs.

I remain alert, but when I see the first star, I join the shadows and fade like the day.

20. Mt. Fuji from Inume Pass

Through fog and above it. It rained a bit earlier. And there is Fuji, storm clouds above his brow. In many ways I am surprised to have made it this far. This view, though, makes everything worthwhile.

I sit upon a mossy rock and record in my mind the changing complexion of Fuji as a quick rain veils his countenance, ceases, begins again.

The winds are strong here. The fogbank raises ghostly limbs and lowers them. There is a kind of numb silence beneath the wind's monotone mantra.

I make myself comfortable, eating, drinking, viewing, as I go over my final plans once again. Things wind down. Soon the circle will be closed.

I had thought of throwing away my medicine here as an act of bravado, as a sign of full commitment. I see this now as a foolishly romantic gesture. I am going to need all of my strength, all of the help I can get, if I am to have a chance at succeeding. Instead of discarding the medicine here I take some.

The winds feel good upon me. They come on like waves, but they are bracing.

A few travelers pass below. I draw back, out of their line of sight. Harmless, they go by like ghosts, their words carried off by the wind, not even reaching this far. I feel a small desire to sing but I restrain myself.

I sit for a long while, lost in a reverie of the elements. It has been good, this journey into the past, living at the edge once again . . .

Below me. Another vaguely familiar figure comes into view, lugging equipment. I cannot distinguish features from here, nor need I. As he halts and begins to set up his gear, I know that it is the photographer of Shichirigahama, out to capture another view of Fuji more permanent than any I desire.

I watch him for a time and he does not even glance my way. Soon I will be gone again, without his knowledge. I will allow this one as a coincidence. Provisionally, of course. If I see him again, I may have to kill him. I will be too near my goal to permit even the possibility of interference to exist.

I had better depart now, for I would rather travel before than behind him.

Fuji-from-on-high, this was a good resting place. We will see you again soon.

Come, Hokusai, let us be gone.

21. Mt. Fuji from the Tōtōmi Mountains

Gone the old sawyers, splitting boards from a beam, shaping them. Only Fuji, of snow and clouds, remains. The men in the print work in the old way, like the Owari barrel-maker. Yet, apart from those of the fishermen who merely draw their needs from nature, these are the only two prints in my book depicting people actively shaping something in their world. Their labors are too traditional for me to see the image of the Virgin and the Dynamo within them. They could have been performing the same work a thousand years before Hokusai.

Yet it is a scene of humanity shaping the world, and so it leads me down trails of years to this time, this day of sophisticated tools and large-scale changes. I see within it the image of what was later wrought, of the metal skin and pulsing flows the world would come to wear. And Kit is there, too, godlike, riding electronic waves.

Troubling. Yet bespeaking an ancient resilience, as if this, too, is but an eyeblink glimpse of humanity's movement in time, and whether I win or lose, the raw stuff remains and will triumph ultimately over any obstacle. I would really like to believe this, but I must leave certainty to politicians and preachers. My way is laid out and invested with my vision of what must be done.

I have not seen the photographer again, though I caught sight of the monks yesterday, camped on the side of a distant hill. I inspected them with my telescope and they were the same ones with whom I had traveled briefly. They had not noticed me and I passed them by way of a covering detour. Our trails have not crossed since.

Fuji, I have taken twenty-one of your aspects within me now. Live a little, die a little. Tell the gods, if you think of it, that a world is about to die.

I hike on, camping early in a field close to a monastery. I do not wish to enter there after my last experience in a modern holy place. I bed down in a concealed spot nearby, amid rocks and pine tree shoots. Sleep comes easily, lasts till some odd hour.

I am awake suddenly and trembling, in darkness and stillness. I cannot recall a sound from without or a troubling dream from within. Yet I am afraid, even to move. I breathe carefully and wait.

Drifting, like a lotus on a pond, it has come up beside me, towers above me, wears stars like a crown, glows with its own milky, supernal light. It is a delicate-featured image of a bodhisattva, not unlike Kwannon, in garments woven of moonbeams.

"Mari."

Its voice is soft and caressing.

"Yes?" I answer.

"You have returned to travel in Japan. You are coming to me, are you not?"

The illusion is broken. It is Kit. He has carefully sculpted this epigon-form and wears it himself to visit me. There must be a terminal in the monastery. Will he try to force me?

"I was on my way to see you, yes," I manage.

"You may join me now, if you would."

He extends a wonderfully formed hand, as in benediction.

"I've a few small matters I must clear up before we are reunited."

"What could be more important? I have seen the medical reports. I know the condition of your body. It would be tragic if you were to die upon the road, this close to your exaltation. Come now."

"You have waited this long, and time means little to you."

"It is you that I am concerned with."

"I assure you I shall take every precaution. In the meantime, there is something which has been troubling me."

"Tell me."

"Last year there was a revolution in Saudi Arabia. It seemed to promise well for the Saudis but it also threatened Japan's oil supply. Suddenly the new government began to look very bad on paper, and a new counterrevolutionary group looked stronger and better-tempered than it actually was. Major powers intervened successfully on the side of the counterrevolutionaries. Now they are in power and they seem even worse than the first government which had been overthrown. It seems possible, though incomprehensible to most, that computer readouts all over the world were somehow made to be misleading. And now the Osaka Conference is to be held to work out new oil agreements with the latest regime. It looks as if Japan will get a very good deal out of it. You once told me that you are above such mundane matters, but I wonder? You are Japanese, you loved your country. Could you have intervened in this?"

"What if I did? It is such a small matter in the light of eternal values. If there is a touch of sentiment for such things remaining within me, it is not dishonorable that I favor my country and my people."

"And if you did it in this, might you not be moved to intervene again one day, in some other matter where habit or sentiment tell you you should?"

"What of it?" he replies. "I but extend my finger and stir the dust of illusion a bit. If anything, it frees me even further."

"I see," I answer.

"I doubt that you do, but you will when you have joined me. Why not do it now?"

"Soon," I say. "Let me settle my affairs."

"I will give you a few more days," he says, "and then you must be with me forever."

I bow my head.

"I will see you again soon," I tell him.

"Good night, my love."

"Good night."

He drifts away then, his feet not touching the ground, and he passes through the wall of the monastery.

I reach for my medicine and my brandy. A double dose of each . . .

22. Mt. Fuji from the Sumida River in Edo

And so I come to the place of crossing. The print shows a ferryman bearing a number of people across the river into the city and evening. Fuji lies dark and brooding in the farthest dis-

tance. Here I do think of Charon, but the thought is not so un-
welcome as it once might have been. I take the bridge myself,
though.

As Kit has promised me a little grace, I walk freely the
bright streets, to smell the smells and hear the noises and watch
the people going their ways. I wonder what Hokusai would
have done in contemporary times? He is silent on the matter.

I drink a little, I smile occasionally, I even eat a good meal. I
am tired of reliving my life. I seek no consolations of philosophy or literature. Let me merely walk in the city tonight, running my shadow over faces and storefronts, bars and theaters,
temples and offices. Anything which approaches is welcome tonight. I eat *sushi,* I gamble, I dance. There is no yesterday, there
is no tomorrow for me now. When a man places his hand upon
my shoulder and smiles, I move it to my breast and laugh. He is
good for an hour's exercise and laughter in a small room he
finds us. I make him cry out several times before I leave him,
though he pleads with me to stay. Too much to do and see, love.
A greeting and a farewell.

Walking. . . . Through parks, alleys, gardens, plazas. Crossing. . . . Small bridges and larger ones, streets and walkways.
Bark, dog. Shout, child. Weep, woman. I come and go among
you. I feel you with a dispassionate passion. I take all of you inside me that I may hold the world here, for a night.

I walk in a light rain and in its cool aftermath. My garments
are damp, then dry again. I visit a temple. I pay a taximan to
drive me about the town. I eat a late meal. I visit another bar. I
come upon a deserted playground, where I swing and watch the
stars.

And I stand before a fountain splaying its waters into the
lightening sky, until the stars are gone and only their lost spar-

kling falls about me.

Then breakfast and a long sleep, another breakfast and a longer one . . .

And you, my father, there on the sad height? I must leave you soon, Hokusai.

23. Mt. Fuji from Edo

Walking again, within a cloudy evening. How long has it been since I spoke with Kit? Too long, I am sure. An epigon could come bounding my way at any moment.

I have narrowed my search to three temples—none of them the one in the print, to be sure, only that uppermost portion of it viewed from that impossible angle, Fuji back past its peak, smoke, clouds, fog between—but I've a feeling one of these three will do in the blue of evening.

I have passed all of them many times, like a circling bird. I am loath to do more than this, for I feel the right choice will soon be made for me. I became aware sometime back that I was being followed, really followed this time, on my rounds. It seems that my worst fear was not ungrounded; Kit is employing human agents as well as epigons. How he sought them and how he bound them to his service I do not care to guess. Who else would be following me at this point, to see that I keep my promise, to force me to it if necessary?

I slow my pace. But whoever is behind me does the same. Not yet. Very well.

Fog rolls in. The echoes of my footfalls are muffled. Also those at my back. Unfortunate.

I head for the other temple. I slow again when I come into its vicinity, all of my senses extended, alert.

Nothing. No one. It is all right. Time is no problem. I move on.

After a long while I approach the precincts of the third temple. This must be it, but I require some move from my pursuer to give me the sign. Then, of course, I must deal with that person before I make my own move. I hope that it will not be too difficult, for everything will turn upon that small conflict.

I slow yet again and nothing appears but the moisture of the fog upon my face and the knuckles of my hand wrapped about my staff. I halt. I seek in my pocket after a box of cigarettes I had purchased several days ago in my festive mood. I had doubted they would shorten my life.

As I raise one to my lips, I hear the words, "You desire a light, madam?"

I nod my head as I turn.

It is one of the two monks who extends a lighter to me and flicks forth its flame. I notice for the first time the heavy ridge of callous along the edge of his hand. He had kept it carefully out of sight before, as we sojourned together. The other monk appears to his rear, to his left.

"Thank you."

I inhale and send smoke to join the fog.

"You have come a long way," the man states.

"Yes."

"And your pilgrimage has come to an end."

"Oh? Here?"

He smiles and nods. He turns his head toward the temple.

"This is our temple," he says, "where we worship the new bodhisattva. He awaits you within."

"He can continue to wait, till I finish my cigarette," I say.

"Of course."

With a casual glance, I study the man. He is probably a very good *karateka*. I am very good with the *bo*. If it were only him, I would bet on myself. But two of them, and the other probably just as good as this one? Kokuzo, where is your sword? I am suddenly afraid.

I turn away, I drop the cigarette, I spin into my attack. He is ready, of course. No matter. I land the first blow.

By then, however, the other man is circling and I must wheel and move defensively, turning, turning. If this goes on for too long, they will be able to wear me down.

I hear a grunt as I connect with a shoulder. Something, anyway . . .

Slowly, I am forced to give way, to retreat toward the temple wall. If I am driven too near it, it will interfere with my strokes. I try again to hold my ground, to land a decisive blow. . . .

Suddenly, the man to my right collapses, a dark figure on his back. No time to speculate. I turn my attention to the first monk, and moments later I land another blow, then another.

My rescuer is not doing so well, however. The second monk has shaken him off and begins striking at him with bone-crushing blows. My ally knows something of unarmed combat, though, for he gets into a defensive stance and blocks many of these, even landing a few of his own. Still, he is clearly overmatched.

Finally I sweep a leg and deliver another shoulder blow. I try three strikes at my man while he is down, but he rolls away from all of them and comes up again. I hear a sharp cry from my right, but I cannot look away from my adversary.

He comes in again and this time I catch him with a sudden reversal and crush his temple with a follow-up. I spin then, barely in time, for my ally lies on the ground and the second monk is upon me.

Either I am lucky or he has been injured. I catch the man quickly and follow up with a rapid series of strikes which take him down, out, and out for good.

I rush to the side of the third man and kneel beside him, panting. I had seen his gold earring as I moved about the second monk.

"Boris." I take his hand. "Why are you here?"

"I told you—I could take a few days—to help you," he says, blood trickling from the corner of his mouth. "Found you. Was taking pictures . . . And see . . . You needed me."

"I'm sorry," I say. "Grateful, but sorry. You're a better man than I thought."

He squeezes my hand. "I told you I liked you—Maryushka. Too bad. . . we didn't have—more time. . ."

I lean and kiss him, getting blood on my mouth. His hand relaxes within my own. I've never been a good judge of people, except after the fact.

And so I rise. I leave him there on the wet pavement. There is nothing I can do for him. I go into the temple.

It is dark near the entrance, but there are many votive lights to the rear. I do not see anyone about. I did not think that I would. It was just to have been the two monks, ushering me to the terminal. I head toward the lights. It must be somewhere back there.

I hear rain on the rooftop as I search. There are little rooms, off to either side, behind the lights.

It is there, in the second one. And even as I cross the threshold, I feel that familiar ionization which tells me that Kit is doing something here.

I rest my staff against the wall and go nearer. I place my hand upon the humming terminal.

"Kit," I say, "I have come."

No epigon grows before me, but I feel his presence and he seems to speak to me as he did on that night so long ago when I lay back upon the couch and donned the helmet:

"I knew that you would be here tonight."

"So did I," I reply.

"All of your business is finished?"

"Most of it."

"And you are ready now to be joined with me?"

"Yes."

Again I feel that movement, almost sexual in nature, as he flows into me. In a moment he would bear me away into his kingdom.

Tatemae is what you show to others. *Honne* is your real intention. As Musashi cautioned in the Book of Waters, I try not to reveal my *home* even at this moment. I simply reach out with my free hand and topple my staff so that its metal tip, batteries engaged, falls against the terminal.

"Mari! What have you done?" he asks, within me now, as the humming ceases.

"I have cut off your line of retreat, Kit."

"Why?"

The blade is already in my hand.

"It is the only way for us. I give you this *jigai*, my husband."

"No!"

I feel him reaching for control of my arm as I exhale. But it is too late. It is already moving. I feel the blade enter my throat, well-placed.

"Fool!" he cries. "You do not know what you have done! I cannot return!"

"I know."

As I slump against the terminal I seem to hear a roaring sound, growing, at my back. It is the Big Wave, finally come for me. My only regret is that I did not make it to the final station, unless, of course, that is what Hokusai is trying to show me, there beside the tiny window, beyond the fog and the rain and the night.

24. Mt. Fuji in a Summer Storm

COME BACK TO THE KILLING GROUND, ALICE, MY LOVE

1

All the death-traps in the galaxy, and she has to walk into mine. At first I didn't recognize her. And when I did I knew it still couldn't be right, her, there, with her blindfolded companion in the sandals and dark kimono. She was dead, the octad broken. There couldn't be another. Certain misgivings arose concerning this one. But I had no choice. Does one ever? There are things to do. Soon she will move. I will taste their spirits. Play it again, Alices. . . .

2

She came to him at his villa in Constantinople, where, in loose-fitting garments, trowel in hand, spatulate knife at belt, he was kneeling amid flowers, tending one of his gardens. A servant announced her arrival.

"Master, there is a lady at the gate," the old man told him, in Arabic.

"And who could that be?" the gardener mused, in the same tongue.

"She gave her name as Alyss," the servant replied, and added, "She speaks Greek with a foreign accent."

"Did you recognize the accent?"

"No. But she asked for you by name."

"I should hope so. One seldom calls on strangers for any good purpose."

"Not the Stassinopoulos name. She asked for Kalifriki."

"Oh, my. Business," he said, rising and passing the trowel to the man, dusting himself off. "It's been a long time."

"I suppose it has, sir."

"Take her to the lesser courtyard, seat her in the shade, bring her tea, sherbet, melons—anything else she may desire. Tell her I'll be with her shortly."

"Yes, sir."

Repairing within, the gardener removed his shirt and bathed quickly, closing his dark eyes as he splashed water over his high cheekbones. Then his chest, his arms. After drying, he bound his dark hair with a strip of golden cloth, located an embroidered white shirt with full sleeves within his wardrobe, donned it.

In the courtyard at a table beside the fountain, where a mosaic of dolphins sported beneath waters which trickled in small rivers from a man-sized Mt. Olympus, he bowed to the expressionless lady who had studied his approach. She rose slowly to her feet. Not tall, he observed, a full head shorter than himself, dark hair streaked with white, eyes very blue. A pale scar crossed her left cheek, vanished into the hair above her ear.

"Alyss, I believe?" he inquired, as she took his hand and raised it to her lips.

"Yes," she replied, lowering it. "Alice." She gave it a slightly different accenting than his man had done.

"That's all?"

"It is sufficient for my purposes, sir." He did not recognize her accent either, which annoyed him considerably.

He smiled and took the chair across from her as she reseated herself. He saw that her gaze was fixed upon the small star-shaped scar beside his right eye.

"Verifying a description?" he inquired as he poured himself a cup of tea.

"Would you be so kind as to let me see your left wrist?" she asked.

He shook back the sleeve. Her gaze fell almost greedily upon the red thread that was wrapped about it.

"You are the one," she said solemnly.

"Perhaps," he replied, sipping the tea. "You are younger than you would have your appearance indicate."

She nodded. "Older, also," she said.

"Have some of the sherbet," he invited, spooning two dishfuls from the bowl. "It's quite good."

3

I steady the dot. I touch the siphon and the bone. There, beyond the polished brass mirror, sipping something cool, her remarking in Greek that the day is warm, that it was good to find a shaded pausing place such as this caravanserai, my doorstep, in which to refresh themselves—this does not deceive me in its calculated nonchalance. When they have finished and risen, they will not head back to the street with its camels, dust, horses, cries of the vendors, I know that. They will turn, as if inadvertently, in the direction of this mirror. Her and the monk. Dead ladies, bear witness. . . .

*　　*　　*

4

"I can afford you," she told him, reaching for a soft leather bag on the flagging beside her chair.

"You precede yourself," he responded. "First I must understand what it is that you want of me."

She fixed him with her blue gaze and he felt the familiar chill of the nearness of death.

"You kill," she said simply. "Anything, if the price is right. That is what I was told."

He finished his tea, refilled their cups.

"I choose the jobs I will accept," he said. "I do not take on everything that is thrust at me."

"What considerations govern your choices?" she asked.

"I seldom slay the innocent," he replied, "by my definitions of innocence. Certain political situations might repel me—"

"An assassin with a conscience," she remarked.

"In a broad sense, yes."

"Anything else?"

"Madam, I am something of a last resort," he responded, "which is why my services are dear. Any simple cut-throat will suffice for much of what people want done in this area. I can recommend several competent individuals."

"In other words, you prefer the complicated ones, those offering a challenge to your skills?"

"'Prefer' is perhaps the wrong word. I am not certain what is the right one—at least in the Greek language. I do tend to find myself in such situations, though, as the higher-priced jobs seem to fall into that category, and those are normally the only ones I accept."

She smiled for the first time that morning, a small, bleak thing.

"It falls into that category," she said, "in that no one has ever succeeded in such an undertaking as I require. As for innocence, you will find none here. And the politics need be of no concern, for they are not of this world."

He nibbled a piece of melon.

"You have interested me," he said.

5

At last, they rise. The monk adjusts the small bow he bears and places his hand upon her shoulder. They cross the refreshment area. They are leaving! No! Could I have been wrong? I realize suddenly that I had wanted it to be her. That part of me I had thought fully absorbed and transformed is suddenly risen, seeks to command. I desire to cry out. Whether it be "Come!" or "Run!" I do not know. Yet neither matters. Not when it is not a part of her. Not when they are departing.

But.

At the threshold, she halts, saying something to her companion. I hear only the word "hair."

When she turns back there is a comb in her hand. She moves suddenly toward the dot manifestation which hangs brightly upon the wall to her right. As she drops her veil and adjusts her red tresses I become aware that the color is unnatural.

6

"Not of this world," he repeated. "Whence, then, may I inquire?"

"Another planet, far across the galaxy from here," she replied. "Do these terms mean anything to you?"

"Yes," he answered. "Quite a bit. Why have you come here?"

"Pursuit," she said.

"Of the one you would have me slay?"

"At first it was not destruction but rescue that we sought."

" 'We'?"

"It took eight of me to power the devices which brought us here, an original and seven copies. Clones."

"I understand."

"Really? Are you, yourself, alien to this place?"

"Your story is the important one just now. You say there are eight of you about?"

She shook her head.

"I am the last," she stated. "The other seven perished in attempting the task I must complete."

"Which are you, the original or a clone?"

She laughed. Then, abruptly, her eyes were moist, and she turned away.

"I am a copy," she said, at length.

"And you still live," he remarked.

"It is not that I did not try. I went in after all of the others failed. I failed, too. I was badly injured. But I managed to escape—barely."

"How long ago was this?"

"Almost five years."

"A long time for a copy to stay alive."

"You know?"

"I know that many cultures which employ clones for a particular job tend to build in some measure against their continued existence once the job is done, a kind of insurance against the . . . embarrassment . . . of the original."

"Or the replacement, yes. A small poison sac at the base of the skull in my case. I believe my head injury did something to nullify its operation."

She turned her head and raised her hair. There were more scars upon her neck.

"He thinks I am dead," she went on. "I am certain. Either from the encounter or from the passage of time. But I know the way in, and I learned something of the place's rules."

"I think you had better tell me about this person and this place," Kalifriki said.

7

The Alices are singing their wordless plaint. Now and forever. I build another wall, rings set within it, chains threaded through them. For all of them. Come back, come back, Alice, my last. It *is* you. It must be. Make the movement that will commit you, that will transport you. Else must I reach forth the siphon, as I have so many times. Even if it be not you, I must now. You resurrect an older self.

"Good," she says, putting away her comb, turning toward the door.

No!

Then she turns back, lips set in a tight line, raising her hand, touching the reflecting surface. A moment, as she locates the pulses, passes her hand through the activation sequence.

As her fingers penetrate the interface the bowman is suddenly behind her, laying his hand upon her shoulder. No matter. He may bear an interesting story within him.

8

"Aidon," she said. "He is Aidon."

"The one you seek?" Kalifriki asked. "The one you would have me kill?"

"Yes," she said. Then, "No. We must go to a special place," she finished.

"I don't understand," he said. "What place?"

"Aidon."

"Is Aidon the name of a man or the name of a place?"

"Both," she said. "Neither."

"I have studied with Zen masters and with Sufi sages," he said, "but I can make no sense of what you are saying. What is Aidon?"

"Aidon is an intelligent being. Aidon is also a place. Aidon is not entirely a man. Aidon is not such a place as places are in this world."

"Ah," he said. "Aidon is an artificial intelligence, a construct."

"Yes," she said. "No."

"I will stop asking questions," he stated, "for now. Just tell me about Aidon."

She nodded once, sharply.

"When we came to this system looking for Nelsor," she began, "the ship's instruments showed that something on this planet had gained control of a cosmic string, circumnavigating the universe, present since its creation. We dismissed this at the time, for it was actually one of the tiny holes of blackness—an object supercollapsed to an unworldly point, also present since the creation—that we were seeking. For this would lead us to Nelsor's vessel, from which a damage-pulse had come to us. We use the black objects to power our way through other spaces. Do you understand?"

"That part, yes," he said. "I don't understand who or what Nelsor is, let alone Aidon."

"They are the same," she said, "now. Nelsor was her—the original Alice's—lover, mate, consort, husband-relation. He piloted the vessel which had the trouble, and they came down in this general area of your planet. I believe that Aidon took control of the vessel—and of Nelsor as well—and caused the landing here, and that this is what triggered the damage-pulse."

She glanced at him.

"Aidon," she said, "is difficult to explain. Aidon began as one of those small, black, collapsed objects which make a hole in space. We use them as specialized devices. Bypassing space for distant travel is one of the ends for which they are employed. They are set up for most of their jobs—travel included—by swirling a field of particles about them at high velocity. These fields are impressed with considerable data for the jobs they are to perform. The field is refreshed at its outer perimeter, and the data is replicated and transferred outward in waves as the inner perimeter is absorbed. So there is a matching informed particle-feed to equal the interior information loss. The device draws on the radiation from the collapsed object for power and is programmed to be self-regulating in this regard."

"I understand what you are saying," Kalifriki replied, "and possibly even where this is going now. Such a thing becomes intelligent—sentient?"

"Generally. And normally their input is well controlled," she answered.

"But not always?"

She smiled, momently. Kalifriki poured more tea.

"Of all categories of employment, there is less control over the input of those used in space travel," she responded, "and I suppose that the very act of traversing the peculiar domains they must has its odd results. The experts are not in agreement on this. One thing which definitely affects such a construct, however, is that for certain areas of space passage the pilot must maintain constant direct communication with it. This requires a special sort of person for pilot, one possessing the ability to reach it mentally—a telepathic individual with special training for working with constructed intelligences. Such a relationship will infect the construct to some extent with the operator's personality."

She paused for a drink of tea.

Then, "Sometimes such constructs become disordered, perhaps from staring too long into the heart of darkness between the stars. In a human we would call it madness. The vessels often simply vanish when this happens. Other times, if it occurs in known space there may be a signature pulse indicating the vehicle's destruction. As with Aidon, they may digest their operators' minds first—an overlay that could enhance the madness to a kind of schizophrenia."

"So Aidon ate Nelsor," said Kalifriki, raising his cup, "and brought the vessel to Earth."

She nodded.

"Whatever had grown twisted within him twists whatever it acquires. It twisted Nelsor's feelings for Alice. He destroyed the four Alices one by one, so that he might know them in their pain. For this is how he learned love, as a kind of pain, from the twistings of darkness that damaged him, to the pain of Nelsor's passing. Not totally alien, perhaps, for there are people who love through pain, also."

Kalifriki nodded.

"But how do you know that this is the case with Aidon?" he asked.

"Alice was also a pilot," she said, "and as such, a sensitive. She had a strong bond of this sort with Nelsor. All of her clones shared her ability. When she brought the final three of us and came seeking him—for he seemed still alive, but somehow changed—this was the means by which we located the entrance to the blister universe he had created."

"He has his own world?"

"Yes. He formed it and retreated to it quickly after coming to this place. And there he dwells, like a trapdoor spider. Alice entered and was destroyed by him. We all felt it happen. Then, one by one, the three of us who remained essayed the passage—each succeeding in penetrating a little farther into the place because of her predecessor's experience. But each of the others was destroyed in the process. I was the last, so I knew the most of how his world operated. It is a kind of slow killing machine, a torture device. I was injured but was able to escape."

She brushed at her scar.

"What could you have hoped to accomplish?" he asked. "Why did you keep going in when you saw what he was up to?"

"We hoped to reach a point where we could communicate with that part of him which is still Nelsor. Then, by linking minds, we had thought to be able to strengthen him to overcome Aidon. We hoped that we could save him."

"I thought he was dead—physically, that is."

"Yes, but in that place, with that power, he would have been godlike, if he could have been freed even briefly and gained control of Aidon again. He might have been able to reconstitute his body and come away in it."

"But. . ." Kalifriki said.

"Yes. Aidon proved so much stronger than what remained of Nelsor that I saw it could never be. There is no choice now but to destroy Aidon."

"Why not just let him be if he's retreated to his own universe?"

"I can hear their cries—Nelsor's, and those of the ravished souls of my sisters. There must be some release for what remains of them all. And there are others now. The entrance to his underworld lies hidden in a public house on a trade route. When a sufficiently sensitive individual enters there, Aidon becomes aware of it, and he takes that person to him. He has developed a taste for life stories along with his pain. He extracts them both, in a kind of slow feasting. But there is more. You are aware of the nature of such objects. You must realize that one day he will destroy this world. He leeches off it. Eventually, he will absorb it all. It will hover forever in a jumble of images on his event horizon, but it will be gone."

"You would hire me to destroy a black hole?"

"I would hire you to destroy Aidon."

Kalifriki rose and paced through several turns.

"There are many problems," he said at last.

"Yes," she replied, drinking her tea.

9

. . . Passing through the mirror into my world, hand emerging from a lake, slim white arm upthrust as if holding the sword in that story the Frenchman had. And hesitation. Coy, her return, as if waiting for me to reach out, to hand her through. Perhaps I shall. There is amusement to be had in this. Come, siphon. . . .

Fading, faded, gone. The arm. She wavered and went out, like a flame in a sudden draft. Gone from beneath the lake, behind the mirror. Along with the blind monk. To what realm transported? Gone from the inn, from my world, also.

But wait. . . .

10

"You are asking me to pit my thread, in some way, against a singularity," he said.

"How is it that your string resembles a piece of red thread?" she asked.

"I require a visible appearance for it locally," he said, "to have something to work with. I do not like your idea."

"As I understand these things, your thread goes all the way around the universe. It was this that we detected on our approach. There are fundamental physical reasons why it can never have an end. A singularity could not bite a piece out of it. The antigravity of its pressure would exactly cancel the gravity of the energy. So there would be no net change in the gravity of the black hole which tried to take it in. The hole would not grow in size, and the situation would remain static in that regard. But you would have Aidon hooked with the string passing through him. Could you then transfer him to another universe?"

Kalifriki shook his head.

"No matter what I might do with him that way, the hole would remain permanently attached to the thread, and that is unacceptable. It might cause unusual loopings. No. I will not match two such fundamental objects directly against each other. If I am to be retained to destroy Aidon I will do it my way, Alice. Aidon, as I understand it, is not really the black hole itself, but a self-sustaining, programmed accretion disc which has suffered irreparable damage to its information field. That could be the point of my attack."

"I don't see how you would proceed with it."

"I see only one way, but it would mean that you would not be able to return to your home world."

She laughed.

"I came here prepared to die in this enterprise," she said. "But, since the black hole cannot be destroyed and you will not attempt shifting it to another universe, I need to know what your attack will involve—as further disruption of the information will involve Nelsor as well as Aidon."

"Oh? You said you'd given up on Nelsor, that what was left of him was ruined and merged with Aidon, that the only course remaining was to destroy the entire construct."

"Yes, but your talk of my not returning home implied that you wanted my ship or something from it. That could only be its singularity drive."

"You're right."

"So you intend somehow to use one black hole against the other. And it could work. Such a sudden increase in mass without a compensating acceleration of the field could result in its absorbing the field faster than the field could replicate itself. You would make the hole eat Aidon and Nelsor both."

"Correct."

"I don't see how you could get close enough to do it. But that is, as you say, your problem. I might be able to penetrate Aidon's world to a point where I could communicate with Nelsor mentally and make a final effort to save him, to complete my mission. I want you to hold off on doing what you contemplate until I've tried."

"That would narrow our safety margin considerably. Why this sudden change of heart?"

"It was because I saw the possibility when I began to understand your plan. Bringing another singularity into that place might perturb Aidon to the point where he may lose some control over what he holds of Nelsor. If there is any chance he might still be freed . . . I must try, though I be but an image of his lady. Also, my telepathic bond with him may be stronger than that of any of the other six."

"Why is that?" Kalifriki asked.

She reddened and looked away. She raised her cup and lowered it again without drinking.

"Nelsor took no sexual pleasure with the clones," she said, "only with the original Alice. One time, however, I was in her quarters seeking some navigational notes we had discussed while she was occupied in another part of the vessel. He came seeking her and mistook me for his lady. He had been working hard and I felt sorry for him in his need for release. So I assumed her role and let him use me as he would her, giving him what pleasure I could. We enjoyed each other, and he whispered endearments and later he went away to work again. It was never discovered, and I've never spoken of it till now. But I have heard that such things can strengthen the bond."

"So you care for him in a somewhat different way than the others," Kalifriki said, "as he did for you, whatever the circumstances."

"Yes," she replied, "for I am her equal in all ways, not just genetically, having known him as the other six did not."

"So you would undertake an even greater risk for him?"

"I would."

"And if you fail?"

"I'd still want you to destroy him, for mercy's sake."

"And if you succeed, and the world is coming apart about us? It may be harder to escape under those circumstances. I don't really know."

She reached for her bag.

"I brought all the gold bars I could carry comfortably. There are a great many more aboard my vessel. I'll give them all to you—"

"Where is your vessel?"

"Beneath the Sea of Marmara. I could summon it, but it were better to go out in a boat and simply raise it for a time."

"Let me see how much gold you have in the sack."

She hefted it and passed it to him.

"You're stronger than you look," he said as he accepted it. He opened it then and examined its contents. "Good," he said. "But we will need more than this."

"I told you you can have it all. We can go and get it now."

"It would not be for me, but for the purchase of equipment," he told her. "This bag and another like it should suffice for that, if I take the job."

"There will still be ample metal left for your fee," she said. "Much more than this. You *will* take the job, won't you?"

"Yes, I will."

She was on her feet.

"I will get you the gold now. When can we leave for Ubar?"

"Ubar? That is where Aidon has opened his office?"

"Yes. It lies near an Arabian trade route."

"I know the place. We cannot go there immediately, however. First, there are preparations to be made."

"Who are you really?" she asked him. "You know too much. More than the culture of this world contains."

"My story is not part of the bargain," he said. "You may rest now. My servant will show you to a suite. Dine with me this evening. There are more details that I wish to know concerning Aidon's world. Tomorrow I would inspect your vessel and obtain the additional gold we will need for a trip we must take."

"Not to Ubar?"

"To India, where I would obtain a certain diamond of which I have heard, of a certain perfection and a certain shape."

"That will be a long journey."

"Not really. Not as I shall conduct it."

"By some employment of the string? You can do that?"

He nodded.

"How did you gain such control over a thing like that?"

"As you said, Alice, I know too much."

11

. . . But wait. Now they are back. Her arm still extends above the waters of my lake. Likely but some trick of the interface, some roving particle's hit within the nanocircuitry, that fogged the transfer. They come now into my world, wet white garment clinging to the well-remembered contours of her form—nipples above their orbs, curves of hip and back and buttocks, shoulders, thighs—ripe for the delicate raking of claws. And the man . . . he is more muscular than first I thought. A lover, then, perhaps. Then to see those muscles flex when the skin has been removed to the waist . . . there is that to fill the air with the music of outcry and weeping. Dead Alices, give them a song as they come ashore, of welcome to their new home, through crystal forest beneath a sky of perfect blue. How long from that then to this now? Centuries. As entropy here rockets to the sharp curves of my architecture, the contours of its form rake of my desire. The arrow of time passes and returns down sharp geodesies, pierces memory to the rage, impales rage that the love may flow. Why did you come back, form of hatred and its opposite? You will tell me, upon the ground I have prepared for you, tell, to the chorus of your sisters beneath a bleeding sky.

But we must not rush these things, Alice, my last. For when you are done the ages will be long, the glory of your exposed architecture a piece of frozen time, distributed in monument about the crying landscape. Come back to the Killing Ground, Alice, my love. I've many a present to gift you there, the entire universe our angel of record against the long dark time. Set foot upon the shore and find your way.

The ladies sing your nuptials in the Place of Facing Skulls.

12

Kalifriki dropped the anchor and struck the sails of their boat, as Alice moved to the bow and began singing in a lilting language he did not understand. The beginning morning's light touched the waves with flecks of gold and a cool breeze stirred her zebra hair upon her shoulder. He leaned against the gunwale and watched her as he listened. After a time the boat rose with a long, slow swell, subsiding only gradually. Her voice went out across the water, vibrated within it, and suddenly her eyes widened, reminding him of one of the Acropolis Maidens, as the water roiled to starboard and a curving, burnished form surfaced there like the back of some great, mysterious sea creature rising to meet the day.

He stirred himself, fetching a pole with a hook affixed to its end to grapple them closer to the bronzed surfaces. He glanced back at her before he used it, and she nodded. Reaching then, he caught it within one of the stair-like projections which had rippled into being upon its side, leading up to a hatch. He drew them nearer until he felt the scraping of their hull upon metal.

"Grown, not fabricated," he remarked.

"Yes," she replied, moving forward.

He held the grapple until she had crossed over to the alien vessel's companionway. Then he set it aside and followed.

By the time he came up behind her she had the hatch open. She entered and he looked down into a lighted interior, down to a soft green deck which might be covered with tailored grasses, furniture built into niches in contoured walls without corners.

Entering, he descended. Barely visible scenes flashed across surfaces he passed. A small vibration communicated itself to him, through the floor, through the air. They passed rooms both bright and muted, traversing corridors with windows that seemed to open upon alien landscapes—one, where red, tree-like forms scrambled across an ebony landscape beneath a double sun causing him to pause and stare, as if remembering.

At length, she halted before a tan bulkhead, manipulated a hatch set within it, flung it open. Stack upon stack of small golden bars lay within the revealed compartment, gleaming as through a hint of green haze.

"Take all you want," she said.

"I'll want another bag such as the first, for the transaction of which I spoke," he told her, "and another after that for the first half of my fee. I will claim the final payment when the job is done. But we can collect these on the way out. I wish to view the source of the ship's power now."

"Come this way."

He followed her farther into the vessel's interior, coming at last to a circular chamber where watery visions appeared around the walls, including one of the under-side of his boat, off to his right.

"This is the place," Alice said.

Kalifriki did not see what she did, but suddenly the floor became transparent and far beneath his feet it seemed that something pulsed darkly. There came a dizziness and he felt drawn toward the center of the room.

"Open it," he said.

"Move back two paces, first."

He obeyed. Then the floor opened before him, the section where he had been standing dropping to become three steps leading down to a narrow well. Its forward wall housed a clear compartment within which he seemed to feel the presence of something drawing him. He descended the steps.

"What are the dangers? What are the safeguards?" he asked.

"You are safe where you are," she answered. "I can open the panel and give you a closer look."

"Go ahead."

It slid back and he stared for a moment.

"How would you manipulate it?" he asked.

"Forcefield pressures against its container," she replied.

He shook out a strand of the thread from his wrist, snaked it about the opening several times, withdrawing it slowly on each occasion.

"All right, I can work with this," he said a little later. "Seal it in again."

The compartment closed before him.

". . . Pure carbon crystal lattice, antigrav field webbed throughout," he said as to himself. "Yes. I saw something like this managed once, a long time ago." He turned and mounted the stair. "Let's go in and get the gold. Then we can head back."

They withdrew the way they had come in, returning to the boat with two heavy sacks. The vessel's hatch secured, she sang it back beneath the waves. The sun stood now fully risen, and birds dipped toward the waters about them as he weighed the anchor and set the sails.

"Now?" she said.

"Breakfast," he replied.

"Then?" she asked.

"India," he said.

13

Now the monk has fully entered my world, following her. Suddenly, things are no longer as they have been. Things are no longer right. Things seem to collapse like strange wave functions about him as he passes. Yet nothing seems really changed. What has he brought with him into my world, that I feel uneasy at his presence here? Is it a kind of turbulence? Is it that I am running faster? It would be hard to tell if my spin state were affected. Where did she find him? Why did she bring him? An aged tree reaches the end of its growth and shatters as he goes by it. I do not believe I like this man, shuffling unseeing through my gardens of crystal and stone. Yet perhaps I shall like him a great deal when the time comes. Such feelings are often close akin. In the meantime, it is always amusing to observe when a new thing comes to this place. My *arbor decapitant* awaits, but fifty paces ahead. She knows of it, of course. All of the Alices learned of it, the first the hard way. Yet it is good sport to see such things do their business. Yes, he will be all right. New blood must be brought to the game from time to time, else there is no bite to it. I will let them play through, to the end of her knowledge. . . .

*   *   *

14

In Maharajah Alamkara's palace of white marble they were feasted and entertained with music and dance, for Kalifriki had once done some work for that ruler involving a phantom tiger and some missing members of the royal family. Late into the evening a storyteller regaled them with an almost unrecognizable version of the event.

The following day, as Kalifriki and Alice walked amid walls of roses in the royal gardens, the chamberlain, Rasa, sent for them to discuss the business to which Kalifriki had alluded the previous evening.

Seated across the counting table from the heavy dark man of the curled and shiny mustaches, they beheld the stone known as the Dagger of Rama, displayed on a folded black cloth before them. Almost four inches in length, it was broad at the base, tapering upward to a sharp apex; its outline would be that of a somewhat elongated isosceles triangle, save that the lower corners were missing. It was perfectly clear, without a hint of color to it. Kalifriki raised it, breathed upon it. The condensation of his breath vanished immediately. He scrutinized it then through a glass.

"A perfect stone," Rasa said. "You will find no flaws."

Kalifriki continued his examination.

"It may hold up long enough," he said to Alice in Greek, "if I frame it appropriately, using certain properties of the thread to control external considerations."

"A most lovely stone for your lady to wear between her breasts," Rasa continued. "It is sure to influence the *chakra* of the heart." He smiled then.

Kalifriki placed a bag of gold upon the table, opened it, poured forth its contents.

Rasa picked up one of the small bars and studied it. He scratched it with his dagger's point and measured it, turban bobbing above the gauge. Then he placed it upon a scale he had set up to his left and took its weight.

"Of great purity," he remarked, tossing it back upon the table. Then he raised several of the bars from the pile and let them fall from his hand. "Still, it is not enough for so remarkable a stone. It may well have accompanied Rama on his journey to confront Ravan in the matter of Sita's abduction."

"I am not interested in its history," Kalifriki replied, and he brought up the second bag of gold and added its bars to the heap. "I've heard report that the tax collectors have had a lean time these past several years."

"Lies!" Rasa stated, opening a nearby chest and dipping his hand into it. He withdrew and cast forth a fistful of semiprecious stones upon the tabletop. Among them lay a small carved mountain of pale green jade, a pathway winding about it in a clockwise direction from base to summit. His gaze falling upon this piece, he reached out and tapped it with a thick forefinger. "Sooner would this spiral change direction," he said, "than would I undersell a treasure simply to raise funds."

Kalifriki raised his wrist. The thread touched upon the piece of jade, seemed to pass within it. The stone moved slightly. The spiral now wound in the opposite direction.

Rasa's eyes widened.

"I had forgotten," he said softly, "that you are the magician who slew the phantom tiger."

"I didn't really kill him," Kalifriki said. "He's still out there somewhere. I just came to terms with him. Story-tellers don't know everything."

The man sighed and touched his middle.

"This job is sometimes very trying," he said, "and sometimes seems to give me pains in my stomach. Excuse me."

He removed a small vial from a pouch at his sash, as Kalifriki moved his wrist again. As he unstoppered the container and raised it to his lips, Kalifriki said, "Wait."

Rasa lowered the vial.

"Yes?" he asked.

"If I heal your ulcer," Kalifriki said, "you may well bring it back with too much worry and aggravate it with too many spices. Do you understand?"

"Heal it," he said. "It is hard to cultivate philosophy in the face of necessity, and I do like my foods well seasoned. But I will try."

Kalifriki moved his wrist again and Rasa smiled. He stoppered the vial and replaced it in the pouch.

"All right, magician," he said. "Leave the gold. Take the stone. And if you see the white tiger again, let it know that you pass this way occasionally and that bargains are to be kept."

Later, in the garden at twilight, Alice asked him, "How did you do that reversal on the stone?"

"The full circumference of the thread is less than 360 degrees," Kalifriki replied. "The negative pressure of antigravity affects the geometry of space about it. Its missing angle is my key to other spaces. I simply rotated the stone through a higher space."

She nodded.

"I seem to recall something of this property from my training," she said. "But how did you heal the ulcer?"

"I speeded up time in its vicinity, letting the natural processes of his body heal it. I hope that he takes my advice and learns some detachment, from his work and his food."

They took a further turn, into an area of the garden they had not yet explored. The flowers seemed to grow flat upon a flattening prospect along the twisting trail they followed. Then they were gone and it was the dead of night with great winnowings of stars blazing above them as they entered the lesser courtyard of Kalifriki's villa at Constantinople.

"You still smell of roses," she said.

"So do you," he replied, "and good night."

15

. . . Walking through my forest, ridiculous archaic weapon upon his back, his hand upon her shoulder, the monk follows the Alice. This one, I note, is scarred. My last Alice, then. She did escape, of course. And gone all this time. Planning, surely. What might she have in mind for the final foray, the last gasp of the octad? Its aim, certainly, is to free Nelsor. Nelsor. . . . Even now, I feel her reaching out toward him. Disturbing. She is the strongest in this regard. Yet soon she will be distracted. They approach my favorite tree. Soon now. . . . It spins in its socket, each limb a saber of glass. But she drops to the ground at precisely the right moment, and her monk moves with her in instant response. They inch their way forward now, the limbs flashing harmlessly, cold fire above them. Yet Endway's Shoot is next, where I took my second Alice, and the Passage of Moons may take them yet, even aware of the peril. And already she calls again.—Nelsor . . . ?

16

Kalifriki sat all the next day in meditation, his bow before him upon the ground. When he had finished he walked on the shore for a long while, watching the waves come in.

Alice met him on his return and they took a late supper together.

"When do you plan to embark for Ubar?" she asked him, after a long silent time.

"Soon," he said, "if all goes well."

"We will visit my vessel in the morning?"

"Yes."

"And then?"

"It depends partly on how long the work there takes."

" 'Partly'?"

"I think that I will want to meditate some more afterwards. I do not know how long that will take."

"Whenever . . ." she answered.

"I know that you are eager," he said later. "But this part must not be rushed."

"I understand."

He walked with her then into the town, passing lighted residences, some shops, government buildings. Many of the sounds of the city had grown still with the darkness, but there was music from some establishments, shouts, laughter, the creaking of a few passing carts, the stamping of horses' feet; they smelled spices in some neighborhoods, perfumes in others, incense from a church.

"What did you do," he asked her, from across a table where they sat sipping a sharp yellow wine, "in the five years between your escape from Aidon and your coming to see me?"

"I traveled," she replied, "seeking you—or someone like you—and trying to find the surface locus of that string. It had seemed bound to this world, as if it were somehow being employed. I supposed that one who had mastered it could be the one I needed to help me in this. I traveled with many servants—

with some large male always in charge—as if I were part of a great man's retinue rather than owner of the lot. It is difficult being a woman on this world. I visited Egypt, Athens, Rome, many places. Finally, I heard stories of a man called Kalifriki, who had been employed by Popes, Emperors, Sultans. I traced the stories down. It took a long time, but I could afford to pay for every scrap of information. They led me here."

"Who told you the stories?"

"A poet. He called himself Omar, tentmaker."

"Ah, yes. A good man. Drank too much, though," said Kalifriki, sipping his wine. "And locally?"

"A priest named Basileos."

"Yes. One of my agents. I am surprised he did not warn me."

"I came immediately. I hurried. There was no opportunity for him to beat my arrival with a message. He told me to make further inquiry of Stassinopoulos, but I decided to ask for you here by name instead. I suspected by then that you had a second identity, and I was certain that a man such as yourself would be too curious not to give me audience under the circumstances. I was in a hurry. Five years of hearing their cries has been too long."

"You still hear them, right now?"

"No. Tonight they are silent," she said.

The moon fell down the sky, was caught in the Golden Horn.

17

Now, Nelsor, they have reached the Shoot, a mountain hurtling by them, but feet above the ground. They must crawl upon their bellies here, and even then, if one of my small satellites whose long ellipse brings it by here has so rotated that some downward projection rakes the land—*quish!* A pair of stepped-on cockroaches. Too fast? True. But this is but the foreplay, dear companion, my mentor. She calls to you again. Do you hear her? Do you wish to answer her? Can you? Ah! another rock—and a jagged beauty it is!—races its purple shadow above the blood-red way. By them. And still they crawl. No matter. There will be more.

18

They completed the transfer on the Sea of Marmara that morning and afternoon. Then Kalifriki, clad in brown kimono and sandals, meditated for a brief time. At some point his hand went forward to take hold of the bow. Bearing it with him, he walked away from his villa down toward the sea. Alice, glimpsing his passage from her window, followed him at a distance. She saw him walk upon the shore, then halt, take forth a cloth and bind his eyes with it. He braced the bow, removed an arrow from its case, set it against the string. Then he stood holding them, unmoving.

Minutes passed on toward the end of day and he did not stir. A gull flew near, screaming. The better part of an hour went by. Then another gull passed. Kalifriki raised the bow almost casually, drew it, released the arrow into the air. It passed beside the bird and a single feather came loose, drifted downward.

He removed the cloth from his eyes and watched the feather rock its way to the water. She wanted to sing, but she only smiled.

Kalifriki turned then and waved to her.

"We leave for Ubar in the morning," he called out.

"Did you want the bird or the feather?" she asked, as they walked toward each other.

"To eat the bird is not to digest its flight," he replied.

19

They have passed Endway's Shoot, where my moons flow like a string of bright beads. Leaving the passage like a trail of blood behind them, they rise, turning sharply to the left, climbing to the yellow ridge that will take them down into the valley where they must pass through my Garden of Frozen Beings, the place where I collected my third Alice. . . . What is that? A question? A chuckle? Nelsor? Do you stir? Would you enjoy a ticket to this final festival? Why, then you shall have one, if you be able to use it. I have not felt such enthusiasm from you in ages. Come then to me if you can. I touch the bone, your skull. I summon you, lord, my mentor, to this place and time, Nelsor, for you were always my master in the matter of killing Alices. It is fitting that you be present when the collection is made complete. Come to me now, Nelsor, out of darkness. This spectacle is yours. By bone, siphon, and dot, I summon you! Come!

20

They came to Ubar, city of Shaddad ibn Ad, to be called Iram in the Koran, oasis town of lofty pillars, "the like of which were not produced in the land." Alice's hair was red now, and she wore a white garment and a light veil upon her face; Kalifriki had on his kimono and sandals, a cloth about his eyes, his bow upon his back, laquered case beside it containing a single arrow.

Passing amid a sea of tents, they made their way down avenues lined with merchants, traders, beggars, to the sound of camel bells, gusts of wind, and the rattle of palm fronds. Conversation, song, and invective sounded about them in a double-dozen tongues. They came at last to the great-gated pillars through which they passed, entering into the town proper, where the splashing sounds of fountains came to them from within adobe-walled gardens; and white-stuccoed buildings gleamed in the morning sun, bands of blue, green, red, and yellow tiles adorning their palace-high walls.

"I seem to recall the dining area of the inn as being located in a kind of grotto," Kalifriki said, "within a rocky hillside, with the rest of the establishment constructed right, left, and forward of it, using the face of the hillside as a rear wall."

"That is correct," she said. "The cavern keeps the place cool by day. The cooking fires are well vented to the rear. You descend four or five stone steps on entering, bearing to the right—"

"Where is the mirror located?"

"On the wall to the left as you go in, below the steps."

"Metal, isn't it?"

"Brass or bronze—I forget."

"Then let us go in, be seated, have a cooling drink, and make certain that everything is still this way. On the way out, pause and investigate the mirror as you pretend to study your appearance. Lower the veil as you do so. If it attempts to draw you through, I will be near enough for you to take my hand. If it does not, turn away as if you are about to depart. Then return, as in afterthought, and employ that transport sequence you learned from your predecessors."

"Yes. There is the place up ahead now," she said.

He followed, and she took him in.

21

See, Nelsor? They are at the Garden of Frozen Beings now, place of your own design, if you recall—though in your original plan it was only for display. I came across it in an odd memory cache. See how cunningly it is wrought? It holds your studies of living things from a dozen worlds, in all sizes and colors, set upon many levels, in many interesting poses. Impossible not to pass among several at any given time. I added the Series Perilous.

I took an Alice here, crushed by the blue spiral, eighth from the left—where she lay long in two pieces, gasping—for not calculating the death sequence correctly; and one back at Endway's Shoot, smeared to a long streak, though barely noticeable upon the red-stone; and another well flayed and diced in the crystal forest, by my *arbor decapitant*.

The first three, which you managed yourself—before your second disorientation—were so much more elegantly done. . . .

22

Finishing their drinks, Kalifriki and Alice rose and crossed the refreshment area. They passed the metal mirror and mounted the steps. At the threshold, she paused.

"A moment," she said. "I want to check my hair in that mirror we passed."

Returning down the stair, she produced a comb. At the mirror, she made a quick adjustment of several stray tresses, letting her veil fall as she did so.

Kalifriki stood behind her. "We must be at least partway entered before I shift," he whispered, "if I am to lay the thread in that universe so as to benefit our course through it. Remember what I said of the phenomenon. Whenever you are ready . . ."

"Good," she said, putting away her comb, turning toward the door.

Three beats later she turned back, lips set in a tight line, raising her hand, touching upon the reflecting surface. After a moment, she located the pulses, passed her hand through the activation sequence.

As her fingers penetrated the interface, Kalifriki, behind her, placed his hand upon her shoulder, following a small squeeze from her free hand.

Her entire arm passed through the interface, and Kalifriki took them to the Valley of Frozen Time, where he removed his blindfold. He regarded the thread's passage through the placeless time into the timeless place. Its twistings were complicated, the nexuses of menace manifold. Alice tried to speak to him, not knowing that words, like wind or music, could not manifest in this place of sculpture, painting, map. Twisting the thread, he flicked it three times, to see it settle at last into the most appropriate bessel functions he could manage under the circumstances, racing ahead to meet himself down thoroughfares of worlds-yet-to-be, and even as it plied its bright way he felt the tug of Time Thawing, replaced his blindfold, and set his hand again upon Alice's shoulder, to feel them drawn back to the waters of a small lake in the toy universe of the collector of Alices, piecemeal, who must even now be wondering at their interrupted passage.

23

Good of you to have summoned me back to my world, Aidon. What have you done to it? What are these silly games you have been about? Aidon, Aidon. . . . Is this how you read my intention? Did you really think the bitches worth the concerted efforts of an entire universe, to crush them in manners you found esthetically gratifying? Did you think I wanted to construct a theme amusement park? You profane the memory of the woman I love. You should have taken instruction from my disposition of the first three. There was a point to those—a very important point. One which you have been neglecting.

Lord, Nelsor, master, my mentor. I am sorry if the program is faulty. I had it that the killing of Alices was the highest value in the universe, as taken from your own example. See! See how this one must scramble, to avoid the hanging twar? *She has generalized the experience of two of her sisters, to learn it is not the* twar *nor the* twar's *physical position that matters, but rather that position in the sequence of encounters. She had to abstract the series from the previous deaths. See how she must scramble—and her companion after her—to dodge the falling* frogbart, *leap high above the lower limb of the* gride? *When the* bropples *rolled around them she knew just how to dive—and to stand perfectly still till the* wonjit *exhausted its energies. See where the* jankel *has cut her arm? And even now she must pass the way of the* vum. *There is fine sport in her gasping, her bleeding, the tearing of her garments, in seeing the sweat pour from her. And the* slyth *yet remains, and the* fangrace-pair. *Tell me how this differs from the doomed races where you ran the earlier Alices. How have I mistaken your intent? When you ceased being able to function I was proud to take on your role. I am sorry if—*

Aidon, it broke me to do as I did with the first three. I retreated into my second madness over my actions, still unsatisfied. Worse than unsatisfied, actually. I hated them, true, and it made it easier to do what I had to, to learn certain things. Still, it hurt me, also, especially in that I did not learn what I wished, though it narrowed the field. You should have summoned me for the fourth, the fifth, the sixth. There was data that I required there—lost to me now!

Not so, lord! For I recorded them! You can summon them! Have them back! Deal with them further! I have done it many times—for practice. I even bring in outsiders for fresh rites. I have performed the ritual of the dying Alices over and over in your name—hoping to effect your repair in the reenactment. I have been faithful to your procedure—What? You have not employed that command mode since ship-time. . . . You would retire me? Do not! There is an important thing I have yet to tell you! I——

Go away, Aidon. Go away. I would rid myself of your bumbling presence, for you have offended me. Let us say that it was an honest mistake. Still, I no longer wish to have you about, chortling over my undertakings, misreading all my actions, distracting me with your apologies. Before you fade entirely, see how I dismantle your remaining stations of blood. It is not games that *I* desire of the scarred lady I hate. But you are right in one thing. I will have the others back, as you recorded them—messy though the prospect be. She will follow the thread of a new course to the Place of Facing Skulls. By dot, bone, and siphon, this one will give me what I want. Go away, Aidon. Go away.

Come back to the Killing Ground, Alice, my last. The rules you've learned no longer apply. Keep calling to me. You shall have my answer, a piece at a time.

24

Provoking *the fangrace-pair to* attack simultaneously, Alice left them tangled in each other's many limbs. Passing behind the nearer then, she led Kalifriki to a narrow bridge which took them above a canyon whose bottom was lost in blackness. Achieving its farther side, she took him down a twisting way beneath an evening sky of dark blue wherein lights that were not stars burned unblinking at near distances. Vivid, against the darkness, an incandescent rainbow took form.

"Strange," she muttered.

"What?" Kalifriki asked.

"There was never a rainbow here before."

"And it is night, is it not?" Kalifriki asked.

"Yes. It began darkening as we entered that last place."

"In some traditions on Earth a rainbow is the sign of a new covenant," Kalifriki said.

"If that is the message, it is more cryptic than communicative," she said.

Suddenly, the faint sounds of female voices which had been with them constantly since their arrival rose in volume. From sighs to wailings, they had been shaped somehow into a slow, eerie tune which rose and fell as if working toward an ominous crescendo it never quite reached, returning constantly to begin again, yet another variation on plaints of pain, punctuated with staccato bursts of hysterical laughter.

A cool wind came by, gusting among the high rocks amid which they moved. On several occasions, the ground shook beneath their feet.

Reaching the end of their downward way and turning to the left, Alice beheld a deep crater in which a lake of orange lava boiled, flames darting above it, casting its light upon the high, piped walls which surrounded it. Their trail split here, an arm of it going in either direction about the lake's oval perimeter, cinder-strewn between its jagged shores and the rise of the organpipe walls.

Alice halted.

"What is the matter?" Kalifriki asked.

"A burning lake," she said. "It wasn't here before."

"What was?"

"A maze, full of pits and deadfalls, flooded periodically with rushing torrents."

"What now?"

"I suppose we must choose a way and go on, to find the place of which I told you that first night over dinner—the place we have glimpsed but never quite reached. There are bones there, and an open wall. I think it is the place of the singularity. Which way should I go?"

"Let us trust to the falling of the thread. Find a random way to choose."

She stooped and picked up a pebble. Turning, she cast it, hard, back in the direction from which they had come. It struck against the rock wall and bounded back. It rolled past them to the right.

"Right," she said, and they turned and took up their way again, in that direction.

The trail was perhaps six feet in width, light from the blazing cauldron to their left casting their shadows grotesquely upon the fluted wall. The way curved in and out as they went; and they felt the heat—painfully, after a time—upon their left sides. Dark fumes obscured the starlike lights in the sky, though the rainbow still glowed brightly. The chorus of pained voices was partly muted by the popping and crackling from below, by the faint roaring that came in undertone.

As they rounded a bend they heard a moaning.

"Alice . . ." came a soft call from the right.

She halted.

Bleeding from countless cuts, one leg missing from below the knee, the other from above it, left arm dangling by a thread of flesh, a woman who resembled her lay upon a low ledge to the right, face twisted in the orange glow, her remaining eye focused upon them.

"Alice—don't—go—on," she gasped. "It—is—awful. Kill me—quickly—please. . . ."

"What happened? What did this to you?" Alice asked.

"The tree—tree of glass—by the lake."

"But that is far. How did you get here?"

"Don't know," came the reply. "Why is it—so? What—have we done?"

"I don't know."

"Kill me."

"I cannot."

"Please. . . ."

Kalifriki moved forward. Alice did not see what he did. But she knew, and the broken lady did not call to them again.

They passed on in silence then, the lake growing more turbulent as they moved, now shooting great fountains of fire and molten material high into the air. The heat and fumes grew more oppressive. Periodically, niches glowed again in the wall to their right, wherein bleeding Alices stood, eyes staring, unseeing, straight ahead, lips twisting in their song which rose in intensity now, overcoming the lake's roaring. Whenever they approached these figures, however, they faded, though the song remained.

Then, in the flaring light, as they neared the far end of the trail, Alice beheld a rough area amid the cinders and congealed slag. She slowed, as she realized that the mangled remains of a human body were smeared before her, still somehow stirring. She halted when she saw the half-crushed head beside the way.

Its lips moved, and a wavery voice said, "Give him what he wants, that I may know peace."

"What—What is it that he wants?" she asked.

"You know," it gasped. "You know. Tell him!"

Then the lake bubbled and roared more loudly. A great strand of flame and lava leaped above it and fell toward them. Alice retreated quickly, pushing Kalifriki backward behind her. The fiery mass fell across the trail, obliterating the remains, draining, fuming, back into the lake. When it was gone, the ground smoking before them, the remains of the dead Alice had vanished, also.

They halted, waiting for the way to cool, and Kalifriki asked, "What is this knowledge of which she spoke?"

"I—I'm not certain," Alice replied.

"I've a feeling," Kalifriki said, "the question will be repeated in more specific and equally colorful terms at some point."

"I'd guess you're right," she told him.

Shortly, they walked on, treading quickly across the ravaged area, beneath the rainbow, the song suddenly reaching a higher pitch of wailing as they went.

As they neared the farther end of the lake, another molten spume reached near at hand. Alice halted, waiting to see in which direction the flashing tower might topple. But it stood, swaying, for a long while, almost as if trying to decide the matter itself. It took on a spiraling twist for a while before abruptly falling toward the wall perhaps twenty paces ahead of them.

They retreated even farther as this occurred. The spume fell in slow motion above the trail, its tip touching the wall, whence it flowed downward to the right-hand trail's edge. Its upper portion remained in place, ten or twelve feet overhead, spirals working through it in two directions, braiding themselves now into a sputtering yellow-orange fretwork of light and molten material. The archway thus formed ceased its swaying and stood pulsing before them.

"We suddenly have a burning gate ahead of us," Alice stated.

"Is there any other way to proceed?" Kalifriki asked.

"No," she said.

"Then it would seem we have little choice."

"True. I just wanted you to know the nature of this encounter."

"Thank you. I am ready."

They moved ahead, and the archway maintained its position as they approached. Passing beneath it, the air was filled with crackling sounds and the prospect wavered. Alice's next step took her onto a rough silvery way with nothing about her but the starlike lights. Another pace, and Kalifriki had passed through also, the gateway vanishing behind him.

It was not a continuous surface upon which they stood, but rather a forty-foot span of about the same width as the trail they had quitted. It ended abruptly in all directions. Looking downward over its edge, she saw, at a distance impossible to estimate, the twisted surface of the land they had been traversing, cracked, pierced, brightly pied, monoliths darting about its surface, the rainbow still arched above it; and even as she watched, it seemed to change shape, lakes flowing into valleys, flames leaping up out of shadows and crests, new jigsaw pieces of color replacing old ones with less than perfect fit. And about them, still, rang the plaints of the dead Alices. She moved ahead, toward the farther end of the silver way.

"We're high above the land," she said, "walking on the surface of a narrow asteroid. It is like a broken-out piece of a bridge. I'm heading toward its farther end."

"Alice," Kalifriki said as they began to move again, "I have a question."

"What is it?"

"Did you come to Earth on the first vessel or the second?"

"Why do you ask that?"

"You said that Nelsor and four clones came here and had their trouble. Then later, his Alice, learning of this, made the voyage with the three remaining clones, yourself among them."

"Did I? I don't recall exactly how I phrased it."

"Then, when you told me of your bedroom encounter with Nelsor, it sounded as if you, he, and the original Alice all made a single journey together."

"Oh. That happened on a different voyage, elsewhere."

"I see," Kalifriki said, matching her pace.

Tenuous wisps of fog swept by them as they walked, followed by larger puffs. Something massive drifted downward from overhead, possibly on a collision course, possibly about to miss them. It was of about the same shape and albedo as the thing on which they moved.

"Another asteroid headed this way," she reported. "A bit of fog's come by, too."

"Let's keep going to the end."

"Yes."

Just as they reached the extremity of their way, the second piece of spanning slid into place before them and remained there, as if joined with their own. This one curved to the left.

"We've acquired an extension," she said. "I'm going to continue along it."

"Do so."

Several additional pieces moved by as they walked—one of them the section they had quitted, removing itself from the rear and drifting forward to join them again ahead.

"It's extending itself down toward a cloud bank," she told him, as she peered in the new direction it was taking. Then, too, they seemed to be moving, relative to the overall form of the shifting panorama below.

She crossed to another section. The clouds came on quickly; they were of soft pink, pale blue, light lime, streaked through each other in delicate abstract waves.

Several hundred paces later she heard a scream. Halting, and looking to the right, whence it seemed to have come, she beheld nothing but clouds. She began to gnaw at her lower lip as the cry was repeated.

"What is it?" Kalifriki asked.

"I don't know."

Then the clouds parted, and she saw a pair of drifting boulders but a few feet distant. The upper torso, head, and shoulders of a woman resembling herself lay sprawled upon the left-hand stone. Severed from these and occupying the slightly lower right-hand one lay the rest of her, twitching.

"Alice!" the figure cried. "He would know which of us was responsible. None of us could tell him. That leaves only you. Tell him what happened, for mercy's sake!"

Then the two rocks flew off in opposite directions and the clouds closed in again. Kalifriki could feel Alice shaking.

"If you know whatever it is he wants," he said, "perhaps you should tell him. It may make life a lot easier."

"Perhaps I do and perhaps I don't," she said. "I suppose I'll learn when I'm asked a direct question. Oh!"

"What? What is it?"

"Nelsor. I reached him for a moment. Or he reached me. He is gone now."

"Could you tell anything about his condition?"

"He seemed a mix of emotions. Happy that I was coming—in some other way disturbed. I don't know."

They walked again. The singing went on, and periodically they could feel the vibrations as new pieces of their twisted passageway through the sky assembled themselves. The colored fogs parted and came together again, flirting with her vision, providing tantalizing glimpses of some vantage that lay far ahead.

Their way seemed telescoped from break to break in their passage through the fog. Suddenly, Alice halted, stiffening, saying "Stop!" sharply.

"What is it?" Kalifriki asked.

"End of the trail, for the moment," she replied. "It just stops here. We are at the edge, and I am looking down again, through a thinning fog, at the distant land. The fog at our sides is dissipating now, too. That which is ahead of us is still thick. A redness flows through it."

They waited, and the red mist passed by degrees, revealing, first, an almost sculpted-seeming rocky prominence, pointed centrally, descending symmetrically at either hand and curving forward into a pair of gray-blue stony shoulders, and before them a flat yellow oval of sandy stone, raised above lesser step-like formations, irregular, more blue than gray, descending into mist. To the rear, set within the bulk of the prominence, a shelf-like niche was recessed at shoulder height; and at the oval's approximate center lay a well, a low wall of red stone blocks about its mouth. Another structured wall—this one of black stone—stood to the far left and downward of the oval, perhaps twenty feet in length, eight in height. Chains hung upon it. And this entire vision seemed to be quivering, as through a heat-haze.

More of the mist blew away, and the lines of the lower slopes came into view. Watching, as the last of it fled, Alice saw that the base of the entire prominence was an abruptly terminated thing, at about twice the height's distance below the oval, jagged blue icicles hanging beneath, as if a frozen mountaintop had been torn loose and hurled into space to hover against the blackness and the unblinking points of light; and now she could see that the rainbow's end lay within the oval.

Despite this clearing, the entire monumental affair still seemed to be vibrating.

"What is it?" Kalifriki asked at last.

Slowly, she began describing it to him.

25

Nelsor, I had only one thing to tell you before, but now I have two. Please acknowledge. There is perturbation within the well of the dot because another singularity is approaching—also a second peculiar item, of energy and negative field pressure trapped within a tube. Please acknowledge. This is a serious matter. I understand now what it was about the monk which first troubled me. Here at the center of things I can feel it clearly. He is very dangerous and should be removed from our universe at once. Release me and I will deal with him immediately. Acknowledge, Nelsor! Acknowledge! There is danger here!

Oh. The other thing I wanted to tell you concerns the first Alice. I had located some small memory caches for her. They were inadvertently recorded because of a peculiar conflict situation. Nelsor, I am going to begin pushing against this retirement program if you do not answer me. . . .

26

Alice stared at the vibrating landscape in the sky. A final span of bridge came drifting in slowly from her right, streaming colors as it passed through the rainbow. The voices of her dead sisters ceased, and only the wind that blows between the worlds could be heard in its chill passage.

"It is called the Killing Ground," she said then. "It has been transferred here from another location since my last visit. It is the final place."

"You never referred to it so before," Kalifriki said.

"I only just learned the name. I have reached Nelsor again. Or he has reached me. He bids me cross over. He says, 'Come back to the Killing Ground, Alice, my last.'"

"I thought you had never been to the final place."

"I told you I had glimpsed it."

As the last piece of bridge slid into place, connecting their span with the lowest step beneath the oval, she saw the vibrations shake loose a small white object from the niche. With a sudden clarity of vision, she discerned it to be a skull. It bounced, then rolled, coming to rest in the sand near a spreading red stain.

"Kalifriki," she said, "I am afraid. He is changed. Everything is changed. I don't want to cross over to that place."

"I don't believe I can get us out at this point," Kalifriki said. "I feel we are bound too tightly to my initial disposition of the thread, back in the Valley of Frozen Time, to employ it otherwise here. We must pass through whatever lies ahead, or be stopped by it."

"Please make certain," she asked, licking her lips. "He is calling again. . . ."

27

Alice, Alice, Alice. You must be the one. It could have been none of the other wasted ladies. Even if Aidon fumbled in his approach by not putting the questions, there should have been some lapse on their part, some betrayal of the truth, should there not? The guilty one would not even have come in. . . . Why, why are you here at all? And that stranger at your side. . . . What is your plan? If it is you, why are you here? I am troubled. I must put you the questions. Why did you come back, Alice my last? It must be you . . . mustn't it? And why do you hesitate now? Come back to the Killing Ground, where her blood stains the sand and our skills lie in constant testimony to the crime. Come back. No? Then I call upon the siphon to bear you to me, here in the last place, beside the well of the dot that is the center of the universe. Even now it snakes forth. You *will* come to me, Alice, here and now, on this most holy ground of truth. I reach for you. You cannot resist—

Not now, Aidon. Not now. Go back. Go back. I have retired you. Go back.

It comes for you, Alice.

28

"I am sorry," Kalifriki said. "It is as I told you."

Staring ahead, Alice saw a black line emerge from the well, lash about, grow still, then move again, rising, swaying in her direction, lengthening. . . .

"The siphon," she said. "A piece of ship's equipment. Very versatile. He is sending it for me."

"Is it better to wait for it or go on?"

"I would rather walk than be dragged. Perhaps he will not employ it if I come on my own."

She began moving again. The black hose, which had been approaching, snakelike, halted its advance as she came toward it down the final length of silver. When she came up in front of it, it retreated. Step by step then, it withdrew before her. She hesitated a moment when she came to the end of the span. It leaned slightly toward her. At this, she took another step. It backed off immediately.

"We're here," she said to Kalifriki. "There are several ledges now, like a rough stairway, to climb."

She began mounting them, and as soon as she reached the flat sandy area the siphon withdrew entirely, back into the well. She continued to advance, looking about. She came to the well, halted, and peered down into it.

"We are at the well," she said, and Kalifriki removed his hand from her shoulder and reached down to feel along its wall. "It goes all the way through this—asteroid," she continued. "The dot—the black hole—is down there at its center. The siphon is coiled about the inner perimeter, near to the lip. It shrinks, so that one circuit is sufficient to house it. Below, I can see the bright swirling of the disc. It is far down inside—perhaps midway."

"So this place is being eaten, down at its center," Kalifriki said. "I wonder if that is the cause of the vibration?"

She walked on, past the red stain and the skull, to regard the niche from which the skull had tumbled. Another skull rested there, far to the right, and a collection of pincers, tongs, drills, hammers, and chains lay in the middle area.

"Torture tools here," she observed.

Kalifriki, in the meantime, was pacing about the area, touching everything he encountered. Finally, he stopped beside the well. Looking back, Alice saw that the rainbow fell upon his shoulders.

Then, above the sighing of the wind, there came a voice.

"I am going to kill you, Alice," it said. "Very slowly and very terribly."

"Why?" she asked.

The voice seemed to be coming from the vicinity of the skull. It was, as she recalled it, the voice of Nelsor.

"All of the others are dead," he said. "Now it is your turn. Why did you come back?"

"I came here to help you," she said, "if I could."

"Why?" he asked, and the skull turned over so that the empty sockets faced her.

"Because I love you," she replied.

There came a dry chuckling sound.

"How kind of you," he said then. "Let us have a musical accompaniment to that tender sentiment. Alices, give us a song."

Immediately, the awful plaint began again, this time from near at hand. To her right, six nude duplicates of herself suddenly hung in chains upon the black wall. They were bruised but unmutilated. Their eyes did not focus upon any particular objects as they began to shriek and wail. At the end of their line hung a final set of chains.

"When I have done with you, you shall join my chorus," Nelsor's voice went on.

"Done?" she said, raising a pair of pliers from the ledge and replacing it. "Employing things such as this?"

"Of course," he replied.

"I love you, Nelsor."

"That should make it all the more interesting."

"You are mad."

"I don't deny it."

"Could you forget all this and let me help you?"

"Forget? Never. I am in control here. And it is not your love or your help that I seek."

She looked at Kalifriki, and he removed the bow from his shoulder and strung it. Then he opened the case and withdrew its arrow, the spectrum blazing upon its tip.

"If your friend wishes to punch a hole in my head, that is all right with me. It will not let out the evil spirits, though."

"Is it possible for you to reembody yourself and come away with me?" she asked.

Again, the laugh.

"I shall not leave this place, and neither shall you," he said.

Kalifriki set the arrow to the bowstring.

"Not now, Aidon!" Nelsor shouted. Then, "Or perhaps your friend would shoot an arrow down the well to destroy the dot?" he said. "If he can, by all means bid him do so. For destroying the universe is the only thing I know to protect you from my wrath."

"You heard him, Kalifriki," she said.

Kalifriki drew back upon the bowstring.

"You are a fool," Nelsor said, "to bring—of all things—an archer here to destroy me . . . one of the legendary ones, I gather, who need not even see the target . . . against a dead man and a black hole."

Kalifriki turned suddenly, leaning back, arrow pointed somewhere overhead.

". . . And a disoriented one, at that," he added.

Kalifriki held this position, his body vibrating in time with the ground.

"You are a doomed, perverse fool," Nelsor said, "and I will use your sisters in your questioning through pain, in testament against you. They will rend you, stretch you, dislocate you, crack your bones."

There came a sound of chains rattling against stone. The chorus was diminished by half as the restraints fell from three of the Alices and their singing ceased. At that moment, their eyes focused upon her, and they began to move forward.

"Let it begin," he said, "in this place of bloody truth."

Kalifriki released his arrow, upward. Bearing its dark burden, the Dagger of Rama sped high and vanished into the blackness.

29

Nelsor! She has brought with her a being capable of destroying our universe, and it is possible that he just has, I must perform some massive calculations to confirm my suspicion— but in the meantime our survival depends upon our acting as if it is correct. We cannot return to our alpha point and start again if I am destroyed. And if I am destroyed you are destroyed, along with this place and all of your Alices. We are facing the end of the world! I must confer with you immediately!

30

The three Alices advanced upon the first stair.

31

Aidon! Whatever it is, this is not the time for it! I am finally arrived at the moment for which I have waited all these years. I find your importunities distracting. Whatever it is, deal with it yourself, as you would. I will not be interrupted till I have done with this Alice. Stay away from me until then!

32

The three Alices mounted the first step. At their back, their sisters' song reached a new pitch, as if the crescendo might finally be attained.

33

Very well, Nelsor. I shall act. First Alice, I summon what remains of you. By bone, dot, and siphon, I call you to embodiment upon the Killing Ground! Perhaps you can reason with him.

34

Alice glanced at her three sisters, approaching now upon the farther stair. Kalifriki lowered his bow and unbraced it, slung it. He reached up then and removed the bandage from his eyes.

"Nelsor, listen to me," Alice said. "Aidon will be destroyed. So will the programs which maintain your own existence—unless you reembody and shift your entire consciousness back into human form. Do that and come away with me, for this place is doomed. No matter what our differences, we can resolve them and be happy again. I will take good care of you."

"'Again'?" Nelsor said. "When were we ever subject to mutual happiness? I do not understand you, clone. What I do not understand most, however, is why one of you killed my wife. And I feel strongly that it was you, Alice my last. Would you care to comment on this?"

From somewhere, a bell began to ring.

"Who sounds the ship's alert?" he cried.

"Probably Aidon," she responded, "as it realizes the truth of what I have been saying."

"You have not yet answered my question," he said. "Did *you* kill my wife?"

The second skull fell from the niche, rolled to the bloody area near to the first. The bell continued to ring. The voices of the three chained Alices rose and rose.

She grimaced. The other Alices mounted another step.

"It was self-defense," she said. "She attacked me. I had no desire to harm her."

"Why would she attack you?"

"She was jealous—of us."

"What? How could that be? There was nothing between us."

"But there was," she said. "You once mistook me for her, and we had our pleasure of it."

"Why did you permit it?"

"For you," she said. "I wanted to comfort you in your need. I love you."

"Then it could have gone by and been forgotten. How did she learn of it?"

"I told her, when she singled me out for reprimand over something one of the others had done. She slapped me and I slapped her back. Soon we were fighting on the ground, here—when this place was elsewhere. She struck me about the head with a tool she had at her belt. This is why I wear these scars. I thought she would kill me. But there was a rock nearby. I raised it and swung it. I was not trying to kill her, only to save myself."

"So you are the one."

"We are the same. You know that. Down to the cellular level. Down to the genes. You cannot have her back. Have me instead. I am the same flesh. You could not tell the difference then. It will feel the same now. And I will be better to you than she ever was. She was rude, imperious, egotistical. Come back. Come away with me, Nelsor my love. I will care for you always."

He screamed, and the three Alices halted at the top of the stair.

Slowly, a haze formed about the skull which faced her.

"Go back, Alices. Go back," he said. "I will deal with her myself."

The skull fell backward—now somewhat more than a skull, as the outlines of features had occurred about it in the haze—and a wavering began beneath it, delineating the form of a body, pulsing it into greater definition. Beside it, however, a similar phenomenon began to invest the second skull. The three Alices at the edge of the oval turned away, began walking back down the stair just as their sisters hit and ran the crescendo, voices changing from wailing to pure song. The three never returned to the wall, however, but faded from sight before they reached the bottom stair. At that time, the chains rang against the wall, and Kalifriki saw that the others had vanished as well.

Shortly, the nude form of a dark-haired, short-bearded man of medium stature took shape, breathing slowly, upon the sand.

Beside him, another Alice came into focus, grew more and more substantial.

"You did not tell me the full story," Kalifriki said as they watched.

"I told you everything essential to the job. Would more detail have changed anything?"

"Perhaps," he said. "You fled after the fight, and this is your first time back then, correct?"

"Yes," she said.

"So you were not party to the other six Alices' journeys to this place, save that you monitored them to learn what you could of it."

"That's right."

"You might have warned them that any of them would be suspect. And after the first of them died you knew Nelsor's state of mind. You let your sisters go to their deaths without trying to stop them."

She looked away.

"It would have done no good," she said. "They were determined to resolve the matter. And you must remember that they were monitoring, too. After the first death, they were as aware as I was of his state of mind, and of the danger."

"Why didn't you stop the first one?"

"I was . . . weak," she said. "I was afraid. It would have meant telling them my story. They might have restrained me, to send me home for trial."

"You wished to take the place of the first Alice."

"I can't deny it."

"I suppose that is her upon the ground now."

"Who else could it be?"

Nelsor and the new Alice opened their eyes at about the same time.

"Is it you?" Nelsor asked softly.

"Yes," she answered.

Nelsor raised himself onto his elbows, sat up.

"So long . . ." he said. "It has been so long."

She smiled and sat up. In a moment they were in each other's arms. When they parted and she spoke again, her words were slurred:

"Aidon—message for you—to me gave," she said.

He rose to his feet, helped her to hers.

"What is the matter?" he asked.

"'Portant, 'im, to talk to. World ending. Arrow."

"It is nothing," Nelsor said. "He shot it off in the wrong direction. What is wrong with you?"

"Cur-va-ture. Perfect vector," she said, "to cir-cum-nav-i-gate small our uni-verse. Back soon. Other way."

"It doesn't matter," he said. "It's just an arrow."

She shook her head.

"It bears—an-other—dot."

"What? It's carrying a singularity around the universe on a collision course with Aidon?"

She nodded.

He turned away from her, to face Kalifriki.

"This is true?" he asked.

"This is true," Kalifriki replied.

"I don't believe it."

"Wait awhile," he said.

"It still won't destroy Aidon."

"Perhaps not, but it will destroy the programmed accretion disc and probably wreck your world that it holds together."

"What did she pay you to do this?"

"A lot," he said. "I don't kill for nothing if I can help it."

"The conscience of a mercenary," Nelsor said.

"I never killed three women who were trying to help me—for nothing."

"You don't understand."

"No. Is that because we're all aliens? Or is it something else?"

Just then, the new-risen Alice screamed. Both men turned their heads. She had wandered to the niche where her skull had lain, and only then seemed to notice her scarred clone standing nearby.

"You!" she cried. "Hurt me!"

She snatched the hammer from the ledge and rushed toward the clone. The Alice dodged her assault, reached for her wrist and missed, then pushed her away.

"She's damaged," Nelsor said, moving forward. "She's not responsible. . . ."

The original Alice recovered and continued her attack as Nelsor rushed toward them. Again, the other dodged and pushed, struck, pushed again. The incomplete Alice staggered backward, recovered her footing, screamed, swung the hammer again as her double moved to close with her.

Nelsor was almost upon them, when a final push carried her backward to strike her calves against the lip of the well.

He was wellside in an instant, reaching, reaching, leaning, and catching hold of her wrist. He continued to lean, was bent forward, fell. He disappeared into the well with her, their cries echoing back for several seconds, then ceasing abruptly.

"Lost!" the remaining Alice cried. "She has taken him from me!"

Kalifriki moved to the edge of the well and looked downward.

"Another case of self-defense," he said, "against the woman you wished to replace."

"Woman?" she said, moving forward. "She was incomplete, barely human. And you saw her attack me."

He nodded.

"Was it Nelsor you really wanted?" he said. "Or this? To be the last, the only, the mistress—the original?"

Tears ran down her cheeks.

"No, I loved him," she said.

"The feeling, apparently, was not mutual."

"You're wrong!" she said. "He did care!"

"As a clone. Not as his woman. Give up the memory. You are your own person now. Come! We should be leaving. I don't know exactly when—"

"No!" she cried, and the ground shook and the chains rattled. "No! I am mistress here now, and I will reembody him without memory of her! I will summon the three recorded clones to serve us. The others were witless. We shall dwell here together and make of it a new world. We can bring in what we choose, create what we need—"

"It is too late for that," Kalifriki said. "You brought me here to destroy a universe and I did. Even if it could be saved, you cannot dwell on the Killing Ground forever. It is already destroying you. Come away now. Find a new life—"

"No!" she answered. "I rule here! Even now, I take control of Aidon! I remember the command modes! I have reached him! I hold this universe in my hand! I can alter the very physical constants! I can warp space itself to turn your silly arrow away! Behold! I have digested its flight!"

The lights in the sky flickered for the first time and jumped to new positions.

"Change the topology and the geodesic will follow," Kalifriki said. "The Dagger of Rama will still find you. Come away!"

"You! You have hated me all along for what I am! As soon as I told you I was a clone you knew I was something less than the rest of you! But I can destroy you now, assassin! For I am mistress of the dot! I can wish you away in any manner I choose! There is no defense!"

"So it comes to that again," he said. "You *would* have me pit my thread against a singularity."

She laughed wildly.

"There is no contest there," she said. "You have already described the entanglement that would result. I believe I will burn you—"

Kalifriki moved his wrist, slowly, to a position above the well.

"What are you doing?" she said. "How can you interfere with my omniscience? My omnipotence? You can't touch me!"

"I told you that the circumference of the thread is less than a full circle," he stated. "I am cutting out a wedge from your disc."

"That close? You can't. If the warp extends to the hole you would violate thermodynamics. A black hole cannot shrink."

"No," he said. "The thread would probably be caused to deliver energy to replace it and increase the mass and the radius in compensation. But I am being careful not to let it stray so near, and not to have to test this hypothesis. My sense is extended along it."

"Then you will not die by fire," she said, slurring her words slightly. "By bone—dot—and siphon—I summon you! Sisters! Destroy this man!"

Kalifriki's head jerked to the left, the direction of her gaze.

The three Alices whose eyes focused were flickering into existence across the oval from him. Slowly, he withdrew his wrist beyond the well's wall.

"Kill him!" she said. "Before he kills us! Hurry!"

The three Alices moved, wraithlike, even before they were fully embodied, rainbow's light passing through them as they came on.

Solidifying before they arrived, they rushed past Kalifriki, to attack the one who had summoned them.

"Murderess!" one of them cried.

"Liar!" shrieked another.

"Cause of all our pain!" screamed the third.

The scarred Alice retreated, and Kalifriki shook out his thread so that it fell among them. A wall of flame rose up between the Alices and their victim.

"There is no time," he called out, "to stain this ground further! We must depart!"

He moved the thread to enclose the three Alices.

"I am taking them with me," he said. "You come, too! We must go!"

"No!" she answered, eyes flashing. "I will shunt your arrow! I will move this place itself! I will warp space even more!" The lights in the sky winked again, danced again. "I will avoid your doom, archer! I will—rebuild! I will—have—him—back! I—am—mistress—here—now! Begone! I—banish—the—lot—of—you!"

Kalifriki retreated with the three ladies, to the Valley of

Frozen Time. There, in the place that is sculpture, painting, map, he laid his way home. He could not speak to explain this, for this was not a place for words (nor wind, music, cries, wailing), nor they to thank him, were that their wish. And while scarred Alice stood upon the Killing Ground and invoked the powers of dot, siphon, and bone against the rushing Dagger of Rama as it cut its way around the universe, Kalifriki transported the three Alices from the land behind the mirror in vanished Ubar, taking them with him to his villa near the sea, though he feared them, knowing that he could never favor one over the others. But that was a problem to be dealt with at another time, for the ways of the thread are full of arrivals and departures, and even its master cannot digest its flight fully.

35

Alice at the end of the rainbow stands upon the red stain and watches the sky. The siphon brings her nourishment as she plies powers against powers in her contest with the inexorable doom she has loosed. A dark-haired, short-bearded man of medium stature sits upon the edge of the well and seems to watch her. Occasionally, she takes her pleasure of him and he tells her whatever she wishes to hear. She returns, refreshed then, to her duel, though it sometimes feels as if the circle of her universe no longer possesses 360 degrees. . . .

THE LAST DEFENDER
OF CAMELOT

The three muggers who stopped him that October night in San Francisco did not anticipate much resistance from the old man, despite his size. He was well-dressed, and that was sufficient.

The first approached him with his hand extended. The other two hung back a few paces.

"Just give me your wallet and your watch," the mugger said. "You'll save yourself a lot of trouble."

The old man's grip shifted on his walking stick. His shoulders straightened. His shock of white hair tossed as he turned his head to regard the other.

"Why don't you come and take them?"

The mugger began another step but he never completed it. The stick was almost invisible in the speed of its swinging. It struck him on the left temple and he fell.

Without pausing, the old man caught the stick by its middle with his left hand, advanced and drove it into the belly of the next nearest man. Then, with an upward hook as the man doubled, he caught him in the softness beneath the jaw, behind the chin, with its point. As the man fell, he clubbed him with its butt on the back of the neck.

The third man had reached out and caught the old man's upper arm by then. Dropping the stick, the old man seized the mugger's shirtfront with his left hand, his belt with his right, raised him from the ground until he held him at arm's length above his head and slammed him against the side of the building to his right, releasing him as he did so.

He adjusted his apparel, ran a hand through his hair and retrieved his walking stick. For a moment he regarded the three fallen forms, then shrugged and continued on his way.

There were sounds of traffic from somewhere off to his left. He turned right at the next corner. The moon appeared above tall buildings as he walked. The smell of the ocean was on the air. It had rained earlier and the pavement still shone beneath streetlamps. He moved slowly, pausing occasionally to examine the contents of darkened shop windows.

After perhaps ten minutes, he came upon a side street showing more activity than any of the others he had passed. There was a drugstore, still open, on the corner, a diner farther up the block, and several well-lighted storefronts. A number of people were walking along the far side of the street. A boy coasted by on a bicycle. He turned there, his pale eyes regarding everything he passed.

Halfway up the block, he came to a dirty window on which was painted the word READINGS. Beneath it were displayed the outline of a hand and a scattering of playing cards. As he passed the open door, he glanced inside. A brightly garbed woman, her hair bound back in a green kerchief, sat smoking at the rear of the room. She smiled as their eyes met and crooked an index finger toward herself. He smiled back and turned away, but . . .

He looked at her again. What was it? He glanced at his watch.

Turning, he entered the shop and moved to stand before her. She rose. She was small, barely over five feet in height.

"Your eyes," he remarked, "are green. Most gypsies I know have dark eyes."

She shrugged.

"You take what you get in life. Have you a problem?"

"Give me a moment and I'll think of one," he said. "I just came in here because you remind me of someone and it bothers me—I can't think who."

"Come into the back," she said, "and sit down. We'll talk."

He nodded and followed her into a small room to the rear. A threadbare oriental rug covered the floor near the small table at which they seated themselves. Zodiacal prints and faded psychedelic posters of a semireligious nature covered the walls. A crystal ball stood on a small stand in the far corner beside a vase of cut flowers. A dark, long-haired cat slept on a sofa to the right of it. A door to another room stood slightly ajar beyond the sofa. The only illumination came from a cheap lamp on the table before him and from a small candle in a plaster base atop the shawl-covered coffee table.

He leaned forward and studied her face, then shook his head and leaned back.

She flicked an ash onto the floor.

"Your problem?" she suggested.

He sighed.

"Oh, I don't really have a problem anyone can help me with. Look, I think I made a mistake coming in here. I'll pay you for your trouble, though, just as if you'd given me a reading. How much is it?"

He began to reach for his wallet, but she raised her hand.

"Is it that you do not believe in such things?" she asked, her eyes scrutinizing his face.

"No, quite the contrary," he replied. "I am willing to believe in magic, divination and all manner of spells and sendings, angelic and demonic. But—"

"But not from someone in a dump like this?"

He smiled.

"No offense," he said.

A whistling sound filled the air. It seemed to come from the next room back.

"That's all right," she said, "but my water is boiling. I'd forgotten it was on. Have some tea with me? I do wash the cups. No charge. Things are slow."

"All right."

She rose and departed.

He glanced at the door to the front but eased himself back into his chair, resting his large, blue-veined hands on its padded arms. He sniffed then, nostrils flaring, and cocked his head as at some half-familiar aroma.

After a time, she returned with a tray, set it on the coffee table. The cat stirred, raised her head, blinked at it, stretched, closed her eyes again.

"Cream and sugar?"

"Please. One lump."

She placed two cups on the table before him.

"Take either one," she said.

He smiled and drew the one on his left toward him. She placed an ashtray in the middle of the table and returned to her own seat, moving the other cup to her place.

"That wasn't necessary," he said, placing his hands on the table.

She shrugged.

"You don't know me. Why should you trust me? Probably got a lot of money on you."

He looked at her face again. She had apparently removed some of the heavier makeup while in the back room. The jawline, the brow . . . He looked away. He took a sip of tea.

"Good tea. Not instant," he said. "Thanks."

"So you believe in all sorts of magic," she asked, sipping her own.

"Some," he said.

"Any special reason why?"

"Some of it works."

"For example?"

He gestured aimlessly with his left hand. "I've traveled a lot. I've seen some strange things."

"And you have no problems?"

He chuckled.

"Still determined to give me a reading? All right. I'll tell you a little about myself and what I want right now, and you can tell me whether I'll get it. Okay?"

"I'm listening."

"I am a buyer for a large gallery in the East. I am something of an authority on ancient work in precious metals. I am in town to attend an auction of such items from the estate of a private collector. I will go to inspect the pieces tomorrow. Naturally, I hope to find something good. What do you think my chances are?"

"Give me your hands."

He extended them, palms upward. She leaned forward and regarded them. She looked back up at him immediately.

"Your wrists have more rascettes than I can count."

"Yours seem to have quite a few, also."

She met his eyes for only a moment and returned her attention to his hands. He noted that she had paled beneath what remained of her makeup, and her breathing was now irregular.

"No," she finally said, drawing back, "you are not going to find here what you are looking for."

Her hand trembled slightly as she raised her teacup. He frowned.

"I asked only in jest," he said. "Nothing to get upset about. I doubted I would find what I am really looking for, anyway."

She shook her head.

"Tell me your name."

"I've lost my accent," he said, "but I'm French. The name is DuLac."

She stared into his eyes and began to blink rapidly.

"No . . ." she said. "No."

"I'm afraid so. What's yours?"

"Madam LeFay," she said. "I just repainted that sign. It's still drying."

He began to laugh, but it froze in his throat

"Now—I know—who—you remind me of . . ."

"You reminded me of someone, also. Now I, too, know."

Her eyes brimmed, her mascara ran.

"It couldn't be," he said. "Not here. . . . Not in a place like this. . . ."

"You dear man," she said softly, and she raised his right hand to her lips. She seemed to choke for a moment, then said, "I had thought that I was the last, and yourself buried at Joyous Gard. I never dreamed . . ." Then, "This?" gesturing about the room. "Only because it amuses me, helps to pass the time. The waiting—"

She stopped. She lowered his hand.

"Tell me about it," she said.

"The waiting?" he said. "For what do you wait?"

"Peace," she said. "I am here by the power of my arts, through all the long years. But you—How did you manage it?"

"I—" He took another drink of tea. He looked about the room. "I do not know how to begin," he said. "I survived the

final battles, saw the kingdom sundered, could do nothing—
and at last departed England. I wandered, taking service at
many courts, and after a time under many names, as I saw that I
was not aging—or aging very, very slowly. I was in India,
China—I fought in the Crusades. I've been everywhere. I've
spoken with magicians and mystics—most of them charlatans,
a few with the power, none so great as Merlin—and what had
come to be my own belief was confirmed by one of them, a man
more than half charlatan, yet . . ." He paused and finished his
tea. "Are you certain you want to hear all this?" he asked.

"I want to hear it. Let me bring more tea first, though."

She returned with the tea. She lit a cigarette and leaned
back.

"Go on."

"I decided that it was—my sin," he said. "with . . . the
Queen."

"I don't understand."

"I betrayed my Liege, who was also my friend, in the one
thing which must have hurt him most. The love I felt was stronger than loyalty or friendship—and even today, to this day, it
still is. I cannot repent, and so I cannot be forgiven. Those were
strange and magical times. We lived in a land destined to become myth. Powers walked the realm in those days, forces
which are now gone from the earth. How or why, I cannot say.
But you know that it is true. I am somehow of a piece with
those gone things, and the laws that rule my existence are not
normal laws of the natural world. I believe that I cannot die;
that it has fallen my lot, as punishment, to wander the world till
I have completed the Quest. I believe I will only know rest the
day I find the Holy Grail. Giuseppe Balsamo, before he became
known as Cagliostro, somehow saw this and said it to me just
as I had thought it, though I never said a word of it to him. And

so I have traveled the world, searching. I go no more as knight, or soldier, but as an appraiser. I have been in nearly every museum on Earth, viewed all the great private collections. So far, it has eluded me."

"You *are* getting a little old for battle."

He snorted.

"I have never lost," he stated flatly. "Down ten centuries, I have never lost a personal contest. It is true that I have aged, yet whenever I am threatened all of my former strength returns to me. But, look where I may, fight where I may, it has never served me to discover that which I must find. I feel I am unforgiven and must wander like the Eternal Jew until the end of the world."

She lowered her head.

". . . And you say I will not find it tomorrow?"

"You will never find it," she said softly.

"You saw that in my hand?"

She shook her head.

"Your story is fascinating and your theory novel," she began, "but Cagliostro was a total charlatan. Something must have betrayed your thoughts, and he made a shrewd guess. But he was wrong. I say that you will never find it, not because you are unworthy or unforgiven. No, never that. A more loyal subject than yourself never drew breath. Don't you know that Arthur forgave you? It was an arranged marriage. The same thing happened constantly elsewhere, as you must know. You gave her something he could not. There was only tenderness there. He understood. The only forgiveness you require is that which has been withheld all these long years—your own. No, it is not a doom that has been laid upon you. It is your own feelings which led you to assume an impossible quest, something tantamount to total unforgiveness. But you have suffered all these centuries upon the wrong trail."

When she raised her eyes, she saw that his were hard, like ice or gemstones. But she met his gaze and continued: "There is not now, was not then, and probably never was, a Holy Grail."

"I saw it," he said, "that day it passed through the Hall of the Table. We all saw it."

"You thought you saw it," she corrected him. "I hate to shatter an illusion that has withstood all the other tests of time, but I fear I must. The kingdom, as you recall, was at that time in turmoil. The knights were growing restless and falling away from the fellowship. A year—six months, even—and all would have collapsed, all Arthur had striven so hard to put together. He knew that the longer Camelot stood, the longer its name would endure, the stronger its ideals would become. So he made a decision, a purely political one. Something was needed to hold things together. He called upon Merlin, already half-mad, yet still shrewd enough to see what was needed and able to provide it. The Quest was born. Merlin's powers created the illusion you saw that day. It was a lie, yes. A glorious lie, though. And it served for years after to bind you all in brotherhood, in the name of justice and love. It entered literature, it promoted nobility and the higher ends of culture. It served its purpose. But it was—never—really—there. You have been chasing a ghost. I am sorry Launcelot, but I have absolutely no reason to lie to you. I know magic when I see it. I saw it then. That is how it happened."

For a long while he was silent. Then he laughed.

"You have an answer for everything," he said. "I could almost believe you, if you could but answer me one thing more—Why am I here? For what reason? By what power? How is it I have been preserved for half the Christian era while other men grow old and die in a handful of years? Can you tell me now what Cagliostro could not?"

"Yes," she said, "I believe that I can."

He rose to his feet and began to pace. The cat, alarmed, sprang from the sofa and ran into the back room. He stooped and snatched up his walking stick. He started for the door.

"I suppose it was worth waiting a thousand years to see you afraid," she said.

He halted.

"That is unfair," he replied.

"I know. But now you will come back and sit down," she said.

He was smiling once more as he turned and returned.

"Tell me," he said. "How do you see it?"

"Yours was the last enchantment of Merlin, that is how I see it."

"Merlin? Me? Why?"

"Gossip had it the old goat took Nimue into the woods and she had to use one of his own spells on him in self-defense—a spell which caused him to sleep forever in some lost place. If it was the spell that I believe it was, then at least part of the rumor was incorrect. There was no known counterspell, but the effects of the enchantment would have caused him to sleep not forever but for a millennium or so, and then to awaken. My guess now is that his last conscious act before he dropped off was to lay this enchantment upon you, so that you would be on hand when he returned."

"I suppose it might be possible, but why would he want me or need me?"

"If I were journeying into a strange time, I would want an ally once I reached it. And if I had a choice, I would want it to be the greatest champion of the day."

"Merlin . . ." he mused. "I suppose that it could be as you say. Excuse me, but a long life has just been shaken up, from beginning to end. If this is true . . ."

"I am sure that it is."

"If this is true . . . A millennium, you say?"

"More or less."

"Well, it is almost that time now."

"I know. I do not believe that our meeting tonight was a matter of chance. You are destined to meet him upon his awakening, which should be soon. Something has ordained that you meet me first, however, to be warned."

"Warned? Warned of what?"

"He is mad, Launcelot. Many of us felt a great relief at his passing. If the realm had not been sundered finally by strife it would probably have been broken by his hand, anyway."

"That I find difficult to believe. He was always a strange man—for who can fully understand a sorcerer?—and in his later years he did seem at least partly daft. But he never struck me as evil."

"Nor was he. His was the most dangerous morality of all. He was a misguided idealist. In a more primitive time and place and with a willing tool like Arthur, he was able to create a legend. Today, in an age of monstrous weapons, with the right leader as his catspaw, he could unleash something totally devastating. He would see a wrong and force his man to try righting it. He would do it in the name of the same high ideal he always served, but he would not appreciate the results until it was too late. How could he—even if he were sane? He has no conception of modern international relations."

"What is to be done? What is my part in all of this?"

"I believe you should go back, to England, to be present at his awakening, to find out exactly what he wants, to try to reason with him."

"I don't know . . . How would I find him?"

"You found me. When the time is right, you will be in the proper place. I am certain of that. It was meant to be, probably even a part of his spell. Seek him. But do not trust him."

"I don't know, Morgana." He looked at the wall, unseeing. "I don't know."

"You have waited this long and you draw back now from finally finding out?"

"You are right—in that much, at least." He folded his hands, raised them and rested his chin upon them. "What I would do if he really returned, I do not know. Try to reason with him, yes—Have you any other advice?"

"Just that you be there."

"You've looked at my hand. You have the power. What did you see?"

She turned away.

"It is uncertain," she said.

That night he dreamed, as he sometimes did, of times long gone. They sat about the great Table, as they had on that day, Gawaine was there and Percival. Galahad . . . He winced. This day was different from other days. There was a certain tension in the air, a before-the-storm feeling, an electrical thing. . . . Merlin stood at the far end of the room, hands in the sleeves of his long robe, hair and beard snowy and unkempt, pale eyes staring—at what, none could be certain . . .

After some timeless time, a reddish glow appeared near the door. All eyes moved toward it. It grew brighter and advanced slowly into the room—a formless apparition of light. There were sweet odors and some few soft strains of music. Gradually, a form began to take shape at its center, resolving itself into the likeness of a chalice. . . .

He felt himself rising, moving slowly, following it in its course through the great chamber, advancing upon it, soundlessly and deliberately, as if moving underwater . . .

. . . Reaching for it.

His hand entered the circle of light, moved toward its center, neared the now blazing cup and passed through. . . .

Immediately, the light faded. The outline of the chalice wavered, and it collapsed in upon itself, fading, fading, gone. . . .

There came a sound, rolling, echoing about the hall. Laughter.

He turned and regarded the others. They sat about the table, watching him, laughing. Even Merlin managed a dry chuckle.

Suddenly, his great blade was in his hand, and he raised it as he strode toward the Table. The knights nearest him drew back as he brought the weapon crashing down.

The Table split in half and fell. The room shook.

The quaking continued. Stones were dislodged from the walls. A roof beam fell. He raised his arm.

The entire castle began to come apart, falling about him and still the laughter continued.

He awoke damp with perspiration and lay still for a long while. In the morning, he bought a ticket for London.

Two of the three elemental sounds of the world were suddenly with him as he walked that evening, stick in hand. For a dozen days, he had hiked about Cornwall, finding no clues to that which he sought. He had allowed himself two more before giving up and departing.

Now the wind and the rain were upon him, and he increased his pace. The fresh-lit stars were smothered by a mass of cloud and wisps of fog grew like ghostly fungi on either hand. He moved among trees, paused, continued on.

"Shouldn't have stayed out this late," he muttered, and after several more pauses, *"Nel mezzo del cammin di nostra vita mi ritrovai per una selva oscura, che la diritta via era smarrita,"* then he chuckled, halting beneath a tree.

The rain was not heavy. It was more a fine mist now.

A bright patch in the lower heavens showed where the moon hung veiled.

He wiped his face, turned up his collar. He studied the position of the moon. After a time, he struck off to his right. There was a faint rumble of thunder in the distance.

The fog continued to grow about him as he went. Soggy leaves made squishing noises beneath his boots. An animal of indeterminate size bolted from a clump of shrubbery beside a cluster of rocks and tore off through the darkness.

Five minutes . . . ten . . . He cursed softly. The rainfall had increased in intensity. Was that the same rock?

He turned in a complete circle. All directions were equally uninviting. Selecting one at random, he commenced walking once again.

Then, in the distance, he discerned a spark, a glow, a wavering light. It vanished and reappeared periodically, as though partly blocked, the line of sight a function of his movements. He headed toward it. After perhaps half a minute, it was gone again from sight, but he continued on in what he thought to be its direction. There came another roll of thunder, louder this time.

When it seemed that it might have been illusion or some short-lived natural phenomenon, something else occurred in that same direction. There was a movement, a shadow-within-shadow shuffling at the foot of a great tree. He slowed his pace, approaching the spot cautiously.

There!

A figure detached itself from a pool of darkness ahead and to the left. Manlike, it moved with a slow and heavy tread, creaking sounds emerging from the forest floor beneath it. A vagrant moonbeam touched it for a moment, and it appeared yellow and metallically slick beneath moisture.

He halted. It seemed that he had just regarded a knight in full armor in his path. How long since he had beheld such a sight? He shook his head and stared.

The figure had also halted. It raised its right arm in a beckoning gesture, then turned and began to walk away. He hesitated for only a moment, then followed.

It turned off to the left and pursued a treacherous path, rocky, slippery, heading slightly downward. He actually used his stick now, to assure his footing, as he tracked its deliberate progress. He gained on it, to the point where he could clearly hear the metallic scraping sounds of its passage.

Then it was gone, swallowed by a greater darkness.

He advanced to the place where he had last beheld it. He stood in the lee of a great mass of stone. He reached out and probed it with his stick.

He tapped steadily along its nearest surface, and then the stick moved past it. He followed.

There was an opening, a crevice. He had to turn sidewise to pass within it, but as he did the full glow of the light he had seen came into sight for several seconds.

The passage curved and widened, leading him back and down. Several times, he paused and listened, but there were no sounds other than his own breathing.

He withdrew his handkerchief and dried his face and hands carefully. He brushed moisture from his coat, turned down his collar. He scuffed the mud and leaves from his boots. He adjusted his apparel. Then he strode forward, rounding a final corner, into a chamber lit by a small oil lamp suspended by three delicate chains from some point in the darkness overhead. The yellow knight stood unmoving beside the far wall. On a fiber mat atop a stony pedestal directly beneath the lamp lay an old man in tattered garments. His bearded face was half-masked by shadows.

He moved to the old man's side. He saw then that those ancient dark eyes were open.

"Merlin. . . ?" he whispered.

There came a faint hissing sound, a soft croak. Realizing the source, he leaned nearer.

"Elixir . . . in earthern rock . . . on ledge . . . in back," came the gravelly whisper.

He turned and sought the ledge, the container.

"Do you know where it is?" he asked the yellow figure.

It neither stirred nor replied, but stood like a display piece. He turned away from it then and sought further. After a time, he located it. It was more a niche than a ledge, blending in with the wall, cloaked with shadow. He ran his fingertips over the container's contours, raised it gently. Something liquid stirred within it. He wiped its lip on his sleeve after he had returned to the lighted area. The wind whistled past the entranceway and he thought he felt the faint vibration of thunder.

Sliding one hand beneath his shoulders, he raised the ancient form. Merlin's eyes still seemed unfocussed. He moistened Merlin's lips with the liquid. The old man licked them, and after several moments opened his mouth. He administered a sip, then another, and another . . .

Merlin signalled for him to lower him, and he did. He glanced again at the yellow armor, but it had remained motionless the entire while. He looked back at the sorceror and saw that a new light had come into his eyes and he was studying him, smiling faintly.

"Feel better?"

Merlin nodded. A minute passed, and a touch of color appeared upon his cheeks. He elbowed himself into a sitting position and took the container into his hands. He raised it and drank deeply.

He sat still for several minutes after that. His thin hands, which had appeared waxy in the flamelight, grew darker, fuller. His shoulders straightened. He placed the crock on the bed beside him and stretched his arms. His joints creaked the first time he did it, but not the second. He swung his legs over the edge of the bed and rose slowly to his feet. He was a full head shorter than Launcelot

"It is done," he said, staring back into the shadows. "Much has happened, of course . . ."

"Much has happened," Launcelot replied.

"You have lived through it all. Tell me, is the world a better place or is it worse than it was in those days?"

"Better in some ways, worse in others. It is different."

"How is it better?"

"There are many ways of making life easier, and the sum total of human knowledge has increased vastly."

"How has it worsened?"

"There are many more people in the world. Consequently, there are many more people suffering from poverty, disease, ignorance. The world itself has suffered great depredation, in the way of pollution and other assaults on the integrity of nature."

"Wars?"

"There is always someone fighting, somewhere."

"They need help."

"Maybe. Maybe not."

Merlin turned and looked into his eyes.

"What do you mean?"

ROGER ZELAZNY

"People haven't changed. They are as rational—and irrational—as they were in the old days. They are as moral and law-abiding—and not—as ever. Many new things have been learned, many new situations evolved, but I do not believe that the nature of man has altered significantly in the time you've slept. Nothing you do is going to change that. You may be able to alter a few features of the times, but would it really be proper to meddle? Everything is so interdependent today that even you would not be able to predict all the consequences of any actions you take. You might do more harm than good; and whatever you do, man's nature will remain the same."

"This isn't like you. Lance. You were never much given to philosophizing in the old days."

"I've had a long time to think about it."

"And I've had a long time to dream about it. War is your craft. Lance. Stay with that."

"I gave it up a long time ago."

"Then what are you now?"

"An appraiser."

Merlin turned away, took another drink. He seemed to radiate a fierce energy when he turned again.

"And your oath? To right wrongs, to punish the wicked . . ."

"The longer I lived the more difficult it became to determine what was a wrong and who was wicked. Make it clear to me again and I may go back into business."

"Galahad would never have addressed me so."

"Galahad was young, naive, trusting. Speak not to me of my son."

"Launcelot! Launcelot!" He placed a hand on his arm. "Why all this bitterness for an old friend who has done nothing for a thousand years?"

"I wished to make my position clear immediately. I feared you might contemplate some irreversible action which could alter the world balance of power fatally. I want you to know that I will not be party to it."

"Admit that you do not know what I might do, what I can do."

"Freely. That is why I fear you. What do you intend to do?"

"Nothing, at first I wish merely to look about me, to see for myself some of these changes of which you have spoken. Then I will consider which wrongs need righting, who needs punishment, and who to choose as my champions. I will show you these things, and then you can go back into business, as you say."

Launcelot sighed.

"The burden of proof is on the moralist. Your judgment is no longer sufficient for me."

"Dear me," the other replied, "it is sad to have waited this long for an encounter of this sort, to find you have lost your faith in me. My powers are beginning to return already, Lance. Do you not feel magic in the air?"

"I feel something I have not felt in a long while."

"The sleep of ages was a restorative—an aid, actually. In a while. Lance, I am going to be stronger than I ever was before. And you doubt that I will be able to turn back the clock?"

"I doubt you can do it in a fashion to benefit anybody. Look, Merlin. I'm sorry. I do not like it that things have come to this either. But I have lived too long, seen too much, know too much of how the world works now to trust any one man's opinion concerning its salvation. Let it go. You are a mysterious, revered legend. I do not know what you really are. But forgo exercising your powers in any sort of crusade. Do something else this time around. Become a physician and fight pain. Take up painting. Be a professor of history, an antiquarian. Hell, be a social critic and point out what evils you see for people to correct themselves."

"Do you really believe I could be satisfied with any of those things?"

"Men find satisfaction in many things. It depends on the man, not on the things. I'm just saying that you should avoid using your powers in any attempt to effect social changes as we once did, by violence."

"Whatever changes have been wrought, time's greatest irony lies in its having transformed you into a pacifist."

"You are wrong."

"Admit it! You have finally come to fear the clash of arms! An appraiser! What kind of knight are you?"

"One who finds himself in the wrong time and the wrong place, Merlin."

The sorcerer shrugged and turned away.

"Let it be, then. It is good that you have chosen to tell me all these things immediately. Thank you for that, anyway. A moment—"

Merlin walked to the rear of the cave, returned in moments attired in fresh garments. The effect was startling. His entire appearance was more kempt and cleanly. His hair and beard now appeared gray rather than white. His step was sure and steady. He held a staff in his right hand but did not lean upon it.

"Come walk with me," he said.

"It is a bad night."

"It is not the same night you left without. It is not even the same place."

As he passed the suit of yellow armor, he snapped his fingers near its visor. With a single creak, the figure moved and turned to follow him.

"Who is that?" Merlin smiled.

"No one," he replied, and he reached back and raised the visor. The helmet was empty. "It is enchanted, animated by a spirit," he said. "A trifle clumsy, though, which is why I did not trust it to administer my draught. A perfect servant, however, unlike some. Incredibly strong and swift. Even in your prime you could not have beaten it. I fear nothing when it walks with me. Come, there is something I would have you see."

"Very well."

Launcelot followed Merlin and the hollow knight from the cave. The rain had stopped, and it was very still. They stood on an incredibly moonlit plain where mists drifted and grasses sparkled. Shadowy shapes stood in the distance.

"Excuse me," Launcelot said. "I left my walking stick inside."

He turned and re-entered the cave.

"Yes, fetch it, old man," Merlin replied. "Your strength is already on the wane."

When Launceiot returned, he leaned upon the stick and squinted across the plain.

"This way," Merlin said, "to where your questions will be answered. I will try not to move too quickly and tire you."

"Tire me?"

The sorcerer chuckled and began walking across the plain. Launcelot followed.

"Do you not feel a trifle weary?" he asked.

"Yes, as a matter of fact, I do. Do you know what is the matter with me?"

"Of course. I have withdrawn the enchantment which has protected you all these years. What you feel now are the first tentative touches of your true age. It will take some time to catch up with you, against your body's natural resistance, but it is beginning its advance."

"Why are you doing this to me?"

"Because I believed you when you said you were not a pacifist. And you spoke with sufficient vehemence for me to realize that you might even oppose me. I could not permit that, for I knew that your old strength was still there for you to call upon. Even a sorcerer might fear that, so I did what had to be done. By my power was it maintained; without it, it now drains away. It would have been good for us to work together once again, but I saw that that could not be."

Launcelot stumbled, caught himself, limped on. The hollow knight walked at Merlin's right hand.

"You say that your ends are noble," Launcelot said, "but I do not believe you. Perhaps in the old days they were. But more than the times have changed. You are different. Do you not feel it yourself?"

Merlin drew a deep breath and exhaled vapor.

"Perhaps it is my heritage," he said. Then, "I jest. Of course, I have changed. Everyone does. You yourself are a perfect example. What you consider a turn for the worse in me is but the tip of an irreducible conflict which has grown up between us in the course of our changes. I still hold with the true ideals of Camelot."

Launcelot's shoulders were bent forward now and his breathing had deepened. The shapes loomed larger before them.

"Why, I know this place," he gasped. "Yet, I do not know it. Stonehenge does not stand so today. Even in Arthur's time it lacked this perfection. How did we get here? What has happened?"

He paused to rest, and Merlin halted to accommodate him.

"This night we have walked between the worlds," the sorcerer said. "This is a piece of the land of Faerie and that is the true Stonehenge, a holy place. I have stretched the bounds of the worlds to bring it here. Were I unkind I could send you back with it and strand you there forever. But it is better that you know a sort of peace. Come!"

Launcelot staggered along behind him, heading for the great circle of stones. The faintest of breezes came out of the west, stirring the mists.

"What do you mean—know a sort of peace?"

"The complete restoration of my powers and their increase will require a sacrifice in this place."

"Then you planned this for me all along!"

"No. It was not to have been you, Lance. Anyone would have served, though you will serve superbly well. It need not have been so, had you elected to assist me. You could still change your mind."

"Would you want someone who did that at your side?"

"You have a point there."

"Then why ask—save as a petty cruelty?"

"It is just that, for you have annoyed me." Launcelot halted again when they came to the circle's periphery. He regarded the massive stands of stone.

"If you will not enter willingly," Merlin stated, "my servant will be happy to assist you."

Launcelot spat, straightened a little and glared. "Think you I fear an empty suit of armor, juggled by some Hell-born wight? Even now, Merlin, without the benefit of wizardly succor, I could take that thing apart."

The sorcerer laughed.

"It is good that you at least recall the boasts of knighthood when all else has left you. I've half a mind to give you the opportunity, for the manner of your passing here is not important. Only the preliminaries are essential."

"But you're afraid to risk your servant?"

"Think you so, old man? I doubt you could even bear the weight of a suit of armor, let alone lift a lance. But if you are willing to try, so be it!"

He rapped the butt of his staff three times upon the ground.

"Enter," he said then. "You will find all that you need within. And I am glad you have made this choice. You were insufferable, you know. Just once, I longed to see you beaten, knocked down to the level of lesser mortals. I only wish the Queen could be here, to witness her champion's final engagement."

"So do I," said Launcelot, and he walked past the monolith and entered the circle.

A black stallion waited, its reins held down beneath a rock. Pieces of armor, a lance, a blade and a shield leaned against the side of the dolmen. Across the circle's diameter, a white stallion awaited the advance of the hollow knight.

"I am sorry I could not arrange for a page or a squire to assist you," Merlin said, coming around the other side of the monolith. "I'll be glad to help you myself, though."

"I can manage," Launcelot replied.

"My champion is accoutered in exactly the same fashion," Merlin said, "and I have not given him any edge over you in weapons."

"I never liked your puns either."

Launcelot made friends with the horse, then removed a small strand of red from his wallet and tied it about the butt of the lance. He leaned his stick against the dolmen stone and began to don the armor. Merlin, whose hair and beard were now almost black, moved off several paces and began drawing a diagram in the dirt with the end of his staff.

"You used to favor a white charger," he commented, "but I thought it appropriate to equip you with one of another color, since you have abandoned the ideals of the Table Round, betraying the memory of Camelot."

"On the contrary," Launcelot replied, glancing overhead at the passage of a sudden roll of thunder. "Any horse in a storm, and I am Camelot's last defender."

Merlin continued to elaborate upon the pattern he was drawing as Launcelot slowly equipped himself. The small wind continued to blow, stirring the mist. There came a flash of lightning, startling the horse. Launcelot calmed it.

Merlin stared at him for a moment and rubbed his eyes. Launcelot donned his helmet.

"For a moment," Merlin said, "you looked somehow different. . . ."

"Really? Magical withdrawal, do you think?" he asked, and he kicked the stone from the reins and mounted the stallion.

Merlin stepped back from the now-completed diagram, shaking his head, as the mounted man leaned over and grasped the lance.

"You still seem to move with some strength," he said.

"Really?"

Launcelot raised the lance and couched it. Before taking up the shield he had hung at the saddle's side, he opened his visor and turned and regarded Merlin.

"Your champion appears to be ready," he said. "So am I."

Seen in another flash of light, it was an unlined face that looked down at Merlin, clear-eyed, wisps of pale gold hair fringing the forehead.

"What magic have the years taught you?" Merlin asked.

"Not magic," Launcelot replied. "Caution. I anticipated you. So, when I returned to the cave for my stick, I drank the rest of your elixir."

He lowered the visor and turned away.

"You walked like an old man. . . ."

"I'd a lot of practice. Signal your champion."

Merlin laughed.

"Good! It is better this way," he decided, "to see you go down in full strength! You still cannot hope to win against a spirit!"

Launcelot raised the shield and leaned forward.

"Then what are you waiting for?"

"Nothing!" Merlin said. Then he shouted, "Kill him, Raxas!"

A light rain began as they pounded across the field; and staring ahead, Launcelot realized that flames were flickering behind his opponent's visor. At the last possible moment, he shifted the point of his lance into line with the hollow knight's blazing helm. There came more lightning and thunder.

His shield deflected the other's lance while his went on to strike the approaching head. It flew from the hollow knight's shoulders and bounced, smouldering, on the ground.

He continued on to the other end of the field and turned. When he had, he saw that the hollow knight, now headless, was doing the same. And beyond him, he saw two standing figures, where moments before there had been but one.

Morgan Le Fay, clad in a white robe, red hair unbound and blowing in the wind, faced Merlin from across his pattern. It seemed they were speaking, but he could not hear the words. Then she began to raise her hands, and they glowed like cold fire. Merlin's staff was also gleaming, and he shifted it before him. Then he saw no more, for the hollow knight was ready for the second charge.

He couched his lance, raised the shield, leaned forward and gave his mount the signal. His arm felt like a bar of iron, his strength like an endless current of electricity as he raced down the field. The rain was falling more heavily now and the lightning began a constant flickering. A steady rolling of thunder smothered the sound of the hoofbeats, and the wind whistled past his helm as he approached the other warrior, his lance centered on his shield.

They came together with an enormous crash. Both knights reeled and the hollow one fell, his shield and breastplate pierced by a broken lance. His left arm came away as he struck the earth; the lancepoint snapped and the shield fell beside him. But he began to rise almost immediately, his right hand drawing his long sword.

Launcelot dismounted, discarding his shield, drawing his own great blade. He moved to meet his headless foe. The other struck first and he parried it, a mighty shock running down his arms. He swung a blow of his own. It was parried.

They swaggered swords across the field, till finally Launcelot saw his opening and landed his heaviest blow. The hollow knight toppled into the mud, his breastplate cloven almost to the point where the spear's shaft protruded. At that moment, Morgan Le Fay screamed.

Launcelot turned and saw that she had fallen across the pattern Merlin had drawn. The sorcerer, now bathed in a bluish light, raised his staff and moved forward. Launcelot took a step toward them and felt a great pain in his left side.

Even as he turned toward the half-risen hollow knight who was drawing his blade back for another blow, Launcelot reversed his double-handed grip upon his own weapon and raised it high, point downward.

He hurled himself upon the other, and his blade pierced the cuirass entirely as he bore him back down, nailing him to the earth. A shriek arose from beneath him, echoing within the armor, and a gout of fire emerged from the neck hole, sped upward and away, dwindled in the rain, flickered out moments later.

Launcelot pushed himself into a kneeling position. Slowly then, he rose to his feet and turned toward the two figures who again faced one another. Both were now standing within the muddied geometries of power, both were now bathed in the bluish light. Launcelot took a step toward them, then another.

"Merlin!" he called out, continuing to advance upon them. "I've done what I said I would! Now I'm coming to kill you!"

Morgan Le Fay turned toward him, eyes wide.

"No!" she cried. "Depart the circle! Hurry! I am holding him here! His power wanes! In moments, this place will be no more. Go!"

Launcelot hesitated but a moment, then turned and walked as rapidly as he was able toward the circle's perimeter. The sky seemed to boil as he passed among the monoliths.

He advanced another dozen paces, then had to pause to rest. He looked back to the place of battle, to the place where the two figures still stood locked in sorcerous embrace. Then the scene was imprinted upon his brain as the skies opened and a sheet of fire fell upon the far end of the circle.

Dazzled, he raised his hand to shield his eyes. When he lowered it, he saw the stones falling, soundless, many of them fading from sight. The rain began to slow immediately. Sorceror and sorceress had vanished along with much of the structure of the still-fading place. The horses were nowhere to be seen. He looked about him and saw a good-sized stone. He headed for it and seated himself. He unfastened his breastplate and removed it, dropping it to the ground. His side throbbed and he held it tightly. He doubled forward and rested his face on his left hand.

The rains continued to slow and finally ceased. The wind died. The mists returned.

He breathed deeply and thought back upon the conflict. This, this was the thing for which he had remained after all the others, the thing for which he had waited, for so long. It was over now, and he could rest.

There was a gap in his consciousness. He was brought to awareness again by a light. A steady glow passed between his fingers, pierced his eyelids. He dropped his hand and raised his head, opening his eyes.

It passed slowly before him in a halo of white light. He removed his sticky fingers from his side and rose to his feet to follow it. Solid, glowing, glorious and pure, not at all like the image in the chamber, it led him on out across the moonlit plain, from dimness to brightness to dimness, until the mists enfolded him as he reached at last to embrace it.

HERE ENDETH THE BOOK OF LAUNCELOT,
LAST OF THE NOBLE KNIGHTS OF THE
ROUND TABLE, AND HIS ADVENTURES
WITH RAXAS, THE HOLLOW KNIGHT,
AND MERLIN AND MORGAN LE FAY,
LAST OF THE WISE FOLK OF CAMELOT,
IN HIS QUEST FOR THE SANGREAL.

QUO FAS ET GLORIA DUCUNT.